# the dog boy

by
## Noel Anenberg

To my wife, Nooshie, our children,
Geoffrey, Nicole, Allan,
and especially to our beautiful grandchild,
'Mac'
and to
our beloved Howie
2002 - 2012

# ACKNOWLEDGEMENTS

I wish to thank my dear family, especially my wife who has put up with my fits of acute crankiness and self-doubt, and friends, including "Perk," who have countenanced and even suffered my oft times awkward apprenticeship to the writer's craft. I am loath to list all out of the fear that I shall overlook one. I have thanked each and everyone. You know who you are. I could not have completed this novel without your friendship, love, and patient kindness. I thank you here again.

I also thank the USC Master of Professional Writing Program and in particular professors Syd Field, Aram Saroyan, Ken Turan, Shelley Berman, and Donald Freed for their wisdom, guidance, and encouragement. I am grateful to my Pierce College writing students whose hard work, determination, and courage, are an inspiration.

Gabe Robinson provided gifted editorial services. Thank you, Gabe.

Stan Corwin provided excellent marketing guidance.

The Montford Point Marines, American-black men who volunteered to fight for their nation's freedom during World War II when they were not yet free have been most gracious and generous in sitting for oral histories and providing research materials that have informed my work and my person. The Marine depicted on this book's cover is Eugene Groves, a private at the instant the photograph was taken. Mr. Groves retired from the Marines with the rank of master sergeant. Thank you for your service to our nation, Mr. Groves.

Finally, I am grateful for the sacrifices, big and small, direct or indirect, courageous or incidental, made by our ancestors who through their undying courage, unending persistence, and steeled determination have passed on the precious gift of liberty. Our beloved nation may be flawed, compared to any other it is the very best. Where else may a kid from a broken home on the wrong side of the tracks work his way to the right side, be part of a wonderful family, build a business, follow his "bliss," and even write a whole book without fear of reprisal.

And, my dear readers, I am honored by your reading my work.

God Bless the United States of America!

# Table of Contents

# Chapter 1

## *Horrific News and a Journey*

The telegram from the War Department arrived late Thursday afternoon. I was pressing linens for the Hutchinson family of Seeley Street. I could barely sign my name let alone read way back then. I thought Mrs. Hutchinson and I both would likely pass out as she read the message.

> *December 9, 1945*
> *Mrs. Phosie Mae Eaton:*
> *(Mother)*
> *Deeply regret to inform you that your son, William L. Eaton, Gunnery Sergeant, U.S. Marines, has been wounded in action during the performance of his duty and in the service of his country. The Major General Commandant appreciates your great anxiety and will furnish you further information promptly when received. Your son has been transferred to the Pershing Army Hospital, Barry Ward, Los Angeles, California. To prevent possible aid to our enemies, please do not divulge the name of his ship or station.*

In the three days that followed the telegram's arrival, I rode the Super Chief, the first train ride in my life, from Galveston out to Los Angeles. The only other trip I had taken, aside from riding the bus to Reedy

Chapel or to shop at Calichi Corners, was in 1923 when my husband, Isaac, may the good Lord bless and keep him, drove us down to
Galveston from Uniontown, Alabama, in his daddy's rheumy Model
T truck. Will was born in Galveston during the fall of that year. Will
filled our days with sunshine.

By Sunday afternoon I was in California, stuck to the protective
vinyl covering  the front seat of my brother Babe's shiny-new, two-tone
DeSoto. Babe and his wife, Pearl, Sis' Pearl, had picked me up at Union
Station and carried me across town to Pershing Army Hospital where I
tried to stop the tears from spilling down my cheeks as we waited in a
line of cars at the main gate.

I was thinking about how Will was the last living remnant of the
love Isaac and I shared. If I lost my Will I felt there would be nothing
left to live for. If he died I believed it would have been because of me.
I was not able to stop him from enlisting in the Marines. I tried, the
Lord knows how I tried. Just before he went to the recruiting office
with his friends—they all loved that dress-blue Marine uniform on the
posters all over town—I said, "Why do you wants to go fight dis war
for people who won't even 'low you to vote?"

Will, bless his heart, was stubborn like his father. "Mama, daddy
told me, 'Don' pay no mind to how we got here, son. That's past. You
live for today and for the future, here? This is our land just like it is
anyone elses, no matter what color de is.' It's time to fight to earn our
place, mama, and that's exactly what I intend to do!"

As I sat silently in Babe's car frozen in time with the low rumble of
the De Soto's motor soothing me, I thought of all the people I missed
who were once in my hard scrabble life. My grandparents, my mama,
my daddy, my aunts and uncles, all the Alabama cousins had all passed
except old Abe Eaton, who was living in the Bayou La Batre Crippled
Peoples Home in Bayou La Batre Alabama after he fell out of his skiff
and broke his neck while clearing his crayfish cages.  I had three older
sisters. I lost them all to the Spanish flu in July of 1919. One died right
after the other. It broke my mama's heart, and she passed, too. You just
never know what's going to happen from one day to the next. I felt like
the Kansas girl who was picked up by that twister and set down in a

dream. One thing I knew, if I could have taken Will's place in the hospital and freed him from whatever his pain and suffering were, I would have done so without hesitation.

I was sitting like a child between little Babe at the wheel—he was just five feet four inches tall—and his wife, Sis' Pearl, a battleship of a woman with dark-chocolate skin and eyes like a raccoon's. She was wearing a snow-white Sunday dress and a hat that could have passed for a funeral spray. Babe insisted on keeping the windows rolled up to preserve his DeSoto's new-car smell. The December sun was baking through the rear window as if through a magnifying glass. Perspiration brought on by travel sickness from the rocking train and my brother's tentative driving was trickling down my back as Pearl lackadaisically worked over a dip of her chewing tobacco like a cud-chumping cow. I felt like I was in a swamp. Each time Pearl reached for her canning jar to spit out the tobacco juice in her mouth, its bitter smell and the brown particulate swirl it made at the bottom of the jar made me feel that I would spray the Chinatown lunch Babe had treated us to all over his showroom-clean dashboard. The teardrops started to fall. Not knowing how serious Will's injuries were was just too much.

"From all that you've written me about Will, he's a strong young man, Phosie Mae. I am sure he will be fine," Babe said as he handed me his handkerchief. Sis' Pearl said nothing, but I could see by her bulldog sneer she was not partial to his showing me or anybody else sympathy. I don't recollect her having one ounce of love to share anywhere in her nearly three-hundred-pound body. That's how some heavyset people are, you know. They can't help themselves. Some did not get the love they needed as children and grew up trying to fill their empty hearts with food.

Babe's gentle voice never failed to comfort me. The tears stopped. I dried my eyes and looked out through the windshield at the mottled brown mountains to the north and wished I could turn back time.

"They'll be bright green come spring," Babe said. "Won't they, Pearl?" Sis' Pearl grunted.

"Well, I reckon I'll be back down in Galveston by then," I said without too much conviction. My roots were in Galveston. Los Angeles was too big and strangely too free. I knew my place in Galveston. I felt comfortable in my skin. Everyone knew you. There were so many people rushing to get somewhere in Los Angeles it seemed no one cared where you were going or what you were thinking about doing once you got there. I suppose it's like the feeling a bird that's lived its entire life in a cage has if one day the cage door is left open and it flies away. Even though the cage was confining it, the bird felt safe. There was no worry about food or safety. Now it is free to fly wherever it pleases. But the freedom terrifies it so that it loses itself and can't find its way home.

A cloud that had momentarily shaded the sun sailed past. The blue sky brightened to a sparkle. The ocean was near. I made a silent promise to myself that I would find out where the colored beach was and take Will as soon as he was back on his feet. He loved going to the beach in Galveston. More little white clouds frisked by. They reminded me of the cotton Isaac and I picked when we first arrived in Texas. Even though we did not have two pieces of kindling to rub together to start a fire and there seemed to be a Klu Kluxer with a rope behind every tree, life felt light and easy. We were young. We felt the warm sun on our shoulders and laughed all the time. Our days were filled with love.

I looked at the hospital's main administration building. It was made of big, dull-gray cement blocks like the buildings on a picture postcard of Washington, D.C. The bright red-and-white stripes of the biggest American flag I had ever seen lazily waved in front of the building's entrance. Determined to be positive, I leaned forward and felt the back of my dress peel from the plastic seat cover. I took a deep breath and sighed. Pearl grimaced. I looked around the hospital grounds. A sense of pride welled up in my heart. Two Marine guards in their dress blues were standing watch at a gatehouse that looked like a little red brick castle. The beautiful green hospital grounds were behind them. I remembered what my mama used to say about always looking for the good in life, and suddenly I felt part of something big like Will's dream of a better life to come. I thought that was what Will must have been feeling when he enlisted. I began to feel reassured. But, as usually happens when I get a good thought, a bad one came and chased it away like a dog after a squirrel. Before I even realized what I was thinking about, I had already started looking for other colored folks and realized there were none. The people occupying automobiles in front of us, the marines at the gate, the nurses in their starched uniforms and pert white caps, the blue-robed patients sitting in wheelchairs, on benches, or in forest-green adirondacks with footrests on the emerald-green lawn, and their visitors, were all white as fresh-fallen snow. My hope dissolved like a teardrop in rainwater. A terrible fear overtook me. How could my child be receiving the same medical care as the white boys?

"Lord have mercy!" Sis' Pearl opined. "This sure look like the country club that Calvin Coolidge Jr. works at!"

"All right now, Pearl dear, let it go, no need to get Phosie more upset than she already is," Babe said as he edged the car up to third in line. Babe never showed his anger. He said it was because he never took things personally. He knew he could not control what others thought of him. So, except when they got in his way, he ignored them. And unlike most of our kin, he did not stay angry and blame white folk for his shortcomings like an adult child blames his once abusive parent. Babe allowed nothing, especially the past, to get in his way. Aside from my Isaac, he was the kindest, gentlest man I had ever known. It was my hope that he would have some influence on Will.

Pearl, on the other hand, reminded me of my grandmother, Rayleen Johnson, who folks called Johnny because she was a bull in a woman's skin. Grandma Johnny Ray looked after us, me and Babe and our sisters, when our parents were out working. We felt safe with Mama Ray, but everyone said she could start a fight with a statue. I think that's why Babe married Pearl, to feel safe. Sis' Pearl was, after all, a truant officer for the Los Angeles City Schools and carried a pearl gripped pistol and a badge in her purse.

Right then, an old, swaybacked, gray-bearded Negro wearing a tattered khaki Cavalry tunic with a frayed red chevron on its right sleeve limped out of the back door of the guardhouse carrying a mop and pail.

Pearl clapped her meaty hands and shouted, "Well, thank the baby Jesus for buckets and mops!" then spat another squirt of tobacco juice into her canning jar.

"What are you talking about, dear?" Babe asked Pearl politely.

"What am I talking about?" snapped Sis' Pearl. "Look over yonder at that old gray mule comin' out the back of the guardhouse with a bucket and a mop. If you two had any common sense you'd realize that if it weren't for buckets and mops, there might not be a need for colored folk at all!"

"Now, Pearl dear, what about me?" Babe said as he inched the car forward toward the guardhouse and second place. Babe spoke with authority because he was one of the highest-paid engineers of any color with the Los Angeles Department of Water and Power.

"Don't you 'Pearl dear' me, Pleas Beaumont!" Pleas was called Babe because of his baby face. "We are here to visit your sister's chile, who for all we know nearly lost his life fighting in a war for all these white folk, and for what? To come back and carry a bucket and mop like old Stepin Fetchit over there? Where are our boys? Probably in some animal shed?" Like many of us, Pearl was an intelligent and angry woman trapped by the color of her skin.

The car at the gate pulled forward. We were next. I reached into my handbag and clutched the telegram. "Pearl! Don' you start fussin'!" I said with a slight quiver in my voice.

The guards at the gate were sharp-looking marines in dress blues. They reminded me of how proud my Will looked in the photograph taken of him in his dress blues at his graduation from Montford Point, the colored boot camp next to Camp LeJeune in Jacksonville, North Carolina. I carried that picture in my pocketbook and showed it to everyone. I still do to this day.

"Fussin'? You haven't seen fussin' yet, Phosie Mae. I do not like what I see," Sis' Pearl said.

"Pearl!" I said in a commanding voice that surprised even me.

"Yesssss?" she answered under hitched eyebrows as she stuffed a fresh chaw of tobacco into her cheek with the nicotine-stained tip of her plump pinky.

"I hope you will not say anythin' dat stop me from seeing my chile," I said in a tone that a parent might use with a spoiled child in a fancy restaurant.

"Ummmmmph!"

"Because if you open dat big mouth of yourn agin I will personally twist your fat tongue right out and feed it to those three black crows sittin' on de telephone line over yonder!"

"Phosie Mae, that's no way for a Christian woman to talk," Babe said, biting back a grin as he drove up to the gate.

I leaned forward and smiled when the Marine guard bent over, placed his white-gloved hand on top of the DeSoto's roof, and looked in through the crack Babe conceded by lowering his driver's side window.

"How may I help you, sir?" the marine asked politely.

Babe nodded at me and said, "My sister's boy is in the hospital."

"Here's de telegram I done received," I said, holding the mustard-yellow envelope up with a trembling hand.

"Colored visiting hours are over, ma'am."

"Over!" Sis' Pearl shouted. "What about all those white folk? When do they leave?" I mashed my foot down on her toes.

"Yes, ma'am. No entrance for anyone is allowed after five. Colored visiting hours are twelve hundred hours to seventeen hundred hours, Sundays, in the Barry Barracks. That's the colored ward, ma'am," the guard said politely while using his white-gloved hand to motion in the direction the Barry Barracks were located.

"What about the cars you just let in?" Sis' Pearl said with a lisp caused by the lump of tobacco tucked behind her lower front lip.

"They work on the hospital grounds, ma'am." He was trying to be courteous.

"Well, thank you kindly," Babe said. "We'll come back next week." As Babe spoke, the old graybeard passed silently into the back door of the guardhouse like a ghost.

"Jus' one second," I said, silencin' Babe with a wave of my hand. "How do we get to de Barry Barracks?"

"You'll enter through the employee entrance at Gate C. Gate C is about one thousand yards north of Wilshire Boulevard across from the cemetery entrance. But like I said, visiting hours are over, ma'am."

"All right den," I said.

The guard now swept the palm of his white-gloved hand in the direction he wanted us to drive and said, "You may turn around behind the guardhouse, sir."

"Well," Babe said as he pulled away, "looks like we'll have to return next week then."

"I shore 'nough didn't come all de way out from Galveston, Texas, to wait one whole week while all dose white folk are visitin' their kin. Take me to Gate C. Now!"

# Chapter 2

## *Colored Needles*

Babe drove us north on Sepulveda Boulevard toward Gate C. This gate allowed access to the service side of the hospital's grounds. No fancy lawns or flags, just gray warehouses and a sign designating the official "Colored" entrance. The National Cemetery for Veterans was on the right. It was peaceful, like a park. Its lawn stretched on and on and on. There were not many graves, though. The thought that there was room to bury so many more of the dead distressed me. *What if my baby dies?* I thought. *I wants him near his daddy. How will I afford that?* A violent shiver shook me.

"Are you cold, Phosie?" Babe said. "I'll turn on the heater."

"No, I'm fine," Sis' Pearl said absentmindedly.

The freshest row of graves was just a little ways up the street. There the traffic was stopped for a beautiful white stallion pulling an ebony carriage from the hospital to the cemetery. A gleaming maple coffin with polished brass fittings and a fresh-pressed American flag draped over it was resting in the carriage's bed. The driver, a soldier in a dress uniform, sat stiff backed, and the horse marched slowly across the lanes as though it understood how solemn was its duty. A small gathering of the fallen soldier's kin huddled on one side of the grave like a little flock of lost sheep. A tall mound of rich brown earth was on the opposite side. Two chrome shovels were standing at attention in the soil. The pallbearers, two sailors, two soldiers, and two marines in full dress uniforms were standing ready to carry the coffin to the grave. One raised a bugle to his lips and played taps. We could hear it clearly even though the windows were up.

"Oh, please let my baby live. Take me if'n you has to take someone," I prayed as Babe drove by.

"He'll live, Phosie. Will has a strong constitution like his father, Isaac," Babe said.

Two colored marines were standing guard at Gate C. They were dressed in green fatigues, not dress blues like the marines at the main gate. Babe studied them as he waited to turn in from Sepulveda.

"Drive on in there, Babe," I said.

"What are you going to say to those boys when I do?"

"Never you mind, just pull in. I'll think of something." Nothing on the face of the Earth was going to stand between my child and me.

A black Buick big as a tank, driven by a little canary of a white lady with bright red lipstick and jet-black hair hitched up in a beehive, came down Sepulveda from the north and turned right in before us. A skinny little girl with pigtails was sitting on the seat next to the woman, licking a lollipop. Even though it was getting dark and chilly, all the windows of their car were rolled down. As Babe pulled up behind the lady's car, we saw the reason. The trunk lid had been removed and wooden crates bursting with crazed chickens were stacked in it. The lady passed a gray cardboard flat with two-dozen eggs to the guard. He smiled and waved them and the chickens through.

"Go ahead on, Babe," I said.

"I don't like this, Phosie. This is the federal government you're playing with here, the military! They might take us for spies and shoot us!" Babe said.

"Spies!" Sis' Pearl said. "Now just what kind of spies do you think they are going to make us out to be, Japanese? Pull on up."

The guard waved us up. There was a big white sign behind the guardhouse:

Barry Colored Hospital Visiting Hours
Noon to 17:00 hrs
Sunday

Babe crept up slowly as guilty man might and rolled his window down an inch. The guard said, "May I help you, sir?" It felt good to deal with one of our own.

Before Babe could speak I leaned forward and said, "We're here to pick up bakin' pans from de colored ward."

"May I see your I.D., ma'am?"

"We don't have no I.D., darlin'. We jus' heping out on a temporary basis," I said. And like magic, the thought of Sis' Pearl's tobacco came to mind. "I have a tin of tobacco you can have, sugar. Would you like that?"

The other guard answered, "Yes ma'am!"

The hard part was separating the Pearl from the tin.

"I still have to telephone Barry," the younger guard said then turned toward the guardhouse and a telephone hanging on the wall.

"It's Sunday. Nobody answers on Sunday. Let 'em go, Mac."

As the guard waved us through he smiled and said, "Much obliged for the tobacco."

Babe drove along a narrow lane lined by grim gray buildings and dying lawns. The buildings, wards of the hospital, resembled the main hospital building but were much smaller. A small, lonely Christmas tree topped with a red cross and an American flag stood at each entrance. The scarred and wounded men who were not lucky enough to have visitors that day were gathered in the courtyards of these buildings, some in wheelchairs, some on crutches, some had an empty pajama leg or arm or both neatly folded and pinned where limbs once hung. Others were so covered with bandages they looked like the walking dead. They were all huddled in small groups smoking Lucky Strike cigarettes.

"It's the Red Cross give them cigarettes and blood, don't hit?" I said.

"Don't they have newspapers down in Galveston?" Sis' Pearl said.

"Why?"

"Because," Sis' Pearl said bitterly, "if you had been reading the paper you'd know that the Red Cross does not give cigarettes, or coffee, or blood to Negroes."

"They do? I means they don't? I gave them money."

"For their Jim Crow blood," Sis' Pearl said.

"How dey tell de difference? It's all red!" I said with a shake of my head. I knew better. I knew in my bones "they" could do just about anything they wanted.

"The funny thing is," Babe said, "the Red Cross and the military and everyone else have a Negro doctor to thank for blood transfusions in the first place."

"That sounds 'bout right," Sis' Pearl said as we drove through a park-like area shaded by grandfatherly eucalyptus trees. My thoughts were with Will.

"Charles Richard Drew, M.D. They wouldn't let him study medicine down here. He had to go to McGill University in Canada to get his medical degree. But he came back and helped the Red Cross and the military set up his invention, the blood bank. It's saved thousands and thousands of lives already, and Lord knows how many in the future. Yeah, most of these white boys are alive because of a Negro."

"I wonder if they would give the blood back if they knew," Sis' Pearl said.

"I don' care one way or t'other long as my baby gets his."

"He's not a baby, Phosie Mae, he's a man now. You have to stop calling him a baby."

Pearl had crossed the line. I said, "Pearl, has you ever had a child?"

"No, but I've chased enough of them down to know what it's like to deal with them. Don't forget, I *am* a truant officer."

"Well, if'n you ever happen to have one, you will realize dat no matter how old dey get dey is still dey mama's baby."

Pearl reached into her purse for her tin of tobacco to freshen the wad already in her mouth, but the guard at the gate had it. She pumped herself up with indignation and stared out the windshield. I felt badly that I hurt her. It wasn't her fault that she and Babe had not had kids. She had been expecting three times but miscarried each one. Finally, her doctor advised her not to try again. Pearl was too proud to adopt. I think the lack of children in their lives opened a deep wound in their hearts and the only thing they could do about it was to suffer in polite silence.

We passed another building. "Most of dese here boys don' look old 'nough to shave," I said, trying to lighten the atmosphere.

"That's exactly right," Sis' Pearl said. "I'll be tracking them down for missing school 'fore anybody knows it." I had a thought that most of the boys would choose to go back overseas and fight the Japanese again over trying to dodge my sister-in-law. I got tickled and chuckled.

"Was it something I said that is funny?" Sis' Pearl said. I ignored her.

"That must be it right there," Babe said.

A dusty, dark wood building with a green roof appeared at the end of the unpaved section of street we were now driving on. A knotty old Spanish pepper with an inviting canopy stood next to the building. There were rickety benches and old chairs under its boughs. They were occupied by an assortment of colored patients and their kin.

"Looks like there's nothing but dirt for blacks!" Sis' Pearl mumbled.

"Hush!" Babe said.

The sign over the door read: "Barry Hospital Colored Ward." A dull brass plaque on the right side of the door was engraved with:

Dedicated to the Courageous Men of the
California Cavalry Battalion
Shenandoah Valley
1861 - 1865

"Shenandoah Valley! Lord have mercy," Sis' Pearl said. "That's the Civil War! Maybe they found Noah's Ark and they keeping some of our boys in that, too!"

A timeworn ramp for wheelchairs stuck out from the front door like a sick man's tongue. The windows, upstairs and down, were small, like the windows of a prison. A boxy old ambulance that must have been used in the First World War was parked next to the ramp. It had a fresh coat of white paint. Bold red crosses were painted on its sides. The word "COLORED" in big black block letters appeared over the crosses. A faded red and green "MERRY CHRISTMAS" placard was tacked over the entrance to the hospital building, but it was so covered by dust it was barely visible. If buildings had souls I would have said this building had lost its long ago. I said, "This look like de place dey takes you to die."

"Well," Babe said, "let's not pass judgment until we get inside and see Will."

"I don't have to wait to make no judgment. I see what I see and I don't like what I see," Pearl snapped.

Babe was driving very slowly to avoid dirtying his car. I said, "Why don't you two stop fussin' and park this car 'fore I crawl over Pearl and climb out the window!"

"I'm not sure if this is a good idea, Phosie Mae," Babe said as he stopped and Sis' Pearl got out and marched us across the gravel lot toward the dilapidated entrance. "I think we're headed for trouble."

I lost my temper and said, "Sometimes it better not to do too much thinkin', Babe. Sometimes hit better just to do. And dis is shore 'nough one of dose times! So if you can' stand de heat go back in de car and stay 'way from de kitchen."

Babe said, "What will you tell them if the guard called 'fore we got here?"

"Lord have mercy, I don' reckon I cares. We will make somethin' up."

Pearl spat a large wad of tobacco juice out onto the lot. "Even it he did, they have no idea what we look like. We'll tell them we were through the gate on time but we got lost. Now let's go see Will." I am not certain what was more important to Pearl, showing the military no one could push her around or seeing her nephew.

"Look here, visitors are still coming out," I said as a nicely dressed man, his wife, and a pretty caramel-skinned girl who was probably their daughter walked down the ramp. The girl reminded me of Ella Dupre, the girl Will was seeing before he left for the war. Ella had the gentlest eyes of any of the girls in Will's high school class. Her hair was so beautiful, soft, light brown, long, straight, and wavy. I believe she inherited her hair from her mother, a Comanche who had strayed into south Texas. Ella had a ready smile, just like Will's. You could not help but like her. I looked twice to make sure it wasn't her having come to visit Will. It was not. This girl's eyes were clouded by fresh tears. I felt sad for us both and said, "God bless," softly as we passed one another. She nodded. I felt good that I was able to say something comforting and proud of myself for not rolling over and playing dead like some dog when the guards told us visiting hours were over.

I thought of Mrs. Hutchinson, one of the finest white ladies there ever was. Her husband, Captain Earl Beauregard Hutchinson III, was killed when his Navy destroyer was sunk by a Japanese torpedo in the Battle of Leyte Gulf. She understood what it was to lose someone you loved deeply. On her way driving me to the train station in Galveston, she'd said, "Phosie Mae."

"Yes, 'um?"

"There's something you need to hear."

"All right."

"It's a confession," she added in a whisper.

"Well, I've had to make a few of those in my lifetime, so you're not alone."

"My daddy was a fine man. But I feel badly about certain things he said."

"He was a kind man, he treated us all well."

"But he misled a lot of people. He misled you."

"How do you mean?"

"Remember how he would speak to the colored staff in his kind and fatherly tone when they first hired on?"

I remembered word for word. I roughened my voice and recited his lecture. "'Now you listen and you won't have a single solitary problem down here on the panhandle. See, if you have any kind of problem with a white man or a white woman then you just turn and walk right on by. Pretend that no basis for disagreement ever existed. Just smile, say 'Good day' or 'Evening,' and walk away. You know why? It's because I don't want to see any of my Hutchinson people, good as you are, getting into trouble with the law. It's something you don't want and something you definitely don't need. Because there's no way on earth you'll win that argument.'"

"That wasn't right, Phosie Mae. You can't go to Los Angeles thinking like that. You can't get on in life pretending you don't exist. You have to stand up and fight for your rights no matter where you are. If you do there will be people who will help you."

"All right den. But you don' have to 'pologize for somethin' your daddy said or did dat you could not control. He meant well, bless his heart. He pay well too, and gave us our Sundays for church. 'Sides, we was free to go if'n we pleased. No, don' worry 'bout dat."

Just before I stepped up onto the steel ladder of the railroad car, Mrs. Hutchinson took me in her arms, gave me a hug then a kiss on the cheek, and said, "I hope that you will fight for what you believe in, Phosie Mae, just like Will did, just like my husband did. What's happening down here is a sin. You're a good woman. You deserve the freedom to make everything you can out of this life." Then she passed me my "suitcase," a brown paper bag wrapped in twine, and started to cry.

"You'll start me to crying, Mrs. Hutchinson," I said as the train's lonely whistle blew and a conductor along the line shouted, "Passengers to Dallas-Fort Worth, all aboard! Dallas-Fort Worth, all aboard!"

Mrs. Hutchinson waved and shouted "Write!" as the train pulled away.

The memory had me in a trance. Sis' Pearl took me by the hand like a mother takes a frightened child's and said, "Come on, Phosie, let's go see how that boy of yours is doing." And we marched to the hospital entrance. Her better angel had finally arrived. The question was how quickly it would depart.

The lower floor of Barry Hospital had two rows of ten beds with an aisle down the middle. More boys and men with bandaged head wounds, casted limbs, or limbs missing occupied each and every bed. Even though visiting hours were officially over, nicely dressed family members and friends hovered around the beds or sat in chairs set in small circles. The thick aroma of home-fried chicken and collard greens boiled with ham hocks and black-eyed peas mixed with conversations and laughter. It took the chill right out of the early evening air.

A prissy-prim colored nurse about Pearl's size was standing behind the nurses' station at the other end of the ward like she was the President of the United States gettin' ready to make a speech. She had light skin and eyes like a Doberman Pinscher. Her hair was pressed and waved like a white woman's. Her uniform was starched and white. When we arrived at her counter, she said, "Yes?" with an uppity tone and an angry scowl. She was the kind of woman, or man for that matter, who, like many powerless people, if given the least bit of power and, God help us, a uniform, will use that power to elevate themselves to an imaginary status over the very people they have been hired to serve, the very people who pay their salaries. That happens only in government. They'd be fired any place else.

Babe smiled. I felt intimidated.

Sis' Pearl stepped forward and said, "My sister-in-law here"—nodding back toward me—"is looking for her boy, William, Gunnery Sergeant William Eaton. He's a marine."

"Eaton?" she said.

I said, "Dat's right, E-A-T-O-N, ma'am," as delicately as I could. You can't tell people like her what you're feeling because you won't get what you want, unfortunately.

"It's past five. How did you people get past the gate?"

"Well—" Babe started then stopped when I jabbed my elbow into his ribs.

"Oh," I said, ignoring her referring to us as "you people," as though she was white and we were some kind of trash the wind blew in, "we came in 'fore five but my brother's car broke down outside de white burn ward." I grimaced and said, "I apologize if'n dey is any inconvenience," to feed her starched white ego. That did the trick.

"Well, let me see," she said suspiciously as she walked to a file cabinet next to a white porcelain water fountain with the sign "Colored Water" hanging on the wall above it.

She thumbed through the record jackets and said, "I don't see any Eatman. You aren't the people with the delivery?"

"No mam. Like I said, ma'am, we're hear to see my boy, it's Eaton, E-A-T-O-N."

"Here it is. But as I said, visiting hours are over. You'll have to come back next week."

"Looky here," Sis' Pearl said, leaning over the counter, "this woman just rode the Super Chief in from Galveston to see her baby. So why don't you tell us where her boy is and step out the way!"

"If we make an exception for you then we'd have to make an exception for everyone," the nurse said with a smirk. "Is that fair?"

"Dat nonsense!" I said, surprising myself. "You cain't treat everyone 'xactly de same 'cause dey ain' two people on de face o' dis Earth dat is de same. Dere has to be exceptions!"

"That's right!" Babe said.

"I'll say this," I said, "if you get two mamas who just rode a train out from Texas, from Galveston, Texas, to see their one and only chile who fought for this country only to be shot, wounded, then sent back to this dilapidated old shed to heal, then you treats them de same. But 'til you do, I wants to see my baby. Where is he?" A premonition of death came over me again. My chest tightened. I imagined the funeral we had witnessed as we drove to Gate C was Will's funeral. That it was Babe, Sis' Pearl, and my poor dead Isaac standing next to me alongside the grave and the mound of moist brown earth and the two chrome shovels. A fat, shiny earthworm slithered out of the mound and crawled down into the Will's grave. I shivered at the thought. I had to do something. I said, "Please, I'm beggin' you, show us you has a heart. Where is my baby?"

"Is this him, Eaton, William, 4592143, Marines?" the nurse said coldly without expression on her face.

"Dat's him!" I shouted. "Thank the Lord, he's alive! That's him!"

"He's in bed seven, port side, second deck," the nurse said and turned away.

"What?" I said.

"Come on," Sis' Pearl said and pulled me away.

The rickety old stairway creaked and moaned with each of our steps. It must have carried memories of great pain and deep sorrow in its worn timbers. It was ten degrees colder upstairs. There were hardly any visitors. Many of the boys were unconscious; others were too weak or in too much pain to have visitors. There was no laughter. There were no aromas of home-cooked meals and the love that went into preparing them. Except for an occasional groan, cough, snort, or snore, there was nothing but a cold, grim silence. The piquant aroma of Lysol mixed with the ghastly stench of cigarette smoke and the putrid odor of bandages sodden with blood, puss, urine, and excrement from unchanged bedclothes. Sis' Pearl whispered, "Lord have mercy!" and placed her handkerchief over her mouth and nose.

A young white nurse with a sunny smile unclouded by the misery around her greeted us. "May I help y'all?"

"We here to see my son, Will Eaton, if you please."

"Will Eaton! He's a sweetheart. I'm your boy's nurse, Millicent Thompson," she said with a sweet Texas accent. "But you can call me Millie." I didn't care about what she was saying. I was searching the beds for my baby. I gasped when I saw him. He was lying on his back with his head turned in our direction. I did not see light or life in his eyes. His body was there, but it seemed his mind was someplace else. His skin, usually the shade of rich coffee, was dull with a waxen hue. A wool blanket covered him from the waist down. His abdomen was bandaged.

"That's my son! That's my Will!" I screamed as I ran past the nurse. When I reached his bed I placed the back of my hand on his forehead, fearing it would be cold. That he would be dead. He was warm. He had a temperature. I was never so joyful that he was running a fever. He was alive! I covered his forehead with kisses, but he did not stir. I stepped back and watched him. He was hiccupping faintly. His chest barely rose with each breath. When he exhaled there was a rasp. "Oh, my baby, my baby, what happened to you?" I said. I started to cry. "Let me take this pain from you."

I noticed Babe, Sis' Pearl, and the nurse were at my side. I looked at the nurse. I am sure my eyes were begging for some good news, some message of hope. I asked her, "What's wrong wit him? Will he be...will my baby live?"

"Well, as you can see, darlin'," the nurse said gently, "your boy's suffered a critical gunshot wound to the abdomen. Lucky for him there was a hospital ship right off Iwo Jima. The corpsmen transferred him right out for a blood transfusion and surgery. He sure enough is one of the lucky ones."

"Praise the Lord! But why is he so weak?"

"Well, see, when they have a gunshot wound to their stomach it leaks and that can cause an infection in the abdominal cavity, the space around the stomach. They call it peritonitis."

Will hiccupped. "Why is he hiccupping so?" I said.

"It's his diaphragm," the nurse explained. "The muscles of his throat and upper GI tract are still stirred up. But we're getting that under control. His hiccups were much more pronounced when he first arrived. I know he looks bad, but this will all clear up as soon as we are able to administer penicillin."

"Isn't there any penicillin?" Sis' Pearl asked.

"Yes," the nurse said as she looked away, "there's plenty of penicillin."

"Then," Pearl continued, "why aren't you able to *administer* it?"

The nurse was obviously embarrassed and had trouble finding the words. "See, the thing is, well, as soon as the war ended in Europe and now the Pacific, all the men that were fighting over there, they started to celebrate with the women that lived in those countries, and the rate of venereal disease skyrocketed."

"What in de Lord's name does dat have to do wit' my baby?" I asked.

"See, the best drug to treat venereal disease is penicillin. And needles are used to inject it. All the surplus needles are in use overseas. That leaves us with penicillin but no colored needles to inject it with."

"That's the craziest thing I have ever heard, no 'colored needles!'" Pearl said. "Did the Jap who shot this child use a colored bullet?"

"When do you expect to receive them?" Babe said.

"We're hoping for sometime later this week." The nurse looked at me with soothing eyes and said, "Don't worry, ma'am, he'll be fine. Just you wait and see."

I felt as though we were in a little sailboat at sea and Will had fallen overboard. We were circling him and trying to reach for him, but each time we did he drifted further away. All we could do was watch helplessly and hope that the good Lord would help us find a way to save him. I have always believed the Lord helps them that help themselves.

For now, I had to pray for colored needles and a job. It seemed I would be in Los Angeles for some time.

# Chapter 3

## *A Japanese Spy Dog*

As I watched the nurse walk away I noticed the boy in the next bed was smiling at me. His right arm was missing at the shoulder.

"And how are you doin', darlin'?" I asked softly.

"I'm fine, ma'am, just fine," he said without hint of sadness or anger.

"You mus' be in a lot of pain."

"There's a lot worse off than me. How's Gunny doing?"

"Who?" I asked thinking of what I could do to comfort him.

He nodded toward Will and said, "Our Gunnery Sergeant Will Eaton. Is he your son?"

"Yes, he is. He goin' to be fine, just fine," I said, trying to avoid anything that might be discouraging. "Where is your kin?"

"Oh, the Spanish flu took my parents. I live with my Uncle Moses down in Money, Mississippi. It's right there in the center of Leflore County. Have you ever heard of it?"

"Well, if it called Money then we ought go down and pick some off the trees!" Sis' Pearl said, thinking she was funny.

"I wish there was money growin' on trees down there, ma'am. Colored folk poor as possums."

"Well, I don' cook creole style, sugar, but when I brings a dinner basket for my son, I'll pack somethin' up special for you."

"That will be fine, ma'am. Thank you," he said.

"Well," I said, "you looks like you can use a good meal. Can I get you anything? A glass of water?"

"I wouldn't mind a glass of water my own self!" Sis' Pearl said, "When I was in the hospital—"

"Pearl, this is not about you," I said, tossing the words right back at her.

Suddenly, a dull shadow of hopelessness fell over the boy's face. He looked so alone and sad I took him into my arms and gave him a hug. "God bless you, darlin'," I said. His eyes welled up with tears. "What's yur name, sweetheart?"

"Gustavus Taylor Hawkins, but everyone calls me Hawk, ma'am."

"Well, Hawk, I shore do 'ppreciate you bein' my Will's friend."

"Yes, ma'am. We do have some stories, me and Will. Did he ever write you about the dog we saved on Iwo Jima?"

"No, no he did not. But Will he loves dogs, you know, um um."

"Oh, I know. He told me all about his little mutt, Blackie. I don't know if you want to hear the story about the dog we saved just now, though."

"Yes! I certainly do. Please, tell me."

"We want to hear, too!" Sis' Pearl said as she and Babe drew closer. Hawk's eyes filled with light. His face became animated.

"See, we weren't supposed to be up along the line fighting because they thought us colored boys would cut and run soon as shots were fired. But one morning on Iwo Jima as we carried ammo and supplies up to the front and transported the dead white boys back, Gunny, your son Will, and I marched right into a Jap shootin' gallery. Bullets were whizzing by in every direction like angry hornets. Some seemed like they were going in circles when they ricocheted off the lava behind us. There was lava everywhere, and where there was no lava there was sand, and that sand was so hot you could bury a can of baked beans in it and take them out piping hot. So, like I was sayin', Japs were all over the place. Gunny motioned with his hand toward a big chunk of lava and we took cover behind it. Then we started shooting the ammunition we had been carrying up."

"Is that when Will was hit?" I asked.

"No, ma'am. But just after the shooting stopped this dog came up from behind and barked at us. It near about scared the life out of us. I was about to shoot it when Gunny, Will, pushed the barrel of my rifle away. The dog was smaller than a German shepherd and had little peaked devil ears and slits for eyes, just like the Japs had. Its tail was coiled up like a hatband. It stared at us and we stared back until it lay down, let its tongue droop out, and wagged his tail slowly.

"I said, 'It's a spy! We better shoot it before it goes back and gets us killed.'

"Will screwed the cap from his canteen, cupped his hand, and let the dog lap water from his palm. Then he said, 'That's no spy. He's just thirsty.'

"So I said, 'We're goin' to catch hell from the louie, I swear.'

"Well, the dog followed us back to the beach where all the white boys were callin' us 'black angels' because we saved their skin by killing a platoon of Japs. Everyone loved the dog. We named it Tojo, you know, after the emperor. We fed it and played with it some until our lieutenant returned to our bivouac. He was not happy. I can't repeat what he actually said, but the order was for Will and me to take the dog down to the beach and shoot it or he'd have us shot ourselves for bringing a dog back to our position. Everyone protested, but the lieutenant said, 'This dog is a *Namatsu-gawa* Akita, you blockheads! Don't you know what that is?' We all shook our heads. 'It's a Jap spy dog,' he told us. We all looked down at his innocent little face as he lay at Gunny's feet like a kitten waiting for a bowl of milk.

"One of the white boys said, 'Sir, if it's a spy dog, then why can't we train it to be our spy?'

"'Hell no!' our louie shouted.

"Another marine asked, 'Sir, why?'

"And our lieutenant shouted, 'Because none of you people speak Japanese, and I don't think the dog speaks English! So, like I said, either Eaton and Hawk take the dog down to the beach and shoot it, or I will personally take them down to the beach and shoot them!'

"So Will, he fished a fingertip's worth of pork loaf out of a K-ration can that he had heating up in the sand and led the dog down to the beach with me following. The dog had no idea what was happening, I swear. Down at the beach some white boys, sailors, were sitting on a LCVP, that's a boat with a flat bottom they use to move men and material from ship to shore. They watched as Gunny chambered a round in his pistol and ordered the dog to lie down.

"To my surprise it did exactly as it was told. I said, 'Wait a second, Gunny. You said "lie down" and it lay right down. Maybe it's not a spy after all. Maybe he's one of ours!'

"And Gunny said, 'I don't want to shoot it any more than you do, Hawk, but an order's an order.'

"One of the white boys, he was no more than eighteen or so, said, 'Hey, what's the skinny on the dog?'

"I told him, 'It's a Jap spy dog, squid. Our louie gave us the order to shoot it.'

"So the sailor shouted, 'Shoot it? What's with you jungle bunnies? You gotta' shoot everything what moves. Orders from the fleet are that all possible Jap spies are to be taken out to the officer of the deck for interrogation.'

"And Gunny said, 'Then why don't you carry it back to your boat?'

"The sailor answered him, 'Well, see, I don't need no more son-of-a-bitchin' problems than I have already.'" Hawkin's said, "Excuse my language, ma'am."

I let him know it was okay, and he continued.

"So Gunny said, 'Son, I'm ordering you to take this Jap spy dog back to your OD for interrogation.'

"Them two boys laughed and said, 'Load it up!'

"So Gunny, Will, he led the dog to the boat, and it jumped right over the rail."

My eyes filled with tears. I said, "I'm sorry, sweetheart, I interrupted your story."

"Was it something I said, ma'am?" the wounded boy said.

"Oh Lord, no. See, Will, he had him a dog down in Galveston. Blackie, de one he told you 'bout. Hits tail wagged nonstop like an electric fan. It was a wild, scrappy lil' thing. Will's daddy say Will cain't keep it at furst. But Will, he kep' de dog out behind our shed and trained hit 'til it was smart as a college professor. Den his daddy could not find no reason to give hit away. Dat dog and Will, bless dey hearts, dey was 'tached at de hip."

Babe smiled at me then turned his attention to Hawk. "What a wonderful story, young man! You should write it out and send it to a newspaper."

"No sir," the young man said. "The newspapers won't write about us or print pictures of us fighting. War Department wouldn't let them film us either."

"Why on earth not?" Sis' Pearl asked.

"See, newspapers and magazines won't touch us colored boys. The War Department forbade it. They thought that if white folks at home saw us fighting they would have believed the war was lost and stopped buying war bonds. That's why you did not hear about any of us receiving medals or battle commendations. It was a good thing the white boys called us 'black angels' because we did not exist as far as the Marine Corps and the government were concerned!"

"Why, ain' dat a cryin' shame."

Just then I heard a weak voice behind me. "Mama, is that you?" it said.

I turned and looked at my Will. He was gazing back at me as though in a dream. I walked to his bed and held his hand. He smiled, but his smile was tinged by pain. "Mama's here, honeychile," I told him. "I's goin' tah make sure you gets everythin' you needs, hear? All you needs to do is get better and get out dat bed." His smile brightened. I felt the weak pressure of his hand squeezing mine.

Sis' Pearl whispered, "Praise the Lord!"

Babe said, "That's a good sign, Phosie Mae, a good sign. He's going to pull through, just you wait and see. The good Lord won't let you down."

"Ummm-uh. That's right," Sis' Pearl said.

Will closed his eyes. I thought he was dying. I put my hand on his chest to see if he was still breathing. He was, but weakly.

The nurse returned with a small white earthenware jar like the kind they used for mustard or horseradish. It had a yellow sticker on its side with the letters "RP" in red. The handle of a little wood spoon extended out through a slot in its top. She walked to the opposite side of Will's bed, smiled at me, and said, "This is the salve we are using in place of penicillin until our needles arrive."

She folded the gauze bandage back from Will's wound. The edges were coated with a brown crust of dried puss and blood. "We change bandages once each day," the nurse said. "It's the best we can do with what we have." The odor gagged me but I would not, I could not, let myself get sick. *Take dat 'way from my chile and give it to me, Lord. My baby don' deserve hit! He never had a mean bone in his body!*

Sis' Pearl read the label on the jar and said, "RP? I don't know what 'RP' is, but that concoction smells like Billy Goat Cologne!"

"It's Russian Penicillin," the nurse said as she scooped crushed garlic out on the spoon then spread it along the wound's edges.

Will's face twisted up from the sting of the paste, his back arched, and he slid his left heel back toward his hip. I took his hand and said, "I'm sorry, baby. I'm sorry."

"The sting goes away quickly, poor baby," the nurse said.

Sis' Pearl said, "My mama used to use Billy Goat Cologne for cuts, scratches, earaches, sore muscles, the toothache, and piles. I can't believe that in this day and age."

"We mix in a sulfanilamide solution now. The sulfanilamide prevents peritonitis, and the garlic keeps the wound dry."

Will arched his back again and winced. His eyelids snapped up like window shades do when they're pulled down and released too quickly. But once the worst of the sting was over he flattened out and looked over at me and smiled gently. A sob rose up from deep inside me. It was like a wave of nausea. I choked it down.

With lips barely moving, Will said, "Mama, what are you doing in Pearl Harbor? Are you and Daddy all right?"

"Don' you worry, honeychile," I said. "De important thing is that I am here with you. Now you rest, hear?" I did not want him knowing about his daddy's passing.

"But, Mama, how did you get way out here to Hawaii with the war on?" he said.

"We in Los Angeles, baby. de miserable war's over!"

"It is?" Will said.

"Dat's right, it is," I said as I continued to dab his forehead.

He tried to lift his head, but the pain was too great. "Who won, Mama? Who? Did we win, Mama?"

"We sure 'nough did, sugar. We won both ways."

Will smiled. Then he grew serious. "What about Gray, Hawkins, Brooster, and Williams? Where are they?" He tried to lift his head again but could not.

"I'm right over here, Gunny," the young man in the next bed said.

"Hawk?"

"That's right."

Will looked as though he wanted to talk. His cracked lips moved, but no sound came out.

"You rest up now, baby. You'll talk wit' yur friend later." I patted Will's lips with the moist washcloth. "Here you go, sugar."

I stepped away from the bed so that Will would not hear me and said, "When did you say the needles are 'riving'?"

"I see them coming in toward the middle or end of this week at the latest. Your boy will be all right till then if he follows my orders," the nurse said loudly enough for Will to hear her. Will managed a slight grin. "I'm sorry. I know how difficult this is. But on the bright side, strong as your son is, soon as we get penicillin in him he will blossom like the slender aster in the fields outside of Galveston. Just you wait and see."

"Are you sure?" I said.

"Most with this kind of wound don't make it this far. And we did manage to find some colored AB positive. That was a stroke of good fortune. The Lord wants this boy to live."

"What is colored AB positive?"

"AB positive is a very rare blood type, especially among Negroes. There must be white ancestors on your family tree."

"Well, I don' knows nothin' 'bout no white relatives."

"Your job is to just keep thinking positive! And prayer won't hurt either."

"Think positive!" Sis' Pearl bellowed. "My sister-in-law's boy can't get the medicine he needs because there are no *colored* needles and you want us to think positive?"

The nurse said, "I'm sorry, really," then dropped her chin. "You just have to think positive and pray."

"She cain't hep it, Sis' Pearl," I said. "She doin' her best." I could tell by the way the nurse was carrying herself that Will's chances were not as good as she was making them out to be.

It was time to say good-bye.

"I'll be back next Sunday, baby," I said as I patted Will's head one last time. He was already fast asleep again and hiccupping lightly.

"We'll be back!" Sis' Pearl said.

"That's right," Babe echoed.

Hawk waved good-bye with the only arm he had left.

As Babe drove away from the colored ward we passed a little white bus terminal building with a gabled roof, white columns, and arched windows. There was a "Colored" sign on one side and a "White" sign on the other.

"Well, look at that!" Sis' Pearl said as she reached into her purse for her tobacco tin, forgetting again that I had bartered it off for our entry through the gate. "They have them a colored ward, colored water, a colored ambulance, and a colored bus. No colored needles, though. But the Japanese, they're smart, they made bullets for every color. That way they did not have to make duplicates."

"I just hope my baby's going to be all right," I said. "He's the onliest thing I have left in this life."

"He will, he will by and by," Babe said. "We'll pray for him. Won't we, Sis' Pearl?"

"Yes, we will. And while we're at it, take me over to the store so that I can buy another tin of tobacco."

There were fresh guards at Gate C. They paid no attention to us. As Babe turned onto Sepulveda I looked through the dusk toward the cemetery where I'd seen the solider being buried. The family was gone. The mound of dirt was back in the grave. A beautiful white seagull dove from a tree limb, opened its wings just over the top of the sodden grave, and soared high up toward the clouds lit blood orange by the setting sun. I imagined the bird was carrying the soldier's spirit to a better place.

"We'll carry Phosie Mae over to Mrs. Fonteney's to find her a housekeeping position first thing tomorrow morning, dear," Sis' Pearl said casually.

I thought that after spending one night at my sister-in-law's two-bedroom palace in the Crenshaw District, I too would be ready for a better place.

# Chapter 4

## *Mrs. Henrietta Duke*

I felt confident on the drive over to Mademoiselle Fonteney's office. Besides turnip farming and raising up Will and the children of the families I kept house for, I was an expert at washing, sewing, pressing, waxing, sweeping, dusting, and polishing, picking, peeling, pickling, canning, frying, baking, boiling, women's issues, cuts, bruised feelings, nightmares, sleepwalking, colds, sore throats, earaches, the chicken pox, storytelling, and the mumps. I was a good listener, too. Every one of the white ladies I kept house for couldn't wait till I started cooking supper so they could sit in the kitchen and pour their little hearts out before their husbands came home.

"Pearl, is you sure dis lady has jobs over to de Westside near de hospital?" I said.

"Oh my Lord, yes. Why, the Mademoiselle is on the *Westside*! She's placed a lot of our Sisterhood in the best homes with the highest salaries. Oh yes. You should hear them talk about how nice their employers are, um-um, yes. Mademoiselle Fonteney is a fine, gentle woman."

"Well, long as she has jobs near de hospital, dat's all I cares 'bout."

"Oh, I know personally she takes only the best placement opportunities in the best areas."

"Has you met her?" I said.

"Well, not exactly. But everyone says so."

The agency office was located in a posh two-story red brick building on Beverly Drive and Charleville one block south of Wilshire Boulevard. There were two large white columns, one on each side of the main entrance, a big white double door capped by a pair of white scalloped angel's wings.

Stepping out of Babe's car on Beverly Drive in Beverly Hills was like stepping onto a movie studio lot. I felt like a turnip in the asparagus section of a produce market. Each store was prettier than the next. Every person we saw was better dressed than the last. No one looked too poor, too fat, too skinny, too ugly, or too old. We were the only colored folks except for the waitresses in starched white uniforms behind the counter at a hamburger café across the street. I made a joke to ease my nervousness. "God as my witness, hit look to me like every single one of dese people is on de way to a movin' picture screen test."

"No, they just have money, and loads of it," Sis' Pearl said, rubbing her index finger against her thumb to indicate wealth. "And they have class, too!"

"They has to have somethin'," I said, suspecting there was something shallow about all the glamour. People dress up in all sorts of costumes to hide their insecurities. The only costume I could afford was a two-dollar dress from the Salvation Army store. It couldn't hide a thing. I turned toward the tall white doors.

"It's in the alley," Sis' Pearl said, pointing to the corner of the building. We traipsed around back and into a grimy, potholed alley lined by oil-coated telephone poles with a retinue of wisecracking crows perched on their lines. I imagined they thought they were fabulous Beverly Hills crows.

*I wish't I could jus' pick up Will and carry him back to Galveston. I don' like dis city. Hit don' seem real.*

We stood outside the office door and knocked, and a woman dressed like a fortune-teller on a circus midway greeted us. Her long hair was dyed jet black, braided, and pinned with a red silk rose. Her eyes were light green and cunning, like cat's eyes. Her cheeks were painted with bright red rouge to match the rose. Her lipstick covered an area nearly twice as big as her lips. She was wearing sequenced reading glasses and enough costume jewelry to sink a battleship. Mademoiselle Fonteney was not the delicate French woman I expected. Turned out she wasn't even Mademoiselle Fonteney. She looked at Sis' Pearl and said, "I'm Mrs. Henrietta Duke, new owner of the late Mademoiselle Fonteney's Exclusive Domestics. If you've come looking for work, you've come to the right place at the right time. So don't be shy, don't be shy, come right on in and take a seat!" We walked slowly into the tacky little office as if it were a pigeon trap. "That's it. Come right on in, come right on in. There's no one going to bite you here," she said as she closed the door behind us and fastened the bolt lock. The place smelled of stale cigarettes, liniment, and rose water. The walls were covered with faded pink-and-white-striped wallpaper. A small Christmas tree with red, green, and white lights was set on top of the file cabinet so that passersby could see the flashing lights through the small transom window. There was a frayed green sofa with a dusty lopsided picture of the French palace at Versailles hanging over it. A tattered occasional chair and a gurgling water cooler with a coffee can perched on its top were next to the lady's desk. I had worked for one of the most exclusive Galveston families. Nothing about Mrs. Henrietta Duke's place struck me as "exclusive."

It tickled me when the woman took immediate interest in Sis' Pearl. She said, "So tell me, what's your name, honey?" with a nice big smile that exposed front teeth stained with nicotine and lipstick.

Sis' Pearl said, "Oh, my name is Pearl Eaton. I'm secretary of the Sisterhood, ummm-ummm. I brought—"

"We'll find you something real nice, a woman of your stature, bright skin, and such beautiful white teeth. Yes, real nice," Mrs. Henrietta Duke said in a dry, gravelly voice as she lit a cigarette, "Folks pay a premium for a woman reminds them of Aunt Jemima." Pearl was fit to be tied. I looked down at the floor and bit my lower lip hard as I could to keep from crying out laughing.

Sis' Pearl said, "Oh! I'm—"

Mrs. Henrietta Duke brushed Sis' Pearl's comment off with a pudgy hand. "No, no problem finding something real-real nice for a lady of your stature, long as you don't eat too much. No problem at all. These people," she said as she swept her arm around the points of an imaginary compass to show us the territory she covered, "you'll look beautiful in a night white uniform and a red head scarf, oh yeah! She laughed until she started choking and coughed till her watery eyes looked like they would pop out of her skull. I was shaking from laughter thinking how some little white child would walk into his mama's kitchen and see a big old colored woman looking like Aunt Jemima right off the box of her pancake mix and then being scared out of its skin when Sis' Pearl turned around and scrawled at it. I declare I would have taken the train out just to watch Pearl be compared to Aunt Jemima even if Will was perfectly healthy.

Sis' Pearl had had enough. She pointed at me and said, "I don't do housekeeping. It's her." I tried to smile, but my lips were quivering.

"Well, if you ever change your mind, you call me right away. I can always find something for a full-figured woman such as yourself," Mrs. Henrietta Duke said. "You know, they pay more for a larger woman. I don't know why, but they do!"

Turning to me, Mrs. Henrietta Duke shook her head wearily and said, "Now, let's see if we can find anything for *you*." She made "you" sound like "pew," as if I were something pulled out of a garbage can. She looked at my secondhand clothes. "You look like you just fell off the hay wagon! Whereabouts are you from? Louisiana? Mississippi? Alabama?" she said loudly as if I was hard of hearing or could not understand simple English.

"I'm originally from… I was born in Uniontown, Alabama, but I've spent most of my adult life in Galveston, Mrs. Henrietta," I said, trying to follow old Mr. Hutchinson's advice and not take anything a white person says to heart.

"So, tell me what brings you out to the coast at your *ripe* age. You looking for a man?" she said and chortled.

"Oh no, madam. I've done all my looking. My boy, he was, he *is* a marine." I was so nervous I could barely string my words together. "He was shot in de stomach. He in de military hospital in West Los Angeles. Dat's why I came up from Galveston to look after him. Now, I needs work, if you please." I was talking in the submissive tone of a house Negro. I hated playing that role.

"Well, we have to find *you* something PDQ then?"

"That's right!" Sis' Pearl said. "That's right, she needs a PDQ too!" My sister-in-law did not even know what she did not know.

"Come 'round this side of the desk," Mrs. Henrietta Duke said, directing me with the motion of a hooked finger that carried an aqua octopus ring with a red ruby eye and glass beaded tentacles. I felt nauseous looking at it.

I stood at her side as she opened her desk drawer and removed a set of small wooden tiles strung on a chain like shaded stain samples found in a hardware store. The shades ranged from very light tan to very dark chocolate. A white rabbit's foot was linked on the chain between the tiles.

"Let's see now," she said as she placed one of the tiles against my skin. "This is a number five, and you're darker than that! Know what?"

"What?" I said.

"You're too damned dark to work this side of town."

I pulled my arm away, stepped back, looked at her, and said, "What in Jesus' name is you doing testing my skin shade like I was some cow being sent to auction for its hide?"

"I'm checking your shade, hon, because if you want work in this town we have to know what your shade is."

I felt shocked and humiliated. I yanked my arm from her grasp and walked out of the office and waited on the landing. I would have walked right down the steps, but I had no idea where I would have gone. I took a few deep breaths to calm myself.

Sis' Pearl opened the door and said, "Phosie, you need a job. You need to come back in. It's nothing personal against you. They do this for all the women. Think about Will."

I knew Sis' Pearl's interest was not in Will but in in getting me hired so that she could hold bragging rights with her Church Sisterhood. But that really did not matter. My interest was in Will. He was lying alone in that hospital, close to dying. I had no choice but to walk back in. Mrs. Henrietta Duke had already selected the matching tile. She laid it down against my skin. "Look," she said, "you're a perfect seven." She held it there so that I could study it.

"That's two shades too dark for the old-money penny-pinchers of Holmby Hills, Bel Air, and Beverly Hills. They like their *coffee* light, with a little cream and lots of sugar, the good-for-nothing cheap bastards," Mrs. Henrietta Duke said, laughing at her own bravado.

"I knows, I knows," Sis' Pearl said.

"This shouldn't be a problem too big to solve," Mrs. Henrietta Duke said as she flicked through a stack of cards in a red satin box. "Are you willing to travel?"

I said. "I jus' did travel."

"Oh, I don't mean that kind of travel. I mean travel out to the Heights, Boyle Heights."

"Boyle Heights?"

"Yeah, Boyle Heights, a fine little residential *enclave* north of Chinatown. Mostly Jews, Mexicans, and a handful of Japs now that the Italians and Russians moved to greener pastures. The Jews will be gone too before you know it. But I'll tell you what," she said, leaning over her desk waving a blue index card with my future employer's information on it, "a job with one of the *Heebs* is a thousand times better than one your sister here could get with one of the tightfisted old-money pikers in Hancock Park. Those Jews, they bathe their help in honey."

"That's right!" Sis' Pearl said. "Yes, they do!"

Mrs. Henrietta Duke picked up the card and read. "Let's see, this listing is for a divorcee. I actually met her. She's a beautiful woman, tried to be an actress but only made it to cocktail waitress. Name's Mrs. Lucile Goldberg, but she told me she goes by the name "Lucky." Spends a lot of time in Las Vegas, she said. There's a kid, a five-year-old, who's been having some difficulties adjusting to his daddy's leaving. And like I said, she's a Jew. It's a live-in, six days, off Sunday morning for church, back Sunday evening, uniforms and meals included, if you don't eat too much. See, you'll have Sunday for church and a visit with your boy at the hospital," Mrs. Henrietta Duke said as she picked up a sequined pen and tabulated a row of figures on a little pad of paper. "And the pay is…let me see. The pay is seventeen dollars and fifty cents per week, cash on the barrelhead. That's after you pay me my cut of two dollars and fifty cents. You know, that's not too bad for you. Think you can handle it?"

"Oh, I can handle anything that comes through the front door of a house, but how will I get over to de hospital?" I said.

"No problem. You'll ride a Red Car then a Yellow Car right to the hospital," Mrs. Henrietta Duke said.

"Red car? Yellow car?" I said.

"Don't worry, Phosie Mae, we'll carry you over to the hospital," Babe said.

"If she rode the train clear out from Texas, sweetheart, she can certainly ride the trolley to the Westside," Sis' Pearl said in a pleasant tone laced with disapproval.

"Not from Boyle Heights! That Mexican White Fence gang is running wild over in that part of town!" Babe said.

"Mexican gangs?" I said.

Mrs. Henrietta Duke chuckled. The jowls of fat under her chin shook. "Look," she said, leaning toward me, "if you take this today, I'll give you a five-dollar signing bonus." She dropped her chin and lowered her voice. "I just won't take the two dollar and fifty cent fee for the first two weeks," she said then cleared her throat.

"I see."

"Then when I have an opening out here on the Westside, voila, I'll send you over for an interview. Think of this as just temporary."

"That sounds too good to be true," Sis' Pearl said. "You can buy some things to wear to the hospital with the money."

"I might even get you a little more salary. The client is desperate. The last girl, a Mexican, took her kid out to her boyfriend's mariachi bar every time the lady went out on a date with one of her gentleman callers or when she worked nights at a neighborhood bar. And the one before that, another Mexican, slapped the kid. The kid's a handful. Oh, this lady, she'll take to a nice little colored gal such as yourself right away, no questions asked. So, what's it going to be, doll?"

*Lord have mercy, what kind of mother lets womens like dat come within ten miles of dey childrun?* I thought. *Not my kind!*

"When would I start?" I said.

Mrs. Henrietta Duke scribbled the lady's name and New Jersey Street address on a piece of paper and slid it across the table. "When do you start? Today!"

# Chapter 5

## *White Camellia Knights*

As Babe and Sis' Pearl carried me out to Boyle Heights and my new job, I kept thinking, *Boyle Heights, Boyle Heights, Boyle Heights.* It sounded like something ugly needing lancing. I felt the blind fury of a storm had ripped my life out by its roots and was sweeping me toward a dark abyss. It was a merciless storm trying to tear my Will, the only love of my life, away like an exasperated mother yanks a dirty spoon from the hand of an innocent child. It made no difference whether I had prayed or did not pray, whether I had sinned or did not sin. I felt the good Lord had turned his back on me. Hoping for Babe to say something to help me through, I said, "Oh Lord, why has dis all fallen on my shoulders? What did my baby do to deserve dis? What did I do wrong?"

"Well," Sis' Pearl said, "nothing works like the healing power of prayer, you know."

"Pearl, don' you thinks I knows 'at? I been prayin' all my natural life and look where I is!" I felt like shoving my fist down her throat.

"The good Lord works in mysterious ways, Phosie Mae," Babe said.

"Well, I reckon he best work faster den. My baby has jus' one week to get de peni…de peni…de medicine he need."

Babe took Wilshire Boulevard to show me the sights. At La Cienega Boulevard, right in the middle of the intersection, glistening oil-sodden workers were scuttling over a tall, dank wood derrick like beetles.

I watched them toil and remembered how Isaac had worked and died on a wildcatter's rig in Texas. I thought about how life can feel as fixed as granite yet at the same time be as fragile as the filaments of a spider's web. Like Adam in the Garden of Eden, one day we feel we are the masters of our destiny, the next day we realize we are not. Yet the good Lord designed it so we still have to keep on living, choosing good over evil, light over darkness, no matter how much difficulty we face.

As we passed the May Company, a streamlined department store big as the Queen Mary cruise ship, with the three of us still riding on the front seat and with me in the middle like their child, I glanced up into the rearview mirror. The sun, glowing like an ingot of molten steel, had paused on the horizon as if to take one more look at its day's work before night descended to deposit all the good and the evil acts of that day into the dark well of the past as if they never had happened. I prayed that my faith would return when the sun rose up again the next day.

Babe cleared his throat and said, "The Miracle Mile starts here at The May Company Department Store." He waved his open palm as if he were showing me a city of miracles. And sure enough there was a MIRACLE MILE sign along the sidewalk announcing we had arrived. "And, there on our left, are the famous La Brea Tar Pits. That's where they have found fossils of the giant prehistoric beasts that roamed the earth before man arrived." Sis' Pearl was protesting our presence by refusing to take in the sights. I glanced at her. She was staring indignantly down the middle of the boulevard looking like a water buffalo as if there was no room for joy in her heart. *Dey jus' might have dug my sister-in-law up out dese pits de way she carry on.*

"Don't look like any kind of miracle to my eyes!" Sis' Pearl said. The businesses had switched on their neon signs. The twinkling lights in their windows let customers know they were welcome to come in out of the looming darkness and be comforted with some new something that would temporarily shield them from the silent anguish we all feel over the uncertainty of our lives. The sun had cast an orange hue on the red and white Christmas bells dangling over the boulevard. There was so much life in the dusk I felt I was dreaming. We passed another department store called Orbach's, and this one was covered in white marble like a temple to a Roman god. There where so many well-dressed white people coming and going from it that Sis' Pearl broke her vow of silence and said, "Least some people have all the money they need to shop."

I tried to imagine how it would be to have the money and the time to shop in a fine department store, to wear new clothes, or just to be able to enter and walk around without a broom, a dustpan, and a rag covering my bristly hair. I was struck by the thought that I did not have the money to buy Will a nice present for Christmas. I sighed and thought, *There are no miracles for my kind on this mile.* I plunged deeper into hopelessness. The hill felt too high to climb and the river too wide to cross. I remembered something my mama taught me as she was walking me to school one morning along the shoulder of Highway 21 past Pitts Folly House.

"Phosie Mae!" she had said.

"Yes, mama." I was a good little girl.

"See how dese trucks and wagons come rumbling by us one after de next?"

"Yes, mama."

"Sum be filled wit cotton, sum wit turnips, and others wit corn. All headin' one way or de other. Our thoughts and feelin's run jus' like dese trucks and wagons, honeychile. Some be happy and some be sad."

"I try to stay happy, mama."

"See, every one of our thoughts and feelings pass through our minds one after de other jus' like dese wagons and trucks pass on de highway a life. Dere somethin' different yet de same coming over and over agin. That's just the way our thoughts and feelings do, come and go all de time. Come to think on it, dey jus' like de weatha'. You can't stop them comin', but you can do something 'bout dem."

"What's that, mama?"

"When dark thoughts has you feelin' down, I want you to remember dat dey nothin' but thoughts and feelings passing through yur mind jus' like dese trucks and wagons are passing on de road. Dey come and dey go and dey come 'round again. If'n a bad thought or feelin' come into yur mind, don't let it carry you away too far down de line. Place yur mind on somethin' else and get movin'. There is always somethin' good to be done. Doin' somethin' good will carry you right through de good times and de bad."

"All right, mama."

A cow in the pasture next to the road mooed as if to confirm that what my mama was saying was right.

It was cold that morning. Our breath and that of the cow formed little puffs of clouds each time we exhaled. "Now, you buttons up dat coat all de way 'fore you catch your death!"

"Yes, mama, I will. I love you, mama."

"I loves you too, honeychile."

I felt comforted by the memory and wished my mama were still alive as I watched the white folk along the Miracle Mile rushing to do their shopping. I thought, *I don' need de miracles on dis mile. I needs my baby to get well. I needs dis job to keep me 'til he do.* I looked up at a jolly Santa driving his sleigh over the boulevard from one lamppost to another and prayed silently again, *Lor' have mercy! Please! I cain't do dis alone. I need yur hep'ng hand now!*

A fire truck with its siren on screamed by us. There was a billowing plume of dark smoke ahead. As we drove, I could see what looked to be a burning building in the distance. My thoughts were carried back to a night in Galveston when the Klu Kluxers set Ella Dupre's parents' place, on the lot next to ours, ablaze.

That was in October of 1938. Around that time a number of the Negro leaders in Texas were trying to get the Democrats to open up what they called their "white primary" for the upcoming governor's election to all races. The Democrats called themselves a "club," and that enabled them to hold a private, invitation-only vote. The polling places were their clubhouses.

The fight went to court and the Democrats lost. The Democrats were outraged. A small group of white men resurrected an old Kluxer chapter from northern Texas called the "White Camellia Knights." Their plan was to scare us. These so-called "Knights" drove through the colored neighborhoods with a loudspeaker announcing, "If you are a law-abiding *Nigrow*, a good Christian, and if you don't try to stir up any trouble with the federal government, there is nothing to fear! No harm will come to you, your, family, or your property." We did not bow. They burnt a few crosses in the front yards of blacks, Jews, and any of the white folk they thought were their enemies, folks who believed in equal civil rights. When the burning crosses failed they hung empty nooses from the limbs of trees lining the county's roads. That terrified us, but we stood our ground. We wanted to vote just like everyone else. Truth be told, the Knights' patrols did keep the drunks, both black and white, off the streets. Crime went down all over the city. They should have taken jobs at the police department.

On this chilly October night Will and I were having our supper when we heard gunshots and the Dupre girls' screams. A loud explosion followed. Mr. Dupre, a wildcatter just like my Isaac, kept dynamite in a shed next to the house. Ella Dupre, the Dupre's youngest daughter, was, I have written, Will's secret sweetheart. I say secret because he was too frightened to tell her of his affection. Ella lived in a two-room tenant shack no bigger than ours with her mother, father, and her two sisters.

Will dropped his fork and charged out the door. I chased after him screaming, "Come back here!" There was a second explosion. A tower of flames lit up the night. I ran after Will and screamed, "Will! Will, you come!" But I tripped over a rough patch of caliche, fell, and skinned my knees.

By the time I reached the Dupres', I saw the spineless White Camellia Knights wearing white sheets and hoods speeding down the road in the bed of a red Fork pickup like a load of chickens. Ella's mama had taken Ella and her two sisters to the front gate to shelter them from the flames consuming their home. Will was on his knees near the house holding Mr. Dupre's limp body in his arms. I could see blood on Will's shirtsleeve and screamed, "Will, is you shot?"

"No, mama, but we need to get Mr. Dupre to a doctor before it's too late. It's him dat's shot."

"How are we goin' to do dat?" I shouted over the fire's roar.

Mrs. Dupre shouted at Will, "Our truck in de shed 'hind de house, but it broke down." I don't know where he learned to fix a car, but Will had that truck out of the shed and ready to go before we realized what was happening. We loaded Mr. Dupre onto a bed of hay on the truck's bed and Will drove him to a colored clinic in West Galveston.

From that day forward Will confided that he was definitely going to work on getting up the nerve to ask Ella Dupre to dance at the next church social. He was almost as shy as his daddy when it came to women.

"What are you thinking about?" Babe said as he turned onto Los Feliz Boulevard. Sis' Pearl had nodded off and was snoring lightly.

"Oh, I was thinking 'bout Galveston, 'bout how brave Will was when de Klu Kluxers burnt our neighbors', the Durpres', house to de groun' and shot de daddy. Will was a hero shore 'nough dat night, but he was still too shy to ask de beautiful Dupre girl, Ella, to dance at de church social. Dat was back in thirty-eight, seven years ago now. Hit amazin' how life trickles out drop by drop and then you look back and realize you've lived through an ocean of time and change."

"Well," Babe said, "that's why mama used to tell us to live as though every breath was our last breath!"

"That's right."

Babe drove us through a white area where beautiful homes with big front lawns and gardens overflowing with red roses, yellow roses, orange poppies, and sunset manzanita like we had down in Texas, lined the street. They were not as big as the houses they had on Broadway down in Galveston. Most of those houses had a staff. Even without looking at the inside of the houses I was now inspecting I felt even if my new employer's house was the same size I would be able to keep it running and everybody happy with one hand tied behind my back.

Babe made an announcement like a tour guide. "This is the Las Feliz area. Griffith Park is just down the road. There are some nice shady picnic places in the colored section. We'll be crossing over the Los Angeles River soon."

A little further along I noticed a handsome young family out in front of one of the fine homes. The husband and his wife were leading their two little adorable towheaded twins, who were walking like bowlegged old codgers, out to their car. The entire family was dressed beautifully. A foolish hope surged up in me. I pictured Will and Ella Dupre coming out of a house just as fine as the one I was looking at with their two kids. *It no use,* I thought. *Even if Will were to have a profession, dey still wouldn't allow a colored man to buy in a white area, marine or no marine.* I looked at Babe; his Department of Water and Power job actually paid quite handsomely. *But Babe's job won' be 'round time all de white mens come back from de war. Dey'll take back de good jobs and save de servin', sweepin', scrubbin', and moppin' for de colored mens. Here I goes getting' down for no good reason. I ain' no fortune-teller. Will and Ella, if'n Will ever do get de courage to ask her to marry him, don' need one of these miracle places to be happy. Isaac and I were happy in our little tenant shack.* I thought of Will lying there in the hospital bed and whispered, "God bless you and keep you, darlin'."

"Who are you talkin' to?" Sis' Pearl asked.

"Oh, I was just thinking aloud," I said.

"Well, it looked like you were thinking with a whole head full of people."

Babe saved me. "That's the Mulholland Fountain over on the right opposite the entrance to Griffith Park," he said, pointing with his free hand. "Kids swim in it during the dog days of summer."

I could have cared less. I just wanted to speed up so that I could start my new job; housework helped me to clear my mind. "Why, dat's de most beautiful fountain I have ever seen!" I said. "But cain' you drives a little bit faster so we get dere 'fore midnight?" I realized I had sounded cross and said, "I's sorry, Babe, I'm just all knotted up on de inside."

"Don't worry about me, Phosie Mae, I understand."

"Umph!"

New Jersey Street was no Las Feliz Boulevard. Doctors, lawyers, bankers, businessmen, and people from the movie industry lived in the big homes on Las Feliz. The little cottages and bungalows on New Jersey Street looked to be occupied by the carpenters, plumbers, and barbers who built the Las Feliz folks' cabinets, mowed their lawns, fixed their toilets, and cut their hair. The curtains on all the windows were drawn halfway, giving the street a sleepy look.

I chuckled as Babe parked the car out front of Mrs. Goldberg's place at the 1937 address. It was nothing at all as big as the Las Feliz-style house I had built up in my imagination. I felt confident I could keep the place and the child up blindfolded.

I was a little excited because this would be the first time I would meet someone of the Jewish faith in person, let alone work for one and live in their home. I didn't believe the people down in Galveston who gossiped that Jewish menfolk wear black fedoras to hide the horns on the tops of their heads and long black coats to hide their tails, just like I didn't and don't believe the myth that Negroes are shiftless and lazy. The Lord knows I wasn't. And if other Negroes were so shiftless and so lazy, then why were the plantation owners willing to pay so much for them back before emancipation and why were white workers so frightened of losing their jobs to colored folks?

The first thing I heard when Babe opened Sis' Pearl's door was an eerie, unnatural sound I will carry in my memory till the day I die. It was like the savage barking of a little dog trying to keep a much bigger dog in its place. Yet there was a menacing, human pitch to it. It was like no dog I had ever heard before.

"RRRRRRR-YIP-YIP-RRRRRRR-YIP-YIP-YIP!"

"Lordie, what kind of voodoo dog is that?" Sis' Pearl said as Babe helped or rather hoisted her up out of the car like they'd hoist a big fish up onto the deck of a Gulf fishing boat. "It sound like it wants to talk!"

"RRRRRRR-YIP-YIP-RRRRRRR-YIP-YIP-YIP!"

The slowed cadence of this last utterance reminded me of Will's hiccups. A thousand needles of fear stung me.

"There appears to be more than one residence at this address," Babe said after he had Sis' Pearl settled on the sidewalk on her own two feet.

"What?" I asked as I looked up the buckled cement path to the lady's front porch. The path's misshapen cement reminded me of the crooked tombstones wrenched about by storms in the graveyard behind our South Galveston church.

"There appears to be more than one residence at this address. There are two front doors up there, with no markings," Babe said again.

"That's a duplex!" Sis' Pearl announced as my brother draped a brand-new six-pelt honey-brown mink shawl across her shoulders. "I declare, them Jews must be real small like if two of their families can live in that tiny place with a dog to top it all!"

"RRRRRRR-YIP-YIP-RRRRRRR-YIP-YIP-YIP!"

"We cain' do no good standin' out chere like scaredy crows. Let's march up onto dat porch and figure out which door to knock on twixt de two."

Each of the minks' heads hung down and over the right side of Pearl's chest. Their little black demon eyes followed me as I followed my brother up to the porch.

"Pearl, I don't thinks whatever it is barkin' on de other side of dat door is going' to take to dat shawl. Those minks look alive, mean, and ready to eat someone or somethin'!" I said with a chuckle.

"Well, cold as it is, I am certainly not taking it off for no fool dog."

*Thank you, Jesus, for letting me find this job! At least I don't have to suffer living in her home!*

I looked up at the man in the moon. The cold cast a silver halo of mist around his face. His eyes looked doleful, as if from a premonition of a painful event.

"RRRRRRR-YIP-YIP-RRRRRRR-YIP-YIP-YIP!"

I felt shivers of fear gripping my spine like jolts of electricity. *Lord, I'm beggin' you, please look after my baby, please! I'll never axe you for 'nother thing long as I lives.* I looked behind me. I felt that the neighbors were standing behind their half-drawn blinds, watching each and every one of our steps.

We walked past a black Ford pickup truck with four greasy rendering barrels and a boom crane on its bed. It was parked in the narrow driveway along the left side of the house. Its sweet, rotten aroma was so strong I could taste the grease.

"Whew! It smell like somethin' died in those barrels. I can sure enough taste it. I wouldn't let anyone park a filthy thing like that out front of my house, not in a million years!" Sis' Pearl said as she stumbled on a crack in the walkway and nearly fell onto her face.

"Well, I'm glad we cleared dat up!"

Sis' Pearl stopped and looked back at me. "What did you say?"

"I said, 'Is this the way December freezes up?'"

"It's supposed to snow tonight for the first time in thirty-nine years," Babe said.

"Snow! In Los Angeles?" I said in disbelief.

"No need to worry, though," Babe said. "The weather's almost always clear and beautiful by New Year's Day no matter what. That you can go to the bank with."

"Well, that pretty white *Rose Queen* has to have her *Rose Parade!*" Sis' Pearl said as she plodded on.

The little dog's barking grew louder and more wild. "RRRRRRR-YIP-YIP-RRRRRRR-YIP-YIP-YIP!"

We stopped at the bottom of the red steps to get a closer look at the two homes. Through a cracked window, we could hear a Billie Holiday record playing softly in the unit on the right. The unit the dog was in.

*The more I read the papers*
*The less I comprehend*
*Nothing seems to be lasting*

"RRRRRRR-YIP-YIP-RRRRRRR-YIP-YIP-YIP!"

We stood between the two doorways, each lit by lights dimmed by soot and dead moths inside the lily-shaped glass shades that covered them. *Those are coming down for cleaning first!* I thought. I could not help myself.

There was a dim light along the edges of the left unit's window such as might be seen around the edge of a garage door when a light's on inside. I leaned toward it and realized there was a wall, literally a wall, of stacked newspapers blocking the view from the street into the house. *That's a barricade!* I thought.

The other unit's windows were covered with jungle-green drapes decorated with wavy palm trees and bright-colored parrots. The drapes were parted just enough in the middle to display a small Christmas tree standing on a lamp table. Silver bells on the tree's branches reflected the little twinkling red, green, and blue lights that were strung around its branches like stripes on a candy cane.

Sis' Pearl noticed me leaning over and said, "That must be the place with a nod toward the window with the barricade."

How could hit be? Why would a woman live behin' a barricade of old newspapers wit' her chile?

As if in answer to my unspoken question, Sis' Pearl said, "Maybe she afraid her former husband going to come attack her."

I felt a heavy weight pressing against my chest. *It just can't be!*

"Why doesn't someone just knock on the door and see before we dig ourselves a deeper hole and freeze while we're at it?" Babe said in a very rare display of impatience.

I knocked on the door on the left. A light switched on. The dog next door growled. A specter slipped across the channel of glaring light between the barricade and the door. I sensed someone standing behind it.

"I don't like this one bit," Sis' Pearl said.

I knocked harder. "Hello?"

# Chapter 6

## *Mr. Jakie and De Voodoo Chile*

A strange man opened the door just enough to peek our and spy on us. We could see one half of his unshaven face. He said, "I'm ain't interested in being saved, we're Jews."

The dog next door was also not pleased by our proximity.

"GURRRRRRRRRRRRRRRR."

The reeking stench of stale cigarette smoke choked me. The un-shaven man's skin was tanned, and he had lake-blue eyes. His hair was cut marine style, high on the sides and tight on the top. He was wearing government-issue eyeglasses, khaki overseas uniform pants, and a time-washed T-shirt with his dog tags hanging down over it. A fresh, unlit cigarette, then only clean thing about him, was propped up behind his right ear like a baby in a bassinette. I studied his eyes. An eerie glaze covered any spark of life that may have been in them. Bitter smoke curled up from a cigarette he was holding in his left hand. His right arm was hanging at his side. I looked down. He was holding a black pistol, like the police used. I stepped back onto Sis' Pearl's fat big toe.

"For Jesus's sake, watch where you're stepping," she said and el-bowed me back toward the man with the gun.

"GURRRRRRRRRRRRRRRR."

"We're not from de church. I's lookin' for Mrs. Goldberg. May I speak wit' her?"

The man smiled, but it seemed the smile was a mask rather than a reflection of a feeling.

"That's my sister. She lives next door. Are you the new girl?"

"Yes, sir, I believe I is," I said, feeling as though I were about to stick my hand into a wild animal's cage to feed it raw meat. I shook the feeling. I would have walked into a den of lions if it meant saving my Will.

"I'm her brother, Jakie," he said with a slight smile. He pointed the barrel of the gun at the other door. "You'll find my sister there. I hope you have better luck then the others!" He laughed.

"Thank you kindly, thank you very kindly," I said as we shuffled away.

The man called out after me, "What's your name, sister?"

"Mrs. Eaton," I said. "Phosie Mae Eaton."

"That's a pretty name."

He was clearly troubled but trying to be nice. I felt sad for him. He must have suffered something terrible in the war. "Thank you kindly."

"Just knock if you need anything, Phosie Mae."

"GURRRRRRRRRRRRRRR."

I dashed around Sis' Pearl to put her between the man and me. Babe tapped on the next door so lightly we could barely hear it and we were standing right next to him. Pearl, indignant, said, "Oh my Lord, let me by 'fore I freeze!" and brushed Babe out of her path with a sweep of her forearm. She rang the doorbell three times then rapped the iron ring of the door knocker so loudly I looked back at the neighbors' houses to see if they would answer their front doors.

"*Com-ing*!" a lady said in a singsong voice as if her world was one big theatrical production.

"RRRRRRRR-YAP-YAP-RRRRRRRR-YAP-YAP-YAP!"

I inadvertently glanced back at Mrs. Goldberg's brother's door. He was ogling me with a coy smile. *Last thing in the world I need now is some shell-shocked white man with a loaded gun comin' after me!* I turned away without giving him the satisfaction of a nod.

A little door protected by black rod iron burglar bars had been cut out of the front door for viewing guests. It reminded me of a speakeasy in a James Cagney movie. The toasty aroma of marijuana cigarette smoke weeped out and spiced the icy air.

The dog's growl grew more vicious.

"RRRRRRR-YAP-YAP-RRRRRRR-YAP-YAP-YAP!"

Sis' Pearl backed up against the porch rail, shouting, "That is definitely not like any dog bark I ever heard! Somethin' must be terrible wrong with it!"

"I would take dat shawl off or go back to de car, one, if I was you, Pearl. 'Cause if'n dat dog sees dem lil' black-eyed animals hangin' 'round your neck, Lord knows what hit may do." The sounds of Billie Holiday singing drifted out to us.

*Oh yeah, life is bad*
*Stormy weather*

The lady's face appeared in the viewer. She had satin auburn hair and beautiful white skin. Her fetching green eyes were like cat-eyed marbles except for their being scored with red lines like railroad maps. She sang "Hi!" in the same fabulous voice. But before she could open the door, the telephone rang. "For Christ's sakes," she laughed, "why does everything have to happen at the same time? Can you wait?"

"Certainly!" Sis' Pearl said with a cheery air. She was, after all, representing her Church Sisterhood.

The phone rang again.

"RRRRRRR-YAP-YAP-RRRRRRR-YAP-YAP-YAP!"

Through the viewer, I heard the lady shout, "Quiet, goddamn you!"

I thought that was harsh because the scared little thing was probably just trying to protect her.

Again the phone rang.

"GURRRRRRRRRRRRRRRR."

She left the flap open and answered the phone in a steamy bedroom voice. "Darling! Where are you? Did you let another little surgery keep you away? If you did, I'm going to have to put you in bed and spank you!"

That dog must have had some idea who the caller was and clearly did not like him one bit.

"RRRRRRR-YAP-YAP-RRRRRRR-YAP-YAP-YAP!

"GURRRRRRRRRRRRRRRR."

The lady's tone switched from hot and steamy to wicked and vicious. "Oh, it's you! Waddyawant, you lying, two-timing, no-good son of a bitch?"

The lady sure did not like the caller, but the dog changed its tune.

"YAP-YAP-YAP-YAP-YAP-YAP!"

"Oh, so now you're drunk and you wanna come by and see the kid, do you? I'll tell you what, you send me my fucking alimony and child support then maybe, just maybe, you'll see the kid."

"YAP-YAP YAP-YAP-YAP-YAP!"

"Don't you threaten me! Oh yeah? I'll tell you what, you violate the restraining order, you step on this property, Jakie will put a bullet through your thick skull, you lying, conniving bastard!"

Now she had my attention. *Lord have mercy! My baby just got home from one war and these people are fighting another one!* "Maybe we came at de wrong time," I said to Babe and Pearl.

"YAP-YAP YAP-YAP-YAP!"

The lady shouted, "Shut up!"

"We'll just let this blow by," Sis' Pearl said with the great confidence people who watch other people about to face danger have in them.

"That's not your dog! You want to know where your dog is? I'll tell you where it is. Jakie took it away for rendering!"

"YAP-YAP YAP-YAP-YAP!"

"I've heard enough of your bullshit, Mr. High Roller. Now you listen to me! You want to see the kid? You send me a stinking check for my alimony and child support! No tickee, no washee! You dig?" The receiver crashed down. "Son of a bitch!"

Without the lady shouting anymore, Billie Holiday's blue voice drifted came drifting out and mixed with the still scent of marijuana.

*Stormy weather, stormy weather*
*Me and my daddy ain' together*
*Stormy, stormy, stormy, weather*

"She seems upset," Babe said.

"Upset?" I said, "She 'bout to kill somebody!"

"Well, I wouldn't worry too much about it. She is one of Mrs. Henrietta Duke's clients, you know," Sis' Pearl said.

I looked up at Sis' Pearl. "I wouldn' worry none neither if I was not de one 'bout to pass through dis door!"

Sis' Pearl just huffed at me, and right then the phone rang yet again.

"YAP-YAP-YAP! YAP-YAP-YAP! YAP-YAP-YAP!"

"What!" the lady shouted into the telephone.

*Here we goes again!* But she switched into her bedroom voice. "*Darling*, I thought you'd never call. Listen, darling!"

"RRRRRRR-YAP-YAP-RRRRRRR-YAP-YAP-YAP!

"GURRRRRRRRRRRRRRR."

"Yes, darling. Listen, I'm getting dressed. What time are you coming? You want to *come* twice? *Ummmm!* We'll see what we can do about that, you bad little boy."

"RRRRRRR-YAP-YAP-RRRRRRR-YAP-YAP-YAP!

"GURRRRRRRRRRRRRRR."

"Why does he want to come twice?" Sis' Pearl asked.

If she did not know the answer at her age, I wasn't about to explain it.

"Listen, baby, my new girl just arrived. Yes, I had to let the other one go. I'm trying a colored one this time. Those Mexicans are good for nothing! So I have to be a bad little girl and say good-bye so that I can show her around and finish dressing. An hour? Fabulous! Listen, I'm wearing the new dress you bought me. Wait till you see it. You'll flip. So don't be late!"

"GURRRRRRRRRRRRRRR."

As soon as she hung up, the lady turned back to nasty like there was a switch in her. "Shut up, goddamn it! Don't you spoil this too!" We heard the sharp report of a palm striking something, then another, and then another. "Stop! Stop or I'll kill myself! You want me to kill myself?"

"RRRRRRR-YAP-YAP-RRRRRRR-YAP-YAP-YAP!"

Babe and I stared at each other. I said, "Lor' have mercy, I hope de chile can't hear her talking like dat. Hit's not right, even to a dog."

Sis' Pearl said, "I have never heard of Mrs. Henrietta Duke placing a woman in a place like this!"

"Well, one way or de other, dis has to work out."

"RRRRRRR-YAP-YAP-RRRRRRR-YAP-YAP-YAP!"

"That's it! You're going into your cage!" The living room became silent. We heard the tinny report of a metal gate closing from somewhere back in the house.

"I'll teach you to screw up my life! Now stay there!"

"Well, least ways she keep that animal caged so it won't get into your hair, Phosie Mae."

I watched the little colored lights merrily twinkling on the Christmas tree. *Dis is no place to be come Christmas. Please, Lord, let Will be out of dat hospital and let us be headin' back down to Galveston by then.* I looked over at the other door. The man was still watching us. He seemed to be enjoying our reaction to his sister's volatile personality.

Finally, my new employer's door opened. Her face was lit up by a star-studded smile She was wearing a million-dollar smile, a pink dressing gown, matching pink slippers, and had red rouge painted on her lips. Without hesitation she extended her hand to Pearl and said, "You must be Phosie Mae. I love that mink shawl. Come in!"

Sis' Pearl shoved me to the front with such force I nearly fell flat on my face. "Matter of factually, this here is Phosie Mae. I'm her sister-in-law just come to drop her off."

"Oh," Mrs. Goldberg said with some disappointment. She looked like Rhonda Flemming. She was one of the most beautiful, glamorous women I had ever seen. Tall, slender, breathtaking. I could not think of what to say.

She was about to invite us in when the dog ran back into the living room and hid under its mother's robe.

"RRRRRRR-YAP-YAP-RRRRRRR-YAP-YAP-YAP!

"GURRRRRRRRRRRRRRRR."

He stuck his head out. We were shocked. The dog was not a dog at all but a little boy of about five years of age.

"RRRRRRR-YAP-YAP-RRRRRRR-YAP-YAP-YAP!

"GURRRRRRRRRRRRRRRR."

He scooted out on his hands and knees with one of his mother's pink slippers clinched between his teeth.

Pearl screamed and backed up.

The lady screamed, "Billy!" but to no avail.

As soon as that dog-child spotted the little black eyes and pointy white teeth of the angry-looking minks hanging over Sis' Pearl's shoulder, he dropped the slipper and scooted right up under Sis' Pearl's Sunday dress.

The way Sis' Pearl screamed you'd have thought she was being skinned and scalped both by Apache indians. "Get that devil thing out from under my dress!" Then she passed out and slumped down onto her haunches. It was a wonder she didn't crush the child.

Mrs. Goldberg screamed, "Billy! For Christ's sakes, get out from under there!" She turned to me. "I'm so sorry! I don't know how he got out of his cage!"

*Cage? What on earth kind of cage is she keeping this poor little thing in?*

The child crawled out from under Sis' Pearl, looked up at the savage minks' heads on her shawl, and brought Sis' Pearl back from the dead by biting down on her exposed ankle until Sis' Pearl screamed again. The situation tickled me so I again had to use every last bit of my self-control to avoid splitting in two for laughing. I couldn't blame her for screaming as she must have been in pain. But that little child's bringing my pretentious sister-in-law down then biting her ankle was just too much to take. *Lordie, was'n' sendin' my Will to de hospital enuff? Why did you have to test me wit dis?*

The child decided he was through with her ankle and scrambled up onto her bosom, where he growled at the minks' heads and waited for them to growl back. When they did not respond he took one of the minks' head between his teeth and tossed his head from side to side while backing down from his perch on Sis' Pearl's chest. When he freed the shawl he dragged the minks back into the house like a victorious predator and disappeared.

"Oh, for Christ's sakes!" Mrs. Goldberg shouted. A small curl of ash at the end of her cigarette broke off and exploded when it crashed on the hardwood floor. She ran over to Jakie's place and beat on his door. "Jakie!" Jakie opened it before she could knock twice. "You got to help me with the kid! He has this woman's goddamned mink shawl, for Christ's sakes."

Jakie looked proud of the boy's mischief. "Where is he?"

"Somewhere in my house, goddamn it! Hurry!"

"Phosie, help me with Pearl!" Babe said. I turned and found him trying but failing to pull her up onto her feet. "Come on, let's lift together!" I took hold of one hand, he took the other, and we tried to pull her up, but we weren't strong enough. She had to roll over onto her hands and knees then stand up without help. I was clinching my jaw so hard against the laughter that tears were seeping out of my eyes. I felt like lying down and rolling around and laughing. It was a blessed release from the fear and pain of the last few days. *I wish my Will was here to see dis. I can' wait to tell him all 'bout it.*

Mrs. Goldberg's scream echoed through the house. "Give me that goddamned mink, you little son of a bitch! Jakie!"

Sis' Pearl held onto the porch rail like a drunk. "If I had a child act like that I reckon I would just kill it and that would be all there is to it!"

*That's why the good Lord did not see fit to give you one!*

"Are you hurt, Sis' Pearl? Lord knows, you coulda broken a hip!" *As fat as you are!* "And lookie chere, you still bleeding. We bes' do somethin' 'bout dat."

Jakie, still with the unlit cigarette tucked above his ear but now wearing a frayed flannel robe over his military-issue clothing, slipped silently up on us. He looked up then down the street like a gangster in a movie, like he was checking to see if anyone was on the lookout for him. Then he walked into his sister's place.

"This house must be haunted. There's something wrong with everyone that live in it!" Sis' Pearl said as she straightened her dress.

"We need to dress that wound," I repeated.

"Are you going to be okay with working here, Phosie?" Babe asked with eyebrows raised.

Sis' Pearl answered before I had a chance to think. "Phosie Mae has plenty of experience working with children, dear. I am sure she can handle this one good as the others."

"Do I has a choice?"

Jakie came back out carrying the shawl with the minks' heads draped over his forearm like a maître d' at a pricey white restaurant and extended his arm out to Sis' Pearl.

Sis' Pearl said, "Thank you!"

Jakie tilted his cigarette-bearing ear toward his shoulder, pinched up his mouth and eyes, and raised up the palm of his hand like a policeman ordering cars to stop at an intersection. He apparently was not interested in our gratitude.

He grinned coyly at me then he slipped back into his place without a word.

# Chapter 7

## *Mrs. Lucile Tells How Things Got the Way they Got to Be*

"Jesus Christ on a bicycle, are you sure you're okay?" Mrs. Goldberg said to Sis' Pearl after we returned from her bathroom, where I had washed and dressed the jagged wound the boy's teeth had carved into my sister-in-law's ankle.

"I hope I don't come down with no rabies or tetanus!" Sis' Pearl said while adding a little hint of a limp to her walk for drama's sake.

Babe looked at Sis' Pearl. "That will be fine, dear."

*The child's more likely to get the rabies from you den de other way 'round!* I sighed. I just wanted Babe and Sis' Pearl to be on their way so that I could start to find solace in my work.

*"G-R-R-R-R-R-R-R-R-R-RUFF!"*

Mrs. Goldberg drew her shoulders up till they touched her ears, and said, "Billy, *goddamn it, no!*" with a vengeance no mother ought to show toward her own flesh and blood.

*Lord, why do you lets jus' anybody have a chile?*

Babe, Sis' Pearl, and I sat silently on Mrs. Goldberg's dark-green sofa with our hands folded in our laps like three scared schoolchildren waiting to see the principal.

"I know this looks horrible, really horrible," Mrs. Goldberg said with a sweeping wave of her hand. "I feel like I'm being pulled down, like in this dream I keep having, you know. In the dream I'm trying to crawl up the steep slope of a black muddy pit, and each time I reach the top, a hand, my ex's hand, grabs my ankle and drags me back to the bottom."

"Well, life's full of challenges for us all, you know," Sis' Pearl said.

Mrs. Goldberg's body shuddered. "You know, sometimes, when I'm driving, if I see a tall building or a bridge, I get this voice in my head that says, '*You're going to jump if things don't get better, you'll see.*' If I try to argue with the voice it says, '*You're no good, you're weak, you're shit. Nobody can stop me, I'll get you someday.*' Sometimes I feel it's going to take over, the voice, and make me do something horrible. I shouldn't have said that. I'm sorry. I mean, don't take what I'm saying seriously. I'd never ever do anything like that, never in a million years."

*Sweet Jesus, dis lady don' need no housekeeper, she need a head doctor. She trouble wit a capital T.*

Mrs. Goldberg glanced at her wristwatch. "*Oy vey!* Am I late! The doctor's coming at seven. *Double fuck!* I forgot to pick up my dry cleaning. Oh Jesus, look at the way I'm talking! I'm sorry. I was thinking out loud."

"*G-R-R-R-R-R-R-R-R-R-RUFF!*"

"It's just that the goddamned kid makes me crazy. I don't know what to do with him!"

*Ask what kind a doctor he is! Ask!* I thought, thinking I might have me a way to get some needles. *How cain it hurt jus' askin'? It ain' askin' for anythin' special. Ask!* "What kind a doctor is de doctor, if you don' mind my askin'?"

"Dr. Buzzbee? Oh, he's a big eye surgeon! Everyone goes to him. People travel from New York and Europe to see him, he tells me."

*I'm going to ask him for needles!* I heard a voice in my mind. Then another voice: *Don't you dare!*

"*G-R-R-R-R-R-R-R-R-R-RUFF!*"

"Billy wasn't like this all the time."

"Don' you worry bout de child none," I told her. *Dis woman's doctor friend cain get Will de needles.* With confidence born of desperation, I said, "You has things pullin' at you from every which way, Mrs.

Goldberg. All de young mothers I knows do. I's good wit de chilrun ev'ry shape and size. I knows I cain hep you out with de boy."

*Ask! No!*

"Now, that's the best offer I've heard all day!" Mrs. Goldberg said then started a fresh conversation with herself. "I wanted to wear a new red dress I bought at Saks, but it's at the cleaners. I'll wear the black with the low-cut neckline, the one he got me. That will catch his eye. Men! They're like little fish in a bowl. You throw a little food in and they swim right up to the surface."

Mrs. Goldbeg bent over to pinch a fresh Chesterfield King from a sequin-studded cigarette box sitting in the middle of her coffee table. Babe's eyes lit up like two flashbulbs on a camera. I looked to see what had Babe so excited. The collars of the lady's terry cloth robe had opened wide like pearly gates. Her billowy white breasts were exposed right down to their nipples. Babe tried to avert his eyes, but Sis' Pearl caught him in the act and jabbed him in his ribs with her elbow so hard I thought he'd break a rib or fly off the sofa, one.

Mrs. Goldberg, unaware of her state of undress, said, "Oh, what's wrong with me? Cigarette?"

"Thank you very kindly," Babe said, momentarily forgetting he didn't smoke.

Sis' Pearl jabbed him again. "Why, Pleas darling, you know you have never smoked a cigarette since the day you were born!"

"I've been trying to quit. It's a lousy habit, and cigarettes, they just went up to fifteen cents a pack! You'd think they'd go down with the war over. What are you going to do, right?" Mrs. Goldberg said as she nervously stroked the wheel of her glass black leopard lighter. There were sparks but no fire. "Christ, sorry, does it bother you if I say Christ? I always get confused. I have to remember to pick up lighter fluid." She pinched a book of matches marked "Ciro's" from a brandy snifter the size of a fish bowl. It was filled with matchbooks from all the famous nightclubs of that day: "The Bandbox," "The Café Trocadero," "The Melody Room," "The Macombo," "The Villa Nova." Places where Hollywood stars and gangsters socialized. She lit her cigarette, inhaled hungrily, then switched the radio on. Perry Como was singing:

*I got it from a guy who was in the kno'*
*It was mighty smoky over Tokyo*
*A friend of mine in a B-29 dropped another load for luck*
*As he flew away, he was heard to say*
*A hubba-hubba-hubba, yuk yuk!*

"Thank God Truman dropped those bombs so our kids could come back in one piece!" Mrs. Goldberg said.

"Yes, 'um," I said. I couldn't help myself. I started sobbing.

"What? What's the matter?" Mrs. Goldberg asked. "What did I say?"

"It's my boy, Mrs. Goldberg, he in bad shape. I'm sorry."

"No, don't be sorry. Tell me about your son. What happened to him?"

I was crying too hard. Babe had to answer. "Her son's at the military hospital. He was shot in the stomach on Iwo Jima."

"Oh my God! I'm so sorry," Mrs. Goldberg said. She looked genuinely sad. "When will he be getting out?" I could see she was hedging about something.

"We hope soon, but there is no way to tell just now," Babe said.

"Well," she said, "at least you'll be here for him over Christmas and New Year's."

I collected myself and said, "Well, I can't rightly say, madam." I meant to say ma'am, as madam felt like the wrong word to use.

"They don't have needles at the hospital!" Sis' Pearl volunteered.

"What? No needles? That's the craziest thing I ever heard, 'they don't have needles.'"

"Things will work out by and by," I said, not wanting to give any more details than necessary. Women I'd worked for, except for Mrs. Hutchinson, would say they wanted all the gory details of my personal life and travails, not that there were many, but I knew they really did not want to be bothered when it came right down to it. They were too caught up in their own lives to care.

I took a deep breath and wiped the tears away. "De little white nurse say de white needles be comin' anytime, Mrs. Goldberg, but dey say anytime in de military can mean forever."

"Colored needles? Your kid fought in the war for Christ's sakes! Who ever heard of such a thing?"

*"G-R-R-R-R-R-R-R-R-R-RUFF!"*

"Billy!"

"It all depend," I said. "But I's ready to work now."

"See, Phosie Mae says she wishes she could take Will out of the hospital and carry him back down to Galveston to get the medicine he needs!" Sis' Pearl said.

Mrs. Goldberg tapped her cigarette on the edge of a jade-green lily-shaped ashtray next to the cigarette box. A plug of wilting gray ash tumbled into the ashtray. "If those lousy government stooges don't get your kid the colored needles, you let me know. I'll ask the doctor…no promises, of course, but I will ask him. Sons of bitches."

"Thank you kindly, but I don' want you puttin' yourself out, Mrs."

"Like I said, no promises, of course."

"Of course," I said. *Maybe she not such a bad woman after all.*

Mrs. Goldberg jerked her head to the left and blew another plume of smoke back over her shoulder, "Even so, you let me know. Maybe I can help if you're here. I mean, he wants to marry me." She looked both ways to check if anyone was listening and whispered, "If his old lady grants him a divorce without taking him to the cleaners. It's the squeaky wheel, right?"

"Dat's right! Lord heps dem dat help demselves." I said with arched eyebrows. I had never ever met anyone like Mrs. Goldberg. She was nothing but a child trying to make sense out of her life, trying to survive. But she had a sweet, loving heart. I couldn't help feeling sympathetic.

"I need a drink!" Mrs. Goldberg said, strutting toward the radio cabinet and a silver-plated serving cart parked next to it. It was a miniature bar with all the best vodka, bourbon, and scotch, shot glasses, stir rods, tumblers, and tall glasses on display. She poured a three-finger shot of Crown Royal on the rocks.

"There I go again, thinking of only me! Can I pour any one else a drink?"

"No, thank you kindly. We're fine, just fine," Babe said with new found religion. I loved my brother but he might as well been living in a Mississippi prison.

"Well, now that you mention it, I wouldn't mind a glass of cold water," said Sis' Pearl. She sat there with one fat leg crossed over the other like the trunks of two fallen trees.

Mrs. Goldberg flew to the kitchen to fill Sis' Pearl's order.

"G-R-R-R-R-R-R-R-R-R-RUFF!"

She screamed at the child, "Shut your trap!" *Smack!* "Don't screw this up!"

"G-R-R-R-R-R-R-R-R-R-RUFF!"

"Don't you shit on my parade! I'm warning you! I've got a doctor coming over who wants to marry me and get us out of this dump! If you know what's good for you, do not *fuck* this up!"

"G-R-R-R-R-R-R-R-R-R-RUFF!"

"Here you go!" Mrs. Goldberg said as she walked back into the living room, smiling as if her life was filled with sunshine and roses. She passed the drink along with a fancy cocktail napkin to Sis' Pearl. My mouth was dry as a parched prairie bone, but I wasn't going to send Mrs. Goldberg back into the kitchen.

"Does the bite hurt? I can't tell you how sorry I am," Mrs. Goldberg said as my sister-in-law slurped her water down. She could not drink normally because her false teeth were too loose. She set the empty glass on the coffee table.

"Well, it's not feeling too good, but long as my mink is fine, that's all."

"It is, isn't it?" Mrs. Goldberg asked.

"Ummm-um. It look that way," Sis' Pearl said. "But for the rabies, I pray I don't come down with no rabies and have to get a shot in my stomach."

*Dere isn't a needle long 'nough or deep 'nough to get through yur fat stomach!*

Mrs. Goldberg inhaled, the tip of her cigarette grew bright red, then she swirled the whiskey and ice in her tumbler, exhaled, and took another sip.

"G-R-R-R-R-R-R-R-R-R-RUFF!"

Mrs. Goldberg shouted, "Billy! Quiet, goddamn you. Quiet!" She looked at us like drunks do when they are about to throw themselves at your feet and beg for mercy, hoping for forgiveness just one last time. "It's so hard."

"I knows," Sis' Pearl said. "Seems like de mountain always gettin' higher and de river always gettin' wider. Praise de Lord. But I am sure you have an interestin' life story. I can tell by just lookin' at a person."

I said, "Sis' Pearl, why don' you and Babe go home for supper so Mrs. Golberg can show me 'round and finish gettin' dressed?"

But, Mrs. Goldberg loved the attention Pearl was paying, "Oh, that's okay, they can stay a while longer."

*"G-R-R-R-R-R-R-R-R-R-RUFF!"*

Mrs. Goldberg took Sis' Pearl's avowal as an invitation and began telling her life's story. "I just have a few more minutes. See, Leo, my ex, Billy's daddy, is twenty years older than me…than I…or is it me? I always mix it up, stupid me. We met before the war when I waitressed at a bar on Brooklyn Avenue that he and his brothers owned. He was a fabulous sport, a real big tipper, nothing but first cabin all the way. I always like to give a nice tip, too. You know, keep it in the family. Us, or we, cocktail waitresses got to look out for each other! We all have to hustle. No, I don't mean *hustle* hustle, I mean work hard for a buck. So, where was I? So, I went out to dinner a few times with him. He took me to all the most fabulous places, The Coconut Grove, The Macombo, The Players, I ate steak and lobster till it was coming out of my ears. I never had it so good. I felt like a real queen. He was real nice, a real doll, Leo was. I thought he was a great catch, you know, someone who would take care of me. Then the war came. He joined the Navy, and I thought that was that, you know. But, lo and behold, as soon as he came back from the war, that was in forty-four, they transferred him to Port Hueneme up near Oxnard, have you ever been up there? It's nice."

*I might start drinking after this story.*

"No, I'm afraid we have not," Babe said.

"So, what do you think? Surprise surprise! He drove all the way down here one Sunday and asked me to marry him. My mom was alive then. She liked him. What was not to like? But the funny thing was that he could have…he was old enough to have dated my mother! See, I lost…my father died when I was three, they said it was consumption, but who knows. This place was my mother's place. Now that she's gone, she died during the war, it's my brother, Jakie's, and mine, you met Jakie. Well, my brother wasn't back from the war yet, and I didn't have two nickels to rub together. I was flat broke. I couldn't even pay the taxes on this place. I mean, how could I say no to Leo's offer? I didn't want to lose the place my mother gave me, right?"

"No, ma'am," we sang like three caged canaries on a perch.

Mrs. Goldberg picked a speck of tobacco from her lower lip and flicked it away. "So, we, Leo and me, I mean Leo and I, we went to Vegas, have you ever been to Vegas?"

"No, ma'am," I said. *Maybe she think that dressed as poor as I is I just came back from losin' everything I had in Las Vegas!*

"We eloped because his brother, my ex-brother-in-law, Morrie, who was like a father to Leo—Leo's father died when he was nine, tuberculosis—didn't like me. No, he hated my guts! You know why? Because I'm a Galitziana, and they're Litvaks. We're different types of Jews, like Cubans are different from Mexicans. We came from Poland, they came from Russia. They think they're better than us! But I got news for them, they're not. There are twice as many Glitz lawyers and doctors than there are Litvaks! So we eloped, and I thought it was all good. And then…"

*Lor' have mercy! This woman 'bout to tell us her whole family history startin' back with Adam and Eve!*

"The minute Leo moved in," Mrs. Goldberg continued, "everything went to hell in a handbasket." He started drinking, like a fish! Like two fish! I never saw him drink like that before the war. But it's not like I knew him all that well to begin with. Turns out he was a just another drunkard. Then he brought a stray dog home from his gas station, and Billy came along. That dog, it was a filthy little thing, and Billy were attached at the hip. Billy wouldn't go anywhere without the dog and vice versa. They even took baths together. Then Billy started having asthma attacks. The kid would gasp for air like he was drowning. The doctor was coming out every week. I felt like offering him one of the bedrooms for an office. He would give Billy a shot of penicillin, tell us to make Billy a cup of coffee with honey and sugar to loosen his chest up, and put Billy in an oxygen tent."

*I wants to talk to dat doctor.*

"If I complained, you know, to Leo, he would say, 'The kid's wheezing because you're on his goddamned back all the time. Let him be a kid, for Christ's sakes.' Then *he* moves out, well, the truth is I threw him out, the chippy bastard. I caught him running around with a hostess from The Airliner on North Broadway, absolutely no class, I mean a real slut there ever was one. The day after he was gone I took the dog for a ride to the merry-go-round at Griffith Park, let the dog out of the car to run around, and drove away like a bat out of hell. I thought that was that. Then the minute Billy found out the dog was missing he decides he'll be the dog! If I was smart I should have kept the dog and driven Leo and my kid to Griffith Park! There's the story of my life. It's a regular shit parade."

"Have you taken de chile to see de head doctor?" I said.

"Oh yeah. I took him to three. The last was a psychiatrist, Dr. Elvin Buzzbee, the bald twin brother of Dr. Lewellyn Buzzbee, the gentleman coming by later. Dr. Elvin's head shines like polished mahogany, and he has bushy black eyebrows. He's spooky, like one of those doctors in a Bela Lugosi 'I vant to suck your blood' movie. But listen," she continued after another drag from her cigarette, "I don't like all that mental stuff. I think people who start looking too deep into their feelings are the ones who wind up crazy in the nut farms getting that electric shock whatever you call it. Pass. That's not for me, baby. Oh no! Christ, I have to get dressed soon." She laughed. "You should see him. His head shines like polished mahogany. And those eyebrows! You could die!"

Sis' Pearl had finally had it. She started to wiggle forward to get up and said, "Well, I'm sure the doctor will help your son by and by."

"He already has. See, Dr. Elvin said Billy is suffering from an 'hysterical identification,' whatever that is," she said. "He's explained it several times, but I still don't understand what the hell he's talking about. And, get a hold of this,"—Mrs. Goldberg leaned toward us— "he wanted me, *me,* to come in and talk about my feelings, my feelings! I told him, 'Look, I'd love to talk with you. We could have lunch or meet for a cocktail sometime. But I'm not the one acting like a dog, for Christ's sakes! My kid's the problem. Don't you have a pill for this type of thing?'

"And Dr. Elvin told me, 'No, there is no pill. However, it is my opinion,'—he always speaks like a college professor—'that if Billy desires to be a canine, he should be treated exactly as a canine'—a canine's a dog, you know—'would be treated, exactly. Nothing more! Do you understand? Feed him kibble, no pie, no candy, give him water in a bowl to drink if he's thirsty, no fancy sugar pops, no ice cream, no malteds, not even a glass of milk. Let him sleep in a cage and take him out only if and when he's on a leash. Wash him with a hose and dress him in the simplest of garments. He'll soon be whistling another tune!'

"'Fine,' I told him, 'I'll do anything for my kid!' And that's what I've been doing. See, the real problem is, like I said, is that I'm like a prisoner because of it. I can't keep a housekeeper, I can't leave for work, I can't even get away for cocktails with a friend unless there's someone to watch the kid. It's jail, baby, jail. Three Mexican women, one with a gold front tooth, a real wetback, have worked here and quit in the last four months. Billy bit the pinky finger of the last one right off at the second knuckle and spit it out under the couch you're sitting on! I think it's still there!"

All three of us raised our feet.

"Just kidding. I wanted to see if you were paying attention. I kid a lot. It's good to have a laugh." She laughed hysterically.

Then Mrs. Goldberg looked at me and said, "Oh, are you good at pressing delicates?"

I was never so happy to be asked about my housekeeping in my life.

"Yes, 'um, I believe I have had plenty of practice in dat department."

Mrs. Goldberg smiled timidly. "So, will you stay?"

*I don' have no other choice but to!*

"Well," I said, hedging my bet, "let me see if'n I can' hep you out."

*"Mazel tov!"*

Babe jotted down Mrs. Goldberg's telephone number, Angelus 2314, and gave me his and Pearl's, Axminster 1121, then I walked them out to their car.

"You watch out for that child, Phosie Mae," Pearl said. "You sure 'nough don't want it biting your finger off."

"It's not the child, Pearl. The child is good as the Lord made him. It's de folks 'round him. Most people treat dey chilrun poorly and when de chilrun reacts dey blames de chile!"

I stood and watched as Babe and my sister-in-law drove down New Jersey Street, turned right on Cummings Avenue, and their car dissolved into the graying darkness. I had my differences with Pearl, but right at that moment in that strange place in the steeled dusk of a strange day, she and Babe were the only two friends I had. I looked at the houses on the opposite side of the street. It seemed that each had a separate style and each was made of a different material. It felt as if they were strangers to one another, too. I thought of Will lying alone in his hospital bed. A sob lodged in my throat. I shivered.

As I walked along the path back up to the house, I noticed a ribbon of light behind the newspaper barricade in Mrs. Goldberg's brother's window. The newspapers stacked in the shadows looked like the layers of dry gray mud you see along the banks of southern Texas arroyos in the dry season. Her broken brother Jakie was watching me from behind his shadowy newspaper barricade. I cleared my throat, kept my head down, and walked up onto the porch as quickly as I could. I did not realize it in that moment but when I crossed the threshold and closed Mrs. Goldberg's front door I was closing the door to my old life and would never be able to pass back through again.

*Dear Lord, if somethin' has to happen, let it happen to me. Please, please, please, I'm beggin' you, don't let anything happen to my Will. I will surely wither up and die without him.*

"Phosie, hurry, I have to finish dressing."

"Yes, 'um, I'm comin', I'm comin'."

# Chapter 8

## *The Color of Blood and an Untimely Visit*

I took my glasses off and silently swept the tears away as I trudged back up through the dusk and into Mrs. Goldberg's. I had never worked in such a small delapidated place. It was just a little bigger and a little better than our tenant shack down in Galveston. I felt embarrassed. I sensed the neighbors were watching me from behind the drawn curtains in their windows across the street. I was carrying all that I owned in the world packed in a wrinkled shopping bag bound in brown twine. I felt like the Lord had set the weight of Job's curse on my shoulders and did not understand why, why our little family, was made to suffer so much when we had had so much love, happiness, and faith. I found Mrs. Goldberg at her little bar pouring another drink. A Benny Goodman song, "Got to be This or That," was playing on the radio. She was singing and humming along until she noticed me. She turned and said, "Are you crying, Flossie?"

"Yes, 'um, Mrs. Goldberg, but don' worry 'bout me none, I fine. But hit Phosie, Phosie Mae, not Flossie."

"Ach! I don't know what's wrong with me. I'm sorry, *Phosie Mae.* Let me finish this drink then I'll show you the place. Shit! I've done this so many goddamned times I should get a job training housekeepers for Chirst's sakes. You can cook, can't you?"

"De Lord knows I can cook jus' 'bout anything der is."

"Good, because I need you to fix my kid's dinner, tonight! I have to get dressed. Phosie, Phosie, Phosie. I read that if you repeat a name three times you'll never forget it. Phosie, Phosie, Phosie. Okay, that's six times. I'll never forget again."

*Dis' woman talk like she chasing or being chased or both by somethen' in her head.* "Well, I might jus' use dat method my own self, old as I is."

"Old? You're still a young woman!"

"I don' feel likes one." I felt awkward standing and talking with my coat and hat on. I shifted my weight from one foot to the other.

"Well," Mrs. Goldberg said, "I'll give you ten-to-one odds that once your son's out of the hospital and you're settled in here in Los Angeles you'll feel a lot better.

"Ten to one?"

"Okay, twenty to one! You know, a bet, like Las Vegas."

"I don' know nothin' about no Lost Vegas or no bettin', Mrs. Goldberg. All I know is to pray."

"You can pray all you want, sister, but you have to have a little fun once in a while, everybody does, you dig?"

"Well, I goes to church regular."

"We'll have to do something about that."

"Yes, 'um, Mrs. Goldberg." I steeled myself for more craziness and thought, *I hopes she don' think I will stop going to church, if she do she out of her mind.*

"Let's get one thing straight right now, honey. I'll call you Phosie, Phosie, Phosie, you call me Lucile, or Lucy, whatever you like, as long as you don't call me late for supper!"

"Awright den. What time do you wants me to call you for supper?"

"It was a joke, just a silly saying." She laughed. "Sorry, I can't help myself. I like to joke around. I mean, life's a ball, right? But most poor working stiffs miss the party because they don't realize it or they're just too afraid to grab the silver hoop or spoon or whatever it is. Between me and you, sister,"—Mrs. Goldberg lowered her voice to a whisper as if someone else was in the room and she wanted to keep the secret from them—"I'm filling my bowl with cherries! Let the suckers have the pits! Screw 'em all!"

"Dat's right," I said as Mrs. Goldberg lit a cigarette. "If'n you makes up yur mind to be happy, den you'll be happy. But if'n you makes up yur mind dat you sad, den that's what you'll be!" *De more you talks, Phosie Mae, de better de chance dis woman will fire you 'fore you cook a meal in her kitchen.*

"I couldn't have put it better!" Mrs. Goldberg said and gave me a big, warm hug. She was a head taller than me. She was wearing her favorite perfume, Mitzuko. It was wild, musty, and sensuous. It took you in and held you tight. "I know we're going to get along, I can feel it in my bones." I could not understand why, but I felt oddly comforted and safe in this funny woman's arms, except for choking on the cigarette smoke that fanned into my nostrils. I sneezed.

"Gesundheit! That means "Good Health!" We say that when someone sneezes.

"Thank you kindly, Mrs. Gold…"

"Remember, call me Lucile!"

"Yes, 'um…ma'am," I said, shifting my weight again.

"No 'ma'am,' it's Lucile! I'm not one of those stiff Hancock Park *goys*, you dig?"

"What is a *goy*?" I asked. "A girl-boy mix't?"

"Oy vey!" Mrs. Goldberg threw her head back and laughed. "I am going to have to teach you some Yiddish!"

"Yiddish?" I asked.

"Yes, that's the language we Jews speak when we're talking about everybody else. Just kidding! Anyways, you have just learned your first word, *goy*, and that means gentile! Say it, *goy.*"

"*Goy,*" I repeated softly.

"*Oy vey!* That means oh my God!"

"*Oy vey!*"

"*Mazel tov*! You're already speaking Yiddish and you've only been here fifteen minutes! We're going to do fine!"

*I hope so.* From my experience, anyone pretending they're perfectly happy is someone with a secret keeping them very perfectly unhappy.

Mrs. Goldberg was desperate, hungry, I could see it in the way her eyes kept searching like a hungry dog's.

"Jesus Christ on a bicycle, I've really got to get dressed now. My date is coming at seven! We have twenty-five minutes. Come on, I'll give you the cook's tour."

"Yes, 'um," I said and chased the patter of her slippers down the dark hallway to her bedroom.

"This is my bedroom, see." It was decorated in red and pink velvet. "Here's the one bathroom, so don't take too long in the shower or I'll cut your hot water off!" She laughed.

*I guess I'll be using the same bathroom.*

We hustled to a door at the end of the hall. She switched a light on. "Here's my kid's room. I wish to hell he would sleep in it!" The little boy's bedroom was decorated in a Western theme, with cowboys on horses chasing Indians around a lampshade on the lamp next to his horseshoe-decorated bed.

We walked back down the hall and turned into the service porch. "And here is your *suite,*" Mrs. Goldberg said. It was cold like a root cellar. She reached up and waved her hand in the darkness until she caught a cord hanging from a light fixture with a bare bulb screwed into it. I had to squint when she switched the light on. There was a small bare cot covered by a gray mattress with black stripes. A neatly folded olive-colored Army-issue woolen blanket was lying at one end. A bare gray pillow covered in striped ticking was on the other end. A short chest of chipped blue drawers was set between the cot and a mop sink, and beyond that there was a narrow broom closet. "There are uniforms hanging in the closet. I like my girls to be in uniform with a frilly French apron. It's classy. The Mexican that just left was too fat to wear them. Thank God she's gone! She nearly ate me out of house and home! The uniforms will fit you perfectly."

She must have seen the disappointment in my face. As poor as I was, I had never worked in a home this scanty. "I know this is not a movie actress's estate in Beverly Hills, but what the hell, right? It'll do for now." There was a door and a window. A cold draft was seeping through both. I sneezed again. "*Gesundheit!*

"Thank you, thank you kindly."

"You're not sick are you?"

"No mam, no. I'm fit as a mule."

"I'll get that window fixed when my ex pays me my back alimony and child support. Okay, follow me. The kitchen's through this door." It was a very nice kitchen for such a small place. There was a white porcelain O'Keefe & Merritt stove with a chrome top, four burners, a nice steel griddle for flapjacks, a oven for roasting, baking, and biscuits, and an under-oven warming drawer. Ringing the room was a new white Formica countertop, and above that French-style cupboards with glass windows in the doors. A small chrome breakfast table with a red Formica top and two matching red Naugahyde and chrome chairs was tucked up against the wall directly across from the icebox. The icebox had one of those new compressors mounted on its top. When it cycled on it sounded like an airplane was coming in for a landing. The iceman with his truck was no longer needed to deliver a five-cent chunk of ice to keep the perishables cool at Mrs. Goldberg's place.

Then I saw the cage she kept the little boy in. It was a thin-gauge wire coop, the kind used to transport chickens on trucks. The cage was tucked under the icebox. Its door, secured by a small bolt latch, was just big enough for the boy to crawl through. A small bowl half-filled with water had been set down near the door. I bent over and peered into the darkness at the back of the cage. The boy leapt forward on his haunches and growled.

"*GRRRRRRRRRRRRRRRRRRRR!*"

I jumped back so fast I flopped onto the dinette chair behind me.

"Lord, I ain' never seen anythin' like dis in my life."

"I know. I know. But the doctor says this is the best way to teach him that acting like a dog doesn't pay. Otherwise, I don't know what I'd do. Maybe send him someplace where they handle problem children like this. The dog pound? This caging thing's made him better, though."

*If knocking Sis' Pearl down, chewing on her ankle, and running off with her mink shawl is better, I would hate to see what he was like before!*

"I know this looks really bad," Mrs. Goldberg said. "I really do. But he'd tear the place apart if I let him. What am I supposed to do?"

I bent over and looked again. All I could make out were the child's big brown eyes and the pudgy outline of his sad little face.

"G-R-R-R-R-R-R-R-R-R-RUFF!"

*Dis chile's mama ought to be de one caged!*

"Let me turn a light on," Mrs. Goldberg said. I heard a switch flip. Light from the ceiling cascaded into the cage. The child switched to his hands and knees and scuttled forward growling until his face was pressed up against the front of the cage.

"G-R-R-R-R-R-R-R-R-R-RUFF!

"G-R-R-R-R-R-R-R-R-R-R RUFF!"

"Billy! Stop it, goddamn it. You'll give me a headache!" Mrs. Goldberg screamed in a tone as vicious as the boy's growling.

"You don' have to growl at me, lil' doggie," I said. "I met ev'ry kind of dog. I bet you're jus' hungry for yur supper."

"G-R-R-R-R-R-R-R-R-R-RUFF! "

"Shut up! Oh, I can't stand this!" Mrs. Goldberg said. "Let me show you what to feed him so I can go get dressed and get the hell out of here before I go nuts."

"G-R-R-R-R-R-R-R-R-R-RUFF!

"G-R-R-R-R-R-R-R-R-R-RUFF!"

I had to scream "Yes, 'um" to be heard over the child's protests. He must have been afraid of me. I might well have been the first colored person he'd ever seen. And I was a stranger in his life, too. Only the Lord knows what kinds of experiences he had had with the other housekeepers.

Mrs. Goldberg opened the icebox door and removed food wrapped in white butcher's paper stamped with the word KOSHER. She unfolded the paper. The biggest, fattest hot dogs I had ever seen were inside. They were strung end to end like sausages.

"G-R-R-R-R-R-R-R-R-R-RUFF!

"G-R-R-R-R-R-R-R-R-R-RUFF!"

"He mus' be hungry," I said again.

"No!" Mrs. Goldberg said. "He's just doing that to get under my skin!" She yanked a pantry door open, jerked out a quart saucepan and skillet, and set them on the stove. "But I got news for him, he's not going to get away with this shit too much longer!" Then she opened another door, removed a can of baked beans, and set it next to the knockwurst. "This is the only thing he'll eat. It's what my ex used to fix him. He won't even touch a cookie. Who knows a kid won't eat a cookie, for Christ's sakes?"

The boy changed his tune.

"YIP-YIP-YIP! YIP-YIP-YIP! YIP-YIP-YIP!"

"Cut one of the hot dogs in half lengthwise and fry it. Heat a half can of the beans. Then mix them in a cereal bowl and set them in his cage. Oh, and be careful! He bites. And if Jakie comes in—he does almost every night before he goes to one of his card games—fix him the same thing. Can you do this?"

"Oh, yes, Mrs. Gol…Mrs. Lucile, I cans."

"Good, I need another drink while I get dressed!"

"YIP-YIP-YIP! YIP-YIP-YIP! YIP-YIP-YIP!"

"Don' you worry 'bout a thing," I said. "You go powder and paint for your gentleman caller. I gots de child." Before I could finish the sentence she was off to the races. I must admit, excitement filled the air.

I glanced down at the cage, feeling sad, angry, bewildered, and, I have to admit, amused all at the same time. "Chile, you sure 'nough know how to give your mama a run for her money, don't you!"

"YIP-YIP-YIP! YIP-YIP-YIP! YIP-YIP-YIP!"

"Don' say anythin'," I whispered, "but from what I see, I can't say I blames you."

"YIP-YIP-YIP! YIP-YIP-YIP! YIP-YIP-YIP!"

"Dat's right."

Mrs. Goldberg stuck her head back in. "Listen, when you hear a knock on the door, answer it. It'll be the doctor. Oh, and put some ice in the ice chest on the bar. He likes his scotch on the rocks."

"Yes, 'um," I said, and she left again.

"No green grass goin' to grow under dat woman's feets."

"YIP-YIP-YIP! YIP-YIP-YIP! YIP-YIP-YIP!"

"Don' you repeats dat!" I said, wagging the knife at the child and smiling.

"YIP-YIP-YIP! YIP-YIP-YIP! YIP-YIP-YIP!"

"Well, let me fix you up some of dese beans wit' Phosie Mae's home-made Texas recipe. I always adds a touch of maple syrup to sweeten de pot. Maybe dat will settle you down."

"YIP-YIP-YIP! YIP-YIP-YIP! YIP-YIP-YIP!"

The boy crawled up to the front of the cage and laid himself out on his belly so that he could watch me prepare his supper. I hummed "This Little Light of Mine" and pretended not to notice him as I spooned the baked beans into the saucepan, added the maple syrup, sliced the knockwurst in half, and laid them out to sizzle in the frying pan. I acted surprised when I looked at him. "My, my, you de onliest dog on de face o' dis Earth dat I knows eats hot dogs and beans! But I has to say you a cute lil' doggie wit dat roly-poly face, dose milk-chocolate eyes, and dat thick, curly hair. You'd make you a fine lil' boy, too!" He let his little pink tongue lap down over his bottom lip.

*"G-R-R-R-R-R-R-R-R-R-RUFF!"*

"You can gruff, sugar, but den I ain' de one in de cage!" I said with a soft chuckle. "I won't pay you any mind."

*"G-R-R-R-R-R-R-R-R-R-RUFF!"*

I stirred the baked beans and turned the knockwurst over with a fork. "Now dat I'm thinking on it," I said, "I do recall a little boy jus' a touch bigger dan you back down in Galveston. You knows what dat boy thought?"

*"G-R-R-R-R-R-R-R-R-R-RUFF!"*

"He thought he was a mule! Can you believe dat? And do you know what his name was?"

*"G-R-R-R-R-R-R-R-R-R-RUFF!"*

Now, I had his attention. "Well, see, de boy in de story was my very own chile, Will." I decided to fudge on the truth a little. There was a boy down in Galveston who had done just what I was about to say in my story, but it wasn't my Will. I just thought saying it was my son would do more to grab Billy's attention and teach him a lesson. A little white lie is acceptable if it does more good than harm. "Matter of factually, Will was a chile who nev'r gave us one lick a trouble. Dat is 'til he got angry 'cause we had to give up old Hoover, our mule, after the stock market crashed in 1929. See, Will would ride dat Hoover all over de place. And when Will wasn't riding Hoover, Hoover would follow Will wherever Will went. Dey were like Frick and Frack. Come night, Hoover slept wit his big head stuck inside de window over Will's bed. You knows de story of Mary and her little lamb? Well, just like Mary wit her lamb, one day Hoover, he followed our Will right to de school door."

*"G-R-R-R-R-R-R-R-R-R-RUFF!"*

I flipped the hot dogs and gave the beans another stir. The sweet perfume of the maple syrup made my mouth water. "Know why we called dat mule Hoover?" I looked down at the child and saw that his head was cocked just a little and his eyes were shining brightly. *How is it dat a mother can't see the precious beauty in her own child? How can she miss de love dat de Lord set in his lil' soul? Why do some folks run everywhere to find love or riches or somethen else when hit right where dey already is? How many applause does it take to make up for the love in a child's eyes, how many diamonds, how many of anything?* The questions made me sad. "Cause dat animal could eat food like a vacuum cleaner sucks up de dust."

*"G-R-R-R-R-R-R-R-R-R-RUFF!"*

"Well, like I said, by 'n by the Crash of twenty-nine came and we lost our little place outside of Galveston. While Hoover was still fit to work, we had to sell 'im to a renderer for soap. No one else had the money to buy him. Will cried and cried as we watched dat ol' mule stand in de bed of de renderer's truck and fade into de dust as de renderer drove away. Will's grown and a marine now, but he was a terrible mess back den. He was so upset over havin' ta get rid of Hoover that he started to act like a mule hisself. He would whinny and bray at his teacher 'til she had to remove him from de class. If he was in de school yard with de other chilrun, Will would back up next to another chile and kick it jus' like a mule would. Dey would not let Will 'tend class it got so bad. We couldn't e'en carry Will to town 'cause he would whinny and bray at passersby. He even whinnied in church till one day de pastor set him outside and tied him off with a rope. We thought we were going to have to send him to de soap factory or lace him to a cart, one."

I sliced the knockwurst and placed the pieces into the bowl. "Dis here smell so good I think I'll have to have me some, too."

*"G-R-R-R-R-R-R-R-R-R-R-RUFF!"*

I had to restrain myself from laughing. Will would not have found my using him as an example of bad behavior amusing as he was naturally such a good boy with an honest heart. Yet it felt good talking about Will, even if I had placed him smack in the middle of a fib. "Oh Lordie, was he full of de devil just like you, that's right."

*"G-R-R-R-R-R-R-R-R-R-R-RUFF!"*

"I wouldn't *gruff* jus' yet. You haven't heard de rest of de story."

*"G-R-R-R-R-R-R-R-R-R-R-RUFF!"*

"So, by and by, Will's ears, dey started to grow high up over his head into points, just like a regular mule's." I glanced at the child; I had his attention. "Dat's right. De Lord knows a body cain't act like somethin' and not 'spect to turn into it. Well, den de strangest thing of all happened—Will started growing a hide. And hit weren't jus' any ordinary hide neither. It was splotched black and white just like a paint mule's is. See, Hoover was a paint and oh Lordie did he smell. Now, dat should give you somethin' to chew on!"

I carried the bowl to the boy's cage. He reared back onto his haunches.

*"G-R-R-R-R-R-R-R-R-R-R-RUFF!"*

I ought to have heeded to his warning, but I really didn't think he'd bite me if I was feeding him. I slid the bolt latch open with my left hand, opened the little door to his cage, and said, "Now here you go. Like I said, you mus' be hungry after all de day's excitement!" I extended my right hand in to set the bowl down. He lurched forward and bit the fleshy part of my palm so hard I dropped the bowl and spilt the knockwurst and beans inside his cage.

"YIP-YIP-YIP! YIP-YIP-YIP! YIP-YIP-YIP!"

"Sweet Jesus! What is wrong wit you, chile?" I said as I stepped back and examined my hand. His teeth had left a bloody half-moon pattern imprinted on the fatty pink underside of my right hand.

"YIP-YIP-YIP! YIP-YIP-YIP! YIP-YIP-YIP!"

I held the hand up and rushed to the sink, washed the wound with soap, and covered it with a paper napkin. "You cain't bite me! I'm going to teach you somethin' right now!" I looked back at the cage, but the door was hanging open and the child was gone. I walked into my room on the service porch, removed a sewing needle from my things, heated the tip in the flame on the stove, and whispered as loud as I could without disturbing the boy's mama and getting myself fired, "Chile, where are you? I'll find you! And when I do, I'm goin' to teach you a lesson you ain' never forgettin'!"

I found him hiding behind the Christmas tree, panting and growling. He put up a little bit of a fight when I took him up under one arm and carried him back into the kitchen like I would a chicken to the coop. I set him down on the floor next to the dinette. I took hold of his little finger, pinched the skin on its tip, and pricked it with the needle just deep enough to allow for a drop of blood to trickle out. "You see dat?" I said. "You see what color dat is? It red! Now,"—I held his finger up against my wound—"you see what color my blood is, chile? It red just like your'n, jus' like everyone. Do you see that? Now, don't you forget dis day. All God's chilrun has de same color blood, our tears have de same salt, and our hearts cain break de same, too. So don' you bite me again! Do you understand?" I saw a little tear fall out of one eye. I think he did understand. He was all out of fight for the moment. "Now, I going to set you in dat cage and fasten de latch so you won't get me fired de first night." I cut a length of string from a ball I found under the sink and tied the latch so that he could not get out. As I was finishing up with that, the doorbell rang.

"Phosie!" Mrs. Goldberg sang in a tone sweet as sugar and smooth as silk. "That must be the doctor! Will you let him in please?"

"Let me get dis den." After I struggled up off the floor, I washed my hands then checked the knots on my stockings to make sure they would not slip down over my knees.

"G-R-R-R-R-R-R-R-R-R-RUFF!"

"Tell him to help himself to a drink!"

"Yes, 'um, Mrs. Goldberg, I means Mrs. Lucile."

Her voice became tense. "And make sure Billy is locked in that goddamned cage!"

"Yes, 'um." I looked at Billy. "Now, if you start to actin' like a regular chile, you won' be in dis situation."

"YIP-YIP-YIP! YIP-YIP-YIP! YIP-YIP-YIP!"

The doorbell rang again. The nylon stocking on my left leg slipped down to my ankle as I started walking toward the living room. I had to stop behind the front door and retie the knot. Then I checked my hairnet to make sure it was covering all my wiry hair. I pasted a plantation smile on my face and opened the door.

"YIP-YIP-YIP! YIP-YIP-YIP! YIP-YIP-YIP!"

The doctor was on the short side and tan, which was unusual, it being so cold. He had a handsome Roman-like nose and artic-blue eyes. His black hair was slicked straight back without a part. He was wearing a tan gabardine Eisenhower jacket, a black silk shirt buttoned all the way up to the collar, chartreuse gabardine slacks, and fine brown alligator shoes. All added up he looked like a real dandy to me. "Come right in 'fore you catch your death, Doctor!"

"I'll give you a doctor. Bend over, sister."

*Lord, dis man a doctor and a comedian all wrapped up in one.*

"YIP-YIP-YIP! YIP-YIP-YIP! YIP-YIP-YIP!"

"New maid, new dog. Money must be flowing like water around here."

"YIP-YIP-YIP! YIP-YIP-YIP! YIP-YIP-YIP!"

"Mrs. Goldberg say *hep* yourself if you wants a drink, Doctor. I'd fix it for you 'cept I don't know de first thing 'bout tending bar."

"YIP-YIP-YIP! YIP-YIP-YIP! YIP-YIP-YIP!"

"What happened to the fat little Mexican with the gold tooth?"

"Oh, I cain' say nothin' 'bout what happened to her. I just hired on."

The doctor glanced toward the hall and said, "I need to see the madam of the house."

"I will tell her you here directly," I said. "Then I has to return to the kitchen. I has food cookin' on de stove. Now my name's Phosie. You let me knows if'n you needs anythin' and I'll see what I cain do to get hit for you."

"YIP-YIP-YIP! YIP-YIP-YIP! YIP-YIP-YIP!"

As I walked out of the room I heard the man say, "For Christ's sakes, another fuckin' dog! She can't even afford to feed the kid!" I started praying that the man would find his way into the kitchen and see the evil the child was suffering. He was a doctor; maybe he would so something to rescue it.

"YIP-YIP-YIP! YIP-YIP-YIP! YIP-YIP-YIP!"

# Chapter 9

## *Spite*

I walked back into the kitchen and found Mrs. Goldberg's brother, Jakie, perched sideways along the edge of a dinette chair like a jaybird on a clothesline. *Look what the cat dragged in.* One leg was crossed over its opposite. He had slicked his hair back with Alberto VO5. I could tell 'cause its pungent, sweet odor curled the tip of my nose. I swerved away from him. *I hope dis man knows de last thing I needs is a relationship with him.* He was dressed to kill in a faded, green plaid robe frayed at the edges and drinking from a longneck bottle of Brew 102 like a boarder in a cheap rooming house. His signature fresh cigarette was tucked up over his ear. An unopened, cellophane-wrapped package of Lucky Strike cigarettes, with its black-and-gold-ringed bull's-eye on the front and back, was lying on the table alongside a red book of matches. The matchbook's cover read "Aladdin's Bail Bonds – Call Angelus 77777" within the outline of a magic lamp. The scuffed leather handle of his blackjack was peeking out over the edge of his robe's pocket like a gopher peeks out of its hole. He wasn't so much a man looking for trouble as he was a man trouble was trying to find.

I felt a chilly draft coming in from the service porch and closed the door between it and the kitchen. *Hit get cold out chere in Los Angeles.* Then it came to me. *I knows what I'll do. I'll sew Will up a patchwork quilt for Christmas, a nice warm quilt.* I felt my heart warm to the idea.

*My quilt will be a better gift dan anythin' anyone could buy on de Miracle white Mile!*

The boy was busy pawing at the latch on the gate of his cage. But the string I had found under the sink and tied the latch up with was holding tight.

"*G-R-R-R-R-R-R-R-R-R-RUFF!*"

Jakie said, "Good evening."

"Well, good evening to you, mister," I said. The boy stopped his pawing and set his little brown eyes on me. "It's good 'n cold like it might snow tonight."

"It's Jakie, call me Jakie," Mrs. Goldberg's brother said with a shy smile, his eyes avoiding mine. The child swung his head over toward Jakie. "Yeah, I don't remember it ever being so cold, and I was born in this house."

"How did you get in here, Mr. Jakie? You must a come down de chimney," I said. The boy looked back at me. He was watching us like we were playing tennis.

"I seen my sister has company, yeah. See, when she's got someone over she doesn't want my sorry as...excuse me, she doesn't want me marching through the living room. I used the back door" *Dat where I sleeps.*

"All right den, Mr. Jakie, de lady say you might be comin' in for supper. Can I fix somethin' up for you? Knockwurst and beans?"

"*G-R-R-R-R-R-R-R-R-R-RUFF!*"

"Don' you worry, chile, I ain' fixin to give your uncle one bite of yur supper!"

"So long as the kid eats franks and beans it looks like I will, too. That's the only thing my sister buys besides booze."

"All right den, I'll fry some up."

"*G-R-R-R-R-R-R-R-R-R-RUFF!*"

"What brings you out to California?" Jakie asked after taking a swig of his beer.

"Well, I don' wants to go too deep into it just now if'n you don't mind."

"I see. I see, sure. It can wait. It's none of my beeswax anyhow. Sure." He was very shy for a man who carried a blackjack in his bathrobe pocket.

"YIP-YIP-YIP! YIP-YIP-YIP! YIP-YIP-YIP!"

"What do you think about the kid?" he asked.

"Oh, chilrun, dey always doin' somethin' crazy, pretendin' dey someone dey ain'," I said in order to hide my true feelings. But I had a bad habit of talking too much, so I went on. "Like my boy, Will. When he had de chicken *pops*, he was 'bout eight, my husband, Isaac, brought in a medicine man from de Karankawa tribe. See, dere wasn't a doctor around for miles. The Indian he carried Will out to the chicken coop and passed him over de chickens and back again eight times, four times over easy and four times sunny side up. I don' know why dey do the way dey do, but dat's de Indian way." *Now that sounded dumb as dirt.* "Then dat medicine man, he carried Will back to bed. He covered de lesions wit a mixture of cool branch water and clay and told Will that if Will scratched any of de sores dey would shore 'nough leave permanent scars de shape of chicken's feet all over his face, body, and hands. Now, Will, he lay out in bed wit his arms outstretched and legs straight like Jesus on de cross 'til de sores were healed and gone."

"Is that so!" Jakie said with a giggle.

The boy resumed pawing at the gate latch. "And what is you tryin' to do, chile?" I said, feeling uplifted by the memory of Will's silly behavior. "Break out of Alcatraz and get your mama all fit to be tied now dat's she finally cooled down?"

"He wants to see his daddy," Jakie said.

"YIP-YIP-YIP! YIP-YIP-YIP! YIP-YIP-YIP!"

"Well," I said, looking at the boy with a gentle smile, "a boy do need a daddy to grow up straight and strong. Mrs. Goldberg say de daddy come by now and again."

"YIP-YIP-YIP! YIP-YIP-YIP! YIP-YIP-YIP!"

"He's here now."

"What does you means 'now,' Mr. Jakie?"

"YIP-YIP-YIP! YIP-YIP-YIP! YIP-YIP-YIP!"

"You just let him in," Jakie said as he pushed the package of Lucky Strikes a few inches to the left then slid the book of Aladdin's matches over next to it like a man playing a solitary game of checkers.

"No, sir. I let de lady's gentleman caller in. De doctor, right?"

"YIP-YIP-YIP! YIP-YIP-YIP! YIP-YIP-YIP!"

Jakie chortled. He took the unlit cigarette out from atop his ear, rolled the clean white paper between his index finger and thumb, both stained yellow from nicotine, then put the cigarette back up over his ear. *Cigarette's must have been precious when he was fightin' in de war.* "Nah, that was Leo, her *ex.* Didn't he say so?"

"YIP-YIP-YIP! YIP-YIP-YIP! YIP-YIP-YIP!"

"No, sir. He jus' said somethen' smart 'bout bein' a doctor, but with de Lord as my witness he didn't say nothin' t'all about being Mrs. Goldberg's ex-husband."

"He's bad, bad news. The fireworks show should start any minute now," Jakie said as he pulled another ice-cold bottle of beer from the icebox.

"Fireworks?"

"YIP-YIP-YIP! YIP-YIP-YIP! YIP-YIP-YIP!"

"You'll see," Mr. Jakie said as I gave him a bowl of baked beans. The fresh knockwurst I had put up were popping and sizzling in the frying pan. "If there's some fresh tomato in the icebox will you cut some for me? I like a nice cold tomato with my knockwurst. And some of that brown deli mustard in the cabinet above the sink, too."

"YIP-YIP-YIP! YIP-YIP-YIP! YIP-YIP-YIP!"

"Sssssh!" I said to the boy. "You'll wake de dead." I opened the icebox and found a tomato in the vegetable bin. "All right, here's one tomato." I sliced the tomato, laid out the slices on a plate next to the knockwurst, and served it to Jakie.

"Aren't you eatin' nothin'?" he said as he sat down. "You gotta be hungry."

"Thank you very kindly! I'm so hungry I could eat a horse and de saddle with hit." I spooned a bowl of beans for myself, took a fork and a napkin, then turned and walked toward my deluxe little suite on the service porch. A prison cell, not that I had ever seen the inside of one, would have been cozier and no doubt warmer.

"YIP-YIP-YIP! YIP-YIP-YIP! YIP-YIP-YIP!"

"You can have a knockwurst. Put one on," Mr. Jakie said from the kitchen.

"That will be fine," I said.

"And you don't have to leave," he snickered. "Come on, pull up a chair, take a load off."

"Oh no, dat would not be proper," I said. "But thank you kindly for de invitation." I did not want to be anyplace near any fireworks, and I did not want to be around when my employer discovered I rained on her parade by letting the wrong man in.

"Come on, you're in California now!"

"No, thank you, Mr. Jakie. Like I said—"

"YIP-YIP-YIP! YIP-YIP-YIP! YIP-YIP-YIP!"

"Shush, chile! Lord have mercy! Shush! It sound like dey a whole kennel of dogs loose in dis kitchen."

"Hey, look, I didn't mean to get out of line or nothin'."

"Oh, don't you worry none, Mr. Jakie." I noticed a shine in his eyes and his giggly laughter. He was high on marijuana.

I was sitting on my cot, ready to take my first spoonful of food since breakfast, when I heard Mrs. Goldberg screech, "What the hell are you doing here?" Jakie started laughing in the kitchen. My stomach knotted up. It was no use trying to eat. I set my bowl down and took a few deep breaths.

"YIP-YIP-YIP! YIP-YIP-YIP! YIP-YIP-YIP!"

Mrs. Goldberg screamed so loudly I was sure every neighbor on the block and all the dead in nearby cemeteries could hear her. It was embarrassing. I dreaded the thought of being seen leaving the house.

"YIP-YIP-YIP! YIP-YIP-YIP! YIP-YIP-YIP!"

"I said what the hell are you doing here? Phosie, I need ice!"

"I came to see the kid. Where are you going? To a coronation?"

"You came to see your kid! Don't pull that crap on me. If you gave one shit about your kid you wouldn't be three goddamned months behind on alimony and child support!" I came from a humble Texas dirt farm, and I'd never heard anyone carry on like they were.

"YIP-YIP-YIP! YIP-YIP-YIP! YIP-YIP-YIP!"

"I'm doing the best I can! When you get a new dog? What the hell happened to Angel?"

"I told you I had to get rid of him. No money! It was either the dog or the kid."

"You were telling the truth? He was my dog! Why the fuck didn't you call me, you phony bitch?

*If dis keep up I'm going out to de backyard to dig a fox hole and crawl in.*

"I did, but you wasn't in, as usual."

I didn't want to, but I went in there and filled up the ice bucket, like Mrs. Goldberg had asked. "Well," I said after finishing up, "I'll be back in de kitchen if'n you needs me, Mrs. Lucile."

"YIP-YIP-YIP! YIP-YIP-YIP! YIP-YIP-YIP!"

I stepped into the dining room, feeling relieved, and took a deep breath. Then I heard something heavy tumble onto the living room floor. Mrs. Goldberg shouted, "Flossie, Fussy, or whatever the hell it is, come back in here. I knocked over the ashtray."

I held my breath and walked back in. If the hanging man was escorting me up to the scaffold I don't think I would have felt any the worse.

"YIP-YIP-YIP! YIP-YIP-YIP! YIP-YIP-YIP!"

"Shut up! Jakie, shut the fucking dog up! Fussy! You let the wrong man in! You were supposed to let the doctor in! Can't anyone do any fucking thing right around here?" Mrs. Goldberg shouted. I thought of explaining, but that would have been like spitting into the wind. "Now clean up this goddamned mess on the floor!"

"Yes, 'um! Right away!"

"I'm so aggravated! The doctor will be here any minute!"

I kept my head low, did an about-face, and left the room to fetch a foxtail and a dustpan.

Mrs. Goldberg yelled so loud as I left that I jumped across the barrier between the living room and the dining room. "You're breaking the restraining order! Get your phony ass out of here now, or I will do what the judge told me and call the coppers. I swear."

The threat did not seem to bother Leo, as he laughed in her face. "Go ahead, you fucking whore, call the cops. Or do you want to know the real reason I came by?"

I was halfway through the dining room. I stopped to hear the truth.

"Truth has the same chance coming out of your mouth as vanilla ice cream has coming out a pigeon's ass."

Mr. Goldberg's tone changed. He started to plead. "No, really, baby! I'm sorry everything got turned upside down. I want to tell you something, baby. I shoulda called first, I know. I'm sorry, baby."

*Lordie! One minute this man calling her a whore and the next he sound like he can't live without her!*

"You *think?*"

"YIP-YIP-YIP! YIP-YIP-YIP! YIP-YIP-YIP!"

"Speak! Fast! You have one minute! Flossy!"

"Yes, 'um," I called out from the dining room.

"YIP-YIP-YIP! YIP-YIP-YIP! YIP-YIP-YIP!"

"My brother's useless. Go in and shut that little bastard up! Then clean this up."

"Yes, 'um, Mrs. Lucile." I walked slowly. I wanted to hear what Mr. Goldberg had to say.

"I been carrying a torch for you ever since we split, baby! I miss you. Every day we're apart I die, my heart dies, a little more."

*Dat sound like vanilla ice cream to me.*

"YIP-YIP-YIP! YIP-YIP-YIP! YIP-YIP-YIP!"

"Don't feed me that bullshit again. I know you like I know the back of my hand. You're busted. What's a matter, you don't have the moolah to run around town playing high roller to your stable of chippies? You got eighty-sixed from your lousy stinkin' bachelor's pad over in Hollywood, didn't you? You son of a bitch! How dare you come in here and bullshit me!"

"Ah, baby, you got it all wrong. Those broads meant nothing to me. I didn't know what the hell I was doing. I thought of you when I was with them, only you, baby."

"You're so full of shit the whites of your eyes are brown! Phosie!"

I had to run over to the far side of the dining room near the kitchen to answer. "I's comin', I's comin' soon as I find de foxtail and de dustpan!"

"There in the closet in the service…your room."

"No really, baby," I heard Leo go on. "You gotta listen to me. I cheated with my body, that's all I ever did. I never cheated with my heart. I love you like crazy, man! I'll do anything to get you to let me move back in. Listen, tell you what. This may sound goofy, but let's me and you blow this place tonight. We'll fly to Vegas right now, tonight, and get married again. It'll be good for the kid and everything, really. It will be like it was for us. Happy, carefree."

"I'm not going to Vegas with you now or never! Get the fuck out of here!"

I could not wait any longer. I hurried back to my room and retrieved the foxtail and dustpan from the cabinet.

"Where's the goddamned ice, for Christ's sakes?" Mrs. Goldberg said as I tiptoed back into the living room.

"I already done put it in. I was comin' to clean de ashes."

"I'm so fucking aggravated. Go ahead, clean. And get under the coffee table, too!"

I dropped onto one knee and began sweeping the nasty butts and ashes. I could not stand the stale metallic smell. I turned my head away.

"So, how about it, baby?"

"Look, Leo, I have a real chance to get out of this phony Mexican shithole. If you fuck this up I swear to God I'll go into the bathroom and slice my wrists wide open with one of the Gillette's you left behind! Do you hear me?"

Mr. Goldberg's tone switched back to anger. "So go ahead, do it! You think anybody will miss your sorry ass? The kid won't. He barely sees you! Your cunt of a mother is dead. Your shell-shocked brother's a good-for-nothing loser. The only reason he sticks around is he knows he can get a C-note or two from me to cover his gambling when he's running cold. That phony sister of yours on the other side of town won't care. She found her prince, that sheenie motherfucker. She has her own life to lead. All your so-called friends who could get out, got out. You're the last fucking Jewish tomato in Boyle Heights! You don't have two nickels to rub together. Nobody will give two shits if you kill yourself, you stupid whore. Go ahead! Go ahead! By the time your body's cold you'll be forgotten. Just make sure you leave the keys to the place with the schwarza so I can pick up the kid and the new dog in the morning."

"YIP-YIP-YIP! YIP-YIP-YIP! YIP-YIP-YIP!"

"Get out, you phony motherfucking bastard! Get out!"

I had already finished the cleanup, but I kept sweeping over the same area to avoid having to rise up and face the shame of their conduct. I felt dirty. They were the parents of a beautiful child. They were sinners. I wished I could have had the courage to say something. I wished I could have stuffed all my things in my sack and walked right out with the child.

"Where's the ice? I need ice in the bucket! What the fuck do I have to do to have an ice bucket filled with ice? Do I have to get it myself? Posse!"

"Yes, 'um, I'll be right back wit more!" I said as I stood and took a step backward. I wasn't about to remind her again that I'd already brought the ice.

"Why don't you take the lousy fuckin' bucket to the kitchen? I mean, how are you going to get the ice in here! Jesus Christ, does everybody on the face of this planet have their heads up their sorry asses?"

*Lord have mercy!* "Yes, 'um, that's exactly right. I don' know what's wrong wit me," I said as I slinked back to the cocktail cart and picked up the handle of the silver-plated ice bucket with my free hand. It was nearly full. "I be right back with it!" By the time I returned, Mr. Goldberg was continuing to plead his case. "Baby, come on, I didn't mean that. You know I love you, baby."

"You don't *love* me."

"YIP-YIP-YIP! YIP-YIP-YIP! YIP-YIP-YIP!"

"Shut the *fuck* up, you little bastard!"

"YIP-YIP-YIP! YIP-YIP-YIP! YIP-YIP-YIP!"

"I don't mean what I say when I get hot like I was, you know that, baby," Mr. Goldberg said, reaching for Mrs. Goldberg's delicate white hand. Mrs. Goldberg pulled it away. "It's just like you don't mean what you say when you say you're going to slit your wrists. You don't mean that, baby, you know you don't mean that." Mr. Goldberg reached for her hand again, and this time Mrs. Goldberg did not pull it away. "So, what's it going to be, baby? A thousand to one all this phony doctor wants is to get into your pants! But me, I want you back, man, I really want you."

"I can't think right now! We'll talk later, but you're going to have to prove, prove, that if I ever give you a chance again things will be different, you hear me? Different!"

"You name it, baby, it's yours."

"I can't think, talk, now. Call me tomorrow."

I walked back into the kitchen. Jakie was feeding the boy Chiclets like an old man feeding crumbs to the pigeons. It tickled me to see the child chewing on gum just like any boy would while at the same time looking up to see if we had noticed that he had slipped out of his doghood.

"I seen a lot a things in my years, chile, but dis is de very first time I ever seen a dog chewin' Chiclets!"

I looked at Jakie inquisitively.

He held up his hand. "Don't look at me. I told her not to get involved with Leo in the first place. You think she'd ever listen to me? My sister don't listen to no one. She does what she wants, when she wants, and says whatever it takes. The only one she cares about is herself!"

Just then there was a knock at the door.

"YIP-YIP-YIP! YIP-YIP-YIP! YIP-YIP-YIP!"

I held my breath.

"Oh shit! My date's here!" I heard Mrs. Goldberg say. "Pussy, will you answer the door?"

Jakie was amused.

"YIP-YIP-YIP! YIP-YIP-YIP! YIP-YIP-YIP!"

"Oh my lord!" I said and wiped my hands on the French-style apron Mrs. Goldberg gave me to wear.

"I can't wait to see this poor schmuck!" Leo said.

Mrs. Goldberg whispered harshly, "He's a goddamned doctor and he wants to marry me."

Leo laughed. "Yeah, and I want to be the fucking king of England."

"I hate you, you motherfucker!"

Mr. Goldberg laughed wickedly. "The only mother I ever fucked was your mother. Best cocksucker I ever knew!" He kept on laughing. He seemed to enjoy prodding people, getting a rise out of them, as if hurting them was funny. He was vile.

We heard, "Lucky? Are you in there?" The gentleman caller had a high-pitched voice like a canary's. He spoke with a Southern accent. "Lucky, darlin', don't you be a bad girl. If you keep your daddy waiting I'll have to spank you!"

"Answer the door!"

"All right then," I said.

"YIP-YIP-YIP! YIP-YIP-YIP! YIP-YIP-YIP!"

"Lucky?" Leo said cynically. "What, he thinks you're a racehorse?"

"You get out of line and we really are through!" Mrs. Goldberg said as she straightened herself out. "Really, you say hello, and then you leave!" Mr. Goldberg laughed cynically.

"Lucky, honey, let me in 'fore I freeze."

"What are you waiting for? Open it!" I opened the door.

The doctor looked like a riverboat dandy. He was wearing a plaid coat and a red bow tie and thick black-rimmed glasses in the style of the day, and he had dyed blond hair combed over the crown of his head like a white duck's wing.

"Well, how do you do, young lady?" he said cordially. "Last time I was here the lady had a fat old Mexican gal with a gold tooth looking after things."

I had no idea what to say, so I just stepped aside.

"I thought I'd catch my death!" the doctor said then noticed there was another man in the room.

"Lewie, this is...I want you to meet my agent, Leo, Leo Kravitz. He just dropped by to discuss a studio offer. Leo, this is Dr. Lewellyn Buzzbee, my date."

"YIP-YIP-YIP! YIP-YIP-YIP! YIP-YIP-YIP!"

"Why, it's a pleasure to meet the agent of such a beautiful rising screen and radio star, sir," the doctor said, the words pouring from his mouth like thick molasses from a jug. He was somewhat drunk and swayed as though he was standing on the deck of a small boat. There was a slight tremor to his hands. "Dr. Lewellyn Buzzbee at your service. But my friends call me Lew."

*How do this man wit palsied hands operate on people's eyes? All his patients mus' be blind.*

"Your friends call you Lew, huh?"

"Yes, and I invite you too as any friend of this beautiful lady is a friend of mine." Mr. Goldberg sneered.

"YIP-YIP-YIP! YIP-YIP-YIP! YIP-YIP-YIP!"

Dr. Buzzbee looked like he didn't know what to say, so he changed the subject. "Billy sounds more agitated than usual!"

"Oh! That's not Billy. Didn't I tell you? I, I just got a puppy, for Billy. Billy's fast asleep." Now Mrs. Goldberg was sweet and cordial as a Deacon's wife at Sunday supper. "Isn't that right, Phosie?"

"Yes, 'um. De chile's sleepin' like an angel from heaven above," I said, playing along as best I could. *Please don't walk in dat kitchen, Mr. Goldberg, and kill me for lyin'.*

"YIP-YIP-YIP! YIP-YIP-YIP! YIP-YIP-YIP!"

"That's a very nice idea. I'm sure he's doing better then," the doctor said with a smile then turned toward Mr. Goldberg.

"What are yah talkin' about, doin' better? What's a matter with the kid?"

"Oh, he has a...a sty that Dr. Buzzbee is treating, Leo. Now, why don't you go, Love, and call me in the morning about that picture deal with Warner Brothers or whatever?"

I tried to inch myself back into the kitchen.

"You know," the doctor continued without noticing what Mrs. Goldberg had said, "lots of girls that come into the office say they came out to Hollywood to be in the movies, but most wind up serving cocktails in some disreputable establishment. Are you a literary man as well as a talent agent, sir? I have been thinking of penning a novel."

"I'm an agent like you're Shakespeare!"

"I beg your pardon," the doctor said in a very dignified tone.

"I'm her ex, bub," Leo said. "Her ex. That's all! My old lady—"

"Ex-old lady and now client," Mrs. Goldberg cut in. "Leo loves to rib when he's had a few too many. You know, catch people off guard."

"YIP-YIP-YIP! YIP-YIP-YIP! YIP-YIP-YIP!"

Mrs. Goldberg looked at me and said, "Will you look in on the puppy and refresh the ice please."

*It like to freeze over if'n I puts any more ice in dis room! But thank you, Jesus, for gettin' me out!* I was never so happy to take an order in my life. I carried the ice bucket I had just filled back to the kitchen, trying to understand what parts Mrs. Goldberg was missing.

Leo was setting the record straight when I returned.

"Yeah, I had a few too many," Leo said, "but what I said is true. I'm not some phony agent. I'm her ex, you son of a bitch, her ex. So welcome to the *nunnery*!"

"I beg your pardon, what do you mean by *nunnery?*"

"I mean another john will be coming around tomorrow night and another the next and the next and the next, so make sure you take all your shit with you in the morning when go back home to your ball and chain in Hancock Park or Beverly Hills or wherever you live. Oh, and make sure you leave a C-note on the cocktail cart."

I started to walk back out.

"Posse, Mr. Goldberg's drunk. Will you please see him out?"

"YIP-YIP-YIP! YIP-YIP-YIP! YIP-YIP-YIP!"

*De front door is right in front a his nose. He can see it his ownself, thank you kindly.* I froze and pasted a grin on my face.

"Agent, ex-husband, or whomsoever you are, I do not think it gentlemanly of you to refer to the lady in that manner!" Dr. Buzzbee said in a sober tone.

"Oh yeah?"

"Leo! Leave, please, I'm begging you!"

"YIP-YIP-YIP! YIP-YIP-YIP! YIP-YIP-YIP!"

"I'm not letting this bum walk into my pad and give me a fuckin' lesson on etiquette."

"It's *not* your pad! It never was. Now leave!"

"I think you ought to follow the lady's advice!" the doctor said.

"I got some advice for you!" Mr. Goldberg said then sucker punched the doctor. The doctor reeled back against the front door then charged at Mr. Goldberg as Mrs. Goldberg started screaming for her brother, who had been sitting in the kitchen the whole time taking everything in as though he was listening to The Mercury Theatre on the Air. "Jakie! Jakie! Come in here!"

"YIP-YIP-YIP! YIP-YIP-YIP! YIP-YIP-YIP!"

Jakie nearly knocked me down as he ran in from the kitchen. The doctor and Mr. Goldberg were standing nose to nose at the front door. The doctor had grabbed Mr. Goldberg's lapels and was trying to keep from being hit again. Jakie must have seen it the other way around. He slipped his blackjack out of his robe pocket and whacked the doctor along the side of his head right over his ear. The blow sounded like a ball-peen hammer striking the side of an oak barrel. The doctor collapsed into a heap on the cold wood floor. He looked dead.

"YIP-YIP-YIP! YIP-YIP-YIP! YIP-YIP-YIP!"

"For Christ's sakes, Jakie, what did you do?"

"What do you mean, 'what did I do?' You called for help, I ran in and helped you!"

Mr. Goldberg was smiling broadly.

"Get the hell out of here, Leo! I'm through with you!" Mrs. Goldberg said. But her tone was unsure. She seemed overwhelmed.

Mr. Goldberg straightened his jacket and said, "Sure, *Lucky*, anything you say. And think about the proposition I made you. We're made from the same mold, baby. His type,"—Mr. Goldberg nodded toward the doctor—"they don't understand people like us. They're squares. They think their shit doesn't stink. What are you going to do, move into Hancock Park and pretend you're white bread? You'd be miserable. You belong with me! No one else will make you happy! You know it, and I know it. I love you, baby."

Mrs. Goldberg cried as Mr. Goldberg walked out. It seemed like a hundred years ago, but I remembered Sis' Pearl seeing the old blackie at the military hospital the day before yesterday and thanking the Lord for the mop and pail because they guaranteed a place for colored folk. Well, I thought these crazy people I was with now better thank the Lord that there was a place for us colored people because without us they would not have a soul to feel superior to.

"YIP-YIP-YIP! YIP-YIP-YIP! YIP-YIP-YIP!"

Mrs. Goldberg, her hair and her makeup mussed, shouted, "You son of a bitch!" as Mr. Goldberg walked out the door. I had never met a man, woman, or child that I came to despise as I despised Mr. Leo Goldberg after so short a time.

"Help me lift the doctor onto the sofa, you two!"

"YIP-YIP-YIP! YIP-YIP-YIP! YIP-YIP-YIP!"

"Shut up, you goddamned little bastard. This is all your fault!"

"YIP-YIP-YIP! YIP-YIP-YIP! YIP-YIP-YIP!"

"I can't take this anymore! I can't!"

After we set the doctor on the sofa, Mrs. Goldberg poured herself another whiskey and gulped it down.

"I swear I'll kill myself if things don't get better! I will!"

"YIP-YIP-YIP! YIP-YIP-YIP! YIP-YIP-YIP!"

"Oh, Mrs. Lucile, you don't mean that. You jus' angry."

Jakie lowered his face, shook his head, and said under his breath, "Don't pay any attention to her. She says that all the time!"

"I do, do I? Well, what are you going to do when I really do it. Maybe I'll jump from a high bridge. Yeah, maybe you'll find my body under the Colorado Street Bridge up in Pasadena, you bastard!" Mrs. Goldberg glanced at the doctor. "Get him a cold washcloth. I'm going to fix my makeup so that I won't look a mess when he comes to."

"Yes, 'um, I surely will, Mrs. Lucile. You jus' go and you take yourself a deep breath or two."

"YIP-YIP-YIP! YIP-YIP-YIP! YIP-YIP-YIP!"

Mrs. Goldberg stomped out of the room.

Jakie and I stood and stared briefly at one another like two survivors of Mrs. Goldberg's train wreck.

"YIP-YIP-YIP! YIP-YIP-YIP! YIP-YIP-YIP!"

Then, we laughed.

It was the first time I laughed since Will left for the war.

# Chapter 10

## *A Shocking Revelation*

Once we were back in the kitchen, Jakie pulled another Brew 102 from the icebox, pried the cap off with a brass bottle key, sat down at the dinette, set the blackjack down crossways above his plate like a butter knife, pushed the sleeves of his robe up past his elbows, and went back to work on his supper.

"De food mus' be col', Mr. Jakie. Let me heat hit up some."

"Nah, that's all right. Hot? Cold? Tastes the same."

I started chipping ice from the block for compresses for the doctor's chin and temple. As the gleaming point of the ice pick split the ice into little shards, I realized how angry I was at the white folks I was now serving as a second-class citizen. A war had been fought and won. My one and only son was lying in a Civil War-era hospital ward without the medicine he needed because white boys overseas were celebrating, and still Mrs. Goldberg, her husband, and the doctor were carrying on as if they were the center of their own little universes and didn't care one wit for anyone else but themselves. My chipping grew furious. The boy protested.

"YIP-YIP-YIP! YIP-YIP-YIP! YIP-YIP-YIP!"

I looked into the cage. He was sitting on his haunches pawing at the string holding the latch. *Poor chile. Dere ain' a soul 'round dis place, 'cept for Mr. Jakie, dat cares for his little self. Maybe de Army need to take dis child out of here and bomb dis place like they did Tokyo and Berlin. Den dese people would know what dey missin'.*

I found the doctor rubbing the side of his head when I carried the compresses into the living room.

"Oh, thank you, thank you very kindly," he said as he placed one on his cheek and the other over his ear. "You know, you remind me of a woman worked for a Charleston family, what was their name, the Bartholomews. Do you have kin down that way?"

I smiled. The impulse to ask him for help with needles for Will was almost impossible to control. "No, sir, Mr. Doctor, no one down dat far south I knows of. I hear hit awful pretty in de fall and even prettier come spring."

"Lovely, it's just lovely. One big garden in the spring. Most beautiful place on Earth." He grimaced as I resituated the compress on his temple.

"Mrs…" I had forgotten her name in all the fuss. "Missus, she say she be in directly. Cain I get you some aspirin or coffee?"

"Yes, a nice glass of Crown Royal neat would be very nice, thank you." I wondered what on Earth this seemingly kind professional man was doing coming way out to East Los Angeles besides looking for trouble. What need did he have? His life must have been so suffocating he had to escape. But he was too naïve to know what trouble looked like. Mrs. Goldberg must have toasted then buttered both sides of his bread and fried his bacon up crisp. He carried the love fever.

"All right den," I said, turning to the bar. "But I don' know what you means by 'neat.'"

He laughed. "Just poor the whiskey into the glass, about three fingers high, and give it to me without ice, straight up."

"All right den, straight up. I've learnt to milk, sew, scrape, cook, hammer, chip, saw and nail, and treat de common cold, I 'spect I cain learn to bartend too," I said with a warm smile that I hoped would endear me to the doctor.

"Just exactly who was the man who was here? The lady's agent or her husband?"

"Oh, I don' know, Doctor. I only been here two hours my own self. You'd best to ask Mrs. Goldberg when she come back out." I wanted to tell him it would be smart to get as far away as he could from the Goldbergs, but I wanted needles for Will more than I cared about protecting him.

"And speaking of Mrs. Goldberg," Mrs. Goldberg announced as though she was the master of ceremonies on a radio program, "here she is, ladies and gentlemen, Miss Lady Luck herself, Lucky Lucile Goldberg!"

The doctor stood up and clapped.

"Flossie, would you mind emptying the ashtray and washing out the leftover glass?"

"No, ma'am, not t'all." I was just happy to be exiled into the kitchen and safety.

"Was that your husband or your agent, Lucky-Lu?" the doctor said as I picked up Mr. Goldberg's glass, moving as fast as I could. A half-smoked cigarette was floating in a shallow pool of diluted liquor amongst translucent slivers of ice at the bottom of the glass. There wasn't much that disgusted me, but that nasty brown concoction did. It reminded me of Sis' Pearl's tobacco juice in the jar she kept under Babe's car seat. I cringed.

"My *ex*. But I don't want you to think about him. He's crazy, and he's a liar, the worst of the worst. I was so young when I met him. You know how those things go, darling," Mrs. Goldberg said.

"Oh, I know, I know. I met Martha when she was just sweet sixteen. It's just too young, too young, I know," the doctor said rapidly in order not to allow any blue sky to open between him and Mrs. Goldberg. *Lord, dis woman could tell dis man she a leper and he would see her as de prettiest leper on de face of de earth.*

Mrs. Goldberg leaned over and whispered something in the doctor's ear. He blushed.

As I walked into the dining room I heard the doctor say, "I've made up my mind, Lucky! I'm going to tell Martha I'm leaving her. How about that?" I froze like a statue in a museum. *Lan' sakes alive, say you pleased.*

"That's fabulous, darling," Mrs. Goldberg answered in a tentative tone.

"You know what that means, it means we can make that trip to Las Vegas. I'll have to go first and rent a motel room until the divorce is processed, but soon as it is you can fly up and we'll hire a great big limousine to take us to one of those wedding chapels they have up there and tie the knot. Won't that be wonderful! You do want to marry me, darling, don't you?"

"Oh baby, you're the most. But let's not spoil tonight by worrying about all that legal stuff. Let's blow this place and go out, live it up, have a ball. The war's over!"

"Whatever you say, darling. I'm just lucky to have you in my life."

*Oh my Lord, I hope dis man is a better doctor dan he is a judge of character.*

"I made reservations at The Players, I hope that's okay. Everybody goes there."

"Anything you want. I'm yours tonight!"

"And I'm *all* yours."

I heard glasses clink.

"Slow down, I don't know if my heart can stand it!" the doctor said with a chuckle. "I don't want to spoil the wedding by having another heart attack."

"You don't have to worry about that, baby, we'll take it slow and easy."

*She's hoping that soon as they marry his heart decides to quit so that she'll be a rich widow,* I thought as I imagined her sitting with the doctor in a plush green leather booth at one of the fancy restaurants or nightclubs advertised on the matchbooks in the brandy snifter on the coffee table. Then it struck me. Each and every one of those matchbooks—there must have been fifty—may well have represented an evening on the town with another sugar daddy. *This woman don' let de grass grow under her feet.*

"Thank the Lord this day is over," I said as I walked into the kitchen. I don't remember feeling so exhausted in my entire life. The boy was lying so far back in his cage I had to stoop to make sure he was inside.

He was asleep or pretending to be asleep, lying on his belly with his head resting on a forearm. He looked so innocent. I couldn't feel angry with him. I felt horrible for him. He was hanging on to the only love that he'd had, and that was the love of the dog his mother had gotten rid of. I whispered, "May de good Lord bless and keep you and cast his smile 'pon you for all of your…" I was about to say "days" when I realized that was the prayer I used to say for Will when I put him to bed. I whispered, "Goodnight, honeychile."

It was so drafty and cold in the service porch that I slept with my topcoat and nylons on. I wrapped a towel around my head to keep my ears from freezing. Lord, I swear I had heard and seen more yelling, hate, lying, and just plain ugliness in the first evening of my employment with the Goldbergs than I had seen in my entire life. Living with the Klu Kluxers, if you minded your own business, was a breeze compared to living with this family. Klu Kluxers wouldn't have allowed such drunken nonsense.

I fell right off into a deep, deep sleep. I dreamt Will was in the stall my daddy kept for his mule, Sally back down in Alabama. The barn in which the stall was located had caught fire and I heard Sally braying until the braying sounded like screaming, but I could not move my body to get up to run and save Will. I felt like I was lying face up under the frozen surface of a creek. I tried to break loose, but all I could move were my eyes. I heard Sally bray again. But now Sally had a woman's voice. She sounded just like Mrs. Goldberg. Next, a dog started barking,

"YIP-YIP-YIP! YIP-YIP-YIP! YIP-YIP-YIP!

I rolled from left to right to break out of the ice until I was finally awake enough to realize that it was my topcoat that was restraining me and that it was the icy cold air in the service porch that had given me the sensation of freezing. I heard Mrs. Goldberg screaming from the living room. Then I heard Dr. Buzzbee trying to settle her down and the boy barking.

"YIP-YIP-YIP! YIP-YIP-YIP! YIP-YIP-YIP!"

I arched up and looked at a Baby Ben alarm clock with nightglow hands on the nightstand. It was 3:23 a.m. *Good Lord, I likely to die for lack of sleep if dis keep up.*

"Rosie, get in here, now!" Mrs. Goldberg shouted.

I heard Dr. Buzzbee with a whiskey-soaked voice say, "It isn't anything the girl can't clean up, pussy cat. Come on over here and give Daddy a kiss?" I fought my way out from under my twisted coat and stood up shivering on the ice-cold linoleum floor, stiff and tired in the pitch blackness of that early morning. "Let's not let the boy ruin another beautiful evening, darling! We have to celebrate. I'm leaving Martha! We're getting married! Come on, bottoms up."

Mrs. Goldberg screamed, "I'm, I'm sending that little bastard to his son-of-a-bitchin' father! I can't take it anymore! Flossie! Phosie! Where the hell are you?"

"Yes, 'um! I coming, missus, I'm a coming!" I said as I ambled through the dark into the living room, losing my balance on every other step. I had forgotten I was wearing my overcoat and had the towel wrapped around my head. *I wish I could jus' walk right out de door, right down de steps, and right back to Galveston to live wit Isaac and my Will in de happiness we had.* The foul odor of human feces was blossoming from the living room. For some reason that made me realize the folly of my previous thought, and I changed my tune. *Lord, please, whatever you do, please don't let this crazy woman fire me! Please! I'll put up with anything, anything. I'm beggin' you!*

"YIP-YIP-YIP! YIP-YIP-YIP! YIP-YIP-YIP!"

I walked into the living room and studied the mess. The front door was wide open, the lamps on the end tables were on, the Christmas tree lights were still blinking, and Mrs. Goldberg was waving a pillow to freshen the air as its white feathers were flying out of it like a flock of geese. Some of the feathers were sticking in her hair. The room looked like a chicken coop with a fox in it. And oh, did it smell to the high heavens. The child had used the living room to do his business. There was a squished brown pile of pooh on the wood floor next to the drink cart. But that was not all there was. Everything—gifts, pillows, cushions—was ripped and shredded. The easiest way I thought to clean the mess up was to set it ablaze, and from the expression on the boy's mama's face, that is exactly what it looked like she intended to do. The doctor had stepped in the boy's mess and was sitting on the sofa holding the soiled shoe in his hand. I raised my arms up over my head, clapped my hands, and shouted, "*Oy vey!*"

"Clean this goddamned mess up! Put the kid back in his cage!"

I had no idea the child had gotten out of his cage. "Yes, 'um, right away! But where is de chile?"

"He's behind the tree, goddamn it!"

The boy was on his haunches behind the tree with a candy cane dangling from his little mouth. *I best get dis child out a here 'fore this woman kill it.* "Come on, chile! Let me get you out dis mess."

"*G-R-R-R-R-R-R-R-R-R-RUFF!*"

"Don' growl at me, chile, you de one made dis' mess. I just doin' what your mama says. Come on now."

"*G-R-R-R-R-R-R-R-R-R-RUFF!*"

I surveyed the room once again. "Lord have mercy on my soul."

"'Lord have mercy!' For Christ's sakes, what's the Lord got to do with it? You were supposed to watch him! What the hell do you think I hired you for? To, to make biscuits?" Mrs. Goldberg screamed, making it clear she looked at me as a smiling Aunt Jemima with a yellow and red do-rag covering my head.

I was so stunned I said, "Who?"

"My goddamned kid! Who do you think? How did he get out?"

"He must a used his teeth to saw through de string I tied de latch up wit, Mrs. Lucile, jus' like you showed me. I wish I coulda stopped hit."

"Tomorrow morning you'll be wishing you had a job!"

"Lucky, it wasn't the girl's fault."

Mrs. Goldberg ignored the doctor. "Take him out of here, clean him up, put him back in that cage, then come back and clean that shit up!"

I wished I had fallen asleep and froze to death in the branch water. "Yes, 'um. Now you," I said to the boy, "come on out from dere, chile! Come to Phosie." He did not budge. "Now you come on now!"

"I said take the kid away and clean this up!" Mrs. Goldberg shouted. She sounded like the infuriated five-year-old sister of a two-year-old boy who had rumbled through her tea party.

"Princess, it's nothing to get so excited about," Dr. Buzzbee said.

"Oh really? I can't find the right help! It's impossible. I've tried whites, Mexicans, now schwarzas, and none of them know the first goddamned thing about taking care of a kid!" I wanted to correct her, but I kept my mouth shut.

"Mrs. Lucile, why don' you take de doctor into de dining room and let me clean dis along wit his shoe up," I said calmly, hoping to settle her down. "Doctor sir, give Phosie dat shoe if you please."

The doctor said, "That's a good idea, Lucky. Accidents happen," as he passed his shoe to me.

"My whole goddamned life is an accident!"

*Oh my Lord. De next thing I am goin' to hear is, "You pack up your things and get out by morning!"*

"You pack up your things and be ready to leave first thing tomorrow. Shit! Now I have to start looking for another girl! No! I'll send the kid to his father's. Let him put up with this."

"Yes, 'um."

"YIP-YIP-YIP! YIP-YIP-YIP! YIP-YIP-YIP!"

"Shut up! You little bastard!" Mrs. Goldberg said as she grabbed a bottle of whiskey and two glasses then led the doctor into the dining room. She stopped before leaving the living room and shouted, "You are going to your father's!"

As I cleaned up the boy's droppings I felt furious about how terrible and unfair it was that my life had been so ruined. Every sure thing I had in my life was gone. My husband was dead. My boy was near death. I was helpless, just flat helpless, to do anything about it. I coaxed the boy out from behind the tree with one of the candy canes that was hanging up out of his reach. "Come on now, sugar, let me change you into somethin' warm and put you back in that cage," I said softly. It wasn't his fault. He and I were both victims of fate just like two little townsfolk living in Tornado Alley. It was just a matter of time before the storm arrived.

I made up my mind I would sneak into the hospital and steal the needles if it came to it. My Will was not going to go without his medicine. I was not going to lose him. I did not care what I had to sacrifice.

# Chapter 11

## *Mud in De Water, Sister*

I tossed and turned until sunrise thinking about what I would say to Babe and Sis' Pearl about my being fired when they arrived to carry me to the hospital. I knew what Sis' Pearl would think. She'd look at me like a dirty old shoe, nicked and scuffed, not worthy of further her attention, and ready for the trash. My failure would shame her. I would be an embarrassment before the Church Sisterhood. Not feeling comfortable using Mrs. Goldberg's bathroom, I washed up in the service porch sink and fixed my hair using the backdoor window as a mirror. I didn't see any sense in putting a uniform on seeing as how I would be taking it off as soon as Babe and Sis' Pearl came to fetch me, so I put my one and only outfit on while imagining how the ride back to their place would be with Pearl sitting right next to me. I felt I'd rather be dipped in hot oil than listen to her snide comments or feel her silent resentment. And there would be Mrs. Henrietta Duke to reckon with too. She would probably demand repayment of the five-dollar bonus she gave me even though I had not worked but one night. It seemed she had already placed me down at the bottom of the barrel. *Only de Lord know where she'd place me de next time. Maybe washin' dishes in a diner.* I did manage to take some comfort in the fact that what was happening to me would not affect Will. I was ready to sleep out on the street outside the hospital or in the cemetery across the street in order to be near him and do whatever I could to help him through his ordeal.

I tiptoed into the kitchen. The boy's cage door was open. That child was loose again. My first inclination was to search for him incase he had made another mess. Then, I thought, *Let Mrs. Lucile take it up,* and started the coffee instead. I took the stainless steel coffeepot from the heating element atop shiny new Perc-O-Toaster—it was a wonder of wonders: made coffee on top, toasted bread on the bottom. I filled the pot with fresh cold water from the tap, scooped coffee grounds into the metal basket inside, then set the pot back on the Perc-O-Toaster hot plate and switched it on. I stared at the elements inside the toaster as they began to glow orange.

As always, the aroma of the fresh coffee was comforting. It announced the beginning of a new day without prejudgment of the events that would transpire. It said this is a fresh new day, perk up and make the best of it. As I took a sip, Jakie shuffled in wearing his robe and slippers with his signature fresh cigarette tucked over his ear. "Lor' have mercy, Mr. Jakie, you musta been waitin' outside de back door! Sit right down. I'll fix you up a fresh hot cup of coffee strong 'nough to take de black out of a crow's feathers." There wasn't any sense in being angry with him. All he was doing was sharing the expense of his mother's place with his sister. He couldn't be blamed for her behavior. And I did not believe in carrying a grudge for all white folk because some acted like animals. Besides, his poor soul was caught back in a sweltering jungle on a Pacific island.

"Yea, thanks, I don't mind if I do," he said after pausing to collect his thoughts.

"Here you go, Mr. Jakie," I said as the silky dark fluid flooded his cup and the aroma made me feel glad to be alive. "Do you take sugar? I believe I saw some sweet sorghum around in here." I opened the cabinet door and saw a pound sack of sugar. "Oh my Lord, dis is de furst sugar I have seen for I don' know how long. How did de missus come by hit?"

"She dates some guy high up in the OPA."

"She shore do get around."

Just then the boy crawled in and laid his head on the scuffed toe of Mr. Jakie's right slipper. I did not acknowledge him, as I believed his behavior had caused me to lose my job. I was not in a forgiving mood when it came to that child.

"Wonder what he been up to," I thought aloud.

Mr. Jakie took a sip of his coffee and looked down at the boy. "Oh, he probably got up into the bed with his mama. He sleeps with her when he's not in the cage. *That cain' be good her being a single woman.* I thought.

"Why are you dressed like that?" Jakie said, changing the subject. "My sister gave you uniforms yesterday."

"Didn't you hear de fussin' last night?" I said.

"Nah, I was out playing cards. What happened?"

"Dat innocent-lookin' lil' chile done chewed his way through de string I tied de latch on de gate of his cage with." Jakie laughed. "Den he up and crawled, or walked, one, into de livin' room, shredded each and every one of de sofa cushions, and chewed his way through all de gift wrapping till hit looked like a pack of coyotes got loose in dat room. Den he did his business on de floor right in front of Mrs. Goldberg's little bar. And de Lord knows it was sum big business for a little chile."

"Where were my sister and the doctor?"

"Well, dey came in twixt three and four dis mornin'. Far as I knows, de doctor must have been feelin' no pain. He likely walked o'er to de drink cart and as he did he stepped right into de mess dat little devil of a chile left for dem. Den, he, de doctor, spread de mess clear 'cross Mrs. Goldberg's rug when he walked over to sit down on de sofa. Lor' it did reeked like somethen' died. But, dey did not notice for de marijuana dey was smoking. Oh Lordy, dey mus' a been real-real high if'n dey missed dat stink."

"My sister must have blown a gasket." Jakie snickered.

"Mrs. Goldberg? De Lord have mercy, she screamed like a body had been found dead skinned and scalped both. Dat's when she fired me. 'Pack your things, sister. You're out of here when the sun rises.'"

Jakie snickered again then twisted up his face, deep in thought. Suddenly he jerked upright. "Hey, listen, this could work out for the best, ya know."

"How?" I said as I pivoted to place my cup in the sink.

"Now that you won't be working here no longer, you and me ought to have dinner sometime. I know all the right places, some are down in the Crenshaw area."

"Well, thank you very kindly, Mr. Jakie. You is a sweet man. But I'm afraid now is not de *right* time. Dey jus' too much going on in my life. Besides, I ain' never been out with no white man *ever*. I don' think startin' up now wit all dat's goin' on will be such a good thing. But I sincerely do appreciate de offer. I really do. At least let me pour you some more of my coffee."

"I know places down on Central Avenue we can go," he said as I refilled his cup. "It won't be a problem, I seen a lot of mixed couples down there when I make my rounds, you know."

"Well, dat's very nice, but like I said, now is not de right time, Mr. Jakie. Thank you kindly," I said.

He looked heartbroken. "So there might be a right time later?"

"Oh lordy, I cain' rightly say."

"I ain' never met anyone like you, really."

I smiled politely.

"I really wish you was staying. I feel like getting out of bed now that you're here. It's like the sun's out all the time."

I continued to smile and tried not to blush.

"It would be better for the kid if you stayed. She's had five women working here since her ex moved out. They left him alone, slapped him, did all sorts of cruel things to the kid. It was lucky I was around at night or he would have gotten much worse."

"When was dat, when did he move out?"

"About eight months ago," Jakie said with a giggle. He was high again.

"Five! Sweet Jesus! Well, I don' know 'bout dem women, but you shore missed all de fireworks las' night."

"You could write a book about the action in this place."

"Why did Mr. Goldberg leave?"

"I think he was just fed up with the setup. I mean, my sister and him should have never married. Them living under one roof, you might as well pour gasoline over the place and throw a match on it," Jakie said. He laughed again. He was a simple man, a plain man, but a likeable man. He turned away and smiled. His smile was nice and warm despite the demons that kept fighting the war in his head. I smiled at him. When he caught me I looked the other way.

Mrs. Goldberg stumbled in looking like a vampire had sucked all the blood out of her delicate veins. I thought of what my mama used to say about beautiful women: *"Chile, dat woman might look pretty right chere right now, but you remember dis, de pretty flowers lose dey bloom da fastest. It better to be more like de hedgerow. Least dey stays green."*

Mrs. Goldberg patted the pockets of her robe. "I need coffee and a cigarette." When she noticed the child lying with its head on Mr. Jakie's slipper, she hoisted the boy up by the back of his pajama bottoms and placed him on the other side of the kitchen, which wasn't more than two steps away. "Don't do that. Those slippers are disgusting."

"May I use de telephone to call my brother to pick me up?"

Mrs. Goldberg looked at me. "Why the hell are you dressed like that? Where the hell do you think you're going?"

I tried to hold back my tears. "Last night you say I should pack den leave  soon as you was up."

"Oh Christ! I didn't mean that! I'm sorry. It's just that when I get mad, you know, I, I run off at the mouth. I say things I don't mean. You look like you're losing the only thing in life that means anything to you."

"Dis here job *is* de onliest thing dat means somethin' to me, Mrs. Goldberg. Hit allows me to stay close to my boy and look after him. I don' knows what I'll do if'n I lose dis."

Mrs. Goldberg hugged me. "I'm really sorry. Is there anything I can do to get you to stay?"

I started to say, "Jus' say de word." But after I said "Jus'" the levy broke and a flood of tears washed down my face.

"Oy! I'm so sorry," Mrs. Goldberg said. "Let me get you a glass of water."

Jakie escorted me to a dinette chair.

Mrs. Goldberg gave me the water and a piece of facial tissue she had tucked under the breast cup of a revealing camisole. Even though I was upset, I felt ashamed for the child. It wasn't fit for a mother to walk through house like that and especially not okay if the child was a boy sleeping with her. Wearing that slinky thing made it all the more damaging. *Dat chile goin' to have him some troubles wit women, and mens too, shore as I am standin' here.*

"Where were you going to go?" Mrs. Goldberg said tenderly.

"Over to my brother Babe and Sis' Pearl's till I cain find work."

"You just want to be here for your boy, I know. You said he's in the hospital?"

I looked down and slowly shook my head. The problem felt too immense to describe to strangers. But Mrs. Goldberg and Mr. Jakie were waiting on an answer. "Yes, 'um, he is. He was shot on de island of Iwo Jimmy," I said, feeling ashamed I had pronounced the name incorrectly. I wiped the remaining tears from my face. "But I cain't say de hospital will hep him." I looked at the child; he was following me with his soft, compassionate eyes.

Mrs. Goldberg brushed her red hair back with the tips of her polished red fingernails. "Why do you say it that way?"

"Remember, like I told you, Mrs. Lucile, my boy need penicillin. Dey has de penicillin but dey don't has de colored needles to go wit it."

"Colored needles?" Mrs. Goldberg and Mr. Jakie sang in unison.

"You just said before that the hospital doesn't have needles. Nothing about 'colored needles.' What the hell *are* colored needles, for Christ's sakes?'" Mrs. Goldberg said not remembering what I had said.

"See, dey say dey using all de needles dey cain get for de white boys who dey say been out celebratin' with de girls overseas. Dey cain't be blamed, really."

"For Christ's sakes! They can't sterilize the needles they use on white soldiers and use them on colored soldiers?"

"No, dey say they cain't. It just like yur white water fountains and yur colored water fountains. Whites cain't drink de colored water and de colored cain't drink de white water, but hit all de same water when it come up out de bubbler."

I could see that Mrs. Goldberg was ready to cry. "Look, you're not going anywhere. You're staying right here with us. I'll work on Doctor Buzzbee for needles. He's a soft touch." She gave me another hug.

"What are they doing for him now?" Jakie said.

"Oh, dey spreadin' Russian Penicillin on de wound till de needles come in."

"Another FUBAR!" Jakie said. "Russian Pencillin. That's the government for you, another FUBAR!"

"What's Russian Penicillin?" Mrs. Goldberg asked.

"Nothin' but garlic," I said. "Dey say it help dry de wound and keep down de bacterialitis."

"You go put your uniform on, Flossie,"

"It's Phosie, ma'am."

"Phosie, you go put your uniform on. You're not going anywhere. I will get those needles from the doctor whether I marry the bum or not. This is just not right, goddamn it!"

"You will?" I said.

"You don't sound convinced," Mrs. Goldberg said.

"Like I told you," Mr. Jakie said, "when my sister sets her mind on something, nothin' gets in her way. She'll get them! I'll lay you hundred-to-one odds!"

"I don' want no odds, I jus want de needles," I said.

I stood up. Mrs. Goldberg hugged me again. "Don't you worry, we'll figure this out!" The stale odor of cigarettes was in her hair and on her nightgown, but that did not matter. I had seen a very beautiful side of her personality. She wanted love and wanted to give love, too. My opinion of her was changing. It takes time to truly know and understand someone. We all have our faults and our virtues.

"Shit!" Mrs. Goldberg said. "He thinks I said yes to marrying him! What the hell am I going to do about that?"

"Marry him!" Jakie said. "You're not getting any younger!"

"Marry de man or don't marry de man, but just get me de needles. If my baby don' make it through I don' wants to either."

"She'll tie the knot, Phosie, you can bet your life on it!" Jakie said. "And if she does, you cash the marker for needles your holding at the peri-mutuel window. My sister never misses her mark."

# Chapter 12

## *Lunch at the Drive in and a Bad Turn*

M rs. Goldberg worked at The Hi Hat Lounge and Supper Club on 7th and Alvarado, Tuesdays through Thursdays from six to two in the morning. She ran out the front door at five-thirty like a convict making a break from jail. She looked glamorous in a clinging cocktail gown she called her "Suzie Wong," outfit. It was tight as a snake's skin and slit up along the outside of her right leg to the hip to expose her thigh. "The higher the slit the more the tip!" she said with a sly smile. "Don't tell anybody, I'm getting paid to go to a party every night! I'd go even if I wasn't getting paid. All the kids I graduated Roosevelt High with show up. They sit around the piano bar, and get loaded. The stiffer they get the better the liars they become, the richer they are, and the more fabulous their lives become, and the more promises they'll make," she explained with a laugh and a snort. "I'm not kidding around here. I mean, get a couple of drinks into some loser on the make and he'll give you the keys to his house with his wife, his kids, and the dog in it for Christ's sake. Somebody's got to listen to their lousy sob stories. So long as the tips are good it might as well be yours truly!"

With Mrs. Goldberg out of the house and the child asleep the first three nights of my employment passed so it seemed the clock was ticking in reverse. By Thursday night I was so worked up, after I fed, bathed, and put the boy to sleep, I washed my things and was about to press my cotton dress for my Sunday visit to Will when the telephone rang. The bell on those old telephones was loud like the bell in a fire station. I started and dropped the iron. It crashed on the floor near my foot and would surely have broke it if it had. "Let me get this before it raises the devil," I said to myself as I walked down the hall. I lifted the heavy black receiver and said, "Mrs. Goldberg's residence, how may I hep you?"

"Phosie Mae?"

"Babe, you sound troubled. What de matter?"

"*G-R-R-R-R-R-R-R-R-R-RUFF!*"

I looked down behind me. The child was sitting on his haunches right behind me, studying me with his sweet little eyes. I had to pretend to be angry. I put my hand over the speaker and said, "Sugar, you supposed to be in dat cage! Now you git off dis cold floor and go back where you belongs 'fore yur mama catches you and talk like she will boil me live."

"*G-R-R-R-R-R-R-R-R-R-RUFF!*"

"What was that?" Babe asked.

"I was talkin' to de chile. Why is you callin' dis late?"

"It's Pearl."

"Has she taken ill? Did she pass?" I said.

"Well, her blood pressure spiked up and the doctor felt it would be best to keep her in the hospital through the weekend, you know, to monitor her progress."

"Well," I said feeling distressed over the news and what it meant for my getting to the hospital to see Will, and guilty for thinking about myself first. "Thank de Lord she in de hospital. He'll look after her, fine a woman as she is. And Pearl, she strong as a bull. She will be fine. You wait n' see."

"Long as they get her blood pressure down. But she likes her food, you know, she likes her food."

*Like a horse like alfalfa.*

"*G-R-R-R-R-R-R-R-R-R-RUFF!*"

"Shush up, chile!" I said.

"I'm sorry, I know how much it means to you, but I don't think I'll be able to carry you over to see Will on Sunday, Phosie Mae. Pearl wants me by her side. Maybe next Sunday."

*"G-R-R-R-R-R-R-R-R-R-RUFF!"*

"Don' worry 'bout me none, Babe. De good Lord saw fit to let me find my way dis far, I'll find de rest of de way on my own. You take care of Sis' Pearl and let her know I's praying for her."

It was freezing the next morning. I was putting up the coffee with all the gas burners on the stove on high flame to heat up the kitchen and thinking about how I was going to get over to the hospital, nothing on the face of the Earth was going to stop me from visiting my son. My intention was to ask Jakie for Red Car directions, the Red Car ran all over the city.

"YIP-YIP-YIP! YIP-YIP-YIP! YIP-YIP-YIP!"

"Shush up, chile! I's tryin' to think."

Jakie walked in wearing his robe and T-shirt. His eyes were bloodshot, his hair was mussed, his face was covered in stubble—he looked like he had one foot in the grave and the other about to slip in. I felt a sudden reluctance to ask anything of him. But it would either be him or Mrs. Goldberg, and I did not want to poke a stick in her bee-hive. "You up bright and early, Mr. Jakie! You mus' has some plowin' to do?"

"Plowin'?"

"It just an ol' dirt farmer's way of talkin'."

"Nah, I got one pickup in San Berdu, one in Anaheim, and another over in Venice near the beach," he said as he tapped an unopened package of his Lucky Strikes on the kitchen counter, then carefully peeled off the red cellophane tag and unfolded the foil wrapper. The fresh tobacco's aroma was delightful. I wished it would smell as good when it was being smoked. Jakie removed a fresh cigarette from the package, and slipped it up over his ear.

"YIP-YIP-YIP! YIP-YIP-YIP! YIP-YIP-YIP!"

"You heard me, chile! Shush before your mama's up and in my kitchen carrying on. Don't any of us need dat."

Jakie coughed.

"Sound like you be in dat truck all de day long, Mr. Jakie. Maybe I oughta fix you up somethin' case you gets hungry 'long de way."

"Nah. I'm picking up from restaurants. I usually give one of the fry cooks two bits and get a ham and egg sandwich."

"All right den, coffee?"

"Yeah, thanks, don't mind if I do."

As I set a cup, saucer, and a spoon and a napkin on the table in front of him and poured the coffee, I braced myself and said, "Mr. Jakie, I am wonderin' if you would kindly give me de directions for taking de Red Car or de bus or both over to de hospital dis Sunday."

"I thought your brother was taking you," Jakie said as he stirred the black coffee with the spoon.

"Well, he would 'cept my sister-in-law she in de hospital and he wants to stay with her."

"It's going to eat up your whole Sunday to get over to that side of town. A lot of the buses don't run and the Red Car schedule is catch-if-catch-can," he said, continuing to stir his coffee without letting the spoon touch the sides of his cup. "And even if you could catch the Red Car it wouldn't be safe. Mexican gangs control big parts of the Heights, now. They fight each other with motorcycle chains and busted beer bottles with jagged edges. Nah, don't let them get their hands on you, the animals, a colored girl like you don't stand a chance alone."

"Den how much do it cost to take de taxi?"

"A taxi? To the Westside? Christ, that will cost you two, three, maybe five dollars with gas still on ration!"

"Well, den I reckon I'll walk if'n you'll tell me de way. I ain' aimin' to miss seeing my boy," I said as I sliced up a knockwurst and put it in the frying pan.

"Listen, I promised my sister I would take care of Billy on Sunday. So if you don't mind riding out with him in my truck, I'll take you over."

"Oh, I don't want to put you out none, Mr. Jakie," I said then instantly wondered whether or not I was losing my mind by playing coy. *Don't be a fool, take de man's offer!* "But, if you're going out dat way it sure 'nough would be awful kind, thank you!"

"Yeah, sure. We'll ride out that way. What time are visiting hours?"

"Noon to five."

"That's it! Noon to five?"

"Those are the colored visiting hours," I said as a speck of hot fat popped and landed on my hand. I jerked my hand back, the fork I was holding flew out of my hand and bounced on the floor.

"I'll get it!" Jakie said, "Careful, that grease is hot!" He handed me the fork, lit a cigarette, inhaled deeply, exhaled slowly through his nose, and said, "There's only one thing."

"What is dat?" I said, ready to agree to anything.

"See, my sister would blow her top if she knew about what we do when I take the kid out for the day," Jakie said as he thoughtfully tapped the tip of his cigarette on the edge of an and watched the ashes tumble in, "and you'd have to sign on. I mean, it's not like we rob a bank or nothin'."

"What is it den?" I said.

"I take the kid over to Dee Dee's Restaurant for a hamburger, fries, and a malt. That's against what the shrink said, you know, about treating the kid like a dog."

"YIP-YIP-YIP! YIP-YIP-YIP! YIP-YIP-YIP!"

"It only takes twenty, thirty minutes. We'll stop on the way to the hospital."

"That will be fine. I will sit in de truck and see de sights while you inside eatin' wit de chile,'" I said as I picked the pieces of hot dog out of the frying pan and pinched them off the fork and into Billy's bowl.

"Dee Dee's is a drive-in restaurant, see. They won't say anything. You can have a hamburger with us."

""Long as I gets to the hospital. What time will we leave?"

"Ten fifteen, ten thirty."

"Okay then." *But don't get any funny ideas because we are eating a meal together.*

They called Mrs. Goldberg in to work on Friday night. Least that's what she told me. It might have been that she called in to work because she did not have a date for the evening. She did not want anything to do with being a mother. From the moment she awoke in the morning she was always getting ready to be someplace else. Motherhood surely did not suit her. But unless she married a man like Dr. Buzzbee, it did not seem her chance at change was all that good. Thank the Lord Mr. Goldberg stayed out of the picture. Dr. Buzzbee came calling for her on Saturday night. The rest of the week played out without too much fanfare.

Sunday morning, Jakie loaded me and the child into the cab of his truck. I rode with my head turned away from the street in order not to draw attention to us. Within minutes of leaving, Jakie asked me where my husband was. I had forgotten whether I had told him and Mrs. Goldberg about Isaac's passing, but in that moment I felt like fibbin' and telling Jakie my husband was alive and kickin' back down in Texas. There was no sense in making up a story though, so I just told Jakie the truth. My husband was dead and I was not interested in a relationship with Jakie or any other man at that time. I did, however, manage to let slip a question that had been in my thoughts. "You're a nice-lookin' man, Mr. Jakie, why hasn't you found some nice white lady to settle down wit?"

"Ah, nuts!" he said. "I had a girl before I left for the Pacific. We were supposed to tie the knot when I got back, but she cut out with some stiff in a three-piece suit who sold one hundred dollar life insurance policies that cost three hundred after all the payments to the Mexicans. Now? I don't know of anybody that would have me." He finished his answer by twirling his finger around the outside of his ear to indicate that something was wrong upstairs.

"Well, dat ain' necessarily so. You're a good looking man. Quiet and handy as you is, you'd make some lucky lady a fine husband."

"Nuts!"

Dee Dee's Drive-In Restaurant was shaped like the hub of a wheel. The cars parked around the hub stuck out like spokes. Nice trim girls dressed up in military-like uniforms, with lips painted bright red were wearing pink hats designed like the Marines' overseas caps. The glided between cars and the kitchen on roller skates delivering food on stainless steel trays that either latched onto the steering wheel or hung from the inside of the door. Jakie seemed to know the girl who helped us. She was nice when she did said the manager had requested that Jakie park the truck in a spot in back of the restaurant, without letting on whether that was because of me, Jakie's rude-smelling truck, or both. No matter. The child sat on his uncle's lap and ate his lunch like a regular little boy. Feeling giddy that I was about to see my own boy who as a child would have loved eating at a drive-in, I watched the boy and said, "Well, I declare, dis is sure enough the first pup I knows of dat eat French fries and drinks a malted milk out a straw." Jakie looked sideways at me. I said, "Don't you worry none, I won't whisper a word." The child ignored the both of us and busily consumed everything on his little tray.

When we arrived at the Barry Ward Jakie ran around to my side of the truck to help me out. As I walked into the main entrance, he carried Billy across a small street to a grass area with benches under a tree.

Will looked terrible. His fever was up, and his hiccups were deep and loud as belches. His lips were chapped. And he was agitated. It seemed he could not lie still.

Rather than the sweet Galveston nurse on duty during my first visit, there was a colored nurse with a physique and an ego big as Sis' Pearl's. I waved her down. She walked toward me with a snippety look on her face and her nose stuck high up into the air in a way that said, "I am too good for this colored ward. I should be on the white ward."

"He my son," I said with a tone of urgency to capture her sympathy. "He was doin' a whole lot better last week. The other nurse say he was comin' along, but he drawn and pale now. What de matter?"

"I'll check his chart," the nurse said without a hint of emotion as she lifted a clipboard with Will's medical record from a hook on the bed's footboard. "We're waiting on needles, colored needles. He needs penicillin." I could feel she was condescending to me.

"He worse dan he was last week! When will de penicillin come?" I asked, trying to keep my temper down as best I could. I felt intimidated by her clean white uniform and the bright red crosses on the lapels of her nurse's jacket. I wished Babe and Sis' Pearl were with me.

"The hospital has the medicine," she said without blinking.

"Well, how long will it be till dey gets de needles, den?" I said. I could feel my heart racing. Panic was setting in. My voice became shrill. "My son goin' to die! Cain't you see dat?"

"We put in the requisition. We're doing our best for all our patients, lady," the nurse said as she began to turn and walk away, "there is no need for anger."

I grabbed her wrist. The nurse tried to pull way. I would not let go. "No, you ain' doing your 'best!' My boy fought for you. He was shot. And now, and now, you tellin' me dey has de medicine and de needles he need across de sidewalk in de white boys' ward but dey don' have dem for de colored boys, for my boy?"

"That's the case, I'm afraid. Needle use is for one race and one race only. No mixing. That's hospital policy," she said and tried again to free her wrist, but I kept my grip.

"Would dat be yur policy, if'n yur chile was lying in dis bed?"

"Madam, I don't have children. I am only in this ward because a nurse called in sick. I work in the white wards. All I can do is tell you what I read on the chart."

"You means to say you wouldn't walk across de way and pick up a handful of needles and syringes to save yur baby, yur own flesh and blood?"

The woman wrenched her wrist out of my grip and stepped back away from me. "If we make an exception in hospital policy for your son, then what will we do with all the other parents and loved ones whose soldiers and sailors need medicine but have to wait their turn?"

"I don't care 'bout any of dem. This is my boy. He is all I have in dis world. Maybe all de others would die even if dey did get de medicine! Maybe dey would. Maybe some knows doctors and nurses in dis place and dey get preferential rather than colored treatment and dey die too. Maybe we would have lost the war and there wouldn't be anybody to save if it wasn't for my son! No! My son is the exception! He is my exception!"

"As I said, we're doing the best we can. That's all I can say," the nurse said as she turned and walked away.

"Well," I said, "dat is not good 'nough. May de devil see you in hell for yur haughty ways." *Dat's it. Go on a make an enemy while you at it!*

"Don't you curse me! I'm a registered nurse!"

"A registered nurse! You're nothin' but a registered house *nigro*!" I was thinking *nigger* but I had never used that term and was not going to lower myself then. "Look in de mirror! You're just as black, if not blacker, dan any one of dese boys lying in any one of dese beds. Registered nurse! You thinks you really somethin' cause de white folk let you change dey linens and empty dey pans." I pointed around the room then at Will. "Yur blood run red as de blood dat flowed from dey veins onto the battlefields dey fought on. Registered nurse nothin'! You a registered nothin'."

She started to walk away again.

"Don't you walk 'way from me!" I shouted. "Let me tell you one more thing. I am going to find de needles one way or t'other! Even if I has to steal dem. Put me in jail, I don' care. My boy goin' to live!"

"Mama?"

I spun around. Will was looking at me.

"Who are you yellin' at, Mama?" He was talking so softly I could hardly hear him.

"Oh, it nothing, sugar. How are you?"

"I'm much better, Mama. Does Daddy know I'm in the hospital? Is he coming?"

"He shore 'nough do, sugar. He's comin' soon as he cain, baby. Now you rest up, hear?" I took his hand in mine and held it tenderly.

"Did Ella answer the letter I wrote her?"

I told him to turn his head sideways and held a cup up to his mouth so that he could take a sip of water. "No, baby, we didn't see no letter yet, but I will check back in Galveston to see if'n hit arrived. When did you write hit?"

"I mailed it from the ship's post office on the Pickens just before we left Pearl."

"Well, maybe dere is somethin' at home, honeychile."

"I asked her to wait and marry me after the war ended."

"You did!" I said as I wiped his forehead with a cool, damp wash-cloth. He closed his eyes and smiled. "Den you best get back on yur feet 'fore she set her eye on someone else."

Will opened his eyes and said, "I'm trying, Mama, I really am. Will you tell her that?"

"I shorely will," I said, knowing it would be difficult. "I shorely will, baby. Matter of factually, when you feelin' better you cain write to her again. "

"And will you tell Daddy I'll be coming home soon?"

"Yes, darlin', yes I certainly will."

I found Jakie and the child across the street playing on a lawn. Jakie was trying to get the boy to fetch a ball. Jakie threw the ball, but the boy stood his ground, making it so that Jakie had to fetch the ball himself. Then the boy started laughing. When he laughed, Jakie made like he was a monster running after him screaming "Me likey eat little dogs for me supper!" The boy rolled up into a little ball on the lawn like a little roly-poly bug and Jakie tickled him till he shrieked with contagious laughter.

I smiled. It was good to see the sunshine in that child's eyes. I prayed I would once again see it in Will's.

# Chapter 13

## *Black-Eyed Peas*

On Tuesday afternoon I set the child into a shiny new Radio Flyer wagon his daddy bought him and carried him up to Katz's Kosher Mart on Brooklyn Avenue, to pick up groceries. Mrs. Goldberg had a charge account there. It was past due according to Mr. Katz. But, it seemed he was in love with Mrs. Goldberg too. He nervously applied the money I carried to her balance and continued to extend credit. "Be sure to let Lucky know I miss her!" Mr. Katz said as I pulled the wagon filled with the child and groceries out of the store.

The child tickled most of the people we passed by barking at them. What they thought they saw was a cute, pudgy, little boy pretending to be a dog. That was until a plump, neatly dressed, gray-haired white lady with a kindhearted smile and misted eyes stepped up next to the wagon as we were waiting to walk back across Brooklyn Avenue.

*"Oy, a sheyner punim. A gesundt af dein kup!"* she said as her eyes grew brighter and brighter. I felt an instant kinship with her. I don't care what color a person's skin is, I don't care what their religion is, I don't care where they came from or where they are goin' to, whether they're tall and thin, short and fat, ugly or beautiful, or what language they speak, there are some people that are good and some that are bad no matter what, and this woman had so much goodness in her soul it was lighting up her eyes. She looked at me and said, *"Velkh iz zayn nomen?"*

I said, "Me no speak you," like someone who believes they can get through to someone who speaks a different language by chopping up their own language.

She reached out to pinch the child's cheek, but he growled at her. She laughed, thinking it was a big show, and pulled her hand away to play along. I shook my finger at her and said while trying not to sound too confrontational, "You no touch!"

"*Vos?*"

I pointed my finger at her and said, "You not to touch." Then I pointed to the boy and added, "Him!" But she paid me no mind and did it anyway. I could see what was coming. The only way to stop it was to shove the woman away or knock her down, one. But then the police would like to lock me up. The only thing left to do was to hold my breath.

"*Oy a tatalah! Velkh iz zayn nomen?*"

"G-R-R-R-R-R-R-R-R-RUFF!"

"*Meiskeit! Gottenyu!*"

Next thing I knew I was bent over trying to pry the child's lower jaw down and free the sweet lady's thumb. I remembered what Jakie and his Chicklets. I reached into my coat pocket and lied. "Chile, take dis piece of yur Uncle Jakie's Chiclets and let go dis poor lady's thumb." His jaws remained clamped down on the lady's thumb, but he rolled his eyes over my way. "Dat's right! He done gave me a fresh box just dis mornin'! Now, you let loose o' dis kind lady's thumb and I'll give you a piece."

The lady screamed, "*Err iz baysik mine grober fingern un du bist offering im a shtekn fun gum?*"

She must have understood "Chiclets." "It's the onliest thing I knows to do less we call the fire or the police!" I said. *Why do you let all this happen to me, Lord?*

"Well, praise the Lord and say hallelujah!" I said when the child let the woman's thumb loose and turned his mouth my way to receive the Chiclets. He looked at me like I was a traitor when he realized I didn't actually have any.

But by now the lady was shaking her finger at me. "*Meshuge folk dos gor shtot iz filled mit meshuge folk!*"

I found myself saying, "I knows. I knows!" even though I had no idea what she was trying to say.

After she walked away, the child stared blankly at me. I said, "I'll tell you somethin' right now, chile, I ain' going to set in no jail 'cause of you. I has a chile of my own, too. I swear in Jesus's name dat if I see any more trouble comin' I'll leave you and dis wagon on de sidewalk and walk away. I means it, too. I will walk away."

*"G-R-R-R-R-R-R-R-R-R-RUFF!"*

On Wednesday morning when Mr. Jakie arrived for his morning coffee, I said,

"Good mornin', Mr. Jakie. Do you wants me to fry you up some eggs and franks?"

"Eggs? Since when are there eggs?"

"Ever since the good Lord made chickens to lay 'um, I 'spect, Mr. Jakie. To tell the truth, Mrs. Goldberg gave me a little extra shopping money and eggs were cheap."

"Sure, I'll take eggs with my knockwurst. Tell me something, Phosie, if you could cook up just one meal, one more meal, what would that meal be?"

"I don' know if I'd care too much if'n it were my last, you know, Mr. Jakie. I wouldn' 'spect too have to much of de appetite."

"What am I saying? I mean what is your favorite meal? Just that. What do you love the most to cook?"

"Fried chicken, hot biscuits 'n gravy, sweet potato pie, and coleslaw. Dat was my husband, Isaac's, favorite meal, may de good Lord bless him and keep him."

"Sounds good to me, Phosie. I'll buy the chicken if you'll do the fryin'."

"Now you have my mouth to waterin', Mr. Jakie."

"You'll have to cook that meal up one of these days," Jakie said with the sheepish grin of someone who managed to get hold of something valuable and did not want to let it go for fear of losing it.

"Well, I don' know if dis little trouble-makin' dog will eat chicken and biscuits."

*"G-R-R-R-R-R-R-R-R-R-RUFF!"*

"He did a pretty good job on the hamburger, fries, and the chocolate malt back at Dee Dee's. Nah, you make something good, he'll eat it. Won't you, Billy?"

"*G-R-R-R-R-R-R-R-R-R-RUFF!*"

"I'll tell my sister we're puttin' it on the menu!"

"Well, I don' know jus' yet."

"Who knows? Her royal highness, Queen of all Boyle Heights, might even sit down and dine with the swine."

"Where will I gets fresh-kilt chickens? See, dat's de onliest kind I'll fry."

"You want fresh? I'll take you over to Peking Poultry in Chinatown. You pick a bird, they kill it, dress it, and flick if for you in ten minutes, and it will only cost about fifteen cents. Best chicken money can buy. And the wait is fun because there's a Mexican behind the counter who speaks fluent Chinese. It's a real kick, man."

"We had us a poultry abattoir down in South Galveston. Mexicans owned it too, but I don' recollect dey spoke any Chinese. My former employer, Mrs. Katherine Hutchinson, had me to buy all her chickens dere."

"What kind of chicken do you like to fry up?"

"De best I knows is de eight-week Cochin."

"Eight-week? Why eight and not nine, or ten, or twelve?"

"Lor' have mercy, Mr. Jakie, you has a lot of questions for a quiet man. See, hit's no good to let a bird get too big 'fore it's kilt. It might dress out weighing more, but de chances are good it'll chew like rubber. No, eight weeks is just right for fryers. Not a day more."

"Who's frying chicken? I love fried chicken!"

*Oh Lordy!*

"*G-R-R-R-R-R-R-R-R-R-RUFF!*"

"Mrs. Goldberg, what's got you up wit de early birds on dis fine December morning?"

"A producer friend got me in to audition for a new movie with Jimmy Stewart. It's called *It's a Wonderful Life*."

"YIP-YIP-YIP! YIP-YIP-YIP! YIP-YIP-YIP!"

"Well," I said, "ain' that somethin'!" Jakie laughed till he had to spit a mouthful of coffee back into his cup.

Mrs. Goldberg threw him a nasty look and said, "What's so funny?" as she poured herself a cup of coffee.

"YIP-YIP-YIP! YIP-YIP-YIP! YIP-YIP-YIP!"

Jakie held out the palm of his hand in defense and smirked.

"YIP-YIP-YIP! YIP-YIP-YIP! YIP-YIP-YIP!"

"What? What the hell were you laughing about you horses ass?"

"YIP-YIP-YIP! YIP-YIP-YIP! YIP-YIP-YIP!"

"*Shut* up, goddamn you!"

Mrs. Goldberg took a sip of coffee, but it scorched her tongue. "*Shit!* This is hot!"

"I'm sorry, Mrs. Lucile, I shoulda said somethin'."

Mrs. Lucile turned her attention back to Jakie. "What?"

"I had a funny thought, that's all."

"Go ahead?"

"I saw you on a stage, but it wasn't in a theater, see. It was the nine o'clock stage to San Francisco!" Jakie laughed as he took the next sip of coffee, and it too came spurting out his nostrils.

"YIP-YIP-YIP! YIP-YIP-YIP! YIP-YIP-YIP!"

*Here we go again! Cain't anybody say anything nice in dis crazy house? Dey like crabs in a basket. One get uppity and try to climb out, de others gonna pinch it right back in.*

Mrs. Goldberg screamed, "I hate all of you! You shit on anything I try then you tell me I can't do anything! I hate you! I *hate* you! I'm going to get dressed for my audition." She stomped out then stomped back in and eyed me with a razor-sharp stare. "And you, get Billy cleaned up and dressed early. My ex is coming to take me out. And make sure to put a goddamned blanket or a sheet over that stinkin' cage! All I need is for him to get hot and try to take the kid away. I'd lose the alimony and child support. She laughed cynically, "Even though he doesn't pay either one, the bastard!"

"Yes, ma'am! I'm right on it! " I said as she dashed out. *I might just as well hide all de knives, pots, and pans, de way dey carry on.*

"YIP-YIP-YIP! YIP-YIP-YIP! YIP-YIP-YIP!"

"Oh, I knows jus' what you thinkin', chile. You lookin' to make mischief. I cain see it in yur eyes."

"What do think about it? A fried chicken dinner? I'll take you down to Chinatown," Jakie said.

"Think? I'm barely gettin' paid enough to clean this house!" I said then turned to the sink to begin my buttermilk biscuits.

Mrs. Goldberg was back in before I could open my box of baking soda. "What did you say you were cooking for dinner?"

"Well, I was fixin' to fry up franks and bake biscuits, but Mr. Jakie, he wants my fried chicken, Mrs. Lucile."

"Really?" she said then wandered off with a scheme lighting her eyes like a searchlight.

"Oh boy! I'll lay a hundred-to-one odds I know what's comin' next," said Mr. Jakie.

"YIP-YIP-YIP! YIP-YIP-YIP! YIP-YIP-YIP!"

*I wouldn't take the bet even if I were the gamblin' kind.*

And I'd have been smart not to, for Mrs. Goldberg waltzed back in with a kitty cat smile and an arc of ashes hanging from the tip of the cigarette dangling from her mouth.

"Phosie, what if I gave you a fin. Would you cook up for one more person?"

"Yes, 'um, I 'spect five dollars will buy food for five."

"Fabulous! I'll call Leo and tell him we're going to eat at home! He'll think I turned into another woman, a regular housewife!" Mrs. Goldberg laughed. "A housewife! The son of a bitch! I'll show him."

"All right den, what time do you want me to serve de supper, Mrs. Lucile?"

"What time do regular families eat supper?"

"'Bout six, I reckon. Least ways dats dah way dey do with chilrun' down in de Galveston area, Mrs. Lucile. Ain' dat right, Mr. Jakie?"

I looked over at Jakie. He was sitting so still and silent that it was hard to tell if he was still breathing.

"YIP-YIP-YIP! YIP-YIP-YIP! YIP-YIP-YIP!"

"And you, you best behave or God will punish you! And, if'n he don' I surely will tan yur little hide!"

"YIP-YIP-YIP! YIP-YIP-YIP! YIP-YIP-YIP!"

Mrs. Goldberg's smile had vanished. "This is perfect! Make it for five at six!" she said and bolted from the kitchen as if a skunk had sprayed in it.

Jakie carried me and the child down to Peking Poultry a little after three that afternoon. The child rode on my lap this time out. There was no fight in him. He seemed comfortable. Little children are that way. They know who they're safe with and who they're not safe with, they know it in their bones. That's the most important part of raising a healthy, happy child. I don't care how much you have or don't have and what part of town you live in. If you treat a child so that it feels safe with you, it will come to you like a lost little puppy. If you don't, it will shy from you and dodge you like a fidgety little squirrel, and it will only pretend to love you.

As it was a pretty nice day for the middle of December, I opened the window and let some fresh air in. The child liked that and rested his chin on the bottom of the door's window opening and watched the people walking in and out of the County Hospital, a massive gray concrete structure with bars on the windows of the upper floors, which Jakie explained were the floors the criminals and the insane were kept locked-up on. *Maybe time up in dat place will help dat sister of yourn."* When the boy tired of looking out the window he leaned back against my chest using my breasts as pillows just like Will used to. I felt his body let go. He felt like someone in a twister who had been holding on for his live that finally felt safe enough to let go and breathe." I matched the tides of my breath to his and placed my palm on his little chest and felt it rise and fall with mine. Our hearts seemed to beat as one. I closed my eyes, let the cool wind blow in on my face, and imagined that Billy was my Will.

"So, how did your son go Marines? Marines recruit whites only, far as I knew. "

"Dey started lettin' colored boys in in forty-three, Mr. Jakie."

"That's really somethen! Yeah."

A low dark sedan riding about six inches off the ground stopped abruptly ahead. When it didn't move, Jakie sat on his horn. When it still didn't move and no one stepped out, Jakie rolled down his window and shouted, "What the hell's wrong with you?"

Two tattooed Mexicans wearing khakis hiked up above their waistlines, sparkling-clean white T-shirts, spaghetti-thin belts, and black leather cap-toe shoes exited the sedan, one from each side. They walked slowly toward us. They had had their heads shaved. The driver was wearing a thick black horseshoe mustache and was waving the end of a motorcycle chain like a watch fob as he walked toward the truck. He had what they called down in Galveston the *viscioso*, or evil eyes.

"Goddamned *pachukos*."

"YIP-YIP-YIP! YIP-YIP-YIP! YIP-YIP-YIP!"

"You shush, chile! Don't you mess wit dese types, dey evil," I said as I rolled up the window, placed my hand over Billy's eyes, and prepared to die.

"I got this, don't worry," Jakie said, reaching under the seat and withdrawing his .38 Special revolver. "They want another Sleepy Lagoon, I'll give it to 'em right here and right now."

"I don' know what dat is, Mr. Jakie, but I hopes we don' go dere."

He kept the pistol hidden below the window behind the door.

The Mexican waving the chain walked up to within a couple of feet of Jakie's door and said, "¿Pendejo, por qué hizo grazna su cuerno?"

Jakie smiled and said, "We ain't looking for trouble, Pepe. I honked because you decided to stop in the middle of the street."

"You disrespect me by honking, gringosso. You disrespect our barrio with the negrita."

"Yeah," Mr. Jakie said, "well see, the last time I checked this was Los Angeles, not Tijuana, pinto."

"Be careful, Mr. Jakie, dese boys looks bad."

"Nah, they just think they're badasses when they feel they have you surrounded."

The Mexican on my side of the truck took a step closer as the Mexican on Jakie's side let out the length of chain one link at a time and said, "¿Qué vas a estar sentado todo el día?"

The Mexican feinted with a shoulder to scare Jakie.

Jakie lifted his pistol up and pointed it right between the Mexican's eyes. "Which one of you frijoles wants to die first? You?"

Now the Mexican was scared. He stepped back.

"Which one, *puta?* Choose!" Jakie said.

The Mexican paused then said, "You better watch who you bring into our barrio. Next time you might be in for it." Then he nodded at his accomplice and said, "Vamos!" They returned to their car and pulled away slowly like two snails sharing a shell.

Jakie said ironically, "I thought I already fought the Japs for this 'territory!' Now I gotta fight the Mexicans? When they get guns, these streets will be like shooting galleries!"

"Lord have mercy, Mr. Jakie, dey jus' lookin' to fight."

"That's why I did not want you taking the bus through here. It ain't safe,"

Jakie said as he drove across the Los Angeles River on an ornate bridge with sculpturesque streetlamps from a more genteel era. The river's not majestic like the Rio Grande or the Mississippi, it's nothing you would want to fish in or have a lazy dream on; it's just a scrappy arroyo tamed by concrete ramparts that run from someplace to no place. Billy leaned forward, turned so that he could watch the other side of the street, then leaned back and settled in. My thoughts ran from one thing to the other: Willy, Christmas coming, fat Sis' Pearl and lil' Babe, and that nasty nurse at the hospital. I made up my mind I would show her who she was dealing with! I don't know where it came from, but as Jakie drove his greasy black truck into the center of Chinatown, I began humming the melody from "Wade in the Water," Isaac's favorite spiritual. *Jakie grinned, and the child started rocking as we passed Chinese out shopping along the sidewalks lined with dragons painted pink and green. There were so many Chinese they were like ants picking through fifty-pound sacks of rice and tables stacked high with lilac-colored eggplant, winter melons, scallions, and white mushrooms. I started to sing.*

*Wade in the water,*
*Wade in the water, children.*

*Wade in the water*
*God's gonna trouble the water*

*Who's all those children all dressed in red?*
*God's gonna trouble the water.*
*Must be the ones that Moses led.*
*God's gonna trouble the water.*
*What are those children all dressed in white?*
*God's gonna trouble the water.*
*Must be the ones of the Israelites.*
*God's gonna trouble the water.*

As I began the last verse the child started to clap. I wrapped my arm around his waist like a cinch belt and drew him near. His clammy, sweet little-boy smell filled my heart with joyful memories of having held Will on my lap when Will was Billy's age.

*Who are these children all dressed in blue?*
*God's gonna trouble the water.*
*Must be the ones that made it through.*
*God's gonna trouble the water.*

# Chapter 14

## *The Innocent and the Damned*

Soon as I finished rinsing and breading my chicken, putting the sweet potato pies in the oven, making up my coleslaw with an extra pinch of sugar for sweetness, and mixing up my biscuit mix, I took a few minutes to get off my feet and work on Will's quilt. I learned quilting from my maternal grandmother, Ida Mae Waters, who took up quilting to improve the lives of her kin when she was still a Mississippi slave. After emancipation, she and her husband moved to Uniontown, where my mama was born. My brother and I were born there, too. Grandmother Ida Mae passed down her quilting skills to Mama and Mama passed them down to me, including the spirit of hope and salvation carried in their design. I remember riding with my grandmother on my grand-daddy's un-sprung pony cart to deliver quilts to her customers. She wrapped the quilts in crocus sacks and tied twine around them with her earth-worn hands. Life was hard back then. But you would never tell it from one of my grandmama's quilts.   She only used patches of pastel blues, yellows, reds, pinks, and greens set on a white background for designs. They were all right out of the natural world: birds singing, flowers blooming, a rainbow, and a small branch of a stream with fish swimming down through it. Looking at one of her quilts made you feel you were standing outside on a warm spring day with the sun baking down on your shoulders. That's how I wanted Will's quilt to come out. I wanted it to warm his heart and lift his spirit.

Jakie was perched on the edge of his seat at the table when I walked back into the kitchen. Billy was laid out on the cold linoleum floor like a skinned animal. "Sugar, you goin' to catch yur death layin' on dat cold floor, hear?"

"*G-R-R-R-R-R-R-R-R-R-RUFF!*"

I took a cast iron skillet, placed it on the stove, and started pouring oil in it.

"Phosie! Phosie!"

"Yes, 'um, Mrs. Lucile."

"*G-R-R-R-R-R-R-R-R-R-RUFF!*"

"Make sure you use the Planters peanut oil for the frying, okay?"

"Yes, ma'am!" *Lord, how does dis woman know about peanut oil? Haven't seen her pass through dis kitchen except for coffee since I arrived. And how she know I was pourin' oil, she bein' on the other side of the house!*

"*G-R-R-R-R-R-R-R-R-R-RUFF!*"

"Oh, and when my ex gets here, whatever you do, don't let him anywhere near the kitchen!"

"Yes, 'um, I shorely will! I means I shorely won't."

Jakie removed the cigarette from up over his ear and studied it as he rolled it between his yellow-stained fingertips and thumb. "Our mother used to use Planters peanut oil."

"Is that so, Mr. Jakie."

"But I ain't seen so much food in this kitchen since before she died."

"Well, I'll bet she happy lookin' down seein' all dese fixins," I said offhandedly. I did not want him getting too cheeky just because I had been in his car twice.

"Lucy never cooks, never has the time."

"Well, I 'spect you'll fin' you a good woman dat cooks 'fore you know it, Mr. Jakie. When you least 'spect it. Dat's de way it is."

"*G-R-R-R-R-R-R-R-R-R-RUFF!*"

"Long as you don't let dis crazy lil' hound scare dem off!"

"*G-R-R-R-R-R-R-R-R-R-RUFF!*"

"Billy, you listen to me! When I puts my chicken in de oil, I don't want you near this stove, hear? It sure to splatter and dat splatter will burn you like de devil would."

*"G-R-R-R-R-R-R-R-R-R-R-RUFF!"*

"Well, start up wit me and I'll have your uncle to put you in dat cage! I don' have time for no foolin' 'round."

*"G-R-R-R-R-R-R-R-R-R-R-RUFF!"*

"And you knows your daddy's fixin' to come for supper! So you best be on your best behavior!"

"YIP-YIP-YIP! YIP-YIP-YIP! YIP-YIP-YIP!"

"And I has to cover yur cage too 'fore I forget."

*"G-R-R-R-R-R-R-R-R-R-R-RUFF!"*

"Lord have mercy, here I am having a conversation with a dog!"

*"G-R-R-R-R-R-R-R-R-R-R-RUFF!"*

"I'll take care of it. I got an extra blanket over in my place," Jakie said.

"Why, thank you kindly, Mr. Jakie." Jakie rose up and adjusted the belt on his robe. "You best take the child with dis oil on de fire!"

"Yeah," Jakie said then picked up Billy by his ankles, twirled him in the air, and laid him back over his shoulder like a sack full of turnips. Billy giggled all the way out the back door.

The blanket Jakie brought reeked so from that stale cigarette odor I couldn't keep it in my kitchen. I did not want to fuss about it so I said, "Thank you kindly, Mr. Jakie, but as you was fetchin' yur blanket Mrs. Lucile came in"—this was a white lie—"and told me 'bout an extra tablecloth in de linen closet. She say a blanket in de kitchen—not dat she know too much 'bout a kitchen—would stand out like a sore thumb. So," I said, pinching the blanket up between my fingertips, "if'n you don' mind, I'll take yur blanket and hang it out back so it can get some fresh air! Everythin' need fresh air time to time."

"I know, it reeks, doesn't it?"

"Like de devil his ownself was sleepin' in it."

Jakie laughed.

I had everything cooked up, the chicken on a platter, the biscuits in a nice basket wrapped in a pretty white napkin, my slaw in a bowl, and the dining room table set including a vase filled with Queen Anne's lace and roses I had picked up from Mr. Katz's market.

Jakie was walking out the back door of the kitchen as Mrs. Goldberg walked in.

*"G-R-R-R-R-R-R-R-R-R-RUFF!"*

"Jakie, where are you going?"

"Back over to my side."

"Why don't you eat with us? It will be nice," Mrs. Goldberg said.

"Nah, I'll only get in the way."

I could tell he wanted to avoid getting in the middle of one of her and the former Mr. Goldberg's bloodbaths.

Mrs. Goldberg looked at me. "I done bought chicken and every-thin' else thinkin' you was eatin' with us, Mr. Jakie. You might as well."

He stood there and thought about it until Billy crawled over and put his little arms around Mr. Jakie's ankle. "All right, let me go put a clean shirt on."

"YIP-YIP-YIP! YIP-YIP-YIP! YIP-YIP-YIP!"

*That's nice. Why should he be alone?*

"Phosie, will you dress Billy in his blue sailor's suit and the match-ing blue shoes? His daddy likes that outfit."

"Yes, 'um, soon as I take dese sweet potato pies out de oven."

Jakie came back wearing a white shirt and a black bow tie. His hair was freshly greased back and he had washed his face but his finger tips were still stained yellow by that nicotine. "Well, you look like a right fine gentleman," I said. "It nice to see you so dapper!" As soon as "dapper" left my lips I realized both that he would probably take it the wrong way and that I was showing him a feeling I did not intend, I thought.

"Where's Leo?"

"Why, it's gone past six, I 'spect he'll be 'round any minute now. Billy's waitin' by de front door."

"Where's my sister?"

"Fixin' herself a drink. I jus' heard de ice cubes tumbling.' I hope dey don't start up fussin' again."

"Oh, they'll fight. They never miss. My sister runs off at the mouth. My ex-brother-in-law runs cold then turns hot as a poker soon as the word money comes out of her mouth. Leo loves you one minute and you feel like he's going to kill you the next. I'll tell you what, spending time with him is like walking through a field of land mines. You'll see."

"Oh my Lord," I said, "dey have dem a beautiful little boy and a nice place to live and all dey know is to fight! *And they think I'm second class.*

"Long as Leo doesn't start hitting the bottle and my sister doesn't start up about her alimony and child support it won't be too bad. They'll be like two birds in a cage.

"Well, if'n you put the wrong two hens in a coop, they'll tear each other's eyes out!"

Mr. Goldberg arrived with a little shine on. He sat himself down at one end of the mahogany dining table with a tumbler half-filled with scotch, Billy on his lap, and a Camel cigarette dangling from the corner of his mouth. Mrs. Goldberg sat at the opposite end. As I poured water, Jakie shuffled back in from the kitchen with his shoulders slumped then took a chair at the middle of the table and sat silently like a referee at a prizefight waiting on the bell for the first round. Mr. Goldberg was talking with, or I should say trying to talk with, Billy, but Billy kept running to the kitchen door and barking. It seemed he wanted to show his daddy the cage.

I was carrying in some piping-hot biscuits when Mr. Goldberg said, "Lucy, when the hell did the baby start acting like a dog?"

"Oh, I don't know Leo, two weeks. He's always got some shtick to aggravate me with."

"Two weeks?"

The atmosphere in that little room suddenly felt charged like August air before a thunder storm. It was heavy and silent.

"You know kids, Leo. They pretend," Mrs. Goldberg said then laughed.

"There's that phony laugh again. He ain't talking, for Christ's sakes. Why?"

"The doctor said he'll grow out of it, didn't he, Phosie?"

I was setting the bowl of my coleslaw on the table. It did not make one bit of sense for me to know what any doctor said as short of a time I had been there, but I said, "Dat's right, I believe he did, Mrs. Lucile."

Jakie opened a steaming-hot biscuit, bounced it from hand to hand to cool it down, and poured honey into its heart. I liked watching folks enjoy my cooking. It gave me the feeling of being nourished.

"I thought you were just hired on? How do you know what any doctor said?"

The lie was getting too deep for me. I started going under.

Mrs. Goldberg said, "I told her, Leo. How the hell do you think she knows, for Christ's sake?"

Mr. Goldberg looked at Billy, brushed the brow of the child's hair with his fingers, and ominously said, "Say something, babe."

Billy looked up at his daddy and barked, "YIP-YIP-YIP! YIP-YIP-YIP! YIP-YIP-YIP!"

Mr. Goldberg winced in disgust and repeated his request with a tone that sounded like distant thunder. "Come on, for Christ's sakes. Say something, already."

"YIP-YIP-YIP! YIP-YIP-YIP! YIP-YIP-YIP!"

"I don't know, but something ain't right!" Mr. Goldberg said. "I can smell it, it smells like bullshit."

"Why don't you try some of my world-famous chicken, mister?" I said as I held the platter for him so that he could serve himself. "Cause once de boy eats he jus' might talk."

Mr. Goldberg picked up a crispy thigh, turned it around a few times then bit into it. A grand smile lit his face. He looked like someone had just told him that he was to be the richest man in the world. "This is some crazy chicken! It's Gee-orge!" He looked at me with a twinkle in his eye and said, "Man, I love that dark meat."

*Love it all you wants, but you won't get any of this dark meat!*

"I'm glad you likes hit, very glad, Mr. Goldberg."

*Now, you enjoy your meal and go on back to wherever you was drinking and take up where you done left off. Don' get in de way of me getting my baby's needles. I will kill you wit my bare heads!*

"Why aren't you eating?" Mrs. Goldberg said.

"Me? Oh, I was fixin' to make up a plate for myself in the kitchen, Mrs. Lucile, thank you."

"That's ridiculous! You don't have to eat alone like some animal. Get your plate and sit with us."

"*G-R-R-R-R-R-R-R-R-RUFF!*"

"Oh, thank you kindly, Mrs. Lucile, but I'll let y'all enjoy yur supper if you don' mind."

"Bullshit! We don't stand on ceremony around here, do we, Jakie?" Mr. Goldberg said, attempting to dominate the dinner and shape it to his liking. "Ain't that right, Jakie?"

"Yeah! Sure! Yeah!" Mr. Jackie said and pulled the chair next to him out so that I would have a place to sit.

*"G-R-R-R-R-R-R-R-R-RUFF!"*

There was no escaping. I was in a river and the current was too strong. It was carrying me along, and there was nothing I could do about it. The moment I sat down to eat Mr. Goldberg pushed his chair back and prepared to get up.

Mrs. Goldberg sprung to her feet like a jackrabbit and blocked the kitchen door. "Where are you going?"

"I'm getting a beer. You wanna beer, Jakie?"

"Okay, Leo, if you're having one."

"I was just going in for some…some…Jesus Christ, butter. We used up the brick on the biscuits," Mrs. Goldberg said. "I'll get the beer, too." I felt Mrs. Goldberg's fear on my skin. If Mr. Goldberg got anywhere near that icebox and discovered Billy's cage, her little charade would have ended along with the alimony and child support even though, according to her, he never paid in the first place. I chuckled. *And you'll be out on de street if'n he let you walk out here alive.* I jumped up and headed toward the kitchen. "I believes we needs more pepper, too. Let me help carry everythin' in, Mrs. Lucile. Dat's what you pays me for."

*"G-R-R-R-R-R-R-R-R-RUFF!"*

Mrs. Goldberg and I paraded back in with the beers, served them, and sat back down.

"Where's the butter?" Mr. Goldberg said, suspiciously holding Mrs. Goldberg in his gaze.

"Butter?" Mrs. Goldberg said anxiously.

"You said you were going into the kitchen to get butter, ya dummy."

"I decided to use honey once I got into the kitchen. It's less fattening. Is there something wrong with that?"

*"G-R-R-R-R-R-R-R-R-RUFF!"*

"What did you do, call one of your phony boyfriends?"

"I did not. And if I did it wouldn't be any of your lousy business, would it?"

*Here we go.*

"Ah, never mind, for Christ's sakes, I don't give five fucks."

I was keeping my head down and eating like a little child waiting for her daddy to come home and send her off to her room for having done something bad.

Mr. Goldberg's mood cooled, and he said, "You ought to have the girl here cook up like this more often, Lucy. The kid likes it." Billy hadn't stopped eating to look up and take a breath once he had chicken and biscuits with honey on his plate.

"YIP-YIP-YIP! YIP-YIP-YIP! YIP-YIP-YIP!"

"I'd love to, Leo. But how can I do that if you never pay my alimony and my child support?"

*Oh Lordie, she done let de fox out de cage now.*

I looked at Mr. Jakie. He had put his hands on the edge of the table as if to push himself away and run for cover. I placed my hands on the table's edge and prepared to push away, too.

Mr. Goldberg's face flashed to red like a Roman candle. He pivoted his head toward Mrs. Goldberg, the veins on his forehead had bulged like they would pop, and he said, "So this is why you invited me over, to squeeze a little more money out of me. I should have known better."

Mrs. Goldberg sipped her cocktail and said, "What the hell are you talking about? It was you who wanted to go out for dinner. I thought you'd like a home-cooked meal!"

Mr. Goldberg slashed right back this time with bits of fried chicken mixed with spit sputtering out of his mouth. "Don't bullshit me, you phony bitch!"

*Lord have mercy, dese people scrap like wild pigs. Dey likely to skin one another 'live.*

I looked at Billy. His eyes were welling up like twin sinks set to overflow. "Well, why don't I take de child and start my cleanup," I said, pushing myself away from the table.

"You keep your ass glued to that chair! I want you to see what a conniving, lying bitch you're working for!"

*Don't you talk to me like dat. I'll hit you upside yur head wit de iron skillet I fried this chicken in,* I thought as I sat still as stone and focused on a tintype hanging behind Jakie on the opposite wall. It featured a stiff, unsmiling groom with a mustache, who it was easy to see was Jakie's and Mrs. Goldberg's father—they had the same exact face. The groom was standing next to his seated bride, who was holding a bouquet of flowers. He was wearing a suit and bow tie and had a top hat resting in the crook of his arm. There was no doubt the bride was Jakie's and Mrs. Goldberg's mother. They had the same face, too. I wondered how she felt hanging up on that wall watching her daughter being tongue-lashed by this drunkard in her own home. *She mus' be rollin' in de grave.* I looked at Billy again. He had stiffened his body till it was straight as a ruler and was trying to slip off of his father's lap, but Mr. Goldberg had his arms wrapped around the child and wasn't going to turn him loose.

"You know what?" Mrs. Goldberg said.

"Go ahead, tell me what."

"You haven't changed one iota. You're the same old suspicious son of a bitch, Leo!" Mrs. Goldberg said. "You think everything I say or do is to squeeze something out of you. It's not. All I was trying to say is that it takes money to raise a kid right, and I don't mean the measly double sawbuck you send me when you feel like it. Shit!" Mrs. Goldberg said, finishing her drink. "You're sick, Leo, sick! You think someone's going to stick a knife in your back at any moment."

*I'm gettin' ready to do that myself.*

"I'm sick? I'm sick?" Mr. Goldberg said. "You know what? Maybe I am sick for getting involved with a broad that wants to be queen every day. That wants a fuckin' parade for herself every time she walks out the door, for Christ's sakes."

"No, I just want my back alimony and back child support, you phony bastard!"

"Maybe if you quit your job serving those lousy drunkards at that joint you work at and get a real job, a day job, you wouldn't be so broke!"

"I work nights because I want to be around for the kid during the days."

"Then get one of your johns to take care of you!"

Mrs. Goldberg lit a cigarette and inhaled deeply. As the smoke streamed out of her nose, she shouted, "Listen to me, you miserable bastard, you want to see the kid? Like the Chinese say, no tickee, no washee, baby, no tickee, no washee."

Mr. Goldberg smiled. His eyes filled with a wicked delight; he seemed to enjoy getting his wife's goat. "So, I guess this means we're not going to patch things up, does it?" He laughed. It was not a kind laughter but a vulgar and evil laughter, the laughter of someone who was amused by their skill at manipulating the people close to them until those folks felt either outraged or devastated or both.

Mrs. Goldberg stood up, picked up an empty coffee cup, threw it at Mr. Goldberg, and screamed, "Get out, you lousy son of a bitch! Go back to those lousy chippies you run around with, you lying bastard! Get out!" Luckily, she threw high and the cup missed both Mr. Goldberg and Billy. It hit the wall behind them, fell to the floor, and exploded just like the family I was sitting with. There was no amount of glue that would put that cup back together again. It was destroyed.

Billy started to cry.

"Let me take de child out de way, Mr. Goldberg. Maybe dat will help y'all settle down some!" I said as I slipped my chair back and stood up.

"Oh, so now I'm the chippy! What the hell were you doing when I was working my ass off trying to make a buck to take care of you, your royal highness?"

"Taking care of the kid!"

"Don't shit me! You were out having lunch and a drink with your phony high school friends."

"Who, Lizzy? Barney? Abie?"

"Yeah, that's right, and all the others. I knew what you were doing, whoring around. I have my spies."

"You're full of shit!" Mrs. Goldberg screamed. "They're my best friends from high school! Weren't they, Jakie?"

I had taken slow, steady steps toward Mr. Goldberg and was just about close enough to rescue the child. All Jakie could do was raise one eyebrow. He was too busy rolling his cigarette over the polished surface of the mahogany table. He stood up to the Mexicans, but for some reason he was no match for Mr. Goldberg.

"And besides, when the fuck did you ever take me out? Only once in the year that we were married, once! And that was when my sister came over for her birthday!"

"Your sister can go fuck herself for all I care, the phony cunt. You're both a couple of phony whores! The whole lot of your Harmatz family are nothing but phonies! I should have run the hell away the first day I set eyes on you. I knew you were trouble, the whole goddamned lot of you!"

"I'll fuckin' kill myself! You hear me? I'll go into the bathroom, fill up the tub, and slit my wrists with the razor blades you left. You know whose fault it will be? It will be yours, you dirty bastard. Yours because your hatred, your ugly, disgusting hatred, drove me to it!"

"Like I said before, go ahead. No one will give a shit. Go ahead!"

"I will kill myself! I will! I will! I will!"

Billy was now crying so hard his little chest was heaving. He was trying to gulp his air like a fish out of water. I could see Mr. Goldberg was fed up with him. I walked over without saying a word and carefully lifted the child out of Mr. Goldberg's arms then slowly walked through the kitchen to my room in the service porch, where I sat on my cot and held the child against my chest and rocked back and forth to soothe him. I felt like hitting both of the Goldbergs upside their skulls with the frying pan. "You cain't pay dem no mind, honeychile, they're jus' hurt and dey takin' it out on each other," I whispered as I stroked his little head. "Dey don't mean to hurt you or each other, dey jus' don' know how to get along, dey both hurt and angry. But dey want love like anybody else and I'm sure they loves you." Then I started humming "This Little Light of Mine."

Once I heard the front door slam I set a nice, clean blanket on the bottom of Billy's cage and put him down for the night. Early the next morning, I found the cage door swinging open and immediately went hunting for him.

"Billy, tsss, tssss, tsss! Where is you, chile? I don' want to wake your mama up. Tsss, tsss, tsss!" I looked over, under, and around everything in the place and was thinking that he must have somehow gotten out of the house when I noticed Mrs. Goldberg's door was cracked. I tiptoed over the rickety hardwood floor and silently pushed the door open.

The first soft rays of the morning's light were glowing along the edges around the curtains. In that soft light I saw Mrs. Goldberg on her bed laid out naked as the day she was born with Billy tucked under her arm with his head resting on her naked white breast. He looked up at me. I motioned for him to crawl out, and he did try, but his mother drew him back up against her.

Horrible as the sight was I wasn't gonna say nothin' 'cause my baby's life was on the line. I had to keep the job.

# Chapter 15

## *A Stitch in Time*

I woke up on the morning of Sunday, December 9, to find my little service porch cold as a root cellar. Clouds of my breath were rising up like torpid fish spiraling to the surface of a frozen lake. There was a thermometer and a mezuzah nailed to the door post. I opened the door and read the temperature. It was dark and thirty-six degrees at six fifteen, thirty-six...so much for sunshine and palms. I looked up into the sky and wondered whether it would snow. The sun had not yet breached the horizon but its light brightened the crisp clean sparkle of the stars. I shivered, closed the door, and wondered if Will was warm enough. Was a kind warmhearted nurse on duty to cover him with another blanket if he needed it? Was he awake and feeling lonely? Not wanting to soil the dress I was planning to wear to the hospital, my one and only dress, I put on one of the uniforms, my nylons, a pair of socks I found in a drawer of the nightstand, and the white shoes, then slipped into my overcoat and hat before I ventured into the kitchen to put up a pot of coffee and wash up if the pipes had not frozen. I could barely button my uniform or coat for my fingers being stiff. Billy's cage door was hanging open like a tooth waiting to be pulled. I knew where he was and tried to stop the image of him lying in bed wrapped in the arms of his naked mother from disturbing my thoughts. I failed. I shivered. *Lord, the way that woman treatin' that child, it don' have a chance to grow up without being touched in de head someways.* A waft of cold air leaked through the window over the sink. I shivered again. *I best get to work finishin' Will's quilt 'fore de worl' freeze over. Let me get this coffee put up first.* I switched on the Perc-O-Toaster turned on the four burners on the stovetop, then let the water from the sink faucet flow to hot so that I could wash and brush my teeth.

It was quiet that morning. Mrs. Goldberg had gone out with the doctor the night before and was slept late. Billy was "sleeping" late too because his mama did not like him getting out of bed until she did because he would make noise and wake her up. She had everything inside out and backward. Jakie didn't get home till just before sunrise. I had heard his truck cough and choke as he pulled it up the driveway.

I stood next to the Perc-O-Toaster rubbing my hands together over the glowing toaster coils and stared at the little glass ball on the stainless steel lid of the coffee pot, and wait for the water to bubble up and over the grounds. The first of the coffee's soft gurgle and smooth aroma seemed to cleanse my spirit and give me hope for this new day. I thought of my design for Will's quilt. I had decided to sew the image of our place on the Hutchinson property down in Galveston as its centerpiece. I had gold satin material for the house, mint-green pearl for the grass in the front yard, rose and peach and scraps of lime green for the flowers and vegetables that grew in our garden, and autumn-brown material for the split rail that ran along the road, sky-blue for the sky, light pink for the clouds, and patches of black and a white diamond for Will's dog's chest—Blackie would lay out on the porch in front of our place, come rain or come shine, and wait on Will to return from school.

Once the coffee was made I poured myself a cup and sat at the dinette with my materials and went to work. The only sounds were the creaks and moans of the house's beams, braces, and studs as they stretched under the warming sun, and the songs of the handful of birds that flew by and pecked through the incinerator in the backyard for bits of food that did not completely burn. My mind emptied of all its worry and stress; focusing on the stitches took all that away. I was so calm I forgot about time passing. When I heard the quick blast of a car's horn, then another, then another, and looked at the clock on the gas range, it read 9:53! The horn blasted again. *That must be Babe!*

I raced through the dining room to the living room on my tiptoes, pulled back the edge of the drapes, and peeked out. It was indeed Babe. Sis' Pearl was sitting in the passenger's seat staring at Mrs. Goldberg's front door, looking ornery as ever. *Look's like she made it! Lord have mercy!* I opened the door and waved my hand until Sis' Pearl saw me. Her eyes narrowed to angry little slits when she realized I was not ready. I ran down to the curb and told them I'd be out in three minutes, and I was because I wore what I had on.

On the way out to the hospital I told Babe and Sis' Pearl all about dinner at the drive-in with Jakie and Billy, Jakie's asking me out, my fried chicken supper and the Goldbergs' savage fight, Mrs. Goldberg's threat to kill herself, and how I found Billy sleeping in his mother's bed with his mother clutching him up against her white cloud-like breasts.

They were speechless, except for Sis' Pearl saying, "I'm saying this as a friend, but I don't know if I'd mess with any white man, Phoise. All that is is trouble. Isn't that right, Pleas?"

I did not give Babe a chance to answer. "Pearl, having a relationship with any man, let alone a white man, is right up dere with traveling to Mars. Dere ain' nothin' too it. It's Will in my thoughts and only Will." Pearl had me heated up so I let a little more steam off, "De Lord knows I been a good Christian woman all my life long! I never done uttered an angry word, never did no harm to no one. If a fly flew into my kitchen, I chased it out de door or window with my spatula. How can de Lord let all dis happen to me? Why is de Lord punishin' me? Ain' dere 'nough bad people dat needs punishin'?"

"What are you trying to say, Phosie?" Babe said.

"I ain' tryin' to say nothin'. I is saying dat my life was shattered like a mirror dat fell on de hardwood floor. I is sayin' dat I don't see de Lord anywhere to help me when I needs him de most."

"Well, he there, I know that," Sis' Pearl said stubbornly. "That I do know."

"Isaac, Will, and I was dirt poor, dirt poor, we hardly owned de dirt on de broken-down shoes we wore, de Hutchinsons owned it. But we was happy as three little clams, and healthy, too. Isaac was makin' him a good salary wildcattin', de Hutchinson family, bless deir hearts, treated

151

me like part of dere own . Will was goin' to graduate high school. De onliest one of our kin beside you, Babe."

"All of my kin finished. I finished," Sis' Pearl said.

"I'm talkin' 'bout my side of de fence. Isaac wasn't but forty-nine, he was strong, and handsome, and he had a smile bright as the sun. We laughed each and every day. It seemed we'd live long like ol' Abraham and Sarah. I kept on dreamin' 'bout how we would grow old and use de little bit of money we tucked away and sit out on our porch and watch de days roll by. Den, like a star suddenly drops out de sky and vanish, dey a knock at our door and my Isaac is gone jus' like dat star. Gone forever. Just like that. One minute our lives seemed solid as a rock, de next everything was crumblin' to dust."

"Well, nothing lasts forever, Sister Phosie. We have to be thankful for what we have and not feel stricken by what we've lost, that's what Reverend Franklin preaches, doesn't he, Babe."

"In time, Pearl, in time, it takes time." Sis' Pearl stuck the tip of her nose up indignantly. "That must have been terrible," Babe said.

"It shore 'nough was. De night Isaac died I stopped trusting everything and anything around me. If'n Isaac could vanish in a breath, den how did I know the earth under my feet wouldn't open and swaller Will and me up both? After losing Isaac I was barely able to let Will out de house to finish his schoolin' for de fear of losing him, too. I was a livin' ghost in a dyin' dream."

"Well, they say losing a spouse is about the biggest loss you can have," Pearl said with careful objectivity.

I ignored her. The only thing she had ever lost was the opportunity to eat another meal. I know I sound harsh, but she wore at me like a tight shoe does a blister.

"And den," I said, "twixt de time I was gettin' back on my feet, we was at war wit de Germans and the Japanese. Lord knows if'n dey wanted de shack we rented for shares, dey coulda had it for de askin'. Why couldn't dey live wit what de good Lord blessed dem wit? Why they decide to attack us? Why? Where was Jesus?"

"God made good and God made evil. Then he cast us out of the womb just like he did Adam out of the Garden. He cast us out and into this mortal life so that we could choose between the two and sometimes even die for our choice. There will always be evil. There's nothing to be done about it, no way to understand it. All we can do is avoid it when we can and smote it when it arises. Praise the Lord," Babe said.

"Praise the Lord," Sis' Pearl repeated.

"And den soon as de Marines soon start 'listing Negroes, my baby signs up! Germans and the Japanese? Dey were de white man's problem, not ours. We didn't have de right to vote and could barely walk on de sidewalk 'longside white folks when Will signed. Coloreds had to walk in de street wit de horses, cows, and pigs, couldn't even ride regular in a bus, sit in a diner or a movie, or use a public bathroom without it bein' set for 'Colored Only.' Forget votin' down in Texas. Texas was for de Democrats. Folks had to join de Democrat Club and de Democrats didn' wan' nothin' to do with us colored folks. I even asked Will, 'Chile, who are you fighting for?'"

"How did he answer?" Babe said.

"He said, 'Dis is our country too, Mama. We might have come here slaves, but we're free as de air we breathe now. Someday we'll be freer. We'll vote and all de rest, jus' you wait and see. But right now we have to protect what we have because if the Germans or the Japs win, things will sure 'nough get a whole lot worse.'"

"Well, I can see what he was saying," Babe said.

"Tell me how things cain' get 'a whole lot worse' if'n de government won't supply colored needles for Will's penicillin? We done won. Why don' dey use de German and de Jap needles?"

"I'm sure they'll be along soon, Phosie Mae," Babe said. "Nurse Thompson said they'd be here by Christmas."

"I'll say one thing," I said. "One way or de other, my baby will get de penicillin he need. Dat's de God's honest truth."

"Do you think your new mistress will come through?" Sis' Pearl asked then tucked a plug of tobacco into her cheek with an index finger. My stomach flip- flopped at the thought of watching her spit into that filthy canning jar of hers. "I think she'll come through," Sis' Pearl said, now in a stuffy tone of voice.

"Come through? How cain dat woman come through when she cain barely tie her own shoes witout trippin' soon as she walk. Come through! Every day she get out de bed is a miracle de way she carries on about killing her own self! And top a everythin' else, crazy as she and de rest are, dey looks down on us like we monkeys and mules! It just ain't right. It just ain' fair. De Lord wouldn't do us this way if he was payin' attention. If he loved us like the Bible say he do."

"You know," Babe said solemnly, "as I've matured I've become a believer in Providence. I don't mean the kind of Providence in which you pray and the Lord answers your prayer by giving you what you want. The Providence I'm talking about is for those who pray then make the choice to roll up their sleeves and work to make their lives better to realize their dreams. The thing is, we never know how exactly our prayers will be answered. We may want a certain something, but Providence might well yield something of the same value but in a different form than that which we had prayed for. But if we don't take care of ourselves, neither will Providence."

"What Babe is tryin' to say," Sis' Pearl said as she moved the plug of tobacco to her other cheek, "is we don't always get what we want, but if we tries, the good Lord makes sure we get what we need."

"That's exactly right," Babe said. "Take when I graduated Tuskegee and decided it was time to find a bride. I prayed for the Lord to help me. But I didn't stop there. I took it upon myself to find the woman of my dreams. I spread the word amongst family and friends. It turned out that one of my college professors, a Dr. Carver in the Mechanical Engineering Department, knew of a family with a daughter. The professor arranged for my invitation to their home for dinner to meet the girl. I knew I was in the right place soon as I walked up to the house."

"Why?" I said.

"What do you think their home address was?"

"I have no idea."

Babe pulled up to a stop sign, stopped, looked at me, grinned, and said, "It was Nineteen Pleasant Way."

"Well, I 'spect dat a nice 'nough address," I said.

"Don't you get it, Phosie? I was born on the nineteenth, and the letters of the street name, Pleasant, contained the letters of my name, 'P-l-e-a-s!' How can you explain that coincidence without mention of a helping hand, the hand of God?"

Sis' Pearl stopped chewing on her cud of tobacco and said, "That's right, Sister Phosie, it was Providence brought Pleas to me." Then she started up chewing again.

I looked at Pearl's reflection in the corner of the rearview mirror. She had turned her head and was looking out the window at a row of nice Victorian houses. She stopped chewing her plug, mashed her teeth to squeeze the juice out of the tobacco, and spit the contents of her mouth into her little jar. It was vile. Then, as if she were a goddess of nature whose every act or utterance was acceptable, Pearl broke wind. It started out rumbling like distant thunder then grew louder and louder like kettle corn popping and popping and popping. I thought it would never end. The car seat vibrated beneath me. The car filled up with an odor like sour milk mixed with rotten fruit. I held my breath for as long as I could. I am sure Babe was aware of his wife's emission; he had to be. But he showed no sign of disparagement. And, he would not roll down the windows.

"See, what I am saying about Providence, Phosie Mae, is we can't know what the future will bring but we can believe that if we try our best the good Lord will help see each of us through to getting what we need no matter what. That's Providence."

I glanced back at Pearl and said, "Babe, I done had 'bout all de Providence I can take for one lifetime."

"You're a fine Christian woman, Phosie Mae, the Lord will light a path for you, you'll see."

"Well, twixt now and de time he does I hopes he at least sends down a candle and a match. My path is awful dark right now."

"Trust in the Lord, Phoise Mae, trust in the Lord," Sis' Pearl said with words strung together by slurps. I felt like extending my right leg and giving her a mule kick on her shin with the heel of my shoe. The only hardship that woman knew was squeezing in and out of her husband's new car.

By the time we arrived at the hospital the sun had warmed the day to a cool but pleasant sixty-eight degrees. Rich white folk were driving their Cadillac convertibles down Wilshire toward the beach with their tops down and their scarves and Hollywood dreams riding the wind.

That's one thing about Los Angeles—no matter how cold it might get at night, it warms up nice most days. By the time we arrived at the hospital it was actually so warm I left my topcoat and hat in the car. At first, it did occur to me that I looked like a nurse.

I was hoping to get an update on Will's condition from our little Galveston nurse, but there was no nurse on duty on the second floor in Will's ward. Within just a few steps I realized that the second bed from the end on the left, Will's bed, was empty. I ran to the bed. Will's friend was gone as well. All that remained was the bed with its bare mattress and pillow and a dark green wool blanket folded over the foot of the bed.

"Where's my baby? Where's my baby?" I ran up and back along the front of each bed and looked for someone who could have given me an answer, but all the boys were too weak to answer or unconscious. Babe and Sis' Pearl followed me down the creaky stairs and over to the nurse's station on the first-floor ward, where a nurse was filling out charts. When I got up to her I breathlessly said, "Where is William Eaton?"

She looked at me calmly and said, "Which ward are your shifts in?"

"What do you means?"

"You're a nurse, aren't you?"

I realized what she was saying and said, "Dat's right, dat's right. But right now I'm lookin' for William Eaton. Has he been moved?"

"Spell the name? Serial number?"

"William Eaton, E-A-T-O-N. I don' recollect his number."

"All right then."

*He's died, I knows it. He's died and gone.*

The nurse nodded to the left and over my shoulder. "He's over there in the fourth bed from the back on the right."

"Thank de Lord!" I shouted. "Thank you, Jesus!"

Will's skin color had regained a healthy hue, he was not hiccupping, and his forehead felt nice and cool. I squeezed Will's hand and wept. "Thank you, Jesus! Thank you for lookin' after my baby, answerin' my prayers! I'll do anything you wants for de rest of my natural life. I don't care 'bout me, just look after my baby."

"Mama?"

"Hi, baby!" I said and kissed his forehead.

"Why are you crying, Mama?"

"Oh, it's joy, sugar. I jus' happy to see you down on dis floor feelin' better."

"I had some soup last night." His voice was still weak. He tried to raise his head up from the pillow but he didn't have the strength.

"Well, dat good, sugar. What kind?"

"Chicken soup. They said it's Jewish penicillin."

"Least they has some penicillin," Sis' Pearl said.

Babe said, "When did they transfer you down here?"

"On Thursday, Uncle Pleas. That's when my temperature dropped and my hiccups were almost gone." Soon as Will said 'gone,' he hiccupped.

"Praise de Lord," I said with joyous, tear-filled eyes. "Praise de Lord."

"Mama?"

"Yes, sugar?"

Will tried to prop himself up on one elbow but again fell back. "I asked the nurse if any mail arrived for me but she said none."

"Well, it take time," I said as I folded the top of his top sheet back over his blanket.

"Will you help me write a letter to Ella and then take it to the post office? I want her to know that I'm almost ready to return home."

"Uncle Pleas can, honeychile. Will dat be all right wit you?"

Will smiled.

"I'd be happy to," Babe said, "but we'll need paper, a pen, and an envelope."

"Ask the nurse, Uncle Pleas, they have all that."

"All right then," my brother said gently. It was too bad they had never had children. He would have been a wonderful father with all the love and patience he had been blessed with.

"Well, it looks like this will take a while, so I might just as well go and find me a seat," Sis' Pearl said.

"There's one over there," I said, pointing to the opposite end of the ward where a single steel chair was resting near a storage cabinet. I was glad to get her out of my hair.

Once we had the writing materials Babe used the clipboard with Will's medical records as a desk and sat on the edge of Will's bed to write Will's words down.

"All right now, I'm ready when you are, young man."

Will smiled faintly—he liked his Uncle Pleas—then he began:

"Dear Ella,

It sure has been a long time since the last letter I wrote to you. I hope that you received my letters. I haven't received yours because our regiment has been moving around too quickly for incoming mail to catch up with us.

Well, how are you? What are you doing with your time now that you've graduated? Did you become a nurse like you were planning? That would be good because right now I'm in the hospital in Los Angeles, California. In fact, my mama is standing next to my bed and my Uncle Pleas is helping me write this letter. Don't worry though, I did not lose my eyesight or my arms and hands. I'm just weak from the wound I received on Iwo Jima.

Hopefully, I'll be heading back to Galveston in early January. I hope that we will be able to visit then.

I have missed hearing from you and seeing you, Ella Mae. I really, really care about you and hope that you care for me in the same way. If you are able, please write to me here at the hospital, please do. The address is on the letterhead."

Will paused here.

"What's the matter, sugar?" I said.

He was starting to doze off. "I don't know what to write at the end, Mama. I want to write 'love,' but I don't want to scare Ella away."

I looked at Babe.

"Why don't you say 'fondly' for the time being?" Babe said.

"That's a good…" Will fell asleep before he could finish the sentence.

Babe finished the letter and signed Will's name so that we could post it as soon as we left.

Another family walked onto the ward as we were fixing to leave. The mother walked up to me and said, "Nurse, can you tell me how we may speak with the doctor about our son returning home?"

I did not want to divulge I was not a nurse. I mustered my best English and  said, "You has to speak wit de head nurse back at the nurse's station, ma'am. I'm only here for today." Babe and Sis' Pearl were stunned, of course. But being mistaken for a nurse twice in the same day made me realize I had a means to smuggle the needles for Will out of the white wards if all else failed. And, I knew in my bones that would be exactly what I would do. I would not let the ignorance and hatred of the people he fought for kill my only child.

# Chapter 16
## *A Big Rock Candy Proposal*

Dr. Buzzbee came around the following night. The Hi Hat was closed Mondays. That meant Mrs. Goldberg was available. The doctor was more sober than he appeared on his last visit. He looked fresh out of the tub and was dressed particularly sharp in a navy-blue suit, a fine white cotton dress shirt, and a big plush red and white silk polka dot bow tie that would have made a circus clown proud. I suppose the doctor it wore believing polka dots would give him a care-free, all caution to the wind, romantic look. He carried a matching bouquet of red and white roses for the missus and lit up the living room with his pearly white dentured smile.

I had Jakie to look after Billy in the kitchen and locked the kitchen's doors to make sure Billy stayed put. But I could still hear that child pawing at the dining room door and growling. That made me nervous, but it did not seem to spoil the doctor's mood. He was riding on Benny Goodman's so-called *A train*, but it felt as though the doctor's train was traveling full speed to a wrecked bridge high up over a deep gorge.

I was feeling lighthearted with Will doing so much better, so I put my bartender's hat on, smiled, and said, "What will it be, Mr....Dr. Buzzbee, the usual?"

"No, thank you, honey."

*Don't you call me honey! That's right! Go right ahead and get angry at this man! Tell him what's on your mind right now! Never mind he might get you the needles your boy might come to need. Lord have mercy!* That was my grandmother Johnny-Rae's voice talking to me. Mama Rae had a tongue so sharp she could lash you until she broke your spirit and made you bleed.

I kept the warm smile and said, "Well then, I reckon I'll let you relax, tell Mrs. Lucile de doctor is in, and find somethen' to put dese beautiful roses up in."

"Thank you kindly, Phosie Mae, but I'd like to present the flowers to the lady myself," the doctor said with a porcelain smile that made my skin crawl.

Mrs. Goldberg sang, "Buzzy, darling!" and the aroma of marijuana wafted out of the hallway.

"Well," I said, "I has my things to do in my kitchen."

Mrs. Goldberg walked in. "Phosie Mae,"—Mrs. Goldberg called me *Phosie Mae* whenever she wanted to impress someone--"did you ask the doctor if he'd like a drink, honey?"

"Yes, indeed she did, Lucky! I've carried a little surprise over for you, my dear," the doctor said while holding the roses out like a little boy offering a gift to his mama.

"It's not the flowers is it?" Mrs. Goldberg said like a little girl thinking her daddy had carried home an ordinary gift that would not excite her.

"Well, they wouldn't be the surprise, now would they?"

"Phosie Mae,"

"Yes, 'um?"

"Will you bring in that fresh ice, please?"

"Yes, 'um."

I arrived back in the living room as Mrs. Goldberg was holding the flowers in one hand and a smoldering cigarette in the other. She was saying, "I made a reservation at Perrino's, darling. I hope you don't mind."

"Mind?" the doctor said. "If that's what you want my beloved, that's what I want, too! It will make a nice setting for the presentation of my other gift."

Mrs. Goldberg chuckled and said, "I can't wait!"

*Lord have mercy, if by sum miracle dey actually do marry, dis talk won't last a day after dis man lets dat woman put a ring through his nose.*

Billy was still pawing at the dining room door. I felt nervous and wanted to be on my way so that they could be on theirs. "If 'n dere isn't anythin' else, I'll get de ice, den I'll be in de kitchen with Billy, Mrs. Lucile."

"We don't need ice, we'll have our drinks at the restaurant," Dr. Buzzbee said.

"Oh okay, forget the ice, Phosie Mae. Give Billy a kiss and a big giant hug for me, will you?" Mrs. Goldberg said with a lavishly forged smile.

"Dat will be fine, Mrs. Lucile, I'll do jus' dat." Everything was so calm and kind and polite I thought for a moment I had died and been brought back to life in some other time and place. "Now, don' you worry 'bout a thing, jus' have a fine time, don't worry 'bout a thing."

The doctor looked back over his shoulder and winked at me as he escorted Mrs. Goldberg to the front door.

Jakie, Billy, and I were in the kitchen the next morning when Mrs. Goldberg and the doctor walked in. I could see she was self-conscious about having spent the entire night out by the way she averted her eyes when she spoke to me."

"GRRRRRRRRRRRRRRR!"

Jakie had to take Billy up onto his lap and wrap his arm around his waist to keep Billy from giving the doctor's pant leg and ankle the once-over like he gave to my sister-in-law, Pearl.

"GRRRRRRRRRRRRRRR!"

"Phosie, thank you for getting Billy up and going for me. We went to Ciro's for dancing after dinner, to celebrate, and we lost track of time, didn't we, Buzzy?" *Gettin' Billy 'up and going,' she's makin' it out to sound like she is in dis kitchen every morning before de rooster crow like a woman on de cover of* Good Housekeepin'.

"Well, there was nothing to worry about, darling. All colored women are wonderful with children. It's bred into them."

*Dey also handy wit a meat cleaver.*

I said, "Why don' you have sum of my coffee, Dr. Buzzbee? It fresh and it hot!"

"Oh no, I'm off to the hospital, early surgeries, not for me, makes the hands shake. But the missus, or I should say 'the *new* missus to be,' has some news for you all. Why don't you show them, darling?"

"GRRRRRRRRRRRRRRR!"

"Aren't you goin' to ask why we were celebrating?" Mrs. Goldberg said presenting her left hand to reveal a diamond the size of a green cocktail olive radiating sparkling light from her ring finger. She tried to smile, but shadows of doubt in her eyes betrayed her. It was clear that she was more worried than pleased.

"GRRRRRRRRRRRRRRR!"

"Lor' have mercy, Mrs. Goldberg, looks like you done hit de jackpot!" I said.

"Isn't it gorgeous?" Mrs. Goldberg said, extending her ring finger toward me and rolling her hand from side to side. "I was really shocked, too!"

"Tell them, tell them what I told you, Lucky."

Mrs. Goldberg opened a drawer next to the stove, removed a bottle of aspirin, swallowed two, and grimaced.

"Go ahead, tell."

Mrs. Goldberg, annoyed, exhaled sharply. "He said he's going to tell his wife he's leaving after his morning surgeries. We're going to elope to Las Vegas. Over Christmas."

"Well, I'm so happy for y'all," I said. *Well, there goes my job!* "It sure is nice to have some good news for a change, isn't it, Mr. Jakie?"

"GRRRRRRRRRRRRRRR!"

"Yeah, nothin' like it, nothin'," Jakie said. He was not happy either. Perhaps he was thinking about losing his cheap place if his sister married the doctor, or wondering if I'd be fired and he'd lose our acquaintance, or both.

"Lordie, dey sure do wrap things up fast out this way!" I said. "Dee-vorce take so long down in Texas most folks jus' wait till de other one give out and die rather den leave."

"Dr. Buzzbee says he knows a judge in Reno who will take care of everything. All we have to do is send him the papers."

"There's something else, darling. You know," the doctor said with a nod toward me.

"Oh, I almost forgot. The only thing is, we need you to stay through Christmas," Mrs. Goldberg said then took a long drag from a freshly lit cigarette.

"Christmas! Well, I don' knows 'bout that, Mrs. Goldberg, wit my son in de hospital, I just don' knows. If he were out and on his feet dat would be fine."

Dr. Buzzbee said, "Wasn't there something about your boy's requiring needles for penicillin injections?"

"Yes, sir," I said without raising my eyes, "he shorely do."

"Well, needles are real-real scarce just now. However, I do have a source in Nevada that I may be able to acquire needles from. If that would be cause for you to stay on with the child through the holiday."

"And I'll ask Jakie to take you to the hospital on Christmas Eve and on Christmas Day. He'd love to," Mrs. Goldberg offered.

"Well, dat seem like an offer I cain' refuse. However, I reckon my brother and sister-in-law kin carry me over on Christmas Day."

"Well," Mrs. Goldberg said from behind a cloud of cigarette smoke she'd just created, "then Jakie can watch Billy."

The air grew tense with their waiting on my decision. The smoke curling from Mrs. Goldberg's cigarette was laced with the scent of her heady perfume. I felt dizzy. "I reckon dey no way I can say no, d'way you is puttin' it, Dr. Buzzbee. My baby need dem needles."

I looked at Mrs. Goldberg; she was still forcing a smile, the strain was still darkening her eyes. There was a slight quake in her right cheek. Maybe the closer she was getting to belonging to one man, just one sugar-daddy, the more afraid she was growing.

"There you go, darlin', we're all good. Are you excited?"

"Yeah, sure!" Mrs. Goldberg said with a toss of her head to shake loose the angst she was feeling.

"You don't look excited, Lucky! Are you sure you're all right?" the doctor said.

"Yeah, sure I'm all right," Mrs. Goldberg said, plucking her shoulders up like a mourning dove does its wings and placing a bright smile on her face. "It's just that I can't wait to go."

"It's right around the corner, darlin'. I'll wrap up the divorce in Reno and we'll be dancing with the stars in Las Vegas, Nevada before you know it."

"I have to get out of these clothes and wash my face, okay?"

"I have the owner of a Ford dealership to operate on this fine morning, so you go right on ahead."

Mrs. Goldberg cupped her hand over the right side of her mouth as if to let the doctor in on a secret and said, "Tell him to send over a red Super Deluxe once he's under, he'll never know what hit him!" Laughing, she gave the doctor a peck on the left cheek. But soon as that man stepped out the door, she started twisting that ring right off her finger like it was a curse or something. Our eyes met. I could see there was something she wanted to say, and I would have listened had she said it. Instead, she spun like an impudent child and marched down the hallway toward her quarters.

I checked in on Mrs. Goldberg after the doctor left. She was in her bathroom, sitting on the toilet with a cigarette dangling from the side of her mouth and a burnt arc of ashes dangling from the tip of her cigarette, and she was weeping. "What am I going to do?" she said with the strained voice of a helpless child, a voice marked by a mixture of anger, confusion, frustration, and fear. "What am I going to do? I don't know. I just don't know." She set her elbows on her knees and leaned forward weeping with her forehead resting on her palms. The ashes plunged and crashed onto the linoleum floor. I thought of being sympathetic, but I did not have the sympathy to spare.

When she bent to wipe the ashes up, I said, "Don't worry none 'bout dat now, Mrs. Goldberg, you has to pull yourself together, chile." When I called her "chile" she looked at me with reverence. I guess that's the way I felt about her, a child in the body of a grown and sensuous woman. You'll knows bye and bye. Jus' be patient and kind to yourself."

"Be kind to myself? Look at me? I live in this shit house, in a shit area, with a shit ex who doesn't pay his alimony! I have a shit brother and a shit child who shits on the fucking rug, and a boring Presbyterian eye doctor who wants to marry me! And you want me to be kind to myself? I hate myself!" she said with a twisted, agonized face.

"Now, you don' means dat, Mrs. Lucile. You jus' has to give yourself time to trust your feelings, dat's all dere is to hit."

"Feelings? What do they have to do with anything! Let me tell you something sister, I'm not stepping into that goddamned feelings crap! I don't want to go crazy thinking about how I feel and wind up in some nut jar. No thank you! You can keep your feelings! I'll take a Sidecar."

"Well, bye and bye…" I said.

You heard Leo. He said he would kill me if I did not go back with him. Leo has killed, Leo will kill me, and the doctor, and you because he'll think you talked me into marrying the God dammed doctor!

*He shore 'nough won' kill me for I will be back home in Galveston wit Will twixt now and de time he find out."*

"Don't you remember that? And the doctor's leaving his wife! Then there's the kid, the goddamned kid! And my brother who can't get out of his own way! Leo's crazy! I don't want to die! I'm scared. I might as well be locked in a goddamned prison. Shit!" Mrs. Goldberg thought about what she had said and doubled over into a fit of laughter.

*Lord, I am scared too! I don' want dat crazy man around me neither!*
"Well," I said, "folks say funny things when dey angry, Mrs. Lucile." I tried to dab her brow with a cool washcloth but she waived my hand away. "Mr. Goldberg done probably turned his mind somewhere else and don' even remember what he said in de heat. Dat's de way de mind work, you know. See, right now you focused on all yur troubles so you feels like you drowning in dem." Mrs. Goldberg's laughter faded. "But if'n you looks some other way and see somethin' good, like de love your boy has for you, den yur mind will follow dat vision and you'll feel better. Den you can go out for a walk or somethen'. What we thinks and what we do makes up how we feels. Come on, Mrs. Lucile, let me hep you into bed. You need to rest, dat's all." *Cause I need dem needles.*

"What is this, some kind of a Jesus thing?" she said droopily.

"No, ma'am. It's jus' common sense, dat's all, common sense," I said as I pulled Mrs. Goldberg up into her bedroom. I helped her with her nightgown. She crawled under the covers and said, "I, I just don't know what's wrong with me! What's wrong with me? Why is this all happening to me?"

I felt like saying, *Cause you afraid of seeing who you really is, seein' what you really needs, then gettin' yurself up and going on from dere.* "Well, you get some sleep, Mrs. Lucile. We can talk about all dis later."

Mrs. Goldberg whimpered twice then, like a bruised little girl, and said, "Can we talk when I get up?"

"Why sure 'nough, Mrs. Lucile, we surely can."

Mrs. Goldberg said, "I just don't know what's wrong with me! What's wrong with me? Everything I do turns to shit," and the tears rolled again.

Her sadness touched me. I understood her pain. I had mine, too. But I had come to know how she grew to look for happiness along the surface of things like a mosquito skimming on the still, reflective waters of a lake. Sadness welled in my eyes. No matter our skin color, we were women awash in separate torrents of despair. I cried.

*Sometimes it seems all that women possess is their tears.*

# Chapter 17

## *A cold gray sky*

December 23, 1945
Sunday

Dr. Buzzbee arrived with all his feathers puffed and picked up Mrs. Goldberg just before seven Sunday the day before Christmas. I let Billy sleep where he was in Mrs. Goldberg's bed till just before eight, which gave me time to dress for my visit to Will. I gently jiggled Billy's shoulder and said, "Come on, sugar, time to rise and shine." I dressed him then carried him next door to Jakie's. "Chile, if you get any bigger you'll have to carry me!" My love for him was growing.

Babe pulled up and tooted his horn as I tapped on Mr. Jakie's door. I waved at Babe then resumed trying to roust Billy's uncle. "Mr. Jakie, come out de door and get Billy, we're set to freeze!" We heard his smoker's hack as he shuffled to the door. He opened it with a fresh unlit Lucky Strike pinched between his lips. "Mr. Jakie, it shore 'nough harder to wake you den de dead!" I passed Billy to him and said, "Now, here you go. I'll be back 'fore supper. I left you and the baby breakfast and dinner fixin's in Mrs. Lucile's kitchen. Don't do anything crazy and get me fired."

Mr. Jakie snickered.

"I means it! Don't you go and get me fired," I added with mock severity.

"I might take the kid to the merry-go-round and the minature train over to Griffith Park around lunch," he said as he took Billy from my arms and wrapped him in his.

"Well, it look like it goin' to warm up, so you have yourselves a fine day. And, thank you kindly for looking after the boy."

"Ah, that's nothing," Jackie said as he brushed his hair back with his fingers and started hacking. He managed to say, "Maybe I'll get another dinner for my effort!"

I smiled and said, "I wouldn't raise up my hopes too high!" Then I turned and   hurried down to the curb and Babe's car. Just before I slipped in I looked back up to the house. Jakie was still at his front door, smiling, holding Billy in his arms.

Babe had dropped Sis' Pearl off at their church so that she could help the Sisterhood prepare Sunday Christmas dinner. As the Rose of Sharon Baptist Church was way down on Western Avenue, bless his heart, he drove down to the church then back up to Boyle Heights and then back down to the church so that I wouldn't miss the last Sunday of Advent service. It was bad enough I would miss attending on Christmas Eve and Christmas Day. As Babe walked me into the chapel, the very first thing I noticed was Sis' Pearl sitting up in the front pews with members of the Church Sisterhood. Most of the Sisters were chatting and laughing like canaries in a cage, but Sis' Pearl sat silent and stoic like a cigar store Indian at the entrance to a saloon. I thought of a line from Scripture, *Wives, be subject to your husbands as you are to the Lord,* and I smiled. Sis' Pearl had it the other way around, for she had Babe working for her and the Lord too. I wanted to sit someplace along the back of the sanctuary, but Babe insisted on introducing me to the Sisters. Once we were in front of their pews, Sis' Pearl's expression changed to a look someone might have upon discovering a dead cat or dog that had been rotting in the cellar. "Pearl, dear, why don't you introduce Phosie Mae to your Sisters while I help distribute the Bibles?

While they smiled graciously, my sister-in-law said, "This is my husband's sister. She's the one working for that crazy Jewish lady with the boy thinks he's a dog out in Boyle Heights." The Sisters nodded and smiled but did not seem so aggrieved as was Sis' Pearl.

"How do you like workin' for dat Jewish woman way out there, Phosie Mae? Has de boy bit anybody else again?" one sister asked. The others Sisters chuckled politely under Pearl's scrutiny.

"No," I said, "I declare Sis' Pearl's ankle was so sweet he be waitin' on her now."

The Sisters fell into a fit of laughing, howling and slapping their thighs to catch their breath. I wished I had had a camera to capture the expression of indignation on my sister-in-law's face. "Well, that devil child will be grown and out of that house before I return." The sisters laughed again.

They were nice and friendly. Another one of the Sisters, a slight woman with gray hair and round silver eyeglasses glasses, smiled and said, "Why, I work with a Jewish family out that way, the Schumers. They're very nice. Maybe your lady know them."

"I don't 'spec she do. She a different breed a cat," I said. The Sisters said "ummm-huh" in chorus.

"What brings you out to Los *Angeleese*?" another of the Sisters asked.

"My baby…well, he's a grown man now, but I still think of him as my baby." Again, the Sisters nodded and repeated "um-huh." "He was shot in de stomach on Iwo Jima. Now he over to de military hospital in de colored ward. I came up from Galveston to look after him, bless his heart."

"Well, we'll certainly pray for…" one Sister said then paused for his name.

"William, William Carlyle Eaton."

"For William Carlyle Eaton then. Our prayers will pull him through, hear!"

"Thank you kindly," I said, tearing up. "See if you cain't also pray up some colored needles so that he cain get de penicillin he needs."

"There's always somethin'!" another Sister said.

And another said, "We'll give the deacon a prayer request for your son. That way he will be in everyone's prayers."

I started to cry then looked at Sis' Pearl. By the look on her face you would've thought she had just taken a swallow of sour milk. I had stolen her show.

We arrived at the hospital near two. There were so many visitors we had to park out on Sepulveda next to the cemetery. Babe and Sis' Pearl crossed the street while I observed several burial services in various stages. The cemetery, a twenty-five acre plot of land, was not half-filled. I looked at all the white alabaster crosses and Stars of David and could not fathom how many more boys would fall till the cemetery was filled up. I hoped that never happened. I noticed a ceremony to the right near the fence. A coffin was being lowered to the bottom of a fresh-dug grave. An honor guard fired a three-gun salute. The leader of the guard picked up the spent cartridges and carried them over to the soldier's weeping mother, who was holding the triangular flag on her lap with the stars pointed up. He slipped the cartridges between the eleventh fold of the flag, the fold of Abraham, Isaac, Jacob, and the Hebrews, and the twelfth fold that represents the Father, the Son, and the Holy Ghost. As the bugler started taps, I took off across the street in order not to hear another ode to death.

Barry Hospital was overflowing with people. Some were well dressed; others were wearing Salvation Army suits and dresses with ties, tacky accessories, hand me down hats, and second hand shoes just like me.

As we walked to Will's bed, I heard a frantic voice calling my name.

"Mrs. Eaton! Mrs. Eaton!" It was Nurse Thompson. "I'm so glad I caught you."

"Why?" I said, filled with terror.

She took my hand in hers and gently said, "I'm sorry, Mrs. Eaton, Will's had a setback."

"A setback? What setback?" Sis' Pearl asked.

"It seems that the infection worked its way to the spleen and that's causing his, Will's white blood cell count to increase," Nurse Thompson said, placing her other hand over mine. "Your son needs a blood transfusion but we don't have any more of his type, AB positive, it's so rare."

"I'll give my blood," I said. Babe and Sis' Pearl volunteered as well.

"That will be fine, but you'll have to be tested. Why don't you have a visit with him first then I'll send you over to the lab. Listen, we're not done fighting yet, and the needles ought to be arriving any day now," Nurse Thompson said, "Don't give up!"

I thought of my plan to wear one of Mrs. Goldberg's maid's outfits to sneak into the white wards and steal needles. "Well, one way or t'other he'll have his needles, one way or t'other."

"What are you saying, Phosie Mae?" Babe asked.

"Never you mind. I just ain' goin' to let my baby die when dey have needles in the other building that are the same needles we need but dey say dey are for whites only. It's like I said, if'n the bullets weren't marked 'white only' and 'colored only,' then the good Lord knows there's no reason on the face of this Earth the needles should be."

"Amen," Sis' Pearl said.

Will was pallid as before. His skin was clammy and his pajamas were damp. The hiccups were quick and shallow, he was groaning softly, he did not have the strength to groan loudly.

I dabbed his head with a damp washcloth and tried to talk with him. "Will baby, can you hear me?" He smiled.

"Hi, Mama. Why are you still here?"

"Never you mind, sugar. I'm just makin' sure you doin' fine."

He smiled. "Yeah, Mama, I'm fine, really. You don't have to worry about me." Hiccup.

"Are you thirsty, baby?"

"We just had us a pitcher of ice-cold lemonade. Do you want some?"

"No, no, I'm all right, baby, I'm fine."

Will turned his head and looked at me with unfocused eyes. "Ella just left, mama. It's too bad you missed her."

"She did!" I looked at Babe and Sis' Pearl. Babe said, "You must have enjoyed seeing her, Will."

"She must have received my letter."

"Dat's right, chile, she shore 'nough did." I uncovered the basket of biscuits and held them up even though Will would probably not look at them. "Are you hungry, baby? I done carried some of my biscuits and honey for you."

"No, Mama, I don' have much of an appetite. Have you heard from Ella? Did you get her letter?"

"No, baby, as soon as..." I was about to repeat what I had said but stopped, realizing that Will was delirious.

"When I close my eyes I can see her, Mama. She's right next to me or she's walking down the road alongside the cotton rows toward the schoolhouse. She steps so lightly I doubt the ground even feels her presence. She's like an angel. If I think on it long enough, she stops and turns and smiles at me. Her eyes are so filled with love and joy. They take me in, mama. I feel warm deep down inside me. Complete."

"You keeps watching for her, baby, keep watching. She'll come out in her skin and bones to see you 'fore you knows it, and if she cain't I'll go to Galveston my own self and carry her out here." I was making a promise I had no way of keeping, but I did not want my baby to lose his will to live. If seeing Ella kept him fighting, then so be it.

I waved at Nurse Thompson. When she arrived at Will's bedside I cornered her and whispered, "I don' knows if I can trust you with this, but you're the onliest one I know to talk to."

"What is it?" she whispered.

"See, my employer, Mrs. Lucile Goldberg, is returning from her honeymoon on Christmas Day."

"Well, isn't that a nice Christmas present, a husband. Wish I could get one!"

"See, de groom is a doctor, an eye surgeon. And he promised dat if I stayed on wit Mrs. Goldberg's chile through de Christmas holiday he would carry needles and syringes back from a doctor friend a his dat lives in Las Vegas, Nevada."

The light in Nurse Thompson's eyes intensified. "And you want me to help you smuggle them in for your son."

I looked one way down the ward then up the other, and while watching the entrance near the stairs, I said, "Matter of factually, I was hopin' that you could hep me get into the white wards and find de penicillin my baby needs 'cause dey holdin it back till de needles arrives. Den we'll sure 'nough have everything we needs."

"Now how do you expect me to help you find a way into the white areas with you dressed that way?"

"See, my employer, she keep maids' uniforms for her housekeepers, look like what a nurse wears. I already been mistaken for one. I would look jus' like a registered nurse. Den you could show me where de medicine is."

"Now that is a rather tall order, sweetheart," Nurse Thompson said. "I don't know how many laws we'd break."

"But will you hep me save my chile?"

Now it was Nurse Thompson looking both ways. "I'll tell you what, you bring those needles and we'll see what we can do."

"Oh, bless your heart! Bless your heart, sugar! You are my angel," I said as I took her in my arms and gave her a big, warm hug. "I'm goin' to make you a fine quilt after all dis! Bless your heart, darlin'."

Nurse Thompson escorted us to the lab on the corner of the main hospital building where our blood was drawn for testing. None of us was a match.

On the ride home, Sis' Pearl asked, "Just what exactly do you have in mind, Phosie Mae?"

I could tell by the sarcastic tone of her voice that her intent was to pick my plan apart, so I said, "It's just something I've thought up."

"Well, if you are plannin' to sneak your way into the white ward and steal penicillin, then I think you better think twice."

"You been spyin' on me, hasn't you?"

"I done heard every word."

"Well, you best not speak a one of dem, hear? My baby is lying in dis hospital at de door of death. For as big a woman as you is, you don't have a bitty ounce of compassion in you, do you?"

"Come on, ladies, there's no sense quarreling," Babe said as he slowed to let a white couple cross Wilshire Boulevard.

"Well, as a matter of fact, I do have an ounce of compassion, and if you'd hear me out maybe you would let me show it to you."

"What?" I said with a good measure of suspicion. "What do you wants to show me?"

"The reason I don't think you should try to sneak into the white ward is because you are too scrappy looking to be one of those starched colored nurses they have over there." Babe laughed. "It's not funny. Phosie Mae looks like a pea picker, not some regulated nurse like the one that gave us attitude! If anyone should sneak over there, it should be me!"

Babe and I said "You!" in chorus.

Then Babe said, "Where will you get a nurse's outfit, darling?"

"From Sister Beatrice Brown. She's a registered nurse, and she's about my size. In fact, I know she is. She borrowed my floral-print dress for a church garden party and never has returned it. So, if it comes down to it, I will help you out."

"Why do you want to do this?" I said.

"Well, Phosie Mae, it's like this. I am not going to stand by and watch one of our brave, young colored men die because the devil doctors running this hospital won't lift a finger to help. I mean, they claim to be so high and mighty, but they are low and feeble sinners through and through. What kind of people let a young man who fought for their freedom die of a wound they have the medicine and equipment to treat? Evil people, that's what kind. They evil, that's all there is too it. It's past time we put them in their place. Come to think of it, if I run into that fat sassy colored nurse marching around in that starched white uniform of hers like she own the place, I'll smack her across her face. I'm no angry woman, but I'll tell you what, I will enjoy lowering her a notch or two. Um-hum!" Then she pushed a plug of her tobacco under her lip and started to chomp away. For the first time it did not bother me.

Just as the pleasant thought of Sis' Pearl coming to Will's rescue heartened me, the thought of her on the loose in the white wards terrified me. She was just as likely to have us all arrested. But there was no mistaking it she did have a heart under all her fat and fury.

"All right den," I said. "Let's see what happen wit Mrs. Goldberg's new man's promise. Then we'll know what needs doin'. Least ways we have us a plan."

It was dusk by the time we returned to Mrs. Goldberg's. Something was terribly wrong. Both Mrs. Goldberg's and Jakie's front doors were wide open.  Both apartments were dark.

Sis' Pearl said, "Look like the hen ran off and all the chicks got loose."

"I don' know nothin' 'bout no hen, but with all de enemies Mr. Jakie has, he usually careful to keep his place locked up like de bank."

"Seem like most of the enemies that man has are in his head, if you ask me."

"Pearl, get out the way so I cain get out dis car and investigate."

"Maybe the child opened the doors while playing a game," Babe said.

Sis' Pearl grunted her way up off the front seat and out of the car. She said, "All that child do is bite, and dig, and soil."

I walked up the path, calling, "Mr. Jakie? Billy? Where is you chile?" The silence of the cold gray sky spooked me. I quickened my step.

I looked into Jakie's place first. He was lying facedown in a pool of blood. I thought he was dead. The cigarette he kept tucked above his ear was blood soaked and crushed by a blow to the side of his head. "Jakie! Jakie!" I realized in that moment that his shy interest in me meant more than I had thought. He had touched my heart. I had very little in my life to hold and call my own; I did not want to lose anything more no matter. I'd always heard that love is blind. Well, apparently it's colorblind, too. "Jakie! Wake up!"

Babe and Sis' Pearl arrived as I kneeled down to see if Jakie was still breathing. I placed my hand on his chest. It rose and fell gently. I felt his heart beating. "Oh my Lord, what happened? Who did this to you?"

"He dead!" Sis' Pearl shouted. "We better call the operator and get the police out here before they 'rest us!"

"No! Can't you see his chest heavin'? He ain' nothin' but knocked out cold. Last thing we needs is the police when dis man laying out cold like a dead fish and bleedin', de baby missin', and his mama out of town. Dey would shorely lock us up and throw 'way de key 'fore dey even ask our names. Hep' me put this man on the sofa. Then let's find that chile!"

Once we had Jakie laid out with an ice pack on his head, I said, "Pearl, you go into Mrs. Goldberg's and see if you cain' find Billy."

"I'll help," Pearl said, "but there is not a chance in this life or the next of me taking one step near that crazy child! Babe, you go."

"All right then, you stay with Mr. Jakie and make sure de ice stay on his skull. I'll look inside. Babe, you look on de outside."

"Will you be all right with Mr. Jakie, dear?" Babe said to Pearl. I felt like slapping both of them.

I looked all through Jakie's place, behind the sofa, under the bed, in the closets and cupboards. I had not noticed, but the place was filthy and there wasn't but two or three cans of beans in his pantry. He only had one pair of shoes, one pair of slippers, two pairs of Marine-issue khaki pants, one dress shirt, and an old navy-blue suit with shiny shoulders. He was living a pathetic, loveless, and empty life. I felt terrible for him. As I walked around I called, "Billy, where are you, sugar?" as loudly as I could without giving the neighbors cause for alarm. "Billy! You come to Phosie right now, hear?" Billy was not there. I searched Mrs. Goldberg's place the same way, no luck. Babe came in and reported the child was not anywhere around the property. "Did you look in de shed?" I said.

"I looked all through that garage, and the child is not in there either, Phosie. Maybe we'd better call the police now."

"Did you look in that truck?"

"Yes, I looked all through that truck, under the seats, and in those barrels, too."

I said, "Let's walk 'round the neighborhood and see if we cain't find him."

"At night? I don't know if that is such a good idea in this area."

"That's right. Then let's drive."

"Let me tell Pearl," Babe said.

"No! We don't have time. Let's go."

Babe and I drove up one street and down the other through most of that night, but the child was nowhere to be found. We drove past the parks too and would have gotten out, but in the end we figured that would have been too dangerous because if the Mexican gangs didn't get us the police would have. You could not be out and colored just anywhere in the city at that time.

The sun was rising by the time we pulled back up to Mrs. Goldberg's place. Jakie was awake holding the ice pack on his wound while Sis' Pearl was sleeping on a chair next to the sofa. She was a sight to behold. Her head was tilted so far back over her shoulders and her mouth was so far open a bird could have built a nest on her tongue if the top bridge of her false teeth had not slipped down and blocked the entrance to her mouth. Every time she inhaled her head fell back further, the loose top bridge clicked against the bottom bridge, and she snorted like a sow. Then, her nerves must have kicked in. Her head jerked back up with her lips pursed. I don't know how she did but she made a delicate tapping sound like a teaspoon clinking against the side of an empty teacup. Only the Lord knows how she made that sound. Babe was watching her affectionately. I said it before and I'll say it again, love is blind.

Jakie waved at me and smiled. My heart swelled with emotion seeing that he was conscious. I blushed.

"What done happened to you?" I said.

"Ah, just a couple a bums came by to pick up on a wager I couldn't pay on. I gotta stop gamblin'."

"Yes, you surely do. Cause now de boy's missin'."

"What do you mean, missing?" Jakie said. "Isn't he with you?"

"No, sir."

"Shit!" Jakie said as he struggled to sit up.

"That's what I feel like sayin' too."

"Where did you look?"

Sis' Pearl snorted, and her head jerked again.

"High and low, far and wide!" I said.

"We've been out driving most of the night," Babe said.

"Did you look under the house?"

"Under the house?" Babe and I said in unison.

Sis' Pearl's head snapped back up and her eyes opened. "What's under the house?"

"No, we surely has not," I said, "but we goin' to 'fore another minute pass."

Jakie got up, put on his robe, slipped into his slippers, snapped a fresh cigarette up behind his ear, and led us to the cement path that ran alongside Mrs. Goldberg's place. We stopped at a small wood-framed screen covering the crawl space. The screen was ajar.

"He's under there. We just have to coax him out," Jakie said.

"What about those Chiclets Phosie say you give the child?" Sis' Pearl said as she took a step back toward the service porch.

"Once he crawls under the house, it's hell to get him out! Hell! I've been meaning to nail the screen shut. I just haven't had the time to get to it."

I squatted down as far as my knees would let me and bent over to put my face as close to the opening as I could get it. "Billy, you bes' come out now 'fore your mama get home. 'Sides, dey spiders, worms, rats, and I don't know what else to bite you up under there."

"He doesn't care about any of that," Jakie said.

"Well, how have you gotten him out in the past?" I said.

Jakie said, "I just wait till he gets tired of hiding. Then he crawls out."

I heard Sis' Pearl's handbag snap open. "Maybe this will help?" she said, passing me a candy shaped like a little bell and wrapped in bright foil.

"What is that?" I said.

"It's a chocolate kiss! Toss a couple near the opening and the child will come right out. They all loves chocolate."

I threw the first chocolate kiss in. "Here you go, sugar. Here sum chocolate. Dere 'ain nothin' to be 'fraid of now! Dose bad men, dey all gone. Your Uncle Jakie is standing right chere waiting on you. Now, come on out now."

The telephone started ringing.

"Lord have mercy, that's probably Mrs. Goldberg now! Let me get that," I said.

I rushed into the house and picked up the phone. "Goldberg residence, may I hep you?" I could hear crying on the other end. "Mrs. Lucile, is dat you? What has you so cryin' so?"

She could barely speak for crying. I was not too surprised.

"Now, why don' you take you a moment to collect yourself. Breathe in slow and breathe out slower." I heard her inhaling. "Dat's right, cain't be nothin' that bad to stop you from breathin'." Now she was crying again. "Come on now. Take you another breath in slow as you can." She tried again. The crying settled to a whimper. "Now, dat's better. Suppose you tell me why you so upset on your Las Vegas honeymoon?"

I heard Sis' Pearl shouting, "Now come on out from there and I'll give you somethin' sweet!" I cupped my hand over the receiver and said, "Shush!"

"I'm not in goddamned Vegas! I'm at Whiteman Airport."

"They has a white man airport top everthen' else?

"Not white man, White-mon!"

"Probably de same thing. Why is you there at dis hour?" I asked, feeling Will's chances for getting his needles were dead and gone.

"That...that no good bastard was a liar!"

"Dr. Buzzbee, a liar?"

"The son of a bitch!"

"Way he was talking that's the last news I 'spected," I said, trying to soothe her, but since he was cheating on his wife with Mrs. Goldberg I was not really too surprised. I wanted to ask about the needles but she was crying so it did not feel right. "Well, it for de best you found out now rather den further down de road where it gone too far to turn back 'round and come back home."

"That lying son of a bitch! They're all a bunch of lying sons of bitches!"

"Come on now, crawl out from under there!" Sis' Pearl bellowed.

"Who's that?"

"Oh, it just my sister-in-law playing with Billy."

"Billy? I thought she was afraid of Billy."

"Oh my, oh my, dey just like peanut butter and jelly now, Mrs. Lucile."

"Where's Billy?"

"He under de sofa. You know how he play. Is you all right, Mrs. Lucile?"

"No, goddamn it. I'm not all right. I'm at this stinkin' airport and I don't have a goddamned penny to my name! I need a ride! Is Jakie there? Get Jakie!"

"Yes, 'um, I will.

I went back out and gave Jakie the news, and he went back in to speak with Mrs. Goldberg. "Yeah," I heard him say, "I'll spot you a fin, take a cab. You'll be here in thirty minutes."

*Thirty minutes! Dis chile is going to be filthy as a pig in a sty.* I ran outside and found Sis' Pearl bent over with her head in the opening and her backside exposed to God and nature. "Move out de way!" I said, pulling her away by her arm. "Dat chile has to come out now!"

I crawled under the house, over dank, musty earth and past spider-webs, a cat's skeleton, and old elixir bottles, to the far corner and found

Billy sitting with his knees pulled up against his chest and his arms wrapped around his knees. "Come on now, chile, it safe now. Dem bad men dey gone, hear? And your mama's on her way home." I crawled up to him, stroked his little brow, and said, "Come on now, sugar." He still did not move. I said, "All right den, you climb up on my shoulders and I'll carry you out of dis nasty place. You don' belong down here, sugar!" I turned my backside toward him, and he crawled up my back and wrapped his arms around my neck. "Lor' have mercy, what else besides being a mule am I goin' to have to do to keep dis job!" I said, laughing. What I was doing was just too difficult to take in without laughing about it. "Let's get you cleaned up and in some fresh things. Your mama shore 'nough don't want to see you filthy as a little pig!"

Billy did not say anything. He did hold on a little more tightly, and I could feel the perspiration from his little arms on my neck, bless his heart. As I crawled, the realization that Mrs. Goldberg would be coming home without the colored needles hit me like a two-by-four, and I barely found the strength to carry Billy out. My will and hope had given out.

# Chapter 18

## *In the Eye of the Storm*

Christmas Eve, 1945

Mrs. Goldberg looked beaten, battered, and fried as she stumbled up the walkway from the taxi. Her hair was mussed, her eyes were dark as an owls', and her clothes looked like she had crawled through a storm drain. Besides her handbag and the two small pieces of baggage the driver was carrying, one being a pink makeup case, there were no other packages. No needles.

I had cleaned up Billy and put his muddy clothes to soak in the sink and forgot about straightening myself up, let alone putting on a uniform. I really did not care, to tell the truth. My dress was smeared with the damp brown earth from the crawl space under the house. I did not look much better than my employer.

"What the hell happened to you?" Mrs. Goldberg said.

"Me?" I thought she had broken her promise and that relieved me of having to answer to her, but just in case a miracle happened and Will turned around and I still needed work, I said, "I fell comin' out the hospital and didn't have a chance to change. I'm..." I stopped short of apologizing. She did not look like she cared either way. Her fabulous fun-loving divorcee act had not only failed to bring her happiness, it had made her downright miserable. Now she was suspicious of and me too. Misery likes company.

*"URRRRRRRRRRRRRR."*

"Shit! Where's Billy? What did he do now?"

"Oh," I said, tightening up my facial muscles, "he ain' done nothing 'cept play 'roun the house, Mrs. Lucile, nothin' t'all. Matter of factually, he in de kitchen restin' in dat little den a his."

Mrs. Goldberg looked around suspiciously, "Where are your brother and sister-in-law?"

"Oh, dey left directly after you called, Mrs. Lucile. They had a church breakfast to attend, it being the last day of de Advent." Once again I felt like gathering up my things and walking right out the door. I would have except there was no place for me to go. I was stuck with Mrs. Goldberg for the time being, whether I liked it or not. That's how it had to be, for Will. It felt strange to feel so alone in a city with so many people. "Well, let me hep you with dose bags, Mrs. Lucile. You go on and take you a warm bath and settle yourself down."

*"URRRRRRRRRRRRRR."*

"Oh, for Christ's sakes, he has to stop that or I'll blow my top!"

"Don' you worry 'bout de chile, Mrs. Lucile, I'll take care a him. Like I said, you go take yourself a warm bath and collect yur nerves."

"The needles are in my makeup case," Mrs. Goldberg said as demurely as if she were talking about the weather.

"I knows, I knows," I said, assuming she was giving me an excuse for not having delivered on her promise. "Women cain't depend on a man like dey used to, no ma'am." *My Isaac would have come back dead before he came back without those needles.*

Mrs. Goldberg lit a cigarette, inhaled as if she were taking her last breath, then exhaled a foul cloud of smoke. "Don't you want the needles?"

"What needles, Mrs. Lucile?"

"The needles I said I'd get for you. They're in my cosmetic case, like I just said. Open it up, they're on top."

"Oh my Lordie!" I said as I knelt and undid the two brass snaps on the front of the pink leather case. The needles and syringes were in two boxes right on top, just like she said. "I thought since—"

"You thought wrong. Go ahead, take them. They're yours."

"I don' know what to say, Mrs. Lucile, I..." Tears were streaming down my face.

"You don't have to say nothin'. Just count yourself lucky because the bastard wanted to stop in Reno to check his eye clinic *and* pick up the divorce papers, the lying bastard. That's where he had the needles."

"I wants to hug you!" I said, and before Mrs. Goldberg could respond I had wrapped my arms around her waist and pulled her against me. I could feel her pained body let go and accept the love I was giving her. We both cried. I slowly released her from my embrace and said, "What did happen in Lost Vegas?"

Mrs. Goldberg laughed. "It's 'Las,' not 'Lost,' but it should be 'Lost,' because most of the people there don't know whether they're coming or going. You want to know what happened?"

"Yes, ma'am, jus' like I say," I said as I picked up the two small suitcases. "Tell me on de way to your bedroom." I had absolved her of all her sins.

She said, "We arrived at the hotel and dressed for the evening, he spent twenty minutes at the crap table, then we went for a drink before going to see Sinatra. It was like a first date all over again. He likes champagne, you like champagne. He thinks it's too warm, you love it when there's a chill in the air. You like a charbroiled steak, that's all he ever eats. You can't drink a rum and Coca-Cola because it's too sweet, he can't stand anything too sweet except you. You know the game."

"I don't, but go 'head, keep tellin'."

"So, I duck into the lady's room and take a couple of fast puffs from the dragon because I'm nervous, you know, and when I return to the table the drinks are served, martinis dry, and he says, 'Listen, darling, I have some good news!'"

"'I'll take all the good news I can get, and whatever I can't use now I'll box it up and take it home,' I told him."

"Well, what did he tell you, Mrs. Lucile?"

"He says, he tells me about his attorney, Marv Geltman, Gittleman, Geller...some Jewish shyster—Jews make the best attorneys, you know. They know how to argue. Anyways, so Buzzbee tells me Marv told him that he will be able to keep all the assets from the clinics for our enjoyment when the divorce goes through. He says his wife and the kids will be set for life of course, and besides that, she has the money she inherited from her parents. 'She'll be fine,' he says."

"What else did you say, Mrs. Lucile?"

"Hey, I'm no home wrecker. I told him I wouldn't have it any other way, I told him I would hate to see his family suffer. I felt like the biggest bullshitter west of the Mississippi. Then I extended my martini glass for a toast.

"But before he clinks his glass with mine, he says, 'There's one little thing Marv wants, though.'

"Well, I looked at the red imprint of my lips on the rim of my glass then spun my glass so that the vodka swirled like a in whirlpool as I waited for him to continue. I had a feeling a sucker punch was on its way. You get that feeling, you know."

"Yes, I knows, Mrs. Lucile, I knows."

"So, he looks around at the people kibbitzing at the other tables and says how about we finish the conversation in our room before dinner, that would be more private up there. So we went up to the room, a comp'd high roller's suite on the seventh floor. I sat on the sofa and he pours himself another drink. Then he starts pacing and says, 'See, Lucky, if we're going to do this thing, I want to do this thing right, remove even the tiniest of possibilities for any problems out of the way now. Because when I say "I do," I don't want anything on my mind except making you happy. How does that sound?'

"'Okay, I say, 'So, go on?' So he walks over to the sofa where I'm sitting and plops down so that the outside of his thigh presses mine. I could feel his hot panting breath on my neck. I shuddered, I'm telling you, I shuddered. So now, he looks me in the eye and he says, 'See, Lucky, Marv wants me to move to Nevada for a year to establish residency before I leave Martha. There's no community property here. Then we'll be home free.'

"I looked at him, and I just said, 'What about me? '.

"And he goes on, and he says, 'That's the beautiful part, darlin'. You can stay right where you are with your boy. You'll have a whole year to get everything ironed out. Isn't that wonderful?'

"'Wonderful?' I say to him. 'Wonderful? Fuck you, wonderful! I'll tell you what I want, I want to get the hell out of this place now, you lying, conniving son of a bitch! Now!'

"Then he reaches into the side pocket of his suit jacket and says, 'I thought you might be upset, darling. So I bought you a little something as a gesture of my love.' And he opens a small red box about the size a ring might come in and inside there's a gold horseshoe on a chain.

"So I told him again, 'Fuck you! I don't want your goddamned lucky charm to tide me over, you bastard!'

"Then he tried to put his arm around me and said, 'Calm down now, calm down, let me help you relax.' But I shrugged his arm right off and jumped to my feet."

I was proud of Mrs. Goldberg, and I let her know. "Dat's exactly right," I said. "Get away from de man, he no good."

She continued with her story. "Now I'm on my feet and pacing. I tell him, 'You fly me all the way to Las Vegas like we're getting married then you tell me your goddamned Jew attorney wants us to wait a year? Then you think some trinket will make everything okay. I'll tell you what you can do with the trinket, you can shove it up your fat drunkard ass! You lied to me, you miserable bastard! Fly me home!'

"Anyways, he stood and walked up to me. He tells me he doesn't want me to do anything rash, that I should sleep on it. He says we'll have dinner, see Sinatra, and spend the night there. Then he says if I'm still angry in the morning he would fly me home on the very first flight. Then he tried to take my wrist in his hand, but I pulled my arm away again and stepped back.

"I told him, 'I don't want your stinkin' drink, I don't want to sleep on anything, I want to get the hell out of this hotel room and out of this town, now, or I call the cops and tell them you got me drunk and tried to rape me! Then your wife will know what kind of a louse she's sleeping next to!'"

I was shaking my head. "Lor' have mercy!" I said. "That was sure some honeymoon! No wonder you're so stirred up. You really do need a warm bath. You get out your things, and I'll run de hot water."

"*URRRRRRRRRRRRRR.*"

"I'm comin', Billy, I'm comin'. Soon as I settle your mama down I'll come see what I need to do for you! If it isn't one thing it's de other," I said with a lighter heart, with hope.

"*URRRRRRRRRRRRRR.*"

I telephoned Babe as soon as I looked in on Billy.

"This is the Beaumont residence," Babe said when he answered the phone. "Who is callin' please?"

"Babe, it's your sister, Phosie Mae!"

"Of course, of course. What is it? I hope there's nothing—"

"No, dere is nothing wrong. Listen to me, hear? See, Mrs. Goldberg jus' came back from Las Vegas carrying de needles! We have de needles!"

"Well, I told you the good Lord has his ways, didn't I?"

"I needs to find a way out to de hospital, tonight!"

"Tonight? What are you planning to do out there tonight, Phosie Mae?"

"What do you think? I'm goin' to carry dose needles over to the hospital and see if one of de nurses won't give Will the first shot of his penicillin."

"We better think this through, Phosie Mae. I mean, first of all, we'll have trouble passing through the gate after visiting hours and all the staff have left. It would be far better to drive out first thing tomorrow morning when the Galveston nurse is on duty. Don't you think?"

"Babe, I can't think, I just have a bad feeling, and sittin' here on my hands feeling helpless to do anythen' is making things worse. I don't know what to do."

"I just don't want to see you having a run-in with that nurse who thinks the hospital administration appointed her to keep the Negro in his place. That would be disastrous. Why don't we go first thing tomorrow morning?"

"All right den, I'll wrap de quilt I made for him and we'll carry it out with the needles."

"That will be nice. Now, try and get some rest or before you know it you'll be in the bed next to him! You have to stay healthy!"

"Dat's right, Babe, dat's right. Thank de Lord I have you."

The telephone rang just after three a.m. I lay in bed with my eyes closed pretending I did not hear it. I tried to believe it was either the doctor, or Mrs. Goldberg's ex, or some other man she met at The Hi Hat calling. I tried, but I could not wish away the harsh reality of Mrs. Goldberg coming into my room and gently shaking my shoulder to awaken me as someone would awaken a child who was pretending that there really wasn't any school on a particular day.

"Phosie, Phosie," Mrs. Goldberg whispered, "it's the nurse at the hospital calling. She says it's urgent that she talks with you."

I jumped off the cot, threw my coat over my shoulders, and ran to the phone, thinking, *Maybe if I had not given that nurse this telephone number she might not have had the need to call me! Why did I do that? Why?*

By the time I reached the phone my lips were quivering and my hands were shaking. "Hello? Yes, dis is Sergeant William Eaton's mother. His spleen? Dey has to take his spleen? Can I come see him before dey take him in? I'll come right now."

When I hung up the phone Mrs. Goldberg said, "What is it? What happened?"

"De nurse say Will need a surgery for his spleen 'fore it busts." My head was so filled with thoughts and feelings I could not recall exactly what the nurse had said. "I don' recollect what all she said, but I needs to get to the hospital. Let me go get my brother's telephone number and see if he cain't carry me over."

"There's no time for that. Come on, I'll take you!"

"What about Billy?"

"Shit! We'll take him. No, I'll wake Jakie up, he'll come over. Go get dressed."

Within minutes we were in Mrs. Goldberg's Pontiac racing down North Broadway through Chinatown past painted sleeping dragons.

# Chapter 19

## *A very colored Christmas*

Something had clicked in Mrs. Goldberg's spirit. I think it was the opportunity my situation presented to her—an opportunity to be needed, truly needed. If loving is caring, then in order to love there needs to be someone or thing that needs our love. In that moment Mrs. Goldberg found an opportunity to be my hero, to feel important, to feel needed and not used. Gabriel could not have opened the gates to the hospital grounds any better than Mrs. Goldberg's Hollywood smile. Will was downstairs on a gurney, waiting on the operating room nurses, when we arrived at Barry. His face was twisted with pain. The pain seared through me. A mother can watch a stranger suffer and feel compassion, but if that mother's child is suffering and she's helpless to take the pain away she feels twice the pain, her child's pain and the crushing unbearable pain of impotence against the wrath of nature or of man, wraths that more often than not choose their victims, young or old, righteous or sinful, charitable or greedy, loved or unseen, without just cause and sweep them away like fallen leaves lost to the wind. *Lord, please take me instead. Please tell me what to do. I'll do anything. Please.*

He seemed to be asleep. I took his hand in mine and put my face close to his. "Baby, can you hear me, baby?"

He groaned.

"Baby?"

Will opened his eyes. The hint of a smile lit up his face. "Mama, what time is it? What are you doing here?"

"I just came by to see you, honeychile."

"Who's that?" Will asked after noticing Mrs. Goldberg.

"Oh, dat' de lady I work for, sugar. I'll introduce you later when de sun come out."

Fear and pain twisted Will's sweet face. "What time is it, Mama?"

"Oh, it's early, baby, very early. But don' you worry none 'bout dat."

Two nurses in scrubs with cloth masks over their faces walked in. "We have to take him now," one of them said flatly. They both seemed exhausted.

Will squeezed my hand and did not want to let go. "Where? Who are they? Where are they taking me, mama?"

"Oh," I said, "dey just taking you across de way to patch a little somethen up. It jus' like de time you stepped on dat nail and we had to carry you over to de hospital. You'll be fine, baby, you close your eyes and let dem take care of you. You'll be fine, hear?"

"All right, Mama," he said calmly. My voice had soothed him. Even though my heart was crushed I felt some relief comforting him.

But then the fear returned. I don't recall ever having seen him scared, ever. I swallowed a sob. I wanted to raise up my fists and scream but I could not set my mind on who or what to scream at. The war? Isaac for dying and leaving me feeling hollow as if all of my insides had been eaten away? The crazy Goldbergs and their dog-boy? The white folks at the hospital? No colored needles or blood? And God? Where was he when all of this happened? I felt like screaming but I did not know who to scream at. I felt helpless.

"I love you, Mama."

I dropped my anger as if it were a rotten fish. "I love you too, baby!" I bent over and kissed his forehead just as the nurses rolled him away. "I loves you, baby! I loves you more den anything in de whol' wide worl'. You remember that!" I noticed he did not have a blanket covering him and shouted, "Wait!" The nurses stopped. "It's cold. Don' you have a blanket for my son?"

"We don't have blankets in the surgical theater," one of the nurses said.

There was a neatly folded blanket at the foot of an empty bed. I ran over and grabbed it then ran back and draped it over Will. "Now you's ready, baby!"

Mrs. Goldberg and I followed Will and the nurses across the street and into the hospital's rear entrance where one nurse looked back and said, "The surgery waiting rooms are next to the elevators. You'll have to wait there."

We found a white waiting room and a colored waiting room. I couldn't sit in the white room and Mrs. Goldberg could not sit in the colored room, so we made up the difference and sat on a bench in the marble elevator lobby. The cold was unforgiving. Each wind gust shook the doors so that the icy air outside blew right in. There might as well have been no doors at all.

An elevator's bell dinged. I looked up with the wild eyes of an animal looking for her lost young. One of the elevator's doors opened smoothly and silently. It was one of the nurses who had carried Will to the surgery. She removed her surgical mask as she walked past us.

"Excuse me," I said.

She was clearly tired and anxious to get home but kind enough to stop. She smiled gently. "What is it?"

"When dey called, when de nurse called, she tried to 'splain but I did not understand what happened to my boy."

"His spleen ruptured."

"How did it rupture? I thought he had de sepsis," I said, rising to my feet.

"We had so many patients that needed transfusions that we got behind, and we had to end up using blood from every source we could find. Some of the blood was contaminated with Hepatitis C. It wasn't just the colored boys, it was with the white boys, too." She removed her surgical cap. Her pretty blonde hair cascaded down onto her delicate shoulders.

"So, what does all that have to do with her son's spleen?" Mrs. Goldberg said.

"Undetected, Hepatitis C sneaks up and damages the liver and causes cirrhosis. When that happens, the veins that supply blood to the spleen swell shut and the spleen fills up and bursts just like a balloon filled with too much water would. That's what happened to the lady's son."

"Is he going to, going to…" I said and started to cry before I could finish.

The nurse's eyes softened, and she lowered her voice. "We don't need our spleens. So if he hasn't lost too much blood and his liver is not too damaged, then he ought to come through just fine."

"When can we speak with the doctor?" Mrs. Goldberg said.

"Honey, I wouldn't hold my breath. They've been working the surgeons around the clock." The nurse looked at me and said, "I'm sorry I can't give you any better news, but the surgeons are terrific here. They're working miracles. If they can't fix the problem, nobody can."

A gust of ice-cold air swept through the lobby when the nurse walked out.

"Come on, let's get the hell out of this icebox," Mrs. Goldberg said then led me into the colored waiting room and took a seat. I looked at her, feeling that she was crossing a line, and that this might in some indirect way affect the outcome of Will's surgery.

"It don' feel right, Mrs. Lucile, a white woman like you sittin' in de colored waiting room."

"It doesn't matter. Who the hell's going to see us at this hour?"

"I don't knows, Mrs. Lucile, but it jus' don't feel right."

"Fine, you stay in here and I'll move to the white waiting room, but I think it's all a bunch of crap!" She realized she was upsetting me, that the time for protest was not then, and she said, "I'm sorry, I'll be across the hall. You call me if you need anything."

"Yes, 'um. Thank you kindly, Mrs. Lucile."

She stood up, softly placed her hand on my shoulder, and said, "I can't imagine how hard this must be for you."

"Oh, it hard, Mrs. Lucile, harder dan anything the good Lord ever choose to test me with."

Mrs. Goldberg leaned over, gave me a hug then kissed my cheek softly. Her tenderness reminded me of how Mrs. Katherine Hutchinson, my former employer back in Galveston, used to treat me so affectionately. We were all mothers. Even though Mrs. Goldberg was running as fast as she could away from being tied down by motherhood, I thought in that moment that there must be a bond deep within us. A bond shared by no one else. That's only natural for any woman who has carried a little soul clinging for its life against the wall of her womb, a being that grows to depend on her cord for its air, its nourishment, and on the warm and fluid protection against the vagaries of an unforgiving world. A fetus haplessly bound to her serenity or distress, who rides on the emotions of her love or her hate, her courage or her fear, the exaltations or disappointments life delivers blindly without prejudgment. Who but a mother could understand the vitality of a new life as it kicks the wall of her womb and presses the print of its little hand or foot on the surface of her belly, and who in the last days of the fetus's development relinquishes it into the world kicking, screaming, gasping for air, and taking its first breath of a new life in which it will someday leave her behind.

I was thinking how cowardly it was for me not to stand up against the foolishness of the separation of a white mother and a Negro mother by the color of their skin, when Mrs. Goldberg walked in and said, "To hell with this. We'll freeze to death in here, for Christ's sakes. I'm going to see if there's a warmer place we can sit." She strutted out of the room and knocked on a pair of doors marked "Administration." There was no answer. "Goddamn them!" She knocked again, still no answer. She charged back into the colored waiting room, fit to be tied. "Listen, if we have to sit and freeze in separate goddamned rooms, why don't we wait in my car. I'll put the heater on. We'll come in and check on your son's progress every twenty minutes or whatever."

"No, that's fine, Mrs. Lucile, you go 'head on. I'd rather stay right chere jus' in case, you know."

"Okay," she said nervously, lighting a cigarette, "but you come out and get me as soon as your boy's out of surgery!"

"Yes, ma'am, I shorely will."

"Are you going to be okay sitting all alone?" I could see that she felt guilty about not having the thickness of skin to sit and be treated like an animal herded into one corral or the other. She was Jewish and the Lord knows there was plenty of hatred for Jews, but she was also white and beautiful and that combination gave her freedom to go anywhere and do anything she pleased so long as she was willing to paint over the origin of her blood.

"Yes, ma'am, you has my word. You go 'head and get your own-self warm. I'll come get you, I will," I said tenderly.

"Here," she said, taking off her coat and draping it over my lap. Even the cold could not defeat the scent of her perfume. I inhaled deeply. "I won't need this." She took another drag from her cigarette. Its tip glowed molten orange. Its warmth was seductive. I had never taken up the smoking habit, but in that moment I felt like asking for a cigarette. When she exhaled, the smoke hung in the murky light like a white cloud hangs frozen on a gray winter's sky. "Okay, I'll be outside. You come get me."

I turned up the collar of my overcoat, pulled the lapels together, leaned back against the cold, unforgiving marble, and stuck my hands under her coat and into my coat's pockets. Then I closed my eyes and remembered.

*"Sugar baby?"*

*"Don't you sugar baby me, 'less you fed de chickens and took dey eggs, Isaac Eaton. I has work to do. I has our baby to take care of."*

*Isaac came up from behind and wrapped me in his big, thick, muscular arms and drew me into him. A hot tremor coursed through my body. The ends of my nerves tingled; my breath quickened with each beat of our hearts.*

*"You can do the wash later. This baby needs some lovin' too, time to time!"*

*"Well," I said as I twisted and squeezed the soapy water out of one of Will's diapers, "you musta not looked at dat Bulova wristwatch you wears, 'cause your time ain' come 'round yet. Now, let me go 'fore I chase you out dis shack with my broom."*

*He bent over and nibbled at the side of my neck.*

A faint smile lit up my face as I sat there on that hospital bench. I felt the same shudder of warmth I had felt back then.

*"Well, you been a pretty good boy dese last few days. Least I have not had to scold and spank you!"*

*"Dat's right, mama baby!" Isaac whispered as his passion grew hard against my backside. "Every good boy deserve a little sugar sometime!" He nibbled along the edge of my earlobe. I shivered.*

*"Lord, I done given you so much sugar only the Lord knows how you still have all yur teeth!"*

*I let my head fall back, and our wet, hungry lips met. We greedily began to consume one another.*

*Then the baby cried. I tried to pull away.*

*"Baby, Will's awright. Let him be for just this once."*

*"No!" I said. "You already had yur turn being my baby, now hit's your son, Will's, turn. Now turn me loose 'fore I get mad and have to send you out to de coop wit de chickens!"*

*"Cock-a-doodle-do!"*

*"I said, turn me loose now!" Isaac loosened his arms enough for me to wriggle free.*

*He smiled. "Let's go see what dat little beautiful boy is into now. I guess I'll have to wait and see if dere any extra sugar layin' around later."*

*"Dat's right. You jus' bes' remember who de one keeps de sugar jar."*

*We walked over to Will's little crib, an old husking box with a mattress made of burlap sacks covered in a hand-me-down pillowcase made of worn ticking.*

*Isaac lifted Will with his big calloused hands and held him up gently. "Now," he said in a high-pitched voice as though he were a little girl, "what is my beautiful baby boy cryin' 'bout? Ain' yur mama been feedin' you 'nough while I been out workin'?"*

*A big, wide grin lit up Will's little face, and he started to chuckle.*

*"Feed enough? He 'bout to suckle on me to where I jus' might have to take him over to de Hutchinsons' wet nurse. Lord no, dat chile cain't be hungry. Maybe he just heard yur voice and want to see his daddy."*

*Isaac held Will high up over his head and pretended to drop him. Will laughed hysterically. I could see that Will trusted his daddy, and I knew that trust is and will always be the most important thing a parent can offer a child. Where there is trust there can be love. If there is no trust, love will shrivel up and die.*

I heard an elevator ding and ran out to the lobby. The elevator dial stopped on the second floor. I walked slowly back to the colored waiting room, sat back down, spread Mrs. Goldberg's coat over my lap, and prayed, *Dear Lord, I ain' ever asked you for nothin' 'cept when Will was inside me and I prayed he would come out fine, and grow up healthy and happy, and he did. Now, I needs you one last time. Please, dear Lord, I'll do anything you ask of me, but please let my baby live. I have lost most of what little I had, but I cannot imagine going on living without him."*

"Ma'am? Ma'am?"

I opened my eyes. I must have fallen asleep. The sun was just coming up over the cemetery across Sepulveda, and the light fog outside glowed with a soft pinkish hue.

"Ma'am?"

I looked up. A tall white doctor in his surgical clothing was standing before me. The light was coming from behind him. His face was in shadow.

I shoved myself back up onto the bench against the icy marble as if he were pointing a gun at me with the intention of shooting me dead.

"Are you the mother of Gunnery Sergeant William C. Eaton?" the doctor said. His voice was tender despite his flat tone.

"Yes, yes, he my chile." I nervously straightened the lapels of my overcoat.

"I'm Dr. Sawyer, ma'am. I am sorry but I have some bad news for you, dear."

"When will my boy be done wit his operation?"

"I'm afraid he did not make it through the surgery, ma'am."

"Well, once't he rest he'll make it de rest of de way."

The doctor sat down beside me, removed his surgical cap, took my hand in his, and said, "What I am trying to say is that your son died on the operating table.

He was just too weak from his abdominal wound. He'd lost too much blood."

"But the needles! I has the needles!"

"Which needles are those?" the doctor said softly.

"Dey de needles Mrs. Lucile, the lady I work for, done brought back from Reno, Nevada, where she went to marry Dr. Buzzbee. Dey needles for Will, for his penicillin," I said without feeling or thought. "For his sepsis. Dey in de car wit Mrs. Lucile."

"I'm afraid they would not have helped, Mrs. Eaton. Hepatitis damaged your son's liver. That caused his spleen to fill up with blood until it burst. Internal bleeding is difficult to catch, especially with a colored patient."

"My Will is dead?"

"He's with the Lord now."

"I didn't get dose needles soon 'nough. If I had, then maybe he would have lived. If I had just been able to get those needles faster."

"Hepatitis caused your son's death, not the bullet wound, ma'am. The needles would not have helped, I am afraid. Is there someone here with you? Someone we may contact for you?"

"No, sir, I means yes, sir, dere is someone. Mrs. Lucile Goldberg, the lady I works for. She out in her car in de parking lot trying to keep warm." I heard the words leave my mouth but I could not feel a connection to them. It seemed someone else had spoken them.

"Do you have family here in Los Angeles?"

"No, Will was all I had on de face of dis earth." I realized I had overlooked mention of Babe and Sis' Pearl, but I did not think it important to correct myself.

"Well, I'm truly sorry for your loss, Mrs. Eaton. I wish we could have done better," the doctor said then stood up.

"I wish you had, too," I said.

"Would you like some hot coffee or tea to warm you up?"

"No, that will be fine." *There isn't a thing that can warm me up.*

"You sit right there and I'll send someone to help you out to the parking lot."

"That will be fine."

"And an administrator from the hospital's Burial Services Department will contact you later today or tomorrow to make funeral arrangements."

"All right then." My heart was beating, I could see, hear, and speak, but I was already dead. I looked down at the doctor's scuffed black shoes. There were specks of blood on them. I assumed Will's blood. One shoe was already turned toward the elevator lobby.

"But if you're feeling too upset, you tell them to call you back in a day or two."

"All right den," I said again. "You can go 'head on to de others."

The doctor softly placed his hand on my shoulder and said, "Try and be strong for your son as he was strong for you." Then he pivoted and walked away. The rubber soles of his shoes squeaked like sad little birds trapped in a cage.

Before long, two white nurses appeared before me. One of them said, "Dr. Sawyer sent us down to assist you, ma'am."

We found Mrs. Goldberg in her car. The engine was purring and ballroom music was playing on the radio, but Mrs. Goldberg was sound asleep. Her head was hanging back over the top of the front seat and her mouth was wide open. Her left eye was slightly open. I waved my hand back and forth outside the door window, but she did not notice it. One of the nurses knocked on the car window with her knuckle. Mrs. Goldberg flinched. The nurse knocked again. Mrs. Goldberg opened her eyes and looked around until she found us standing at the door. She rolled down the window and said, "What the hell did she do? Why are you escorting her?"

The nurse on my right said, "We were sent to help her find you. Her son died on the operating table."

"Oh no!" Mrs. Goldberg shouted. "No! He wasn't supposed to. I got the needles for him. How could he be dead?"

The word "died" and Mrs. Goldberg's near-hysterical reaction shocked me out of my stupor. I realized my Will's spirit had left his body and that his remains were lying alone, stiff and cold somewhere in the hospital. My entire body quaked. Tears poured down my cheeks like floodwaters running over a river dike.

*My Will is dead! My Will is gone! Gone forever!*

"I wants to see my boy 'fore I leave," I said. "I won't leave till I do."

The nurses along with Mrs. Goldberg walked me back into the hospital, where we took the elevator to the basement and the morgue. Will's remains had just been transferred. I walked over to him. Pulled the sheet back from his head and kissed his cold forehead. He looked like he was at peace. "You rest now, sugar, an' you send me back a sign soon when you meet up wit your daddy, hear? You send me a sign, baby."

I nodded at one of the nurses that it was time to go. She gently took the sheet with both hands and pulled it back up and over my Will's face. *I will never hear his voice, see his smile, or feel his arms around me again.*

Mrs. Goldberg walked me back out to her car, and we drove in silence back to her place.

The sun had set. The sky was cold and bleak when I walked back into my porch. I found Will's quilt where I had left it at the foot of my cot. I didn't bother to take off my coat. I sat down at the edge of my cot, picked up the quilt, pressed it into my face, kissed it, and sobbed.

Billy crawled in. Climbed up onto my cot, kissed my cheek, then lay down and rested his head on my lap. I stroked his soft curly hair and cried and cried and cried.

# Chapter 20

## *A Colored Color Guard*

Will's funeral was held on Sunday morning, January 6, nineteen hundred and forty six, at ten a.m. Colored funerals for the veterans did not enjoy the pomp and circumstance the white veterans' funerals did. All the boys in the color guard were colored, which I guess was not all that bad considering it was a *color guard.* The colored color guards were not allowed to carry real rifles; they had them to carry rifles carved from wood like you'd see boys using to play war. The colored color guard bugle was old and dented, but if you'd have closed your eyes while the colored bugler played taps you would have thought it was Louis Armstrong. Both the horse and the run-down cart it was pulling looked like their days were numbered, too. Babe, Sis' Pearl, the Galveston area nurse, Millie Thompson, Will's friend Hawk, Jakie, Mrs. Goldberg, and Billy attended the funeral service. It was comforting to have them with me even though I did not consider them all like family, even Babe. Prior to coming to Los Angeles, I had not seen Babe since I left Uniontown, and that was before he married Sis' Pearl. I used to think that only relations of close blood, only those people I had grown up with, could comfort me, but I have come to learn that the kindness that comes from a perfect stranger is just as sweet as that which comes from a body you've known your entire life.

As we stood in a line alongside the fresh-dug grave, I looked at the mound of dirt piled on the far side. That mound felt like it was meant to cover my throbbing heart and keep silent the screams for Will that I could hear deep inside. Once Will's coffin started descending into his grave my legs gave out. Babe, Jakie, and Hawk carried me to a folding chair and sat me in it. I broke down and sobbed and sobbed and sobbed. In the middle of it all, Billy walked over and took my hand in his. That just made me cry harder.

One of the colored color guards, a marine, picked up a smallish box the size work boots would come in from the coffin's wagon, and with his perfectly clean white gloves placed it in my lap. The box was wrapped neatly in plain brown paper and tied off with twine. "Madam, on behalf of the President of the United States, the citizens of the United States, and the United States Marine Corps," the young marine said, "I extend my condolences and thank you for the dearest of sacrifices you, your family, and your son have made for the future of our nation and our freedom." Next, he passed the fresh new flag that had draped Will's coffin. I was able to take it and place it in my lap. It was folded thirteen times into a triangle like a big honey bun. Billy stroked it. Then the colored color guard stepped back and raised their wooden rifles three times to fire a mock three-gun salute. As the bugler blew taps I looked at the little saplings that had been planted around the cemetery and wondered what the world would be like when they grew tall, and I remembered Will's words: "Mama, this is our country, too." I tried to feel some hope that things would turn out that way for all the sacrifices that were made, I really did. I just hoped the little trees would receive enough water and sunshine to grow tall and strong, and I cried.

Mrs. Goldberg insisted that everyone go back to her place to "sit shiva," a Hebrew word meaning to gather to mourn the dead. She stopped at Cantor's Delicatessen on Brooklyn Avenue on the way home from the cemetery and bought us a platter of cold meats, potato salad, coleslaw, pickles, cheese, sour tomatoes, and several different varieties of bread and rolls. I told her I would repay her, but she said she would not have any part of taking money from me. Babe and Sis' Pearl carried me back. Billy drove with Jakie, and Will's friend Hawk came out in his car. Nurse Thompson wanted to attend but had to report for a shift in a white ward. She gave me a big hug, a kiss on the cheek, and warned me that if I did not take care of myself she would come find me and give it to me good. She also gave me her telephone number and address. She said she had a place down in Venice near the beach, and that I could call her anytime.

Everyone was very kind. They would not let me lift a finger. I sat in the occasional chair across from the sofa in the living room, and they waited on me. Sis' Pearl made me a cup of tea; I didn't feel like anything strong like coffee. Mrs. Goldberg fixed me a plate with turkey, potato salad, a slice of rye bread, and a pickle, but I had no appetite. She took the plate away and insisted I have a sip of her Courvoisier and I did. It gave me a good jolt, but it did not give me any kind of appetite. Just remembering to breathe seemed about all I could do that day.

When they all left I asked Mrs. Goldberg if she'd look into Will's personal items with me.   She felt honored I'd asked her to do so then she retrieved the box from my cot. We sat side-by-side on the sofa like two sisters. She was to my left with her legs curled under her. Billy crawled up on the sofa and lay down on my right, and beyond him the lights on the little Christmas tree still standing in the corner were twinkling.

"We're going to have to take dat tree down 'fore it explode in flame," I said.

"In all the *tummil* I completely forgot about it," Mrs. Goldberg said. "Do you  need help with the string?"

"No, ma'am, I keep one pinky nail razor sharp jus' for dis purpose."

"You do? Let me see it." I held my pinky out and twisted my hand so that she could see the inside of my nail. She touched it with the tip of her finger and pulled her finger away as if she'd touched a sharp knife. "Jesus Christ, you could kill someone with that! How do you do that?"

"Oh, my mama taught me how, it's a family secret," I said as I sliced the twine and removed it from the box. Mrs. Goldberg and Billy watched intently as I carefully pulled away the folded leafs of wrapping paper covering each side of the box. Once I had them loose I slid the box out, carefully folded the paper, then lifted the lid slowly, peeked inside, and started to cry.

"What is it?" Mrs. Goldberg said.

"Dose are my baby's shoes," I said with hitches in my voice.

"That's some baby," Mrs. Goldberg said. "Just kidding."

I chuckled. "Dat's all right, Mrs. Lucile, I knows you don't mean nothin' by it." I started to cry again.

Mrs. Goldberg teared up, too. "What is it? Why are you crying?"

"It's, it's just that he will never walk in dem again!" I said before breaking down completely as I did at my Will's grave. Mrs. Goldberg was very uncomfortable with the expression of deep feelings. She leaned forward, removed a cigarette from the holder on the coffee table, lit it while I dabbed my tears with one of her dainty silk handkerchiefs, took a puff, and shook her shoulders like she was shaking a bug off. Then she smoked as Billy lay in his place silently while I cried.

"I try to never let myself get too low, you know," Mrs. Goldberg said after a while. "I try to stay high, high on life! On the sunny side of the street with a smile, you know."

I looked at her with stern, unbelieving, tear-filled eyes and said, "I just lost my onliest child. I don' know what else to do but cry."

"I don't know what I'm talking about. Things were so crazy after my father died we never had a chance to feel. We were always too busy trying to find a way to get the hell out of here. There was no time or place for feelings."

I removed three neatly folded regulation T-shirts and three pairs of clean white jockey shorts from the box. I held a T-shirt close up to my face to see if I could detect any of Will's scent, but it had recently been washed.

"Is that...can you smell him?" Mrs. Goldberg asked.

"I wish I could, Mrs. Lucile, but they done washed all these things in Ivory Snow. There ain' nary a hint of him," I said sadly. "I wish there was."

Billy started pawing the T-shirts. I had a mind to stop him but decided that so long as he didn't chew them up or tear them it did not matter, I could always wash and press them again. Besides, I had thought several times that Will would have been a good influence on Billy, and I was happy to let the boy play with my son's shirts.

The next item was a large manila envelope closed by a hasp. I took it out, felt its heft, then opened the hasp and reached inside for its contents. There was a three-by-five-inch photo of Will that must have been taken at his graduation. He was wearing his dress blues and standing so tall and proud and with such a big smile. I gasped.

"Let me see it," Mrs. Goldberg said. "Oh, he's handsome, very handsome!"

"He the spittin' image of his daddy," I said.

"I'll bet the girls came buzzin' around him like bees on a hive. I could go for him!" Mrs. Goldberg said before taking a nervous puff of her cigarette and jerking her head to the left to exhale in order not to blow it in my face. Billy did not take to that.

"*GRRRRRRRRRRRRR.*"

"Matter of factually," I said, "Will was quite shy growin' up. He had him a few school friends he liked to play wit, all boys, and dere was just one girl and one only. Once't he set eyes on her he couldn't even look at anyone else. Lord, he fell head over heels in love."

"That was Ella."

"That's right, you remember."

"You told me about the letter Will sent to her," Mrs. Goldberg said with a nervous smile, another shake of her head, and another puff from her cigarette. "Something about his wanting her to wait for him."

"Dat's right, Mrs. Lucile, dat jus' what he wanted, bless his heart. Jus' exactly what he wanted, um-hum."

The next item in the envelope was a photograph of Will with his boot camp company and drill instructor. In this one the boys were in fatigues and looked like scared children. Will looked so skinny, I had to laugh. "I never seen dat chile so skinny. It's a wonder he could keep his pants up!"

The last item was an envelope of a rose hue. I held it in front of me and stared at the writing on the front.

"Could that be the letter Will was waiting for?"

"I don't know, Mrs. Lucile," I said. "I'm not sure."

Mrs. Goldberg delicately crushed the tip of her half-smoked cigarette into the ashtray and said, "Let me see it." She read the return address.

"Miss Ella Dupre
Alpha Kappa Alpha Sorority

Howard University
Washington, D.C."

"Alpha Kappa Alpha, that's *Greek* to me!" Mrs. Goldberg said with a cynical laugh. "I always thought I'd go to college. But then the war happened, I met Leo and the other war broke out, and now I have a kid on top of everything!"

"You're still young, you still can."

"Listen, my boat already sailed, sweetheart. I got a kid now. What am I going to do, go to college? Join a sorority? Become a Hollywood star? I'm a cocktail waitress, that's all I'll ever be."

"You don' have to beat yourself up over it," I said.

"Do you want me to open it?"

"You might as well," I said.

"Let me get a drink first." She passed the envelope back to me. I slowly passed it under my nose. It carried a soft, smooth floral scent, fresh but not too sensuous. I gave the envelope back to Mrs. Goldberg when she came back and sat down. She swirled her glass and made the ice spin in a small whirlpool of chilled Crown Royal, took a sip, then opened the envelope. "Are your ready?"

"Ready as I can be, Mrs. Lucile."

The photograph of a group of girls gathered in a ballroom fell out of the folded letter. Tall windows with sunlight spilling through open drapes were in the background. The girls, all dressed in trim black dresses with fresh corsages pinned onto the left lapels of their dresses, were posed in a semicircle for the photograph.

"Are all of these girls colored?" Mrs. Goldberg asked. "They're so light."

"Yes, 'um, dey sure 'nough are. You won't find too many real dark-skinned women like me going dat way. Ella was light skinned, too. Let me see the photo. Dere she is." I pointed with my finger at a girl near the right side of the semicircle.

"Oh, she's a natural beauty! I bet she doesn't have a speck of make-up on!"

"I s'pose not."

"Wait a second," Mrs. Goldberg said, holding the photo under the floor lamp to her left. "Do you know who the white lady in the center of the photo is?" She held the photo so that I could study it. Billy edged up for a look, too.

"Why, she look just like Mrs. Eleanor Roosevelt, de president's first lady."

"Holy Christ! You're right!"

"She de one made her husband sign de order to make de Marines enlist Negroes. It strange Ella is posin' for a picture with her now. Read me dat letter, Mrs. Lucile. I has to hear it sometime."

"Dear Willie,"

I laughed.

Mrs. Goldberg stopped and looked at me. "What's the matter?"

"Oh, she callin' Will 'Willie.' That's what they called him at his school, 'Willie.' And he'd come home cryin' that he didn't want nobody callin' him Willie, and I would say, 'Now, you lookie here, de more you say you don' like Willie de more dey goin' to call it. So jus' pretend you don' even notice it. By and by dey goin' to let up, you'll see.' And his friends did, except for Ella. Lordy, she knew it bothered him and she like to tease him with it till he got hot under his collar. Then she would laugh and run away. You knows how kids is."

"Yeah, I know," she said, looking over at Billy. He looked back and let her know he did not like her sarcasm.

"GURRRRRRRRRR-RUFF!"

Mrs. Goldberg shook her head violently as if she thought she could empty her head of Billy's troubles then took another sip of her drink. "Do I ever know how kids can be!"

"Read what Ella wrote, Mrs. Lucile."

> *January 3, 1946*
> *Washington, D.C.*
> *Dear Willie,*
>
> *I hope that you had a nice Christmas and that you will have a happy New Year.*
>
> *I apologize for having taken so long to answer your letters. As you can see by the picture, I am away at college in Washington, D.C., studying to become a nurse.*

*I was happy to hear that you had the opportunity to stop over in Hawaii on your way back from the war. From what I've read it is truly a paradise.*

*Will, I truly appreciate the fond feelings you hold for me. I feel the same way toward you. You will always remain a true friend, always. I hope we will always remain in contact. I want to hear all about what you did in the war and what you'll do after returning to Galveston or wherever you decide you'd like to live. You're bright and kind, and you have a wonderful sense of humor. I'm sure you'll achieve all that you set out to obtain.*

*I won't be moving back to Galveston, Will. And, in fact, I have met a young man up here at college and we are engaged to be married. I know this will be troubling news considering the beautiful letter you sent to me, but in matters of the heart I believe it is best to be direct and above all honest.'*

"Amen to that, sister!" Mrs. Goldberg said then continued reading.

*'Afternoon classes will start soon, so I'd better stop for now and get myself ready. The professors here do not like students who dishonor them by showing up late for lectures.*

*Please write and let me know how you're doing, Will. And please let me know how your mama is doing. She is a fine woman, Will. You are very lucky to have someone like her to return home to.*

*Goodbye for now.*

*Fondly,*

*Ella'*

Mrs. Goldberg passed the letter to me and said, "I'm sorry. Do you want to hold onto it?"

I folded the letter carefully, as if it were written on precious, irreplaceable material, and slipped it back into its envelope and set it down next to Will's other things. "My Will would want hit dis way, wanted Ella happy, you know. Dat's how strong he loved."

Mrs. Goldberg said, "Will would have been torching for her the rest of his life, for Christ's sakes. She couldn't have waited until she knew he was out of the hospital to write this?"

"It's jus' as well," I said, straightening the pile of Will's things and thinking about how I would keep them, where I would keep them, and if I would keep them at all. "Long as she happy. I means, everythen' happen for a reason, I guess. I jus' wish I knew what de reasons were. Isn't dat right, Billy?" I said, stroking his hair.

"*RUFF-RUFF-RUFF!*"

"I reckon dat's de best answer I ever will hear."

"*RUFF-RUFF-RUFF!*"

"Now, I has to find me a way back to Galveston."

"Why?" Mrs. Goldberg asked.

"Dey ain' nothin' here for me now, Mrs. Lucile."

"'Nothin'? What about me? Billy? Jakie? We need you. You can't just pack up and leave. Billy won't let you!"

"*RUFF-RUFF-RUFF!*"

I looked into Mrs. Goldberg's eyes. They shone with love, tenderness, and need. Billy took hold of my hand and held it tightly. I knew I wasn't going anywhere soon.

# Chapter 21

## *Will's Sign*

Losing Will seemed to be too big a burden to bear. When you lose one you loved so dearly, a great void opens inside you. It is a wound that never completely heals. You keep looking for them throughout your days even though you know they only exist in your memory. When I did the dishes for Mrs. Goldberg I'd feel Will's boyish presence yanking on the hem of my skirt, picking at a bowl of berries he was supposed to have left alone, or asking for just one more buttered biscuit. In these moments I would speak to him: "Chile, you goin' tah eat yur daddy and mama right out dis' shack and den eat de shack on yur way out! How big do you wants to get?" If Mrs. Goldberg or Jakie heard me they did not speak a word about it. I talked with Isaac too. I did not want to forget either one of them, ever. The funny thing is that sometimes I'd slip and call Jakie Isaac, but he didn't seem to mind; Jakie just like being called for anything at all. The ache from the loss did not get better or worse; it remained like the sensation someone feels with a ghost limb. When a limb is lost they know it is no longer part of their body but they want to scratch it when it itches or rub it when it's sore nonetheless.

When I'd do my pressing the iron felt heavy as a deep-sea anchor hanging from the bow of a big cargo ship out in Galveston Bay. I had lost Isaac, then Will, our little shares shack in Galveston, all our friends in Galveston, my friendship with Mrs. Hutchinson, and the job I loved.

I felt that my place in the world had vanished, as if my life had been nothing more than a pencil sketch and the artist, God almighty, had decided to erase everything in that picture except me. I was lost like an odd piece of a big puzzle and there was no place left to fit in. I tried to find a reason to go on. I attended church with Babe and Sis' Pearl, joined the Sisterhood. I prayed, yet with each and every word I spoke I felt that I was praying more out of anger for the unjust way life and the Lord had treated me. I was caught between life and death, alone, like someone drowning without strength to claw back to the surface, but still conscious and still aware of a deep voice within that screams, "I want to live, dear Lord, please, help me to find a reason to live!"

I read my Bible every night, and every night no matter where I started I turned back to one phrase in Isaiah for its comfort and strength: "Fear not, for I am with you, be not dismayed, for I am your God; I will strengthen you; I will help you; I will uphold you with My victorious right hand." Maybe the passage comforted me most because my husband, Isaac's, weathered and notched hands were thick, strong, and capable. I felt as though Isaac was Isaiah reaching down and pulling me up out of the stifling deep of my despair.

I had always believed in Providence. Believed that everything happens for a reason. But I could find no good reason for losing my only son to the evil of war. It happens with each generation, because each generation forgets what happened with the last. That's just the way life is. Yes, I believed the good Lord does giveth and does taketh away, but I also believed there was and is plenty we can do in life between all the giving and the taking. I studied what Adam learned after following Eve out of Paradise. He had to face reality, take the good with the bad, choose right from wrong, and fill his aching heart with life and love and hope even though he had learned that his days were numbered. We are all cursed by that same fate. When I realized that, I started crawling back up into life.

I remembered one fine afternoon of an Indian summer when Will was just ten. Our dog, Blackie, had been out lying in the shade on the porch waiting for Will to walk up the road from school. Blackie started barking and howlin' like the world was going to an end. I ran to the door with my heart thumping, thinking it was Klu Kluxers coming, but instead I saw Will walking through our gate with three juicy sun-ripe peaches balanced on his crossed arms. They set my mouth to watering. "Blackie, you 'bout scared de life out me, shush up! And, chile, where did you come up wit de money to buy such fancy peaches? I knows you don' have an oil well!"

"I didn't buy them, Mama, I picked them off one of the Habershams' trees."

"How you 'spect to pay for 'um?"

"They were hanging from a branch on the roadside of the Habersham fence, Mama. Hanging right over the road and about to fall for being so ripe. All I had to do was reach up and take them. It's not like I stole 'um."

"Well, what if one of dem Habersham childrun left them a bicycle outside dey fence, would you take that up and ride dat bicycle home wit de peaches?"

"No, Mama, that's a bicycle. It belongs to them."

"De fruit from der trees belong de same way, sugar."

Will said, "I thought we could have something sweet for dinner, Mama. They are ripe and ready."

"I cain see, but no we cain't. Dey don't belong to us 'less we pay or 'less de Habershams see fit to make us a charity case and give 'um to us. You don' want to be no charity case, do you?"

"No, Mama."

"Dat's right, sugar, we ain' dat type."

"Then what should I do, Mama, go stick 'um back on the tree or throw them back over the Habershams' fence?"

"Let me think, sugar. I'll tell you what, go over to my cookie jar and take you a nickel. Den you take hit and de peaches back over to de Habershams'. And when you get dere, you tells Mr. or Mrs. Habersham that you done already picked dey peaches and wants to pay for 'um."

"But—"

"Dey ain' no ifs, buts, or maybes 'bout hit, chile. You has to choose right from wrong, good from evil. Otherwise,"—I lowered my voice to emphasize the seriousness of the consequences—"you know what dey do to a boy like you dat steal peaches?"

"No."

"De county sheriff will pick you up and de judge will shore 'nough send you to de county jail where dey has real small cells special for chil-drun. Now, I knows you don' wants to go to dat place. Or, maybe you does because when yur daddy find out he will not be happy wit you. You don' want dat either do you?"

"No, Mama, I don't."

"Dat's right. 'Cause once de sheriff get his hands on you he gives you a big ol' sledgehammer dat's 'bout tall as you is standin' right here. Den, dey hooks you to a chain wit de other boys like fresh-caught cat-fish on a stringer and dey dtakes you out under de blazin' sun where you will chop big rocks into little rocks all de day long, so hep me God! Does you understands me?"

"No, Mama, I mean yes, Mama, I do!"

"Den you has to make up yur mind you goin' to choose for the good every wakin' breath of yur life, just like ol' Adam."

"Yes, Mama."

"Ah right den. You carry dem peaches wit dat nickel back over to de Habershams' place and you do what I say. Den yur account for today will be settled wit de Lord, hear?"

"Yes."

"And don' never go to sleep 'less yur account is current wit de Lord and wit dems dat you loves."

Will looked as dejected as if he had lost his best friend. He was in-nocently trying to do something nice for us, after all. The Habershams were good country folk. I had taken in some of their tubs. But I knew how severe Will would have been treated had he taken those peaches or even the pits of peaches from some of the other white folk in our area. Will and Blackie carried the peaches back. He came back with a smile full of sunshine and a burlap sack full of six peaches. "Mama, look what I got!"

"My oh my, you has a bag full of peaches now. A nickel go de long way for de honest man."

"Mr. Habersham wouldn't take my nickel, Mama. He said, 'Your mama and papa are raising you up right, son. I'll tell you what. You keep your nickel. I'm goin' to reward you with six of my finest Tropic

Beauties for your show of honesty. How would you like that, Will Eaton?'"

"Ain't everybody good like Mr. Habersham, sweetheart, but it don't matter one way or t'other if dey is. You has to make up yur mind yur goin' to be good and honest no matter what. Hear?"

"Yes, Mama."

"And you let de good Lord above take care of de rest because de rest is what dey call Providence."

"What is Providence, Mama?"

"Some folk call hit luck, some call hit fate. But de way I see hit, Providence is de Lord's pay for de work you do for de Lord. If you does good you get paid. But if you does bad, why, not only do the Lord not pay you, he jus' might take somethin' away. Hit dat little extra we don' know 'bout 'cause hit is in de Lord's hands."

"How much does the Lord pay for doing good, Mama?"

"Dey ain' no fix'd price, sugar. You jus' keep doin' good den one day de Lord's check will come sure as dat man comes to collect on de twenty-five dollar 'surance policy we bought for Daddy."

"What's a 'surance policy, Mama?"

"Dat's 'nough questions now. If'n you ask me one more my head will surely 'splode. Now don' you has some chickens to feed?"

I recalled other snips of conversations, memories of little moments Will, Isaac, and I had together, almost every hour of every day as I made my rounds at Mrs. Goldberg's. They were always with me. When it occurred to me that I had not done so I would search my memory for something so that I would not forget the sound of their voices or the brightness of their smiles. I'd remember all the little details, like the things Will kept hidden away atop the pallets under his mattress. Lord, that child would keep frogs, little birds with broken wings, worms for fishing, old elixir bottles, rusted nails, string, lightning bugs in a jar, just anything he found. Sometimes in the middle of the night Isaac and I would be awakened by a frog croaking, and Isaac would say, "How dat frog get in dis place?" And as we lay in the dark I would smile and point over to Will's bed where Will would be sleeping like an innocent little angel while that creature sung a frog opera.

Mrs. Goldberg, reeling from her disappointing experience with Dr. Buzzbee, invited Mr. Goldberg over for Valentine's Day. He arrived with a dozen roses and a fifth of Canadian Club. He had been visiting her at The Hi Hat. The missus walked on eggs in order not to say the wrong thing and send Mr. Goldberg blasting off to another planet. She reminded me of an old man that used to live on the other side of a cow pasture. He had to cross that pasture every time he wanted to get to the main road and town. He had to walk two steps left, then one step forward, then three steps to the right to avoid stepping in one of the cow pies. It took him so long to get across that field it was a wonder he didn't just give up and stay put. It was clear Mrs. Goldberg stayed with idle chitchat. If Mr. Goldberg said the sky was green, she'd say it was a nice shade of that color, too. She hated her life and would have done anything to climb up out of it, even going back to living with the devil, and Leo Goldberg was certainly the devil or the devil's kin. He had a frightened and suspicious mind and a hair-trigger temper to go with it. You never knew when he would start thinking you were trying to get something by him then attack you with all the fury his angry soul could muster. Something in that man's past must have made him feel the world was his enemy, that everyone, even those who loved him, were scheming to get something from him. If you tried to do something nice for him he'd get suspicious and say, "Whadya do that for?" I would have had a better chance of getting by with living in a box filled with scorpions than living with that man. But that is exactly what I came to realize Mrs. Goldberg had in mind.

Before he arrived Mrs. Goldberg painted her lips, powdered her nose, strapped on a push-up bra the Army Air force could have used to protect their airplanes from enemy fire, and stuffed herself into a girdle so tight it could have been used for Sunday sausage—I know this because I had to stand on a chair and hold the girdle while she jumped up and down to squeeze into it. Then she dabbed on her fiery perfume, slipped into a red silk kimono, and sent me and Billy out into the wilderness so that she could go to work on Mr. Goldberg.

On this particular day I decided we'd go to a nearby park. I put Billy in his Radio Flyer and like a beast of burden pulled him up a steep little hill to a small park at First and Chicago. As we made our way I kept looking back hoping that it was Will in the wagon, that I had Will back to hold in my arms and kiss just one more time. Then a scream would coil up inside me because I knew I would never hold him or kiss him again. When a child dies they take a big piece, if not the biggest piece, of your heart with them into the grave.

I parked the wagon next to the sandbox as usual, and Billy crawled out and starting digging in the sand as if there was buried treasure underneath it.

"Do you wants to go on de swing, chile?" He paid no attention. Then it struck me that he was digging on account of how his mother was manipulating his father. Bless his little heart, he recognized how his desperate mother was scheming and would say and do anything to lure any man in and was now doing the same thing to lure his daddy back. Billy was a child. He must have felt helpless to change the immutable fact that even if his daddy did come back, his mama and daddy would soon be screaming and hollering so loud that he'd want to bark and howl so that he'd be heard all through the planets, stars, and galaxies. I know because the last time they fought I felt like doing the very same thing. I said, "All right den," and took a seat on a nearby bench, and I am ashamed to say I nodded off.

A little chirp of a bark awoke me. I bolted up and looked at the sandbox. My heart was racing. I thought Billy had run off, but he was right there. A little black mutt was prancing at the concrete curb surrounding the sand. Then he chirped again, stopped, tilted his head, perked his ears up and out, and held them so that they looked like little bird's wings. He had scraggily whiskers around his chin and a small patch of white fuzz the size of a cup saucer on his chest. His hair was bristly all around except on his hind legs; they looked shaved. He might as well have been a Brillo pad with a head, ears, four legs, and a tail stuck into it like a Mr. Potato Head. Billy stopped, looked at the dog, and the dog wagged its tail with some fury. Billy growled.

"GRRRRRRRRRRRRRRRRR!"

The dog slowed its wag to the speed of a pendulum on a clock. For a moment I thought Billy would attack him, so I stood up and took a couple of steps forward and waited to dive in. Suddenly, the dog started wagging its tail so wildly that the little thing's whole body waggled with it. Still, I didn't feel right about a strange dog being so close to Billy. "You bes' get 'way from de chile!" I shouted. "We don' want no Brillo pad dogs givin' us de fleas or rabies. Now shooo!"

That dog was sprightly. It jumped over the curb and into the sand-box like a jaybird and started digging right alongside Billy. Before too long they reached hard pack and both started barking. The little dog's bark made a high-pitched sound that quickly became unbearable. After several moments it dawned on me, the dog looked like a smaller ver-sion of Will's dog Blackie! Now, I wanted to pet it. I started to cry, I dropped to one knee on the lawn, and I said, "Come here, baby, come give me a lick. Come on! I won' hurt you." But just like Will's Blackie he would not come. He stood his small ground and barked at me. I ached to hold him. I felt I had found a piece of Will. "Come on, sugar, I knows who sent you. Come say a proper hello! Come on now." He still wouldn't budge. I opened my purse and offered an Arrowroot cookie. He must have been hungry because a bullet couldn't have moved as fast as he did, bless his little heart. He gobbled down one cookie, then another, then another, while keeping one paw on my knee just exactly like Will's Blackie did, exactly. Tears of joy tumbled down my cheeks. After several more cookies the dog placed his other paw on my other leg, stood up on his hind legs, and licked the tears from my cheeks. And, his licking made me cry all the harder. It was as if Will was tasting the bitter distillate of my sadness. When Billy crawled to my feet I had to feed the two of them. I have no doubt that if Billy had a tail it would have been wagging just as wildly as that dog's was.

When I ran out of cookies I set Billy in the Radio Flyer, looked at the dog, and with a tone of mock anger said, "Now you scoot and go home. Let yur mama and daddy feed you. We'll see you de next time we comes to de park." Quicker than I could blink he jumped into the Radio Flyer. And before I could reach over to remove him, Billy had wrapped his arms around the animal as if it were Billy's long-lost broth-er. "Well, I 'spect we have a Billy and a Blackie now, 'cept your mama goin' t' throw the three of us out de house shore as I'm standin' here!"

As I pulled them away, Billy spoke. It was nothing short of a mir-acle. I stopped and turned back toward the wagon and I listened for

Billy to speak again. When Billy noticed that I was waiting to hear what he had to say he spoke again, and I knew that Will's sign had arrived.

"Blackie!"

I filled my lungs with air and exhaled, feeling alive for the first time since Will had passed.

# Chapter 22

## *The Face of Evil*

May 1946

Mr. and Mrs. Goldberg worked at mending their fence post by post, rail by rail, and nail by nail through the winter of nineteen hundred and forty-six. They had a big surprise for me when Babe and Sis' Pearl carried me back to work after church on Easter Sunday. I walked back into the house and, lo and behold, Mr. Goldberg had moved back and was sitting on the couch reading the newspaper and smoking a Camel cigarette like the king of the castle. The Goldbergs tried their best to get on with one another, but living in that small place—and I don't mean to infer that a space big as the whole universe would have sufficed—was no good from the get-go. They were like two feisty thunderclouds captured, capped, and sealed in a lightning jar. The likelihood of thunder, lightning, and worse was imminent. It would have been a good idea had they added a swinging two-way gate to their mended fence, and those two surely did need a fence.

Helping them with some marital advice for that poor child's sake did cross my mind. I spent the weeks after Will's funeral in a blind fog. I felt as though the sun, the moon, and the stars had vanished and the oceans had filled to overflowing with my tears. I felt one scream for Will after another climbing up in me like a wild beast trying to climb out of a deep pit. It was that horrible kind of helpless feeling that makes you want to tear at your own skin. No matter what you do it does not go away. The only two living things I had any mind to look after were Billy and Blackie.

By late May the pain broke like a fever, but I continued feeling weak and numb. Walking from one end of the kitchen to the other felt like wading waist deep through swamp mud and never knowing if I would sink to the bottom with my next step. I felt like I was dying piece by piece and the biggest piece of me was already dead.

There were certain things I avoided doing because when Will was a boy he would usually be at my heels when I did them. If some of Billy's things needed mending I ordinarily would have enjoyed the sewing. That's what I'd done for the Hutchinson twins, Lily and Porter T. Now, I could not pick up a pair of Billy's dungarees to so much as sew a patch on a knee. If I did I felt they were Will's dungarees and could not make my fingers move. I felt as if there was no need to sew ever again. Will was dead. I could not sing most of the songs I used to love singing. Will and I used to sing "This Little Light of Mine" all the time. I could not bear to even let it play out in my thoughts after losing him.

If there was one good thing that happened through those months, it was how Billy's behavior was changing for the good. That started the day the little mutt we found at the park came home with us. In fact, Billy's behavior improved so much that Mrs. Goldberg had me take the cage out of the kitchen and put it in the shed. I think she might have done that anyway because she was close to patching things up with Mr. Goldberg. But, nonetheless, I was happy to see it go. Every time I had passed it I had the horrible thought of what if it was Will who had had the terrible mother, and it was him she kept locked in a cage. Each time I had that vision my fingers clinched into fists.

On one afternoon, Mrs. Goldberg decided to take me and Billy over to the Catholic nursery school to meet the principal. She, the principal, was a big mean-looking Dominican Sister with jailer's eyes who looked like she shaved with Burma-Shave. I imagined Sis' Pearl would have looked like that had Pearl become a Sister. The school was at Santa Teresita Catholic Church. As we drove over, Mrs. Goldberg confided that she had carried me along because I was colored and that if they saw a colored lady coming in they wouldn't even think to ask about her, Mrs. Goldberg's, religion. I will say this, Mrs. Goldberg had proved over and over again that when she wanted something nothing on the face of the earth would get in the way. It was just too bad she had her mind set on all the wrong things for the right reasons. All told, except for Billy's growling at the Dominican Sister who was wearing a black habit with a white collar and a great big white nun's hat that looked like the hull of a sailing ship, everything went quite well. I understood how she spooked poor little Billy. The Sister did not so much as grin during our entire visit. She was not a pleasant woman.

On the drive back home I asked Mrs. Goldberg why she had chosen a Catholic school over a Jewish or even a public school. She said, "Too Jewish is no goddamned good. Look where it got us in Europe. They slaughtered us like lambs, for Christ's sake. No, I want Italian, I want people to think Billy's Italian. Leo's got that olive skin too, don't you think?" I started to laugh.

Mrs. Goldberg slowed down, looked at me, and said, "What's so funny?"

"Oh, it nothin', Mrs. Lucile. Hit jus' caught me by surprise you wantin' to be Eye-talian. We had us some Eye-talian down in Galveston." As I spoke I remembered hearing them fighting like they would kill one another every time I walked by their little market. If they were outside I'd see them nose to nose, screaming and flailing their arms like they would tear each other limb from limb, but they never did injure one another. I said, "Come to think on hit, Mrs. Lucile, I reckon y'all could fit right in."

"Really?"

"Oh yes, ma'am, I wouldn't lie 'bout dat. Fit right in. Tight like gloves."

"That's funny," Mrs. Goldberg said as she looked into the rearview mirror and adjusted a lock of red hair. "Right after I had my nose job everyone I met thought I had that European look, you know, like Katharine Hepburn in *Break of Hearts*. Did you see it?"

"No, ma'am, Mrs. Lucile, we did not see us too many movies down in Galveston. And when we did go we had to sit up on de balcony in de color section. Problem was we could barely make out de screen for de cigarette smoke coming up from de white seats."

Billy did surely love having his daddy back in the place. Before his daddy moved in, Mrs. Goldberg did not let the child play outside for fear he would bite someone, hurt himself, or get sick, all of which would have caused extra aggravation for her. If Billy was outside I had to be outside with him, which actually was not that bad with all the birds up on the telephone lines singing like they were in a big-city opera. Now, Mr. Goldberg, he was just the opposite. Anything his "kid," Billy, wanted to do was fine with him. Lord, he even brought a razor-sharp fishing knife with a leather sheath home for the child. I think the knife might have been part of a plan to kill off Mrs. Goldberg in the event things did not play out as he had planned. I would not have put it past that man. One afternoon Mr. Goldberg just carried it home, gave it to me, and said, "Here, go out front and play with the kid." Mr. Goldberg would do that, buy something then pay it off on someone like me with the instruction to take the child out and play with it. The truth of it was he did not want to be bothered. We didn't actually play. I pretended to teach Billy the safest use for the knife I could find in Mrs. Goldberg's front yard and that was cutting dead flowers in the little garden Jakie kept along the front edge of the porch.

Just when I thought Mr. and Mrs. Goldberg had turned a corner and were going to make it, they had them a battle royal over where to move. But before I describe it, I want to mention that soon as Mr. Goldberg moved in Jakie became a persona non grata. He stopped coming in for his morning coffee and rarely showed up for supper. He shied away from Mr. Goldberg. Yet it seemed every time I took a tub of wet laundry and wooden clothespins out to hang on the clothesline, or carried a bundle of trash for the incinerator, Jakie would mysteriously appear like a sprite with that cigarette on his ear and that shy smile lighting his face. I remember one afternoon in particular he did just that.

"Hey, how ya' been?" Jakie said as he stepped into the back yard while I was hanging laundry.

"I'm just tryin to be, Mr. Jakie. Takin' hit one step at a time, one step at a time."

"Yeah, I know how it can be. I lost a lot of friends on Luzon, but, I mean, that ain't nothin' like losin' a kid, I mean a child."

"Well, dat's awright, Mr. Jakie, I knows what you means. Some days it seem hard and de others it seem even harder. Hit don' let up. But I'm gettin' through somehow. I want ta say wit de Lord's help, but de Lord's de one got me into dis mess in de first place."

"Yeah, he does that sometimes," Jakie said with a cackle. He pulled the cigarette from his ear and rolled it between his yellow thumb and yellow fingers as he would do when he became nervous, and he said, "Listen, there's been something I been meaning to ask you."

"What is dat, Mr. Jakie?" I said as I hung the edge of a wet sheet on the line and clipped it with a clothespin.

Mr. Jakie took the other end of the sheet down the line and said, "Well, first of all, I wonder if you could call me just Jakie, you know, just Jakie. The mister makes me feel awkward, like I was some kind of officer or somethin', which I wasn't. "

"Dat will be fine," I said, pinning the other end of the sheet. The fresh scent of Ivory Snow gave me a lighthearted feeling. I picked up a pillowcase with two clothespins and stood up on my tiptoes to hang it on the line. I lost my balance, though. Jakie came right up behind me, placed his hands on my shoulders, and steadied me then slid his hands down my arms and together we pinned the pillowcase on the line. When he released me I could feel a quake of heat spread throughout my entire body. The only man I had ever felt that with was Isaac. I was terrified. I tried to push the feeling away, deny it. I thought, *No!* But the harder I tried the harder my body pulled me deep into a dark chasm full of *Yes!* We were both flustered.

"Listen," Jakie said as he tried to set the burning cigarette on his lips with a quivering hand. "What it is that I want to ask you is if you'd like to go out for dinner and take in a show with Louis Armstrong and Ella Fitzgerald."

"Den dey take us straight off to the jail 'fore we eat our desert, Mr., I mean Jakie. No, I don' think that is a good idea t'all, us being seen out together. It again' the law, and if'n it ain't, wit all de rioting goin' on we likely to be skinned alive by folks aroun' dis city of angels."

"No, see, I want to take you…I want us to go to the Dunbar, it's a night club, see, it's the finest *Negro*-owned hotel in the city. All the colored entertainers stay there when they come through to play L.A.. Duke Ellington, Count Basie, that blues singer, what's her name, Billie Holiday. And all the biggest white Hollywood movie stars go there, too! Clark Gable, Myrna Loy, all of 'em. Look, it's the cat's meow, see, and they don't care if you're colored or white or if you have zebra stripes, so long as you make good on your tab."

"Well, I declare, Mr. Ja—I means Jakie. You gonna have to let me think on dat. I don' even have a thing to wear to dat kind of place."

"My sister will give you something."

I laughed. "Mrs. Goldberg? She a head taller than me."

"Well, we'll figure somethin' out. Just let me know, say, by Friday, no, Thursday, because, see, a wartime buddy of mine is the bartender over there. I have to let him know if we're coming. He says it gets real jammed up on Saturday nights, especially with Louis Armstrong on stage."

*Louis Armstrong? I'm going to see Louis Armstrong! I can't believe it.*

"Well, thank you kindly, Jakie, but—"

"Ah, don't say no, just say you'll think about it."

"Ah right den. Like I said, I will think 'bout it and let you know."

He took off like an angel with brand-new wings.

The fight over where to move the family began on a sunny Friday afternoon in late May when Mrs. Golberg and Mr. Goldberg came home, both coincidentally with brochures on new housing tracts. They were having their happy hour, I was chasing Billy around the house, and "Black Tooth"—that was Blackie's new name—he was begging to be let outside. I couldn't call the new dog "Blackie"—that would have been like my having another son and calling him Will. Some don't understand this, but dogs are just like children, and losing one is almost as bad as losing a child. Before too long Billy started calling the dog Blackie Too, which sounded like "Black Tooth," and that's the name that stuck.

Anyway, so that one afternoon I was chasing Billy around the house while Black Tooth scratched at the back screen door and barked at the pitch of a fork being dragged across somebody's dinner plate until he got far enough under Mrs. Goldberg's skin that she yelled, "Phosie, shut that goddamned dog up and bring us some ice please! Son of a bitch! What do I have to do to get a little relaxation around here?" She did not take to keeping Black Tooth, but the dog wasn't going anywhere long as Mr. Goldberg was in the house.

"Yes, 'um," I said as I chased Billy through the living room.

"Billy!" Mr. Goldberg shouted as we rounded the cocktail cart and were heading toward the dining room. "Come over here ya little shit bum, I got something for you." Billy ran back to his daddy, leaned over his daddy's leg, looked up into his daddy's eyes, and waited for his surprise.

Once I caught my breath I said, "Dis chile 'bout to kill me. Some ice comin' right up, Mrs. Lucile," and I scuffled off to the kitchen wearing the hand-me-down white shoes, the frayed white nurse's uniform, and a new black apron Mrs. Goldberg brought home because "it dressed things up." I felt like a peacock in a chicken coop walking around like that in Boyle Heights.

When I returned with the ice bucket, Mrs. Goldberg was taking a real estate brochure out of her purse and Billy was ogling a flashy new silver dollar. "That a mighty fine silver dollar, chile. You bes' to keep hit somewhere safe!" The brochure featured a picture on the cover of a pretty white house with black shutters, a white picket fence, a green lawn, a beautiful garden full of colorful flowers, and a big oak tree with a swing hanging down from a limb in the front yard.

"Phosie, put some ice in a couple of tumblers, will you?"

"Yes, 'um," I said, feeling like the names of the different cocktail glasses represented a new language I had learned. There was something cheap and sleazy about it. *Hit may be sleazy but least you cain' find work keepin' bar if worse come de worse.*"

"Leo," Mrs. Goldberg said, "I was in Beverly Hills getting my hair done and there was this office on Beverly Drive and Wilshire, you know, one of those new 'track' home sales offices, or something, and they, the salesman, gave me this for us to look at." She passed the brochure to Mr. Goldberg and said with breathless temerity, "What do you think?"

"What do I think? First of all, why the hell do you have to drive all the way over to some fucking joint in Beverly Hills to have your hair done? What's a matter? You're too good for a Boyle Heights salon?"

Billy ran over to me with that shiny silver dollar cupped in his little hand and a big smile pasted on his face. "Chile, you bes' to save dat for a rainy day. Now come on now, let's play wit Black Tooth in de back yard so yur mama and daddy can have dem some 'lone time."

Billy shouted, "No!" and ran back to his daddy and wrapped his arms around his daddy's leg as before. Mr. Goldberg laughed.

"I was just…I just wanted to look. I mean, we could buy it for five hundred dollars down and three thousand paid out over thirty years. The payment, the salesmen said, would be under thirty dollars a month. What do you think, Leo?"

Mr. Goldberg was in one of his cranky moods, but he managed a smile for the baby before saying, "Driving all the way to Beverly Hills for a hairdo! Who are you trying to fool? The schwarza?" I did not know what the term meant at the time, but I knew he was talking about me because he nodded at me when he said it. It means black or dark in German and in Yiddish, and I'm not too sure that it was always used in a derogatory way. Still, he let go a wicked and cynical laugh that gave me the feeling he was trying to make Mrs. Goldberg feel low as a snake. He was as angry at life as he was afraid of it, and bitter. I never met anyone like him before that or since, and I never want to. That man was like sulfuric acid. Most everybody that came into contact with him was burned and scarred for life.

"I was just thinking that it would be a nice place for Billy to grow up in, that's all," Mrs. Goldberg said as she set the brochure down on the coffee table for Mr. Goldberg to peruse. As far as their marriage was concerned, the dew was definitely off the rose. "And, the salesmen said the prices in Beverly Hills is going to be a lot someday!"

Mr. Goldberg picked up the brochure and studied the photograph. "What a bunch of bullshit! Beverly Hills will never catch up to Boyle Heights. Boyle Heights is ten minutes from downtown. What's out in Beverly Hills? A bunch of fucking farm property is all."

"Come on, Billy, I got us some fresh cookies in the kitchen," I said and tried to pry Billy loose. But I could not break the child's hold on his daddy's leg. It seemed the louder his daddy screamed the tighter Billy held on. Little children are like that when their life is being scared out of their little bodies. If a parent scares them they'll want to stay close to that parent, believing that if they hold on tighter the parent won't hurt them. Believing that if they let go they will lose that parent's love.

"I did…I do, the salesman said so," Mrs. Goldberg said.

"There never was or ever will be anything that you want that is not for yourself, you phony cunt!" Mr. Goldberg yelled. I cringed.

"Like I said, Leo, I mean, we were talking about buying a house and the salesman gave me that," Mrs. Goldberg said with a nod toward the brochure. She swirled her cocktail then reached for a cigarette. "It's a new track or tract or whatever. It's right above Sunset Boulevard near Beverly Drive. It's a steal."

"How fuckin' stupid can you get."

"Phosie, take the kid and find something to do," Mrs. Goldberg said. Billy would not budge. Mrs. Goldberg turned to her husband. "I'm just telling you what the salesman told me."

"What the salesman told you. Who in the fuck do you think you are, Rockefeller's wife? That salesman wanted to get in your snatch, and you probably teased him along like you do every Tom, Dick, and Harry you bump into. 'He gave me a brochure because he thought it would save us money.' You're so stupid I wonder how you find your ass to wipe after you take a shit."

I had heard more than enough.

"You phony snatches. You get turned upside down, you're all the same."

I stepped toward Billy with the intent of doing whatever it took to wrestle that child loose. "Come, chile, let yur mama and daddy see 'bout a house. We can go back and play wit Black Tooth." Billy would not let go. Mr. Goldberg must have taken Billy's action as a sign of solidarity, because he brushed his fingers through Billy's thick black mop and chuckled.

Except for a twitch in her right cheek, Mrs. Goldberg looked steady down to her hips, but her right leg was shaking so that the toe of her high-heeled shoe was tapping on the wood flood like a woodpecker taps on a tree limb. Anger will have its way. She took a long, deep drag from her cigarette and exhaled so much smoke I thought she might disappear behind the cloud. Then she screamed, "So, now we're not getting a house! So that was just a bunch of bullshit too!"

Mr. Goldberg tilted his head and laughed bitterly. Mrs. Goldberg responded like Mr. Goldberg had tossed a tin of kerosene onto a red-hot fire. Her temper flared. "Are we getting a fucking house or not? Because if we're not, Leo, then who the fuck needs you? Phosie, for the last time, get the kid out of here!"

"Oh, so nowwwww I see why you angled to get me back. You needed some schmuck with a fountain pen, any schmuck with a fountain pen, to finance your move to the Westside! Now I see. You can wipe my ass with that phony brochure."

I tried again to take Billy. "Leave the kid alone," Mr. Goldberg said. Then he looked at Mrs. Goldberg. "Now, you listen to me if you know what's good for you, you phony, ungrateful cunt," he said with spittle flying from his mouth like popcorn. "I'm goin' to say it one more time! Ya better dummy up if you know what's good for you!"

Billy started barking.

*"RUFF RUFF RUFF! RUFF RUFF! RUFF RUFF! RUFF RUFF!"*

"Oh, what are you goin' to do now, knock me around, show me who's the fuckin' boss in my mother's house, in *my mother's house*, you freeloading fuck. Fuck you! You think you scare me? You don't scare me! Fuck you!"

Billy barked in chorus with his mother. It looked like he wanted to drown the screaming out.

*"RUFF RUFF RUFF! RUFF RUFF! RUFF RUFF! RUFF RUFF!"*

"See, that's what's wrong with you, Lucile, you can't even keep your fucking piehole shut long enough to hear what someone else has to say."

"Phosie, the kid!" Mrs. Lucile screamed.

I nodded for Billy to come follow me, but Mr. Goldberg stared me off.

"What?" Mrs. Goldberg said and took a drag from her trembling cigarette.

"I think I found a cool place for us, as a matter of fact," Mr. Goldberg said smugly, pulling out his own brochure and placing it on the coffee table next to Mrs. Goldberg's. She didn't reach for it. Her hands were shaking.

"Oh yeah, I can't wait to hear this! Where is this palace?"

Mr. Goldberg took his time lighting a fresh cigarette, inhaled, and exhaled as casually as if he were out for a Sunday stroll.

"Where's this palace already, for Christ's sakes!"

"Pacoima."

"Pacoima? Where the fuck is that?"

"It ain' no fancy-ass shithole like your Beverly Hills. You won't find any phony Jews driving around pretending their shit doesn't stink like you do over there. And, Pacoima is going to grow like crazy, the skies the fucking limit! It's five minutes from the Ridge Route! Do you realize how many trucks come over the Ridge Route every day? If I had a fuckin' nickel for every one I'd be a Rockefeller! Pacoima is where it's at sister."

"'No Jews driving around pretending their shit doesn't stink.' Of course they don't, there aren't any fuckin' roads!"

"Don't give me your bullshit. I'm giving you the *emmis*. Pacoima's in the north valley. They're selling rancheros with a minimum of three acres. Each spread comes with a brand-new three-bedroom, two-bathroom ranch-style house with a large kitchen, a fireplace, and a pool!"

"A Goldberg with a pool? Don't make me laugh."

"Consider yourself lucky, baby doll. The other Goldbergs don't even have a pot to piss in."

"I don't give two shits about what your shitbird family has."

"We can get the kid a pony! You want a pony, kid?"

*"RUFF RUFF RUFF! RUFF RUFF! RUFF RUFF! RUFF RUFF!"*

"A pony! I've heard everything now!" Mrs. Goldberg said. "Who's going to shovel the horse shit?"

"You will!" That statement tickled Mr. Goldberg, and he laughed and laughed.

"I'd rather die first."

"Don't die so fast, doll face. I want to take you out to see the spread I bought for us."

"You already bought a place?"

"Yeah, why? What's it to you? It's a nicer place than this dump!"

"You can take your shit and move there tonight because it will be over my dead body that I would ever move out there!"

"You know what, go to hell!"

It was clear to me then that if they stayed together one was going to kill the other sooner than later if I didn't kill the two of them first.

*"RUFF RUFF RUFF! RUFF RUFF! RUFF RUFF! RUFF RUFF!"*

# Chapter 23

## *The Hotel Dunbar*

Jackie did his best to clean his little black Ford truck for our date. I told him it wasn't necessary, but he removed the rendering barrels and the crane, too. I poked my head out and watched him and Billy scrub it while Black Tooth licked at the suds all Saturday morning. "Jakie, far as I cain see, nothin' but de paint goin' ta come off if you and de chile keeps scrubbin' hard as you are."

Jakie arrived at Mrs. Goldberg's door to pick me up at seven o'clock sharp. I was sitting on the edge of Mrs. Goldberg's sofa, dressed to kill, I don't know what, in one of her nightclub outfits and terrified like I had never been before. Billy was barking with a high-pitched yap, giving both of us a headache. "Billy, goddamn it! Shut up!" Mrs. Goldberg shouted. She had come into the living room to have a drink and sit with me until Jakie picked me up. Mrs. Goldberg was in a deep trough after the fighting with Mr. Goldberg over their intended purchase of a house. Mr. Goldberg was working, he said, longer and longer hours, staying away more and more, and she was stuck at home because when she did go out to have a drink with her friends at the Airliner or the Hi Hat, her former employer, that would infuriate him. Staying home was the same as death to her. She could barely sit in a chair long enough for the seat to warm.

On her way to answering the door, Mrs. Goldberg said, "Are you nervous?"

"As much as a body can be without shakin' all apart, Mrs. Lucile."

Poor little Billy had turned back to some of his puppy ways as his parents' relationship turned once again to the negative.

"*YAP-YAP-YAP! YAP-YAP-YAP! YAP-YAP-YAP!*"

"Billy, goddamn it!"

Jakie walked in with a shy little smile. He could not seem to lift his eyes up from the floor. Lord have mercy, that man was all dressed up for the rodeo in a chestnut-brown suit with suede drop-down arrow yokes on the shoulders of the jacket, a suit that probably fit him before the war but was now a size or so too big. His shirt was light tan with white pearl snaps in place of buttons. He was wearing a golden-brown bolo tie with a shiny silver dollar adornment on its slide and polished brown goat-skin cowboy boots with snipped toes. He looked to be about two inches taller. His cowboy hat was the same chestnut shade of brown as were his boots.

"Jakie, oy vey es mir! You're a cowboy again! Just kidding. I haven't seen you look so good since Pearl Harbor! Mazel tov!"

Jakie's kitty cat smile evaporated.

Earlier that day, Mrs. Goldberg came into the kitchen and asked me to cut up a grapefruit for her. Then she shared it with me. As we picked at the segments I said, "Are you sure dis is a good idea, Mrs. Lucile? I fear de people in dis city won' 'cept a white man and a colored woman together."

"Screw the people in this city. It's done all the time. You just don't see it, you know. You'll be fine, you'll have a ball. Man, this grapefruit is like candy."

"Sweetest I've ever had, Mrs. Lucile."

"Listen, Phosie, life's a bowl of cherries and most poor slobs are stuck with the pits. You know why?"

"I cain't say I do, Mrs. Lucile."

She finished swallowing a mouthful and said, "Because they sit on their asses and wait for someone to come along and give them something. Well, you know what? Nobody gives you shit! If you want shit you gotta take it!"

"Dat's right."

"It's first come first serve, baby! You gotta fight your way to the front of the line and pick the sweetest fruit before the other slobs grab it if you want your life to be sweet. You dig?"

"Oh, I digs, I digs," I said with a little grin as her mention of sweet fruit brought me back to thinking about the time Will carried the Habersham peaches home.

"Here, have the last segment. Listen, there is something I think you should know about my brother."

"Yes?" I said as I picked up the last piece.

"Thing is, he wasn't always this way, shy, a loner, not too keen on the grooming. Yeah, he had his problems, but he wasn't always like this. See, after our father died, our mother had to send Jakie, who is one year older than me, to a home, something like a reform school, because he was just too wild. She couldn't handle him. Every day was something else. But the school just made him angrier. He left at seventeen and met a girl, Rosie…Rosie Kantowitz. He fell head over heels. Man, they were hot and heavy,"—Mrs. Goldberg smiled wryly—"if you know what I mean. They were going to get married. He had the whole enchilada planned. He even found a place for them, a small apartment on the other side of Brooklyn Avenue. He took me to it and showed me. But what did I know, I had just turned sixteen and never been kissed. Then the war came. Jakie had to be a marine. So they sent him to the Pacific."

"Dat's where my Will was, you knows dat. Maybe dey saw each other."

"If Jakie did he wouldn't remember." Mrs. Goldberg said then lit another Chesterfield. "They had him fight on every goddamned island. I know because he told me everything in the letters he sent me. Then, on Guadalcanal, he and his best buddy, Tony D'Agostino from Brooklyn, were pinned down in their foxhole for three days. On the first night a son-of-a-bitchin' Jap threw a grenade into the foxhole and Tony saved Jakie's life by throwing himself on the grenade. Jakie had to stay in that foxhole for two more days with his best friend, who saved his life, with the friend's blood and body parts all over him. Jakie came back a different man, spooked, his own shadow made him nervous.

That was a year ago. He's a little better now, you know, but he still needs work, a lot of work. You seem to have a real nice way with him, you know. He seems really relaxed when you're around. That's good, you know, real good."

"Thank you kindly, Mrs. Lucile. I am glad I cain help."

She didn't say why she was promoting my relationship with Jakie, but like the headlamp of a distant train speeding toward me, her rationale became brighter and brighter as her cigarette smoke grew thicker there in the living room as Jakie stood before us like he did not want to move out of fear he would wrinkle his outfit. I realized that if Jakie and I married she would lose a housekeeper and the related expenses and in turn gain a sister-in-law who lived a knock on the door away, a woman who could and most likely would continue taking care of Billy and cleaning both apartments. Once it dawned on me I could not help but smile. People do things for the strangest reasons. Plotting to have your brother marry your housekeeper, your colored housekeeper, in that day and age, in order to gain a sister-in-law and an auntie for your child, and keep a housekeeper at no extra charge, was definitely one of the craziest plots I had seen. Then again, if it weren't for folks who were a little bit touched, life would be boring as death or worse.

I rose up on Mrs. Goldberg's high heels like a newborn foal trying not to topple over. I wish I had a picture of the expression on Jakie's face. I had never had anybody look at me with a sense of awe. We just stood there looking at one another then looking at the floor then looking at one another again.

"You two kids better go or you'll miss all the action!" Mrs. Lucile said.

The cab of Jakie's truck was clean as a hospital operating room. Yet when he made the first turn up Cummings to Brooklyn Avenue, the stale odor of nicotine and Mrs. Goldberg's Mitzuko, which she'd made me spray on, were easily overpowered by the sweet and rottten odor of rancid grease. It wasn't that bad so long as he kept driving fast, but I had to hold my breath when he had to turn or stop.

As we passed the neon blue, red, and yellow pagoda gate of Chinatown, Jakie said, "I'm sure we won't have a problem see'n as how it's dark." I would swear he was talking with a Texas draw. "But if we get pulled over by a copper and he asks where we're going, see, we'll just feed him the truth with a lime twist. I'll tell him you're my sister's housekeeper and I'm driving you home. But like I said, no one should bother us at this hour."

"I hopes dey don't," I joked, feeling a little excited, "'cause I doubt any police goin' to believe your sister's housekeeper dresses like I's dressed. What he gonna say 'bout dis leopard-spotted fez? Dis dress? Dese shoes? Most housekeepers I knows of never even seen a leopard! 'Specially one dat looks like a mama hen."

Jakie smiled. "Don't worry, I was just letting my mouth run on automatic-fire."

When I'd first told Mrs. Goldberg that her brother had asked me out to dinner at The Dunbar, she insisted I borrow one of her cocktail dresses, a slinky black rayon thing with a crimped waist and soft draped shoulders. I had to tack the hem. She also insisted I wear a wire-form push-up bra to perk up my flagging breasts. I swear the bra cups were shaped like Cadillac tail fins. I was as uncomfortable as I was nervous. She also loaned me her black patent-leather high heels. Lord, how we laughed when I put them on and took my first steps. I stumbled around like a cheap drunk until I used the wall in the hallway to steady me. Billy laughed till I thought his sides would split. I felt like a scrawny chicken wearing peacock's feathers. Then there was the fez Mrs. Goldberg insisted I wear. Not just any fez. Hers had a faux leopard-skin print. When I looked in the mirror I said, "Mrs. Lucile, 'cept for de cup, I look like de organ grinder's monkey wit dis hat on." Then we all laughed again. Still, Mrs. Goldberg was a magician. Only a magician could have made a homely little thing like me look like some hot dish.

"Nonsense," she told me. "You don't see it, but you actually happen to be beautiful, very beautiful. You're tall, and you have beautiful, soft hazel eyes and beautiful skin tone. Most white women would die to have a deep tan like that all year."

"Well, honey, I don' think dey would wants to look like no Hershey's Bar neither."

"That's sad, but you're wearing the fez anyway, baby. I mean, they'll go crazy for it at the Dunbar. You'll be the bee's knees. Come into the bathroom."

As I followed her into the bathroom I said, "I don' wants to be any bee's knees. I is happy de way I is."

"Is that why you cry yourself to sleep every night?"

"How—"

"I'm a light sleeper. Turn around and lift the hem of your skirt and stand up on your toes."

"Why?"

"Just turn around, you'll see. You need to get your life back on track."

"I jus' lost my son, my husband's passed, Mrs. Lucile, what do you 'spect?" I said as I turned, held onto the sink, and lifted myself up on the balls of my feet.

"Would your husband and your son want you walking around like a ghost, or would they want you to go on with your life, find love and what happiness you can?"

I felt the soft tip of a black eyebrow pencil leaving a line down the back of my leg, past the back of my knee, then along the middle of my calve. "Mrs. Lucile, what is you drawin' on de back o' my leg?"

"Everyone that's anyone will be at the Dunbar tonight. I've made that scene. It's jumpin', baby, jumpin'! All those Dunbar girls will either have nylons on or have eyebrow pencil lines painted down the back of their calves just like the ones I'm drawing on yours. You don't want to be feel naked, do you?"

"No, I reckon I don'."

She started on the other leg. "Keep still or the line on your fake nylons will look like you were drunk when you put them on."

"I'm tryin', Mrs. Lucile, I'm tryin'!"

By the time Jakie drove us down to Central Avenue and Forty-Second Street I was so tired I felt like closing my eyes, curling up, and going to sleep. I yawned.

"You okay?" Mr. Jakie said.

"I'm fine, I'm fine, jus' tired from chasing dat boy and dat dog 'round."

"I think he loves Black Tooth just as much as he loved the last dog, Checkers."

"Checkers, dat a funny name. Too bad hit gone."

"I just hope at least Leo sticks around this time for the kid's sake. Billy's doing much better, right?"

"Lord, yes, he was. Walkin', startin' to talk, eatin' at the table like a chile should. That is 'til Mr. Leo and Mrs. Lucile got to fightin' like caged cocks. De more de fights de more dat chile take to actin' like a dog."

"How have you been doin', you know, with your son dying?"

"I'm jus' takin' life one breath at a time, Jakie, one breath at a time."

Jakie leaned over and switched on the radio. "That's Benny Goodman playing 'Bugle Call Rag.' Ever heard it?"

"Oh yes," I said and began tapping the toe of my high heel on the floorboard as Jakie tapped his index finger on the steering wheel. I felt comfortable as we drove through the colored district near Central and Twelfth Streets. Everyone on the sidewalks was colored. The majority of the men were wearing suits and ties, and the majority of the women were wearing nice dresses and hats. The shops were busy. That was the way it was back then.

"Hit shore 'nough is way down."

"Yeah, we got to cross the Mexican border before we hit it," Jakie said then choked down a cackle and waited for my reply.

"We ain' goin' to Mexico?" I said, looking nervously out the window, "Dey likely won' let me back in if'n we do!" I said with a chuckle. It felt nice to have a little fun.

Jakie laughed. "Nah, we stop at Forty-Second Street."

"Why dey build hit so far down?"

"Property's cheap down here. You know all the best colored talent there is stays at the Dunbar—Count Basie, Duke Ellington, Lena Horne. And all sorts of real high-browed people too—W. E. B. Du Bois, Thurgood Marshall, doctors, lawyers, you name it. See, just because the top colored acts play the ritzy white clubs does not mean they can stay in the ritzy white hotels."

"Well, dey prob'bly feels more comfortable 'mongst der own kind."

Jakie slowed down and looked at me. "You don't feel comfortable around me?"

"To tell the truth, I did not at first, Jakie, but I'm comfortable now."

Jakie smiled and said, "And there it is."

The Hotel Dunbar was a five-story brown brick building with tall Spanish arched windows trimmed in white. Its sign, a red block with its name written out in white neon letters, was hanging on the building's corner over the intersection of Central Avenue and Forty-Second Street. There were lots of people, black, brown, and white, all dressed to the nines and standing around the hotel entrance; they were surrounded by a small army of newspaper reporters and photographers who were snapping so many pictures the flashbulbs seemed like fireworks. And there was a line of cars, big luxury cars, waiting to pull up to the valet. It was like a Hollywood premiere.

*I belongs here like a jackass belong in a church pew.*

"Excited?" Jakie asked.

"I guess, Mr. Jakie. This is the first time I'll be in any hotel, let 'lone one dis' big and beautiful one." *I wish't Sis' Pearl could see me now! Lor' have mercy she would be speechless for de first time."*

"Oh, so now I'm mister again!"

"I means Jakie. I am nervous. I've never been 'round high society 'cept to clean der houses, serve der meals, do dey wash, and change dey children's diapers."

A big black Packard limousine pulled up to the hotel valet as we waited for the only traffic light that far south on Central to turn green.

"You see that? You see him?" Jakie said, pointing at a man stepping out of the   Packard. "You see who's getting out? That's Stepin Fetchit. He's a millionaire! Royalty down here."

"Well, I declare. I did see him in a movie. But he shore move different now." My hands began to shake and my voice quivered I was so nervous. "He jus' a broken-down, lazy, good-for-nothin' fool in de movies. And look at him now," I said as Jakie drove past the awning-covered entrance of the Dunbar at the speed a snail crawls. We had arrived. I smoothed out my dress and adjusted my fez. *Look at him? Look at me, a moth turned butterfly.*

"I'm going to park on the next block. Why give those valets fifty cents? Nobody gives me nothin'."

"I don' mind walkin', Jakie. It will give me practice on dese heels."

"Don't worry, you'll do fine. You look beautiful."

"You really think so, Jakie, I'm beautiful?" I said, looking over at him.

"You're damn tootin'. I'm goin' to be with one of the most beautiful and most sexy dames in the joint."

I thought of what Mrs. Henrietta Duke said when she placed me with Mrs. Goldberg and laughed.

"What's so funny?"

"I've been called lots of things, but not 'beautiful.'"

"You are to me."

We had to walk about two blocks. Jakie held my hand along the way. It was permissible to do that on Central Avenue—everyone was "hip." There were even homosexuals dressed in drag down there. But by the time we reached the hotel's entrance my calves were tight and cramping. "You okay?" Jakie asked.

"I will be soon as we get some place to sit. My legs is crampin'. Jus' keep goin'."

The inside of the Dunbar was a palace. The floors were marble. The furnishings were plush; a big crystal chandelier was hanging in the center of the lobby. A band was playing up on the mezzanine. The band was led by a man playing the xylophone. It was a cool and soothing melody. I felt like I was in heaven.

"Know who that is?"

"No, I don' believes I do, but he look an awful, awful lot like my Will. I'd like to go up and hug and kiss him."

"That's Lionel Hampton. You know his name, don't you?"

"I think I've heard him on de radio at Mrs. Hutchinson's. Dat's right, I did."

We heard a female singing as we walked into the next room. It was a grand ballroom with a bar, a stage, a dance floor, and too many tables to count. Every table was packed with smiling people talking, smoking, drinking, looking like they were without a care in the world. I thought of what Mrs. Goldberg had told me about how people change when they get a couple of drinks in them. The menfolk were in black tie and the women were wearing evening gowns. There were a good many mixed couples, too. We stood in a crowd toward the servers' end of the bar and had to speak over the music and noise with our faces close together. I could smell Jakie's Aqua Velva, and my body flushed. Seeing Jakie out of his greasy uniform or that worn flannel robe he wore, and away from the mess at Mrs. Goldberg's, allowed me to see him in a truer light, to see how handsome he really was, with his deep sky-blue eyes, compared to the other men in the ballroom. Our lips were so close together I felt like kissing him. I had to look away before I lost my way. I changed the subject. "Lor', I ain' never seen so many happy people all in one place 'cept church, and church people look happy 'cause dey sittin' and comparin' demselves to ever'one else and wantin' to look like dey are jus' a little happier and more prosperous den de next. Dat way dey feels better."

"If you had their kind of bread, you'd be smiling too!"

"I don't think we dressed up right, Jakie."

"Don't worry, we're not sitting down here, we're sitting up there," he said, pointing up to a balcony where one table was empty. "Look up at the stage. You recognize the lady singing in front of the orchestra?"

"She has a beautiful voice and a nice smile, but I declare I cain't place her."

"It's Ella Fitzgerald."

"Ella Fitzgerald? You means *de* Ella Fitzgerald?"

"In the flesh!"

"Lor' have mercy, she known all de worl' over."

"Jesus Christ, look over there at the table in the front row center. Count Basie is sitting with Lauren Bacall and Groucho Marx."

I looked at the table Jakie was pointing out. "Oh yes, oh yes," I said, but I really did not recognize the man with the big round eyes and the funny mustache.

"Come on, let's go say hello to my buddy, Detroit, at the bar."

"Detroit? I never have know'd a body named after a city."

"We did that a lot in the Marines. I was California. Get it?"

"Jakie baby, what's you up to these days?" Detroit said when we approached. He was a big dark man with a smile bright as a thousand candles. "Slip me some skin." Detroit held his hand out with his palm up, and Jakie slid his hand over Detroit's.

"Ah, same ol' same ol', Dee. Meet Phosie."

"How ya'll doing, baby?" Detroit asked.

I was afraid to open my mouth and just smiled.

"You gonna kill 'em like a marine with a flamethrower with that outfit, baby girl. Better have California carry you a fire extinguisher around for backup, dig?"

*I don' dig and I ain' no baby girl!* I thought while holding a smile.

"What are you two lovebirds drinking?"

"A couple of Hurricanes, my man," Jakie said before I had a chance to think.

*How strong is a Hurricane?*

"I reserved that table for you, Jakie," Detroit said, pointing to the balcony.

"Thanks, Dee," Jakie said as he offered his friend a five-dollar bill. Dee frowned and pushed it away.

We carried our drinks up to the balcony and sat at the table reserved for us. I felt like a queen sitting up there watching over everything. When Ella Fitzgerald left the stage the orchestra started playing "It Don't Mean a Thing if it Ain't Got that Swing." A whole flock of penguins—that's the men in their black ties—led their women to the dance floor and started dancing like I had never seen before. Every man who remained seated started up tapping and beating anything they could find: spoons, forks, plates, anything to keep beat with the music. I could not believe how good they were. Jakie tapped me and pointed to one man who had slid off his chair and was using its seat as a drum pad. Another used his table as a snare drum. They were going wild. "You know who those guys are playing at their tables?" Jakie asked.

"No, I surely don', but dey shore 'nough has rhythm."

"That's because every one of those kids are in Duke Ellington's Orchestra. 'Ain't Got that Swing' is their number. They'll be on later."

"Well, ain' dat nice," I said as I looked around nervously, afraid someone would recognize me for who I really was, a know-nothing dirt farmer turned housekeeper who did not even own the outfit she was wearing. But when I exchanged glances with two well-dressed ladies sitting at a nearby table, they smiled and nodded up toward my hat. They actually liked it. Mrs. Goldberg knew her fashion. I tapped my foot as the orchestra played and couples seated on the balcony started to dance.

"Come on," Jakie said, "let's swing!" He stood and pulled me up out of my seat. I did my best to keep my body in balance and let my feet go in the direction Jakie was twirling me. It felt good to dance, to let go. I had closed my eyes and lost myself in the music when Jakie stiffened up and said, "Son of a bitch!"

He looked fearful. "What is hit? What did I do?" I had begun to feel a little light-headed from the Hurricane.

"Oh, you couldn't do anything wrong. Look over at the bar near the entrance. See the short little Yid with rat's eyes and a boxer's nose? He's with the tall, dirty blond and the two suits behind them?"

"Yes, I do," I sang. *But I don't see no suits walkin' by dey ownself.* I was even thinking like I was drunk.

"Well, the Yid's Mickey Cohen. The big lug behind him is Izzy Glasser, his juice man."

"Why he need a man for juice followin' him when de sells it everywhere?"

"He don't squeeze juice out of lemons, apples, and oranges, doll, he squeezes money out of deadbeats like I was. See, it was Glasser what knocked me around the day your brother and sister-in-law took you to the hospital. The other guy, the guy with the white hair next to Glasser, is A. B. Phillips, the little rat's bondsman and shylock."

Jakie stopped dancing and drew his black revolver out from under his belt at the small of his back and tucked it into his jacket pocket.

"Maybe we should go, den."

"Nah, Glasser can't see you unless you're standing two feet away from him, he's nearsighted. He won't wear glasses because he thinks it makes him look weak. And Cohen's too busy ogling the dames to notice a two-bit gambler like me."

"Lord, I thought you was out of all dat."

"Oh, I am, believe me, I've had it. Done, through, kaput. But I still have a marker to pay, and until I do I have to keep my eyes open for Cohen and his gorilla."

It was not yet ten o'clock. I had warned myself that when the clock struck midnight Mrs. Goldberg's cocktail dress would turn into my maid's uniform, my high heels would be replaced by the scuffed white hand-me-downs, and I'd be back riding in Jakie's broken-down pickup smelling sweet rancid grease. But it seemed midnight had arrived early. I studied the people on the dance floor and at the tables. They suddenly looked like circus clowns whose makeup was disappearing. I could see behind their smiles and chic clothing and could feel that there was something false about their presence. They were able to dress up and hide from themselves behind the music and the whiskey, but only for a short while. Their champagne was losing its bubble. Their smiles came to look like masks.

A gunshot shattered the sound of music and chitchat and laughter. We looked over the rail of the balcony. There was pandemonium. The people who had just been on top of the world were running for the exits like rats running from a burning house. I saw the "juice man," Glasser, take out his pistol and aim at a tall, skinny colored boy in a busboy's outfit holding a gun and standing at the entrance to the kitchen. The boy shot again before he ran and ducked behind the bar. Glasser shot back. They both missed. Liquor bottles on a shelf over the bar shattered. A woman screamed as a man next to Glasser collapsed over a table. The boy dashed out through the swinging kitchen doors. Glasser ran after him. We heard more shots. Men and women were screaming and running every which way. Everyone on the balcony was trying to run down the stairway. The Hurricane lost its effect, my thoughts focused. "Come on, Jakie, we best get out of here 'fore de police comes."

"Nah, let's sit down and relax. By the time the cops get here everyone will be out on the sidewalk trying to get their cars from the valet. We'll wait till things cool down then walk across the street to Ivy's Chicken Shack for chicken liver omelets, biscuits with honey, and a strong cup of Ivy's Joe with the finest chicory money can buy. You like chicken liver omelets?"

"Matter of factually, I do."

"You'll love Ivy's. She kills all her own chickens in the back. The livers are fresh, real tasty. Let's just take it easy for now. We'll lay low." I sat down, ready to return to the country life. The high life wasn't for me.

"What an evening. Did you have fun?" Jakie asked as we drove back through Chinatown. It was drizzling. The streets and sidewalks were empty, but the reflections of colored lights, Chinese characters, and neon dragons were playing on them. It was magical.

"Yes," I said, "thank you kindly." I took a deep breath. "But I don' 'spect I'll wants to go back to de Dunbar any time soon, Jakie. Hit's not my style."

"I can dig it," he said. "It's not really mine either. I just wanted you to have a good time, is all."

"I was fine parked in de back of dat drive-in restaurant wit you and Billy. Dat's all I needs."

"It's all I need, too. We'll leave the high life to my sister! She likes the sport."

I felt protected and safe for the first time since Isaac had died. I hoped that Isaac and Will would understand. Life does not always give us what we want, but if we try, Providence gives us what we need to get by.

When we arrived back home, I kissed Jakie on the cheek as we stood at Mrs. Goldberg's front door. He smiled and blushed.

"Let's do this again," Jakie said.

"Long as I kin wear somethin' regular next time."

"Yeah, what the hell. It's still us no matter what we wear."

"Ain' dat de gospel truth."

# Chapter 24

## *The Main Event*

**M**rs. Goldberg marched into the kitchen followed by Billy early Wednesday morning, June 19, 1946. I remember the date because Isaac's birthday fell on June 20. She took a seat at the breakfast table, lit a cigarette, and said, "Son of a bitch! That no-good two-timing, lying, selfish bastard!" Billy, now walking all the time, yet still not talking, was mocking her from behind by twisting his cute little face into an angry scowl, rolling his head from side to side, and making a high-pitched *yap* noise that imitated the shrill pitch of his mother's voice.

"*YAP-YAP-YAP! YAP-YAP-YAP! YAP-YAP-YAP!*"

"Look like somebody got up out de wrong side de bed!" I said as I poured her a cup coffee. "Here you go, Mrs. Lucile, some of my finest Southern blend with a hint of chicory to keep de curl in dat beautiful red hair a yours."

"I don't need any goddamned curl in my goddamned red hair!"

"*YAP-YAP-YAP! YAP-YAP-YAP! YAP-YAP-YAP!*"

Mrs. Goldberg turned around and slapped Billy across his face. It sounded like a thunder clap.

"Come on, Billy, yur mama's crossways. I'll take you and Black Tooth out to de back, baby."

Billy had been emboldened by his father's presence. Not necessarily in a good way, the Lord knows, but at least his daddy gave him the permission he needed to fight back against some of his mama's foolish-ness even if he was only capable of putting up just a little biddy fight.

"*YAP-YAP-YAP! YAP-YAP-YAP! YAP-YAP-YAP!*"

"Listen to him! He'll turn out just like his father! Another dog in heat! Shit! Now I have the kid, his good-for-nothing father, my good-for-nothing brother, and another goddamned dog on my back! I hate this. I'd rather be dead!"

"What is it got you so stirred up dis fine June mornin', Mrs. Lucile? You seemed to be havin' a nice evening las' night."

"What got me so 'stirred up?' I'll tell you what got me so stirred up. Leo walked in around three a.m., and when I asked him where the hell he had been he said it's none of my goddamned business where he has been and told me to 'dummy up' and go back to sleep. I hate, hate, hate him!"

"Well, he probably out workin' real hard."

"'Workin' real hard' my ass! He was out running his crap games in the back of his gas station near Chinatown. Every judge, cop, downtown politician, and all the businessmen go there to drink and play. Oh, did I mention the whores? That's right, they stock the place with whores! Would you want your husband doing that? Would you want to be sen-tenced to stay home every goddamned night until death do you part while your two-timing husband was out throwing a God damned party?"

"Well, I cain't say I would."

"No, you cain't, can you? And here's the kicker! This morning, he gets up at five and nudges me awake. He tells me he's got to drive out to Barstow or some shithole to buy a load of retreads. 'So, all of a sudden you're waking me up to tell me you're going to Barstow? What? Do you need my permission?' I say.

"'Nah,' he says, 'but if you dummy up I'll tell you what I need. I'm having some of the boys over to watch the Louis-Conn fight this afternoon and I need you to get two or three…make it three cases of beer for this evening.'

"I say, 'What do you think, I'm running a goddamned saloon? Get your own beer, for Christ's sakes!'

"And he says, 'I don't need any shit at five in the morning, doll. So for once, shut your kisser and do as you're told. And if you do, maybe I'll bring you a little present back.'

"So I say, 'From Barstow? What will it be? Cowshit?'"

"And he says to me, 'So this is what I get for trying to be nice? Cowshit?'

"Well, I'll tell you what, Phosie, he can kiss my ass. He's having 'friends over to watch a fight,' and I'm the one to get the beer, to serve the food. I just quit my job waiting on tables! And now, he's goin' to feed that pack of losers like kings! And he never has an extra fin or a sawbuck in his pocket for the kid. What's next? Whores to entertain his no-count 'friends?' Friends! That's a laugh. If he was lying on the sidewalk dying those two-bit hustlers would step right over him."

"Well, gettin' upset won't help matters, I cain tell you dat."

"Then what will 'help matters'?"

*Lord have mercy, what is I goin' to say now? Throw de louse out de house?*

"Let me see," I began with great caution, "why don' you ax him out for a cocktail someday soon and talk dis over? See if he cain be reasoned wit. Play to his sof' side. You don' wanna stir him up, Mrs. Lucile, he can be a violent man." I had no standing to issue an opinion as I had absolutely no experience with his brand of madness.

"I could talk with him till I'm blue in the face. He's just a selfish, coldhearted son of a bitch."

"Well, maybe if you'd give a little, so would he," I said as I refilled Mrs. Goldberg's coffee cup.

"What are you talking about, 'give a little?' I've already given him an arm and a leg! He lives here for free. What do I have left? The gold in my God damned teeth?"

"I knows, why don' you telephone one or two of your high school girlfriends. Go out and have you a lunch wit dem? Least ways dat would get you out de house for some fresh air. Dere ain' no use waitin' on Mr. Goldberg 'cause it seem he don' care."

"Oh, he cares, when I play hard to get, he cares."

"Well, you take it easy today, Mrs. Lucile. I'll have Jakie to pick up de beer so you don' has to worry none over dat. Now finish your coffee and go take you a nice, long, relaxin' bath that will settle you down shore 'nough."

Strings of glistening teardrops streaked down Mrs. Goldberg's cheeks. I dabbed them with a kitchen towel. "Come on now, Mrs. Lucile, you has yourself all worked up for nothin'."

She smiled and said, "I feel like you're my mom."

"Maybe dat's why de good Lord saw fit to send me here."

"Worst goddamned mistake I ever made in my whole goddamned life letting that lying bastard back in here! I should have made him buy us a place first. But then...ah, never mind. You know what it is? You know what's wrong with me? I'm a loser. I always have been, always will be."

"Don' be so hard on yur own self, you doin' de best you cain, Mrs. Lucile. Life is hard 'nough as it is."

Mrs. Goldberg smiled. "Thank you, Phosie. I'm adopting you as my mother. I don't know what I'd do without you."

I gave Mrs. Goldberg a hug and said, "Dat right, honey, you call me Mom."

Billy came back in as his mama left. I gave Billy Black Tooth's bowl filled with leftovers—liver, onions, cabbage, and kasha from last night's dinner—and said, "Why don't you go out and feed your brother. I bet he hungry as a woodpecker in a forest of petrified trees."

Most of Mr. Goldberg's friends arrived before he came home. They were like the swarm of locusts Moses let loose on Egypt in Exodus. They lounged in the living room drinking all the liquor and smoking every cigarette in Mrs. Goldberg's cigarette box; in the kitchen eating all the food and drinking all the milk and beer; in and out of the bathroom smoking their weed; using the telephone to call in bets on baseball; asking me for this and that; running in and out the front door to pay or collect money from other men who pulled up to the curb; and smoking up such a storm it was a wonder the house itself did not burn to the ground. A couple played with Billy like he was a little pet before I carried the child out to the backyard and set him to play with

Black Tooth. The missus knew most of the men. She would not have anything whatsoever to do with them. She came into my kitchen after most of them arrived and traipsed back and forth like she was ready to take her mother's kosher meat cleaver and chop them into little pieces for stew meat. I sent her into her bedroom and told her to lock the door.

Mr. Goldberg finally came home with platters of pastrami, corned beef, pickles, coleslaw, potato salad, bagels, rye bread, and *challah*—that's what the Jewish call their egg bread but it should be called "cake" because it tastes more like cake than it does bread.

"Mr. Leo, Lord knows it good to see you. Your friends clean'd out de kitchen and I'm worryin' dey goin' t' start working on de house like dey termites."

He grumbled something incoherent that ended with, "We'll need some ice chopped for the beer tub."

"I don' reckon I seen any beer tub 'round de place, Mr. Leo."

"It's in the shed, unless my old lady gave it away. Speaking of which, where is she?"

"Oh," I said, taking a deli platter from him and setting it in the icebox, "she in her room nappin', Mr. Leo. Gettin' ready for de main event."

"Ah, who needs her anyhow! Bring in the platters, will ya!"

*I work for the missus. I sure 'nough ain' your house nigger.*

When I carried the first platter in, Mr. Goldberg shouted, "Okay, ladies, clean the shit off the table so the girl can put the chow down." Those closest to the tables passed the empty bottles to those closest to the front door, and they tossed the bottles out onto the front lawn. Everything else was pushed outward from the center to create an oval space for the platter. "And bring that tub of beer in while you're at it." I had to put a towel under one end of the tub to drag it over the floor. It was too heavy to carry, and I wasn't going to poke my finger into that hornet's nest in the living room by asking for help. You'd think one of those strong young men might have offered to help seeing me stooped over like a broken-down mule dragging that tub. But they were too interested in the Indian Head Test Pattern on the television screen and tossing bets back and forth like they were baseballs and basketballs.

"Phosie, while you're in here, why not give everyone a Brew *One-Oh-Twoski*." All of his friends loved that. One shouted, "You da king, Leo, da king of Brooklyn Avenue!" They all laughed.

"Leo, where's your brother-in-law, Jakie? He likes the action, don't he?" a man with a blond comb-over said.

"He's sewed up his pockets after losing a bundle to Mickey Cohen and his shylock A.B. Phillips," Mr. Goldberg said.

*Lor' have mercy! Dat da man Mr. Jakie pointed out 'fore de shooting.*

"Hey, Leo, what's the over-under?" a nervous little man asked in a squeaky voice.

"What do I look like, a bookmaker? Call Fat Maxie."

A man with a pockmarked face and greasy hair shouted, "I don't give two shits what Izzy thinks, my money's on the nigger in the third." I winced.

Another man said, "Who do you think you are, Hemingway? Putz, when Conn fought Louis in forty-one, the Bomber had at least twenty-five pounds on him and still Conn went toe-to-toe for thirteen. One official had the match tied. The other two had Conn seven-five and seven-four-one."

Mr. Goldberg shouted, "Yeah, Conn had the match won until Louis knocked him out!" as he took a seat in the easy chair next to the sofa.

Everyone laughed.

A diminutive man wearing a ten-gallon cowboy hat and boots like Jakie's said, "All I know is Louis demolished Schmelling twice, defeated Two-Ton Tony Galento, and was the only heavyweight to have his own 'Bum of the Month Club' he defended his title so many times."

Mr. Goldberg said, "That's right, *Tex*, that is all you know." Mr. Goldberg's followers hooted, shouted, and clapped.

"But Louis is, by my arithmetic, five years older," the pock-faced man said.

Mr. Goldberg said, "I'm in Louis's corner. Why? Because he didn't even train for the match in forty-one. He didn't want to be seen as a bully beating up on some dumb little mick!"

I had finished opening long-neck bottles of beer for almost all of the men and turned to walk out when Mr. Goldberg said, "Hey, where are you going? Make me a pastrami on rye and put some mustard and coleslaw on it."

"What's a matter, the old lady too good for this? She hooked you back in like a big tuna?" the pock-faced man asked.

"Ball and chain, ball and chain, ball and chain!" the men hollered.

Mr. Goldberg shouted, "Attention on deck! Here comes the fight."

My mouth watered as I spooned coleslaw on Mr. Goldberg's juicy thick-cut pastrami sandwich. I glanced up at the new television Mr. Goldberg bought not long after moving in. The sound coming out of the speaker in the burnished mahogany television cabinet was nothing but static. I looked at the screen. A black-and-white show card with the ropes of a ring and boxing gloves in the background appeared:

WORLD'S
HEAVYWEIGHT
CHAMPIONSHIP
YANKEE STADIUM – JUNE 19, 1946
PRODUCED BY RKO PATHE, INC.
I kept spooning as the next card appeared:
JOE LOUIS
WORLD'S HEAVYWEIGHT CHAMPION
VS.
BILLY CONN
CHALLENGER

Seeing Joe Louis's name on the television screen gave me goose bumps. I wished he'd jump out of the television and knock out every one of the men assembled in Mrs. Goldberg's living room.

Mr. Goldberg said, "For Christ's sakes, Phosie, leave some coleslaw for the peasants."

"Oh, I'm sorry, Mr. Leo, this is my first time seein' television 'sides outside a store window."

"Who do you like for this fight?" he asked in a voice loud enough to attract the attention of the others.

"I likes de colored boy, Mr. Leo, Joe Louis. He gonna beat Conn 'cause Joe Louis beat everyone he fight!" This brought out more hoots and hollers. "Dat's right, he good for de colored man, too. Klu Kluxers down in Texas don't know what to do 'bout him. He de Brown Bomber."

Mr. Goldberg nodded his head toward me and said, "From the mouth of babes!"

"I ain' no babe anymore, Mr. Leo."

"Make yourself a sandwich, take the load off, and watch the fight! Maybe you'll bring us luck from the Negro boxing gods."

Billy jumped in and hopped up on his daddy's lap.

"Oh, I has my washin,' wipin', and waxin' to do this morning, Mr. Leo. I don' have no time for watchin'."

"Bullshit. I just gave you the time. Make a sandwich for yourself and Billy and sit."

*"RUFF-RUFF-RUFF! RUFF-RUFF-RUFF-RUFF!"*

"Well, all right den."

"Hey, you slobs on the sofa, make a hole for my good luck charm!" The men on the sofa slid over. After I finished making sandwiches for Billy and myself, I took my seat between the white men on the sofa.

After all the cards disappeared, the announcer, a tiny white man wearing a tuxedo and a black bow tie, came on speaking into a steel microphone the size of a miniature milk bottle hanging from a cable. It was like looking into a little world with miniature people in it. I felt like walking up to the screen and looking around the edges to see what else was inside. The announcer started off in in a high-pitched voice like a barker at a circus midway. "This is the telepresentation of fifteen rounds of the heavyweight championship of the world. From Pittsburgh, Pennsylvania, weighing one hundred eighty-two pounds, wearing black trunks, undefeated light-heavyweight champion and the very capable challenger for the heavyweight crown, Billy Conn." The little man pointed his white fight card toward the corner to his left, and the boxer, wearing a long white silk robe, jumped up, spun around, bowed, and sat back down on his stool. There was no cheering. A good long spell of silence followed.

"One hundred eighty-two pounds! You gotta be kidding me!" said another of Mr. Goldberg's guests, this one wearing a Hawaiian-style shirt and a leather five-cigar case in its breast pocket. "He'll be chopped liver by the time Louis gets through with him."

"Clam up, Benny!" Mr. Goldberg said, wanting to hear the announcer introduce Joe Louis.

The little white man turned toward Louis's corner and continued as the men on the sofa shifted around to accommodate me. "And his opponent, weighing two-oh-seven, wearing purple trunks, the internationally famous Detroit Brown Bomber, always a great credit to his chosen profession, and the race he represents..."

Mr. Goldberg had grown impatient. "What is he doing, for Christ's sakes, inaugurating the next President of the United States? Let 'em fight already!"

I mouthed, "That's my race he talkin' 'bout!"

"The heavyweight champion of the world, Joe Louis!"

Wild cheering from the fans at Yankee Stadium spilled out of the television screen like the waters over Niagara Falls

Another announcer, this one with a Western twang, said, "Referee Eddie Joseph gives the fighters their instructions."

"Holy shit, what a fight this is going to be!" the man sitting next to me, a man with one eye cocked, said. I had pushed myself to the edge of the sofa and was leaning toward the television as the fighters returned to their corners and threw their robes off. This was about the most exciting thing I had ever seen. Another show card filled the screen. This one was decorated with a striker bell background and the words:

*Round* No. 1

The bell clanged. The fans at Yankee Stadium and in the Goldberg living room went wild. Louis and Conn strode stridently to center ring and circled one another like wily tigers sizing up their prey.

With the Lord as my witness, before the first punch was thrown Mrs. Goldberg paraded out from the hallway and stopped next to the television set. She had fixed herself up so that there was not a leading lady in all of Hollywood more bewitching. Mr. Goldberg's friends whistled and made catcalls as Louis and Conn exchanged glancing jabs. I don't know where it came from, I had never before used the name of the Lord in vain and have never since, but after seeing how beautiful Mrs. Goldberg looked then seeing fires of vengeance burning in Mr. Goldberg's eyes, I raised my arms up over my head, slapped my hands together, and shouted, "Jesus Christ Almighty!" The man next to me leaned into me and laughed. Now it was like a tag-team wrestling match with both teams going at it. Louis and Conn continued to dance around and test each other with probing jabs while Mr. and Mrs. Goldberg held each other's eyes in a venomous death lock. We watched as Louis and Conn drew close, ducked, and traded inside punches. Then our eyes switched to Mr. Goldberg as he said, "Where the fuck do you think you're going?"

Louis paced and Conn danced as Louis struck Conn with a left then a right. Conn backpedaled.

"I'm going out for a drink with a high school friend, you phony bastard, and if you don't like it you can kiss my ass!"

"Who?"

"Abie Phillips."

Remembering what I witnessed at the Dunbar with Jakie, I shouted, "May de Lord have mercy! Dere goin' to be war!" No one paid attention as they were transfixed by Mrs. Goldberg's hypnotic presence.

*"GRR-GRR-GRR-GRR-GRR."*

"Abie Phillips. Go ahead, hang out with Mickey Cohen's stooge, see what happens," Mr. Goldberg said.

A car's horn tooted twice.

Mrs. Goldberg stopped at the door. She looked back at Mr. Goldberg as if to say, *Screw you! You don't own me!*

Mr. Goldberg's retinue hooted, jeered, then waited for their leader's response.

The car horn tooted twice again.

Mrs. Goldberg opened the door. Mr. Goldberg said, "Step out that door, sister, and don't plan to walk back in, ya hear!"

Mrs. Goldberg said, "This is my mother's house, you freeloading son of a bitch. I'll come and go as I please!"

Mr. Goldberg's knights were silent. The queen had claimed her castle.

The bell ending round one rang. Louis and Conn returned to their corners.

Mrs. Goldberg strutted defiantly out.

# Chapter 25

## *The Last Round*

It wasn't till after midnight that I finished cleaning up after Mr. Goldberg and his retinue. If it hadn't have been for Jakie's coming in and helping after Mr. Goldberg took his liquored-up men to a bar on Alameda to do whatever liquored-up men do in bars on a Wednesday night, I might not have been able to get any sleep. Then again, I did not get too many hours as it was. I felt very pleased as I went to bed. Joe Louis had won. I fell asleep thinking about the White Camellia Knights and how there wasn't a thing on the face of this Earth they could do to take Mr. Louis's championship belt away. Joe Louis was more than a Brown Bomber; he was a Brown Savior for most colored folks back then. Joe Louis was Hope. My exaltation did not last long, though. Billy came in just after five the next morning and tapped on my head. "Sugar, what you thinkin'? Your mama don' pay me 'nough to work all 'round de clock. Lor' have mercy what can it be now?"

He said, "Come on!" then ran to the kitchen door, stopped, looked back at me, and waited.

"All right, den. It better not be dat Black Tooth up to no good! I'll skin it and you alive dis time."

Mrs. Goldberg's scream cleared my groggy mind. "Get away from me, you son of a bitch! Help! Phosie! Jakie!"

I jogged around the dining room table and into the living room. Mr. Goldberg had Mrs. Goldberg cornered near the hallway. She was still in the outfit she had worn out, her hair was mussed, her makeup was faded, and her lipstick was smeared. Mr. Goldberg did not look much better. His hair was mussed, too. The back of his shirt was hanging out over the back of his pants, and from what I could see of it his face was red-hot like steamed crab's shell. Mrs. Goldberg's hand was extended out toward Mr. Goldberg. An eight-inch boning knife with a gleaming blade was in it, its point not more than an inch from his heart.

"Go ahead, you good-for-nothing cunt. Stab me!"

"I will! If you touch me I swear I will!" Mrs. Goldberg cried.

Billy wrapped his little arms around my leg. I quietly said, "Why don't you put de knife down, Mrs. Lucile, so you and de mister cain talk things out."

Mr. Goldberg swiveled his head around to look at me. His face was the living image of the devil. "Get the kid out of here, for Christ's sakes!"

"Come on now, you two don' have to fight like dis. Dere is a better way, I knows."

Mr. Goldberg shouted, "I said get the goddam kid out of here now!"

I took Billy into my room, closed the kitchen and hall doors, let Black Tooth in off the back porch, looked the dog in the eye, and said, "Now don' you let dis chile out yur sight, hear?" Black Tooth looked at me with his ears perked and his tail wagging like everything in the entire world was just fine, bless his little heart. I returned to the living room.

Mr. Goldberg's voice was coarse with rage. "Go ahead, stab me."

Mrs. Goldberg cried out, "You bastard! I hate you! I hate you, you motherfucking bastard! I hate you!" Her words spewed from her mouth like splatters of blistering grease. Her entire body trembled.

"Ya can't, can ya? Know why? I'll tell you why, because you can't even wipe your ass without getting shit under your fingernails. You can't keep a friendship, all your girlfriends deserted you because you kept putting the squeeze on their old men. You can't help yourself, can you? You don't know up from down. You can't even hold down a decent job, for Christ's sakes."

Mrs. Goldberg's voice turned shrill. "Yes, I can, I can. I had a job, before you moved in and told me to quit! They loved me at The Hi Hat."

"They loved you? You're so stupid it's pathetic. Get this through your thick skull, you dumb bitch, they didn't love you. They liked you because you got the sucker fish to swim around the bar with your looks. You were chum. I saw you in action. You smiled, shook your tight ass, showed a little cleavage. You did everything you could to hustle those Johns. You had them eatin' out of your hands, for Christ's sakes. And if that wasn't enough you took a different john every week. The kid must have thought his father was a baseball team, for cryin' out loud."

"They weren't Johns, you bastard! I was trying to find a husband and a decent father for Billy. To replace you!"

"A 'husband and a decent father for Billy.' Kiss my ass. How many times did I tell you, you don't go looking for a blue ribbon in a pig's sty. 'A decent father for Billy.' You wouldn't recognize a decent father if he was standing right in front of you. I know you like the back of my hand, sister. You don't give a shit about Billy, you don't give a shit about me, the only one on the face of this Earth you care about is you. You're in it for yourself and nobody but. And you're a lousy mother to boot."

I could see that Mrs. Goldberg was overwhelmed. "I am too a good mother!" she screamed. "I work at night to be with the kid!"

"You can't bullshit the bull! You work at night to get away from the kid."

"We were doing fine till you moved back in!"

"You were? Then why the fuck did you lure me back? I'll tell you why, you couldn't make it without me. You're a helpless, good-for-nothing, worthless piece of shit!"

"Fuck you! Fuck you! I hate you!"

Mr. Goldberg laughed cynically. "Ah, why don't you shut your trap already."

As it seemed that Mrs. Goldberg was not going to stab Mr. Goldberg, I silently stood my ground.

She hissed, "I'll kill myself!"

"Go ahead. You couldn't even get that right the last time you tried. But whatever you do, stop talking about it and do it, for Christ's sakes.

You want the pills, you want one of my razor blades, a nice bridge, I'll drive you over to Pasadena, all the jumpers love whatever the hell that bridge is called." Mrs. Goldberg was weeping. "Look at you, you can't even kill yourself without my help you're so pitiful. And you know it."

His words were too evil, too vile. "Come on, Mrs. Lucile, give me de knife. You don' means to hurt yourself or anyone else for dat mattah. Mr. Leo don' mean what he say. He drunk."

"I give you this knife I'm dead!" Mrs. Goldberg screamed. I thought of Jakie and wondered if the shouting had awakened him.

Mr. Goldberg snapped. "You want to die? You want to fucking die? I'll show you how to die!" He grabbed Mrs. Goldberg's wrist and twisted until she screamed. The knife fell to the floor. Its needle-sharp point stuck into the wood, a glimmer from the street light glowed on the edge of its blade. Mr. Goldberg stepped toward Mrs. Goldberg. She straightened her arms and tried to push him away, but he reached up between them, grabbed her head, and started banging it against the wall. I ran over to Jakie's and knocked on his door. He answered in underwear and a moth-eaten T-shirt. "Come on!" I said. "He gonna kill her shore 'nough!"

I ran back into Mrs. Goldberg's. Mr. Goldberg had been punching her. Her face was masked in blood, her nose was broken, her lip was split. She was screaming like an hysterical baby crying for its mama. Her helplessness stoked his rage. He banged her head again then he gripped her throat and started to choke her. "I'll show you, you fucking cunt!" I am sure I heard the coarse voice of the devil right then. Bloody bubbles gurgled around Mrs. Goldberg's mouth as she slapped wildly at his hands. Her air was cut off, her lips were turning purple, her eyes were screaming for life. She did not want to die.

I tried to pull Mr. Goldberg away from her. He planted an elbow in my chest, shoved me backward over my heels. I went tumbling over the coffee table and onto the floor. I crawled to the cocktail cart and used it to get back onto my feet. My heart was beating so hard I thought it would surely break my ribs or outright quit. I reached for a whiskey bottle and was about to hit Mr. Goldberg on the back of his head, but Jakie ran in carrying his pistol.

"Leo, for Christ's sakes, you're going to kill her!"

"Shut up, you fuckin' loser, or you'll be next!" Mr. Goldberg said as he continued pounding his wife.

Jakie screamed, "I said let her go!"

"You ain't got the brass to make me, you goddamned shell-shocked son of a bitch!"

Jakie silently raised his black police revolver and pushed the barrel up into the base of Mr. Goldberg's skull.

I screamed, "No!"

Jakie pulled the trigger. The odor of gun powder filled my nostrils. Mr. Goldberg's body crumpled. Chips of his shattered skull were lying about the floor and on the sofa. Bloody chunks of his brain were splattered on the ceiling; others had come to rest in Mrs. Goldberg's hair and on her chest and shoulders. Even my new robe was spotted red. I helped Mrs. Goldberg over to the sofa. She collapsed.

Leo Goldberg's bitter, poisonous presence would no longer stain the lives of those who believed they could trust him and those who wanted, needed, and deserved his love. Leo Goldberg was no more. The repugnant shame he felt for himself and the shame he brought out in the people close to him would be his legacy.

I heard the sirens of approaching police cars and stepped out onto Mrs. Goldberg's front porch. Between the wails of sirens a mourning dove on the branch of a nearby tree sang *cooOOoo-coo-coo*. Another answered from the roof of the house next door, cooOOoo-coo-coo. The brilliant light of a new day gave New Jersey Street a fresh, clean pink hue as the chilled air that rises each morning to greet the sun filled my lungs. I felt relieved. Jakie fought the devil and won. I heard sirens screaming at the edge of my thoughts and walked back in to see how Billy was doing. He and Black Tooth were having a tug-of-war over one of my hairnets.

When I returned to the living room I found Mr. Goldberg's body covered and Mrs. Goldberg on a stretcher waiting to be carried out to the ambulance. The police were interviewing Jakie but not threatening to arrest him. It seemed they could clearly see what had transpired.

I stepped back outside to fill my lungs with air so that I would not buckle.

*CooOOoo-coo-coo.*

*CooOOoo-coo-coo.*

# Chapter 26

## *A New Beginning*

Independence Day, 1946

*YIP YAP YIP YAP YIP YAP YIP YAP*

"Black Tooth, if'n you don' stop dat yip-yapping I's going to pull dose lil' ears of your'n up over your head and tie dem in a knot. Now scat!"
*YIP YAP YIP YAP YIP YAP YIP YAP*

"One dog turn into a boy one day, another come right in to take up after him de next. Billy! Come take dis lil' black pest out a my kitchen 'fore I use my butcher's knife on it!

"I'm listening to the 'Red *Skeleton* Show!'"

"You cain't be listenin' to no 'skeleton,' chile. Far as I knows, skeletons don' talk, cause dey is dead!"
*YIP YAP YIP YAP YIP YAP YIP YAP*

"Lord have mercy, do I have to take care of everyone and everythin' 'round dis place? When somebody goin' to take care of me?"
*YIP YAP YIP YAP YIP YAP YIP YAP*

"All right den, all right!" I looked down at Black Tooth. He looked up at me with his loveable, sad, brown eyes, tilted his head, and perked his ears to make sure he heard everything I was about to say. "I's goin' to give you one more chicken neck, and if dat don't do de trick den I might jus' fry you up wit de rest of de chicken! Here you go." I led Black Tooth to the back door using the chicken neck as a carrot, opened the door, and flung the piece as far out into the yard as I could, knowing full well he'd be at the back door yapping and yelping soon as I stepped back into my kitchen.

Mrs. Goldberg wheeled into the kitchen and passed me a note. The doctor had confined her to a wheelchair as the concussion Mr. Goldberg gave her as his departing gift from this world left her with vertigo. If she stood up she would fall over, it was so bad. And she was communicating in writing because Mr. Goldberg had also broken her jaw and a surgeon had wired it shut. I read the note: "Have you seen Jakie?"

I said, "No, matter of factually, Mrs. Lucile, he mus' be up to somethin'. I haven't seen hide nor hair of him all day." Another note from the little spiral notepad she was carrying around was awaiting me: "'I'm worried, I hope he's okay, the police said he didn't have to worry about the shooting. It was self-defense. But he slips down deep into himself. He gets quiet, lost. It's not good. I'm worried."

"I was too, Mrs. Lucile, but I spoke wit him after supper yesterday and he was chirping like a little bird. He gonna be fine, Mrs. Lucile, jus' fine." I examined the bruising around her broken nose and blackened eyes.

"Does it look any better?" her next note read.

"Each and every day, Mrs. Lucile, each and every day."

She dashed out another note. "The dining room table is set really pretty. I love the gardenias, they smell so beautiful."

"Dat's right, dey do. Maybe you should get some gardenia perfume. You will shorely catch a fine man wit dat."

She smiled and wrote, "I think I caught my limit!"

"Yes, you has, Mrs. Lucile. You don' wants to catch any more of dat kind a fish."

There was a twinkle in her eye. She tossed her head back in a mock laugh then wrote, "What time are your brother and sister-in-law and that friend of your son's from the Marines arriving?"

"Well, I told the Hawkins boy to be here 'bout six. I want Babe and Sis' Pearl to arrive 'bout de same time, but slow as my brother drives I told him to come by at four thirty and dat ought to bring dem in right on time." Mrs. Goldberg started to laugh, but a sharp pain caught her. She grimaced.

Mrs. Goldberg had changed in the weeks since Jakie shot Mr. Goldberg. Before the shooting it was clear she had not grown up by the way she was always on the run from one thing to the next. And if that one thing required her to think of something other than herself she ran away from it twice as fast. She could not stand being anything other than the star of the show. But she was terribly lonely, and hungry for love. I started out believing that she was sleeping late and running out every night because she was looking for the right man. But as time passed it came to me that she was really running away from the child she had given birth to in order to take care of the unrequited needs of the child she still was. Until she had her jaw wired she did not want anything to do with Billy. In her heart of hearts I don't think she wanted to be a mother, as being a mother meant missing out on the glamour and the glitz. It meant staying home and looking after a messy little child, wiping his nose when it ran, holding its head when it vomited, tying its shoes, just being there when the child needed her so that the child would grow to trust her. She felt her glamour was spoiled by motherhood and did not want any part of it. She passed another note: "What's Billy going to wear?"

"Well, I don' know, Mrs. Lucile, I've been too busy fryin', bakin', and mixin' to think on it. Why don' you pick somethin' out." I could see the shame she felt in her eyes, shame that came from the awareness of the difference between what she was and what she should be. She wasn't an evil person by any means, but she had a voracious appetite for life and did not know how to fill herself up other than by running from person to person and place to place like a wild dog in heat. To her credit she quietly wheeled herself out of the kitchen to do as I suggested.

*YIP YAP YIP YAP YIP YAP YIP YAP*

"You shush up now!"
*YIP YAP YIP YAP YIP YAP YIP YAP*

I let Black Tooth back into the kitchen. *"Scoot!* Go listen to Red *Skeleton* wit yur brother, let me suffer in peace!" I said as I waved the carving fork I was using to turn the chicken in the skillet, and thank the Lord he listened, too.

Left alone, I watched the chicken's fat spit and crackle in the hot oil and thought about Will. I wondered what he would have been doing on this holiday if he were alive, and if he would have recovered from Ella's rejection and found a new girl to love in time for the holiday, and if we'd have stayed in Los Angeles. I remembered how Isaac and I took Will down to Seawall Boulevard on Galveston Island to see the fireworks when he was just three, and how scared he was going to bed after the fireworks that night.

"What de matter, chile? Does yur stomach ache from all dat sugar candy?"

"No, Mama, it's the fireworks up in de sky! They scare me. Look at them, Mama!" Will said, pointing up to the brilliant twinkling stars framed by the wooden window over his palette bed.

I sat on the edge of his mattress, stroked his brow, and whispered, "Dey ain' fireworks, honeychile, dey stars. See how dey stay and sparkle where dey at? And you know what?"

"What, Mama?" Will said as his eyelids grew heavy.

"Dey yur lucky stars. Dey be up dere lookin' down after you no matter where you is."

"They stars?"

"Dat's right, sugar, dey yur friends, dey de Lord's way of showin' you de way out de dark. Dey light your path." I bent over to kiss him, but he was already asleep.

A spatter of hot oil pricked the top of my hand, and a terrible thought occurred to me as I flipped a piece of chicken. I imagined Will alone and afraid out on the Pacific island waiting to fight the Japanese. I hoped that he had looked up at the stars and that they gave him shelter from the terror he must have been feeling, that by seeing them he felt my presence, my love, and felt comforted and safe. I pined to see him one more time.

Billy ran into the kitchen and jolted me out of my reverie. "Phosie Mae!"

"Lord have mercy, chile! You 'bout scared me right out my skin! What is it?"

As Black Tooth yapped at the front door Billy said, "There's a big colored man with one arm missing at the door, he says, Billy imitated the man by dropping his chin to his chest and speaking in the deepest voice he could produce, 'Please tell Mrs. Eaton Hawk is here.' Is he a hawk? He don't look like one."

"Landsakes no, chile, he a friend of my Will's, a friend from de Marines. Tell him to come in." Billy tore out of the kitchen as I set the knife down and fixed myself up to walk in and greet the young man. I looked at the clock; it was 5:43. I had not even changed out of my scrappy uniform.

He, as many men were, was still wearing his Marine Corps uniform. "Well, I declare, it's good to see you, chile, and my oh my, don't you look handsome."

He removed his cover and said, "Thank you for inviting me, Mrs. Eaton."

"I been so busy cookin' I ain' had chance to change," I said, nodding at my clothing.

"Oh, I don't care, Mrs. Eaton, it's good to have a home-cooked meal for a change."

"How have you been and what have you been doing?" I said as I ushered him to the sofa and served him an ice-cold beer. He told me had stayed in Los Angeles and was looking for work but having a hard time like the rest of the colored boys were with all the white men returning from the military.

There was a another knock at the door. Billy opened it. It was Babe and Sis' Pearl, and at first I thought I was seeing a ghost but then I realized that Mrs. Katherine Hutchinson in the flesh was standing behind them. I threw my hands up in the air as tears streamed down my face. "Oh my Lord, Mrs. Katherine! How did you find me? Why is you here?" We embraced and kissed one another. She was a welcome connection to Isaac, Will, and Galveston.

*YIP YAP YIP YAP YIP YAP YIP YAP*

"Sweet Jesus! You is de very las' person I thought I'd see come knocking on Mrs. Lucile Goldberg's door! How *did* you find me?"

A tall, willowy young lady with sandy-brown hair and blue eyes just like her mother's followed Mrs. Hutchinson in.

*YIP YAP YIP YAP YIP YAP YIP YAP*

"Do you remember Lily?" Mrs. Hutchinson asked.

"My eyes have seen the glory! Come here, chile, let me see you." Lily stepped toward me smiling brightly with tear-glossed eyes. "I sure 'nough don' remember her dis way. She done blossomed out into a beautiful flower. Give me some sugar, sweetheart." Lily and I kissed and hugged, too.

"I'm sorry about your losing Will," Lily said.

Mrs. Hutchinson added, "I too am truly sorry about your loss of Will, Phosie. I can't fathom how wrenching an experience that must be."

"Well, you both done lost de captain."

"Yes, and Lord knows you helped me and the twins stay afloat after Captain Hutchinson's loss, but losing a husband and even a father, as big a loss as those are, losing a child is of a far greater magnitude. Parents are supposed to die before their children," Mrs. Hutchinson said.

"Well, dat's right, Mrs. Hutchinson, dat's right. Now, you shore lookin' beautiful as ever. If'n I didn' knows you I would think you was dis beautiful chile's sister, not her mama!"

"I feel like I'm a hundred years old," Mrs. Hutchinson said, "with running the farming and ranching, but you look radiant and beautiful, Phosie. It looks like all the California sunshine is treating you right good."

"Well, dey say you cain't judge a book by hits cover, Mrs. Katherine. De wound from losin' Will is still deep as it is fresh, you know."

"Of course."

"Well, I see you already knows my brother, Babe, and Sis' Pearl, his wife."

"Yes, they were kind enough to pick me and Lily up at Union Station this afternoon."

"Well, dat is nice. And dis is Billy, the chile I take care of."

*YIP YAP YIP YAP YIP YAP YIP YAP*

"Now, you shush, Black Tooth! You'll have your time."

Mrs. Hutchinson bent over, smiled, extended her hand to Billy, and said in her Texas twang, "Well, how are you this Fourth of July, young man? You ready for the fireworks?"

Lily smiled and followed, "Pleased to make your acquaintance, Billy."

Billy had turned shy with strangers since he had started back acting like a little boy. "Billy," I said, "what do you say to our guests, sugar?"

"Why do you talk funny?"

Mrs. Hutchinson, Lily, and Gus Hawkins laughed with Black Tooth taking up the chorus.

*YIP YAP YIP YAP YIP YAP YIP YAP*

"Lord have mercy, chile, dat's de way people down in South Texas talks."

I began to apologize, but Mrs. Hutchinson waved the apology away. "You just have not heard a Texan speak before, so it must be a little strange. We understand, don't we, Lily?"

*YIP YAP YIP YAP YIP YAP YIP YAP*

"And we call dat raggedy little creature 'bout to have hits tongue tied and boiled Black Tooth."

*YIP YAP YIP YAP YIP YAP YIP YAP*

"Just like Will's dog, Blackie, right?" Lily said.

*YIP YAP YIP YAP YIP YAP YIP YAP*

Lily mentioning Will and Blackie brought both momentarily back to life. I was stunned.

"I'm sorry if I upset you, Phosie."

"Oh, you didn' do anything wrong, sweetheart, nothin' wrong t'all."

*YIP YAP YIP YAP YIP YAP YIP YAP*

"Willy chile, why don' you…" When I realized I had spoken Will's name I was so overwhelmed with emotion I could not finish the sentence.

*YIP YAP YIP YAP YIP YAP YIP YAP*

"Billy," I said, finally in control of my emotions, "why don' you take Black Tooth out to de back and play?"

*YIP YAP YIP YAP YIP YAP YIP YAP*

Billy was happy to be relieved of having to address Mrs. Hutchinson and Lily and ran toward the kitchen with Black Tooth on his heels.

"Now, Mrs. Hutchinson and Lily, I has de pleasure of introducin' dis young man here who was a good friend of Will's in de Mah-rines, Gustavus Hawkins."

"It's an honor to meet you, young man," Mrs. Hutchinson said as she extended her hand to shake. "Will spent a good deal of time playing with my children when they were all young. I knew him well. You must be a fine young man, Mr. Hawkins, if Will was your friend."

"Yes, ma'am, Gunny, I mean Will and I, we got on like brothers since the day we met at Montford Point."

Mrs. Hutchinson smiled and was about to say something else, but right then Mrs. Goldberg made her entrance from the hallway.

"Oh Lordie!" Sis' Pearl shouted. She had not seen Mrs. Goldberg since Mr. Goldberg had beaten her to the edge of life.

"Well, lookie who de cat drug in!" I said. "Mrs. Goldberg, dis here is Mrs. Hutchinson, my employer from Galveston, and her chile Lily, one of a pair a twins. Only de Lord knows how Mrs. Hutchinson found me."

Mrs. Goldberg's eyes lit with a smile. Her makeup hid the bruising, but her right eye and nose were still swollen. Yet she looked very glamorous. We all waited patiently while Mrs. Goldberg wrote a salutation on her little notebook then ripped out the page and passed it to me to pass to Mrs. Hutchinson. Mrs. Hutchinson read Mrs. Goldberg's note, "Can I get you a drink?" then nodded and said, "Of course, we have to celebrate on an occasion like this, don't we?"

Mrs. Goldberg nodded at me, and I put on my bartender's hat. Mrs. Goldberg had a VO and Seven she sipped through a straw, and Mrs.

Hutchinson had a bourbon and Coke. Babe and the Hutchinson girl had a Coca Cola on *the rocks*. Will's friend had another beer, and Sis' Pearl, ever the lady, joined him. I had a vodka gimlet. People do change.

Just as soon as I had the drinks mixed, Jakie came prancing in holding the door open for another visitor. It was a woman. I felt shattered until she stepped into the living room. I thought he had brought a gypsy to read our palms. But as I studied the woman's face I realized it was Mrs. Henrietta Duke. She flashed a smile, showing her nicotine-stained teeth smeared with the excess lipstick she had applied.

"I declare, Mrs. Henrietta Duke, I reckoned I'd never see you 'gain long as I lived, but here you is at our door."

"I'm glad to see the job worked out, honey."

"I is too, but why is you here, Mrs. Henrietta? And what are you up to, Jakie Kravitz? Why is you been sneakin' 'round all de day long?"

Jakie said, "I'm having a beer, would you like one, Mrs. Duke?" and walked out without answering.

"Dat man has somethin' up his sleeve," I said.

Everyone pitched in to set out the meal while I changed into my new dress. When we sat down to eat, Billy took the chair on my left with Black Tooth tied under it and Mrs. Hutchinson sat on my right. "Lily, remember dat prayer you used to recite for your daddy 'fore supper way back when?"

"Yes, ma'am, I do."

"Would you kindly recite hit?"

"Yes, ma'am."

"All right den, let's all join hands. You too, Mrs. Lucile."

Once the circle was completed Lily began.

*"Thank you for the food we eat,*
*Thank you for the world so sweet,*
*Thank you for the birds that sing,*
*Thank you, God, for everything."*

"'Fore we eat I jus' want to say dat we miss having Captain Hutchinson, Isaac,

Will, and all de other ones we loved dat passed. And may we have peace! Amen." Everyone, including Billy, said amen. Mrs. Goldberg said it by humming "umm-humm."

Once we passed around the platters of fried chicken, the baskets of biscuits, and all the other fixings, Mrs. Hutchinson told the story of how she found me by presenting me with an envelope from the Department of War in Washington, D.C. I must have looked frightened because she said, "Don't worry, Phosie, I believe there is a check inside. I opened the envelope and sure enough found a seventy-five-dollar check payable to me as a death benefit for a surviving mother.

Mrs. Hutchinson told us all her story. "I had no idea what was in the envelope. It had been over at the Calichi Corners post office for some time when Sam Tillman's girl Eloise finally had the good sense to carry it over to us. I recalled the telegram Phosie received from the War Department advising her that Will was in the Barry Colored Hospital out here in Los Angeles. I had to find her. So I telephoned the hospital, and they gave me Babe's number and that was that. I was planning to mail the check to Babe so that he could pass it along to Phosie, but Lily and I were going to be traveling out to Los Angeles anyway to look at the University of Southern California, so here we are.

"University of Southern California?" Jakie said. "Oh yeah, that's the one with the good football team. I used to bet on them."

"I hope you didn't have a bet on them for the Rose Bowl. They were crushed by the Crimson Tide," Gus Hawkins said.

Jakie stood up, picked up his beer bottle by its neck, and walked over behind me. He cleared his throat and said, "I have an announcement," in his shy little tone. Then he waited until everyone quieted down. I looked back over my shoulder. "Go on," I said with a palpitating heart.

He had me stand up next to him and produced a small ring-sized box covered in purple velvet from his pocket. He took my right hand in his, looked around the table, then said, "See, I knew you was all coming, and I, see, I decided to, to make this the time I would ask you, Phosie, to marry me. That's what I wanted to say." I was so stunned I was speechless. Everyone's eyes were on me. "I was out looking for a ring all day long," he continued, "couldn't find one, so I telephoned Mrs. Henrietta Duke here, she told me she knew a jeweler on Beverly Drive what could give me a real good deal." He took the ring out. The gold ring was thin as a hair and the diamond small as a speck of sand, but the thought of what he had done was so beautiful the size of the ring did not matter.

Everyone waited for my to answer.

"I declare I never ever did think I'd marry agin, 'specially to a white man. But Jakie is a good-lookin' white man"—everyone laughed—"and he sure do look after me like a mother hen." They laughed again. "He a man I've grown to love. And, more importantly"—I looked at Mrs. Goldberg and smiled—"I wants to keep this job, so I believe I will say yes!"

Everyone, even Mrs. Goldberg, stood up and applauded and cheered. I noticed Mrs. Goldberg was crying and truly believe they were genuine tears.

When all quieted down there was an awkward moment of silence that Billy relieved by saying, "Phosie, don't you have to kiss the man?" Everyone laughed again.

I said, "Yes I do, chile," and stood up on my tiptoes so that Jakie and I could kiss. It wasn't much of a kiss as I could not tell which one of us, Jakie or me, was more nervous. But it would be a lasting and a private kiss. Mixed race *anything* was not acceptable just after the war. The places we would go together were limited to the colored areas, and Jakie was not always graciously welcomed in those parts either. The fact was that what other people thought or did not think did not matter to us because we had something most of them did not have: our love, and the gentle way in which we treated one another.

Pearl followed Jakie's proposal. A little light-headed from the beer, she stood up holding a chicken leg in one hand and a napkin in the other, pointed the drumstick at Mrs. Henrietta Duke, and said, "I want to say that it was Mrs. Henrietta Duke, of the Mademoiselles Fonteney agency, who helped our Church Sisterhood and me find my lovely sister-in-law, Phosie Mae, a placement out here in California. Without Mrs. Duke, a fine Christian woman if there ever was one, and a long-time friend of our Sisterhood, Phosie would never have met Mr. Jakie in the first place. And, to tell the truth, once I finish up with the city schools—I'm a truant officer, you know—I may just ask Mrs. Henrietta Duke to place me in one of those beautiful homes everyone talks about."

"Okay, Pearl, darling, that's fine," Babe said, trying to grasp Sis' Pearl's wrist. She swept his hand away.

"So," Mrs. Hutchinson said to Mrs. Henrietta Duke, "you have a domestic agency?"

Mrs. Henrietta Duke had a little chicken crisp tagged onto her left cheek, but no one had the nerve to tell her. "I own an exclusive domestic agency in Beverly Hills. You may have heard of us, Mademoiselle Fonteney's Exclusive Beverly Hills Domestics. We are located on Beverly Drive, but we place downtown, Hancock Park and Bel Aire, the real exclusive homes."

"She real, real good," Sis' Pearl said, pointing the drumstick at Mrs. Henrietta Duke. "De best in de West."

"I think that's enough, dear," Babe said.

Lily said, "Nanny,"—she used to call me Nanny—"do you remember that song you used to sing to us when Porter and I were really small?"

"I sung lots of songs, sweetheart. Was it gospel?"

"No, it was something about walking on the grass."

"Oh, 'Walkin on de Green Grass,' is dat it?"

"That is it! Will you sing it again?"

"Oh Lordy, dat was a song my grandmother taught be back down in Uniontown when colored folks were supposed to stay off de green grass in de parks and such."

Everyone cheered me on.

"Let me see if I cain 'member it." I sang slowly at first.

*Walkin' on de green grass*
*Doesie Doesie Doe*
*Wish I had a nickel, wish I had a dime*
*I'd be walkin' on de green grass all de time.*

"Is dat it, sugar?"

"Yes." Lily was smiling. "Sing it again."

This time everyone sang with me except for Mrs. Goldberg, who hummed while using her desert fork as a conductor's wand. Tears filled my eyes.

*Walkin' on de green grass*
*Doesie Doesie Doe*
*Wish I had a nickel, wish I had a dime*
*I'd be walkin' on de green grass all de time.*

"Lordy, dat song make me realize how old I is!"

"You're still a spring chicken," Mrs. Hutchinson said.

"Well,"—my cocktail had gone to my head—"I may be a spring chicken, but I shore 'nough ain' layin' no more eggs or hatchin' no more chicks!"

Billy said, "I thought chickens lay eggs, Phoise?" Everyone laughed again.

As we finished my pecan pie and vanilla ice cream drizzled with caramel sauce and sprinkled with rock salt, we heard firecrackers popping from out on the street. "Let's watch!" Billy shouted.

*YIP YAP YIP YAP YIP YAP YIP YAP*

"All right den, y'all go 'head on. Soon as I clear dese dishes I'll be 'long."

"Oh no, you won't," Mrs. Hutchinson said. "This is your engagement day, you're coming out with us. We'll all take care of the dishes after the fireworks have ended."

"I got something to do next door," Jakie said.

"No sir, dis de end of being shell shocked, darlin'. If'n I'm goin' out and if you is to be my future husband, den I wants you out enjoyin' de fireworks wit me." I reached for his hand and pulled him along. "Come on now. I'll protect you."

We gathered on the front porch. From up there we could see the high spire of Los Angeles City Hall. It looked like the Tower of Babel the Hebrews built after the Flood. The neighbors, some white, some recently released Japanese, some Mexican, were out on the sidewalks of New Jersey Street celebrating the first Fourth of July since Pearl Harbor. Everyone was delirious with relief that the killing had ended. Some carried sparklers that gave them silhouettes of fairies dancing in the dark. Rockets soared high up over the rooftops and burst into a thousand stars, fountains spewed showers of gold and silver sparks, Roman candles, popping spinning wheels, and gaily colored little parachutes that floated down after the little rocket that sent them high burst in a rainbow of sparks. Black Tooth was chasing his tail on the front lawn while Billy was tugging my arm wanting to join the festivities on the sidewalk.

A sharp report hit us like the shockwave of a bomb dropped from an airplane. Jakie dove for cover behind the spindled Victorian ballisters. "Come on up, sweetheart," I said, reaching down and placing my hand under his arm. "Dat ain' nothin' but de start of the show."

Jakie stood up, I took his hand in mine, and we watched serpents of light chased by starbursts of red, white, and blue streak across the sky. Everyone on the street, including us, applauded and cheered. God had blessed us with victory. The next firework rocketed up above the city hall's tower and expanded into a dome of brilliant silver stars that floated silently downward in the dome shape of a weeping willow. It was a beautiful yet sad display. I felt comforted being with people who loved me, but I missed Isaac and Will so and I knew the ache would never leave me. I did not want it to. I did not want to forget them, ever.

Billy tugged at my sleeve. His arms were extended upward. I picked him up and passed him to Jakie. "Chile, you're too big for me to hold." Jakie lifted Billy up over his head, flipped him, and sat the child on his shoulders. Judging by the expression on Billy's face, he looked like he was at that moment king of the mountain. He was awestruck by every pop, bang, and whistle that sang through that night. It was wonderful to see him happy. I looked behind us to see how the rest of our guests were doing. Mrs. Hutchinson and Lily were whispering to one another while they pretended to watch the show. Babe was quietly enjoying the spectacle. Sis' Pearl and Mrs. Henrietta Duke were each having another piece of pecan pie, and Will's friend Gus was oblivious to the fireworks because he was eyeing a pretty Japanese girl across the street. I wondered how his life would turn out, whether he and the rest of the Montford Point Marines would be treated more as an equal after risking their lives fighting for our nation.

We had rolled Mrs. Goldberg's chair near the steps so that she could watch the show without interference from the balustrades. But she wasn't watching the show. She was studying Mrs. Hutchinson and Lily's animated conversation with the expression of a dreamy child looking into the window of a toy store at objects she believed would forever be out of reach. Glistening pearls of tears were tumbling down her cheeks. A miniature reflection of the brilliant fireworks illuminating the sky appeared on each tear like frames of film. I felt terrible for her. I went to her. "How is you doin, Mrs. Lucile darling? Not too good?" She shook her head no. I took up her left hand and held it between mine. She was cold. Her hand was trembling.

"Come on, Mrs. Lucile, de sun goin' to rise up again tomorrah, just you wait and see."

She turned her face away and wept.

"'Member what you told me 'bout how to get de sweetest cherries? Not gettin' left wit de pits?"

No response.

"Well, de Lord knows you done had yur share of sour cherries, Mrs. Lucile, I seen dat. But dat don' mean you cain't find you a sweeter bowl with an earnest man for yurself and Billy."

She turned slowly and looked up at me. "Dat's right. You jus' needs a good man's lovin. You jus' waits and sees."

We heard a series of rapid-fire bursts. I looked up. The fireworks show's grand finale had started. A gossamer haze enveloped city hall's white alabaster tower. The sky above became a dazzling display of color and light.

"Remember what you told me when my Will was in de hospital, Mrs. Lucile? You said, 'Don' you give up hope.' Remember? Well, I am here to tell you, you cain't give up hope neither. You is a mama. Yur child needs its mama's love. And, while I am at it, he need a daddy too, somebody he cain trust, someone who will take him up and love him as he would his own. Dey out there, Mrs. Lucile, long as you know what to look for." We looked at each other as the last of the fireworks exploded, shrieked, and popped. Billy crawled up onto his mama's lap. She looked at me again. I could see the faint glimmer of hope twinkle in her sad eyes.

The fireworks show ended with a twenty-one-gun salute using mortars to honor all the folks that fought and died in the war and all the folks who helped with the war effort. Then there was silence. The fireworks were over. We had our peace. It was time to move on.

Made in the USA
Lexington, KY
19 June 2015